D0876644

The Captain of her Heart

BEST-SELLING AUTHOR ANITA STANSFIELD WRITING AS

ELIZABETH D. MICHAELS

The Captain of her Heart

BEST-SELLING AUTHOR ANITA STANSFIELD WRITING AS

ELIZABETH D. MICHAELS

SWEETWATER BOOKS
An imprint of Cedar Fort, Inc.
Springville, Utah

© 2022 Anita Stansfield
All rights reserved.

No part of this book may be reproduced in any form whatsoever, whether by graphic, visual, electronic, film, microfilm, tape recording, or any other means, without prior written permission of the publisher, except in the case of brief passages embodied in critical reviews and articles.

This is a work of fiction. The characters, names, incidents, places, and dialogue are products of the author's imagination and are not to be construed as real. The opinions and views expressed herein belong solely to the author and do not necessarily represent the opinions or views of Cedar Fort, Inc. Permission for the use of sources, graphics, and photos is also solely the responsibility of the author.

ISBN 13: 978-1-4621-4208-8

Published by Sweetwater Books, an imprint of Cedar Fort, Inc.
2373 W. 700 S., Springville, UT 84663
Distributed by Cedar Fort, Inc., www.cedarfort.com

Library of Congress Control Number: 2021949023

Cover design by Courtney Proby
Cover design © 2022 Cedar Fort, Inc.
Edited and typeset by Valene Wood

Printed in the United States of America

10 9 8 7 6 5 4 3 2 1

Printed on acid-free paper

To my daughter, *Anna.*
I see in you the child I once was.
May your imagination serve you well.
Never, never, never let go of that creative part of you;
let it be one of the brightest, strongest threads
in the tapestry of your life.

Other books written by
Elizabeth D. Michaels

The Horstberg Saga

Behind the Mask
A Matter of Honor
For Love and Country
The Tainted Crown
Through Castle Windows

For a complete list of this author's
books, go to anitastansfield.com.

Too long ago, too long apart.
She couldn't wait another day
for the captain of her heart.

—"The Captain of Her Heart"
The Double

Prologue

itcherd Buchanan threw his cloak behind his shoulders and mounted the waiting stallion. He gave the order for his men to move forward, and the long trek to their appointed battlefront began. The horse beneath him plodded along in perfect time to the drummer's beat, as if the animal had an innate sense of rhythm. The same beat that kept the foot soldiers on cue seemed to measure the pounding of Ritcherd's heart as he contemplated the inevitable. Somewhere at the end of this brief journey, a battle was imminent. Some men would die. Some men would be maimed. And every man would be changed forever. Their preparations had been thorough and absolute, their training complete. But Ritcherd felt unprepared. He wondered what he'd done to warrant being put in charge of these men, many of them little more than boys. They had looked up to him and trusted him, and now he was following orders that would alter their lives. He had taught them to believe in the cause they were fighting for, to honor king and country, and to see these rebel colonists undone. But in his heart, he wasn't sure if he believed it himself. Certainly not enough to die for it. And that's where he had to admit he was afraid. He didn't want to die. He had too much to live for. First and foremost was Kyrah.

Kyrah. Thoughts of her softened his anxiety. From the first time he'd laid eyes on her, he had been fascinated by her in a way he could never explain. He'd often wondered if the timing of her appearance in his life had somehow compensated for the recent loss of his sister. Perhaps that could explain the way he was initially drawn to her. But as time had passed, something rich and deep had kept them close. And being without her now was the most difficult thing he'd ever endured.

As his men pressed on to the never-ending beat of a single drum, Ritcherd wondered what Kyrah might be doing now. He imagined her running over the moors of Cornwall, her dark hair flying in the wind. It hadn't been so many months since he'd seen her, but it seemed like centuries. And he knew it would be a long, long while before he saw her again—if ever. No, he couldn't think that way. He had to live to see her again. He *had* to. She had barely been on the brink of womanhood when he'd kissed her goodbye, and his first order of business when he returned would be to ask for her hand in marriage. He would live to see that day. He *would!*

Please God, he prayed silently, over and over, *Let me live to see Kyrah again. Please . . .*

"Captain." A voice interrupted his thoughts and startled him.

"Yes, lieutenant," Ritcherd replied.

"We're approaching the rendezvous point, sir."

"Very good," Ritcherd said. "You know what to do."

"Yes, sir," the lieutenant said and rode quickly away to see to his predetermined orders.

Ritcherd's prayer stayed with him as the battle proceeded, but he found that he was far more frightened than he'd anticipated. He fought to push the fear away and show the courage he knew these men needed to see in him in order to stand strong. But inside, his heart beat so quickly that he feared it alone would kill him.

Amidst the chaos of the ensuing skirmish, he found himself alone in a patch of trees. Seeing a vantage point ahead where he could get a better view of their situation, he wove carefully between the closely rooted aspens, attempting to ignore the continuing sounds of gunfire, explosions, and anguish floating to his ears. Consciously fighting back his own fears, he continued to pray in his mind and kept pressing forward.

Briefly distracted by a sudden volley of cannon fire aimed toward the largest body of his men, he was surprised to hear a familiar voice speak distinctly behind him. "Get your head down, boy. There's one coming right at you!"

Startled by the presence of someone close by as much as from the warning, Ritcherd immediately ducked and heard a bullet whistle just above his head a split second later. In the moment it took him to realize he could have been dead right then, Ritcherd dropped to his belly and quickly started easing back the way he'd come. Following the time it would take to reload a rifle, another shot rang out. Obviously someone had gotten sight of him and pegged him as an officer. Ritcherd ran as soon as the second bullet whizzed past, knowing it would take the gunman several seconds to reload again. He turned as he gained momentum, wondering who to thank for saving his life, but no one was there. Certain that whoever it was had turned and run for his own life, Ritcherd concentrated on getting to a place where he couldn't be seen.

The battle raged on for hours, and it wasn't until the wounded had been cared for and the dead tallied that Ritcherd sat to record the day's events. He hated the sick knots that tightened in his stomach as he mentally put faces to the list of casualties, but he had to stop and utter a heartfelt prayer of thanksgiving that he was not among them. Recalling the incident in detail, Ritcherd tried to pinpoint the voice of the man who had warned him without a second to spare.

"Stephen," he murmured before he even realized what he was saying. Then he chuckled to himself at the absurdity. Kyrah's father was back in England, caring for his sweet daughter until Ritcherd could return and take over the job. He told himself he needed to stop letting his imagination run away from him, and made a mental note to see which man had a voice that reminded him of Stephen's—if that man was still alive.

Returning to his record, Ritcherd felt something stab at him as he realized that today was Kyrah's sixteenth birthday. Much later, when he finally crawled into his makeshift bed and tried to talk himself out of being cold, his mind drifted to what her day's activities might have entailed. Oh, how he missed her! Tears burned his eyes as he contemplated the reality of what this war had put between them. But he forced the tears back, certain that if he started crying, he'd never be able to stop. And his men needed him to be strong.

Recommitting himself to doing whatever it would take to get him through this, he finally drifted off to sleep, once again thanking God for surviving this day.

Chapter One

First Kiss

Cornwall, England

Kyrah came awake suddenly, as if she'd been startled from a nightmare, but she couldn't recall what she might have been dreaming. Her eyes stung with an unfamiliar dryness, and her every muscle felt strained. She groaned and curled around her pillow, wondering how so much could go wrong in so short a time. Not so many days ago, she had been anticipating her sixteenth birthday and the celebration she would enjoy with her parents. Of course, nothing was ever completely right without Ritcherd, and she missed him dreadfully. Still, life had been good in spite of his absence. But now, her birthday had come and gone, unnoticed amidst the horror of her father's death and the loss of everything they owned.

If only Ritcherd were here, she thought for the thousandth time this week. But he wasn't here, and reality had to be faced. Kyrah would have to find a way to support herself and her mother, or they would be out in the streets. Her mother was too absorbed in her grief to face the inevitable. Kyrah knew it was up to her. But how could she face the gravity of their situation when she couldn't even face the fact that her father was gone?

Needing fresh air to clear her head, Kyrah brushed the wrinkles out of the dress she'd slept in and quietly checked on her mother. Sarah was still sleeping soundly, no doubt aided by a concoction the doctor had given her to keep her calm. Leaving Sarah a note so she wouldn't worry, Kyrah wrapped a heavy shawl around her shoulders and ran down the long drive between the two rows of Cornish elms that stood like skeletal sentinels, bared by the winter wind. Kyrah felt oblivious to the cold as she stood at the crossroad where she and Ritcherd had met nearly every day for eight years. Staring up the lane toward Buckley Manor, she could easily imagine how he would look riding toward her against the backdrop of his home. She lost track of the time as she stood with the wind reminding her that Ritcherd was an ocean away, and she could only pray that he might return to her alive and well—not in a wooden box, as her father had returned.

The thought startled Kyrah, and she wrapped her shawl more tightly around her. Desperately needing peace and solace, she headed over the moors toward the one spot on earth that she considered a haven from the harsh realities of life. Sitting among the church ruins, she could almost forget, if only for a few precious moments, that her life had been turned upside down.

As she absorbed the timelessness of her surroundings, the wind rustled past her like an old familiar friend, escorting her back in time to that fateful day when she had first laid eyes on Ritcherd Buchanan. Her memories were complex and seemed far too insightful for a seven-year-old girl. But it was difficult for Kyrah to know if her insight had truly been present that day, or if it had come through the years of analyzing her memories.

Kyrah's mother had often told her of the beautiful moors of Cornwall, and the church ruins where she had played as a girl. For Kyrah, the highlight of moving from London's crowded streets to the open countryside was learning that the big house they would live in was very near the cottage where her mother had grown up. It was her mother's playground that Kyrah first sought out upon their arrival.

She was immediately fascinated by the ruins, and she felt certain that this church was closer to God than any other, since she could stand anywhere inside the structure and see the sky. There was no longer any roof, and the floor was more grass than stone, although the altar as well as many of the stone pews still existed.

Kyrah was just craning her neck to view what had once been a series of stone archways when she first heard Ritcherd's voice.

"This church was built in the fifteenth century," he stated as if he were a schoolmaster.

Startled, Kyrah turned abruptly to see a young man standing in the doorway, wearing a casual jacket with the sleeves pushed up and a wool scarf hanging forward around his neck. He moved closer, watching her carefully. She glanced at him, then moved her eyes quickly away from his unyielding gaze.

"I'm sorry if I frightened you," he said in response to her silence. "I just thought you'd like to know."

Ritcherd told her the history of the old church that day, and pointed out all of the features remaining of its structure. Kyrah followed him about, listening attentively but saying nothing until he announced that he'd told all there was to tell and sat on one of the stone pews, motioning for her to sit beside him.

"My name is Ritcherd," he said after a long moment of silence. "I'll be thirteen soon." He paused and asked, "So, what is your name?"

Kyrah fingered the stone bench beneath her hands, noting its coldness despite the summer sun. "Kyrah," she said at last.

"That's very pretty," he said, watching her closely while he seemed deep in thought. "It sounds like a lady's name. An elegant lady, with diamonds round her throat. What do you think about that?"

Kyrah smiled. "I'm only seven."

"Does that mean you can't think?" he asked with a chuckle.

"Only that I can't imagine such a thing . . . as being a lady."

"I believe you will," he said in a voice that forced her to look at him again. Even in her youth and naivete, Kyrah felt something significant in that moment, an undefinable sensation that had made it cling distinctly to her memory. It was almost as if fate had tapped her on the shoulder, prompting her to take notice. And she somehow knew that Ritcherd had felt it, too.

He surprised her by taking her hand and leading her from the church. "Come on," he said, almost skipping as he pulled her behind him. "If we go up here, we can see the old church from a different perspective."

They were both breathless when they reached the hilltop. Ritcherd pointed down to the ruins sitting timelessly against an endless stretch of moors, sweeping toward the distant sea like a purple and gold blanket fluttering in the wind, halted only by an occasional stone fence-line. The wind that had rolled gently through the old church now briskly played havoc with their hair and threw the longest part of Ritcherd's scarf out behind him, almost giving the illusion that he was flying.

"Is it always so windy here?" Kyrah asked, gathering her hair into one hand to keep it from blowing in her face.

"No," he said intently. Then he grinned. "Sometimes it's worse."

Kyrah laughed and turned her eyes again to the view.

"This is a beautiful place," he said, and Kyrah silently agreed.

"May I walk you home?" he asked. Kyrah wasn't certain if she should let him, but she was reluctant to part with this new friend, and she nodded her assent. She was surprised when he took her hand as they walked, and she wondered if this was how it might feel to have a big brother. She watched him more bravely now, and thought he was rather handsome. She hoped that he could be her friend forever.

Kyrah expected Ritcherd to take her to the gate and make his departure, but without permission or hesitation he walked to the door with her and asked if he might come in and meet her parents. Although she had no idea how her parents might react to such a visitor, she couldn't bring herself to make any excuses, and he followed her into the entry hall.

Ritcherd glanced around and clasped his hands behind his back. She wondered if he noticed the long-unused air to the house. But signs of renovation promised to bring the century-old edifice back to life.

"It's a fine house," he said. "Nobody's lived here for years, not since old Mr. Greene died."

Kyrah led him to the drawing room, only because her mother had said it was meant to entertain guests. They stepped carefully around the partially unpacked crates and oddly placed furniture and sat down together on a small sofa. When minutes passed and nothing was said, she expected the silence to be awkward enough to make him get up and leave. But he smiled comfortably at her, and for the first time in her life, Kyrah found it possible to be with someone besides her parents and not feel uncomfortable.

"There you are, young lady." A voice startled them both, and Kyrah's mother appeared in the doorway. "We were wondering where you'd gone off to, and—" Sarah Payne stopped at the realization that they were not alone. "Oh, hello," she said to Ritcherd.

For a moment Kyrah feared she would get a scolding for having a boy as a friend. But Sarah's expression turned from surprise to genuine pleasure when Ritcherd stood and introduced himself like a perfect gentleman.

"Hello," he replied, "I'm Ritcherd Buchanan. I met Kyrah this afternoon at the church ruins and asked if I might walk her home."

"How very nice." Sarah turned a chair the appropriate direction and sat down. "I'm Sarah Payne . . . Kyrah's mother."

"It's a pleasure to meet you, Mrs. Payne," he said as if he'd been socializing all of his thirteen years.

"You say you've been at the old church?" she asked, and he nodded as he sat back down. "I went there often as a girl," Sarah mused. "It was always one of my favorite places."

"Did you live here before?" Ritcherd asked.

"Many years ago." Sarah smiled warmly. "I grew up in the cottage on this estate . . . the one just east of here."

"I know the one," he said in response to her expectant expression. "Is your family from here, then?" he asked.

"No, actually," Sarah said. "I lived with the schoolmistress, Miss Hatch."

"I remember her," Ritcherd said, seeming pleased.

"My husband was fortunate enough to acquire the estate so that we could come back," Sarah said. "It's like coming home for me."

"The house has been empty for a long time," Ritcherd said. "It will be nice to have neighbors."

"You live close then?" Sarah prodded.

"Yes," he said, and the bright countenance he'd worn all morning suddenly faded. "Just north of here, at the end of the lane."

"Buckley Manor?" Sarah nearly gasped. "But of course. Buchanan. I should have figured that out. I remember your parents."

Kyrah noticed that Ritcherd's confident aura was briefly dimmed. She was relieved for Ritcherd's sake when her mother seemed to sense something uncomfortable and picked up the conversation, telling more about her childhood in Cornwall.

Kyrah watched Ritcherd more bravely now that his attention was centered on Sarah's conversation. She admired the way he looked so comfortable. He acted much older than thirteen, she thought.

Turning her attention to her mother, Kyrah was relieved to see that Sarah liked Ritcherd. She knew her mother was a good judge of character, and if Sarah liked him, she knew he was worth liking.

"Listen to me running on," Sarah finally said. "I was looking for Kyrah so we could get a bite to eat. It's already far past noon. But we seem to get rather caught up in the work and forget all about—"

"I should be going then," Ritcherd said, coming quickly to his feet.

Kyrah couldn't help feeling disappointed, but it was short-lived as Sarah added warmly, "Would you like to stay and eat with us, Ritcherd? Under the circumstances it's not very fancy, but you'd be welcome. I'm certain Kyrah's father would love to meet you and . . . Oh, perhaps your mother would be worried if—"

"I don't think she'll notice," Ritcherd interrupted dryly. "If you're sure it's all right . . . I'd like to stay."

Kyrah beamed with pleasure, and they walked together to the dining room, which was in a similar condition to the rest of the house. But Ritcherd didn't seem to mind. Stephen Payne was waiting there, and he immediately liked Ritcherd as well. For the first time ever, Kyrah felt that she had found a real friend.

Late in the day, after Ritcherd had helped Stephen tear down some atrocious wallpaper in the library, he finally announced that he should be getting home. He seemed reluctant to go, but Kyrah was relieved when he spoke to Sarah at the door.

"Would it be all right if I come and visit again?" he asked. "I'd be happy to help with the work."

"You're welcome here anytime, Ritcherd." Sarah took his hand, and for a moment Kyrah almost thought he was trying not to cry. But she felt certain she'd imagined it. Surely thirteen-year-old boys didn't cry. "And we'd appreciate the help, but you certainly don't need to feel obligated."

Ritcherd cleared his throat and turned to Kyrah. "Maybe we could go to the church ruins again tomorrow."

Kyrah nodded firmly, then ran up the stairs so she could watch him from an upstairs window as he walked down the long drive between the rows of huge elms.

The following day, Kyrah began watching from the window right after breakfast and completing her chores. By late afternoon, she began to fear that he had changed his mind about wanting to spend time with a little girl. Surely he had just been kind in order to make her feel welcome as a newcomer. But she couldn't expect him to be a real friend—not like those she'd heard about in books her mother read to her.

When she saw him from a distance on a horse, trotting casually toward the house, Kyrah ran down the stairs and out past the gate to meet him.

"Hello, Kyrah Payne," he said with a remarkable smile. She liked the way he said her name.

"Hello, Ritcherd Buchanan," she replied.

"Would you like to ride with me to the church?" he asked without dismounting.

"I would," she replied, glancing away.

"Is it all right with your parents?"

"Mother went into town, but she said if you came today, I could go as long as I'm home before dark."

"Good." Ritcherd smiled again and dismounted, holding out his hand to her. "What's the matter?" he asked at her obvious hesitation.

"I've never ridden a horse before," she said quietly.

"Not to worry," he said and took her hand to help her into the saddle. He mounted in front of her, and she held to him tightly as the horse moved slowly forward.

Ritcherd tied the horse near the church ruins to graze, then he helped Kyrah down. He took her hand to lead her around the perimeter of the church until she saw something in the tall grass and stopped to investigate. Her heart quickened with fascination and compassion as she knelt down and scooped a wounded bird into her hands.

"It's hurt," she whispered and couldn't help crying, even though she wondered if Ritcherd would be annoyed by her tears. The little bird fluttered helplessly, attempting to fly away. Its distressed chirping tore at her heart.

"He has a broken wing," Ritcherd informed her after closer examination.

They took the little bird back to Kyrah's home, where Sarah helped them doctor it as much as possible. Ritcherd stayed for supper and helped Stephen into the evening by tearing out a piece of wall in the drawing room that had to be replaced due to water damage. When it was down, Sarah declared that she liked the room better without it. Kyrah kept watch over the little bird.

The following days found Ritcherd common company at the Paynes' new home. He and Kyrah spent hours feeding and caring for the little bird and watching it gain strength. They helped as much as they could in the house, and gradually it began to show vast improvement.

On the ceremonious day when it was declared that the little bird had healed, Kyrah stood on a pew in the old church and held her hands toward the sky. The bird chirped a moment as if to say something tender, then it flew from her hands, lit briefly in one of the high windows, and disappeared.

Kyrah told Ritcherd how sad she felt to let it go, but she knew its freedom was important, and somehow it would know they loved it. She told him how selfish and unfair it would be for them to expect to keep the little bird from flying just because they wanted it with them.

After the incident with the little bird, Kyrah became fascinated with every bird she saw. She wanted to know what type of bird it was, and speculated about what it was doing and where it had come from. She was delighted when Ritcherd returned from a short trip to London with his parents and brought her a beautiful book containing more information and pictures of birds than she'd ever dreamed existed. The book quickly became as much a companion to her as Ritcherd did, and they would sit for hours in a particular spot on the moors where a cluster of oaks, birches, and elms gave them shady retreat and a perfect view of the birds as they came and went. Kyrah would search out the facts in her book, then she'd make up stories about them as if they were people. She couldn't deny her innate love and fascination for birds, which were second only to her deep admiration for Ritcherd. In her childish imagination, it was easy for her to imagine Ritcherd as the greatest bird of all, soaring over the Cornish countryside, watching out for her.

Nearly every day found them together. Beyond the necessary time spent at their school lessons, they spent every possible hour enjoying each other's company. If they were not watching for birds, they were running over the moors or lying back in the heather to watch the clouds. Still, their favorite pastime was to play among the church ruins. For children, it was full of intrigue and endless possibilities for spurring the imagination. Together they shared a castle with daring rescues, or a haunted house with ghosts at every turn. Or sometimes they just played hide-and-seek among the pews. Even in the depths of winter, when the cold wind howled as if it were one of their playmates, Ritcherd and Kyrah hardly missed a day's visit to the ruins.

They truly became the best of friends, and Kyrah was often surprised that despite their age difference he continued to spend the majority of his time with her. Their friendship existed on a level somewhere between their ages, where her maturity met with something in him that seemed drawn back to childhood, as if he'd never really played or learned to use his imagination prior to Kyrah's coming into his life. He was completely at ease in her home and with her parents, and eventually he became an inseparable part of the family. Kyrah prayed every day that it would always be that way; in fact, she became so thoroughly dependent upon him that she found it difficult to even imagine being able to live without him.

As the years passed, Kyrah felt certain that she could not have survived without Ritcherd for many reasons, although some stood out stronger in her mind than others. It gradually became evident that Kyrah would always be snubbed by those who considered her father's profession and lack of social distinction unacceptable. But Ritcherd not only compensated for her absence of friends, he often rescued her from their cruel teasing. And she always found sanctuary in his friendship. Still, she never realized how thoroughly he protected her until a day came when she found the courage to ask him something she had always wondered. "Why have you never taken me to your home?"

He looked so startled that she nearly regretted bringing it up. "You wouldn't like it," he stated tersely.

"Are you ashamed of me?" she asked. Through nearly four years of friendship, he'd never once suggested that she meet his parents.

Now Ritcherd looked astonished. "No!" he said adamantly.

"Then why?"

"It's not like your home, Kyrah. Personally, I don't find it very appealing."

"But it's so beautiful," she said, glancing toward the magnificent manor situated on the hill. Ritcherd made no comment, so she added, "I'd like to go there."

He seemed tense for several moments while he was obviously working something out in his mind. Finally, he conceded. "If you want to see it, I would be honored to show it to you."

The following morning, Kyrah went by horseback to the crossroad where Ritcherd met her. They rode side by side toward Buckley Manor, and Kyrah was amazed at how far it seemed. The house was so big that it had always appeared closer than it really was. As the distance lessened, the structure became more ominous.

Kyrah was silent as he led her inside. The manor's beauty and size left her in awe. She considered her own home to be large and elegant, but it seemed a mere cottage compared to the massive, elaborate Buchanan residence. The reality of his home was Kyrah's first real indication of what she gradually came to learn about Ritcherd's circumstances. It was difficult to look at him as her friend and comprehend that he was one of *the* Buchanans of north Cornwall. Not only were they by far the wealthiest family in the area, but she learned as time went by that they were also very powerful— one being a result of the other.

A deep impression was left on Kyrah from that first visit to the manor. The great hallways of black and white checkerboard floors, massive staircases, eloquent pillars, and aspiring archways were all awesome and breathtaking. Each room was beautiful and unique. But Ritcherd didn't take the pride in his home that she might have expected.

Puzzling over the reasons, her fascination was quickly diverted when Ritcherd completed his tour by taking her to meet his parents. "It's about time they had the pleasure of knowing you," he said warmly, but she saw something tense in his eyes.

Kyrah felt immediately uncomfortable when they entered the drawing room together, but Ritcherd held her arm firmly and she was reassured by his presence. He gave formal introductions, but they were answered with little more than a curt nod from Mr. and Mrs. Buchanan. Ritcherd escorted Kyrah to a sofa and sat beside her, holding her hand.

In the minutes that followed, Kyrah became more aware of her circumstances than she ever had been. Jeanette Buchanan's cold stare was the most demeaning thing she'd ever come up against. "Is it really true, my dear," the woman finally said with an edge to her plastered smile, "that your father came by his estate as the result of a . . . card game?"

Kyrah felt Ritcherd go tense beside her. "Really, Mother, I don't think that—"

"Yes, it's true," Kyrah interrupted, lifting her chin courageously. The love she felt for her father outweighed her fears, and she defended him with pride. His methods made no difference to her.

At her admission, a slow, hard glance passed between Ritcherd's parents, then their eyes turned back to Kyrah as if she were a leper. Apparently unable to bear looking at her any longer than necessary, their gaze moved to Ritcherd. Kyrah's gaze followed, and her breath caught in her throat. If she had met Ritcherd Buchanan at that moment, from his expression she would have believed him to be the most bitter, hateful young man on earth.

"I'd heard," Jeanette said, breaking a horrible silence, "that you had been traipsing around with this Payne girl all these years, but I really didn't want to believe it."

Kyrah felt her chest go tight, and a painful throbbing struck between her eyes. The relief was indescribable when Ritcherd rose to his feet and urged her along. She sensed that he wanted very badly to retort, but he was fighting to maintain control, perhaps due to her presence. They moved toward the door as his father added, "I think you'd do well to stop and think about where you're headed, son. Oil and water don't mix. I would have expected more of you than this."

Ritcherd stopped at the door, drew a deep breath, and turned back to face his parents, while Kyrah stood half-shielded by his tall frame. "And I would have expected at least a degree of graciousness from my own parents," he said. "You call yourselves the epitome of social grace. Well, I want nothing to do with it. As far as I can see, your social standard stinks, and your priorities sicken me."

"How dare you speak to us like that, young man!" Jeanette came to her feet in a reddening rage. "I'll not stand here and—"

Ritcherd interrupted and pointed a hard finger. "I'll not stand here and listen to your self-righteous drivel. How dare you treat a guest of mine in such a manner! You and your social graces can *rot* for all I care!"

Kyrah moved numbly out of the house, propelled by Ritcherd's hand at her arm, hearing doors slam behind them. In silence they rode to the church ruins, while Kyrah wanted to die inside. She had never felt so humiliated and frightened in her life. And the Ritcherd Buchanan she thought she knew so well was suddenly someone she had never seen before and didn't understand.

By the time they reached the church, the pounding in her head had become unbearable, and it took every grain of concentration she could muster to keep from bursting into heaving sobs. With trembling hands and weak knees, she followed Ritcherd inside, and felt frightened all over again when he turned abruptly and slammed a fist into the stone wall. Kyrah clamped a hand over her mouth, but a whimper escaped as he pressed his bloodied knuckles to his lips and squeezed his eyes shut with a harsh groan. She watched him draw a sustaining breath, but his voice cracked as he spoke, his eyes still closed. "I'm so sorry, Kyrah. I should never have taken you there."

Another whimper escaped, and he turned to look at her. "Are you all right?" he asked.

Her little remaining self-control crashed around her, and she would have collapsed if Ritcherd hadn't rushed to catch her. Helplessly she sobbed against his shoulder while he whispered soothing apologies and reassurances. When her outburst finally quieted to a rhythmic sniffle, Ritcherd grasped her shoulders and looked into her eyes. "It makes no difference to me, Kyrah. Just look at you. You're a perfect lady. To me, it doesn't matter."

Kyrah found comfort in his sincerity, but she would never forget that in his parents' eyes, her lack of aristocratic background left her totally unsuitable for his companionship.

As time passed, Kyrah was amazed at the way Ritcherd continued to outwardly defy his parents' wish that he not see her. She knew there was some deep estrangement between them that he had mentioned briefly, but his adamance in avoiding the subject left her mostly ignorant of the reasons. She suspected, however, because of the way Ritcherd was so compelled to be in her home, and the closeness he shared with her parents, that he found little—if anything—of value in his own home.

When Ritcherd's father died, Kyrah attended the funeral by his side. It was the first time Jeanette didn't bother to throw a cold glare in her direction. But Ritcherd's hope that the absence of his father's stern hand would soften the circumstances was quickly dashed when his mother later ridiculed him for bringing Kyrah to the funeral, saying he should not have done it out of respect for his father. Yet even then, Ritcherd made it clear that he would see Kyrah Payne with or without his mother's approval.

Following his father's death, Kyrah noticed that Ritcherd felt a subtle softening toward him. His only explanation was that some papers had been left with the will which helped Ritcherd understand that, in spite of his father's faults, he'd had a softer side that he'd never allowed his son to see. If only he could have felt the same way about his mother.

Ritcherd continued to protect Kyrah from the harshness of the world, while each day was an adventure to them. Time passed, and their play gradually merged into long conversations and longer walks. Just being together was all that either of them seemed to need. If the moors or the church ruins ever became tiresome, they would walk along the beach with bare feet, or ride to the pier to see the ships, and sit for hours admiring their beauty and speculating over the places they had been. Their conversation often turned to the gulls and curlews flying above them, with their own tales to tell.

Occasionally Ritcherd took it upon himself to dance with Kyrah in the old church, and together they perfected all the moves. They occupied many summer weeks with the minuet and the cotillion, while the wind whistled through the crumbling stones for their accompaniment.

The older Kyrah became, the more her dependance on Ritcherd grew. It became so deep that her greatest fear was the possibility of losing him. As she began to realize that he'd become a man and she was little more than a child, she often feared he would eventually tire of her. She hardly dared voice her fears, if only to keep from giving him the idea. But she often tried to approach the issue through back doors with the hope of gaining reassurance. Inevitably Ritcherd proved to her that any fear was unwarranted. She was continually amazed at his depth of commitment to her, but found that it took little to bring nagging doubts to the surface again and again. One afternoon, however, she was given the chance to overhear a completely candid piece of conversation which gave her a deep peace that helped ease her doubts.

She went to the church ruins to meet Ritcherd, but realized he was not alone and paused outside, not wanting to intrude. Recognizing George Morley's voice, she knew they wouldn't talk long. George had been a casual friend of Ritcherd's from childhood, but he was always on the go.

"You're sure now," George was saying. "This is your last chance."

"Quite sure," Ritcherd replied firmly.

"I don't understand it. You're the only man I know who would pass up a chance like this. Why?"

"I'd rather be here, George. I have what I want."

George chuckled. "You can't say I didn't offer. You may be jealous when I get back and tell you what you missed."

"Maybe," Ritcherd murmured. "But we'll see who's jealous when Kyrah grows up. She means more to me than anything you could ever offer." He chuckled. "Nothing personal."

George's laugh moved closer, and Kyrah backed away to appear as if she'd just arrived.

"Good afternoon, Miss Payne." George bowed gallantly, grinning in his typical way. "Your beloved awaits your arrival with great anticipation."

"Hello, George," she said, quite accustomed to his teasing.

George quickly left, and she found Ritcherd sitting on one of the pews, his arms stretched out across the back. She watched him a moment, trying to comprehend what he'd just said to George. Although it was vague, she felt somehow secure—a feeling that deepened from an intensity in his eyes that was becoming more familiar.

When Kyrah finally came to the conclusion that one way or another Ritcherd would always be a part of her life, news came only days later that threw everything she'd ever felt for him into a whirlpool of fear and confusion. It was an extremely hot day in late summer when Ritcherd came through the front door of Kyrah's home with an abrupt, "Where's your father?"

Stephen quickly appeared, and the two of them were holed up in the library for what seemed hours. Kyrah felt an unspeakable dread, but in no way expected Ritcherd to emerge with the grave announcement, "I have been *asked* to serve my country."

Their eyes met with no need to express the horror they were both feeling. He cleared his throat and explained, "The Americans have declared independence, and King George won't stand for it."

"How . . . long?" Sarah asked, her emotion evident. He might as well have been her own son.

"There is no way of knowing," Ritcherd said. "I've heard all degrees of speculations, but personally . . . I don't think it will be over quickly."

Kyrah wanted to die. It was difficult for her to comprehend that his need to serve stemmed from some unwritten expectation tied to his title and background, and refusing would leave him socially tainted for the rest of his life. She didn't understand it. She only knew she hated it. Still, she couldn't deny respecting him for having the honor and courage to do what was expected of him. She only wished that leaving her and putting his life at risk weren't part of those expectations.

Kyrah's only comfort was seeing the pain she felt mirrored in Ritcherd's eyes. But there was nothing to say that would make any difference, and the days leading up to his departure were filled with unspeakable dread. The future had always seemed so hopeful, so easy. Talk of war had been disregarded as a faraway triviality. Then a day came when Kyrah had to face the reality that war had come between them. This would be their last day together.

She was surprised to arrive at the usual meeting place and find it unoccupied. But she waited patiently at the crossroad, staring up the lane to Buckley Manor as she watched Ritcherd approach against the backdrop of his home. As the dread within her deepened, Kyrah pulled her lightweight cloak tightly around her, feeling more chilled than the air of early autumn warranted.

"Sorry I'm late," he said, halting his stallion an arm's length away to dismount. "I was . . . packing."

Kyrah managed a smile and looked down to avoid having him see the painful tears that she forced back. Determined not to mar their brief time together, she lifted a courageous face toward him. "You look very handsome in that uniform."

Ritcherd gave a forced smile and glanced away. It was evident that he didn't want to discuss his reasons for wearing it any more than she did, but the tension in the air was undeniable. They knew this was their final time together. Just when Kyrah thought the strain might make her scream, Ritcherd reached for her hand. By way of habit, they strolled aimlessly over the moors and walked hand in hand through the ruins of the old church. Kyrah watched him carefully, trying to memorize every detail of his presence as he leaned in one of the partial archways of the church ruins, his blue eyes penetrating, his hands stoically behind his back. Consciously she absorbed his sculptured features and high forehead into her mind. He had a distinct aristocratic look about him, but could by no means be called delicate. Every movement, even his mannerisms, lent an aura of virility to what otherwise might be called a gentle face. His well-groomed downy blond hair was tied back, as usual, into a fashionable ponytail. His hair looked dark in the shadows, although Kyrah knew it had been lightened by the summer sun.

But summer was over now, and he was leaving. Kyrah met his gaze for a timeless moment and saw something unfamiliar there. She turned away and absently put a hand to her heart, puzzled over what he might be thinking. She wished in that moment that she could see herself through Ritcherd's eyes and know for certain how he saw her. But she felt certain she would only see a fifteen-year-old girl who was too tall for her age, and therefore too lanky. In her own opinion, her skin was too pale and her hair too unruly. When she observed her full lips and wide, not-so-brilliant blue eyes in the mirror, it was difficult to imagine the lady with diamonds round her throat that Ritcherd often envisioned. Still, he had told her many times that she was pretty, and she knew he would never lie to her.

Attempting to face what this day would bring, Kyrah wanted desperately to know that he felt for her as she did for him. But the thoughts that she ached to share remained unspoken. Words seemed trite, and silence somehow pure. While she tried to be content with lingering glances and a sense of togetherness, the morning passed with only the continuing wind breaking the stillness of the old church.

He sat beside her on one of the cold stone benches, toying idly with her fingers. She met his eyes and smiled, hoping to ease the tension, but he only squeezed her hand too tightly as he leaned back and looked skyward. All the years they'd spent growing together seemed suddenly too brief as she tried to comprehend what the future might bring.

Ritcherd was, in every sense of the word, Kyrah's dearest friend. But as he turned to look into her eyes, she felt her emotions deepen. She had always found it difficult to comprehend her future without Ritcherd in it, but being so much younger had made her hesitate to ever verbalize how she felt. And for some reason, it had always been avoided. They had always spoken only of the present, as if the world could be this way forever.

Kyrah saw his lips part as if to speak, but he only sighed and stood, clasping his hands behind his back.

"What is it?" she asked, moving beside him.

He turned to meet her eyes, and the intensity of his expression left her breathless as he pulled her, for the first time, into his embrace.

"I will miss you, Kyrah," he whispered near her face. "There's hardly been a day in eight years that I've not seen you . . . and been able to talk with you. How can I go away and have no idea when I can be with you again?"

"I don't want you to leave," she replied quietly. By its own will, her hand went to his face. She thought it strange that with all the time they'd spent together, she had never once touched his face. She could feel the rough shadow of beard that always showed up late in the day, and she recalled how young he'd been when it had first appeared. Even now, barely past his twenty-first birthday, he looked far too mature to be holding a girl so young in his arms.

In silent answer to the gesture, Ritcherd touched her hair with his fingertips, then moved them with determination over every part of her face, as if he was attempting to memorize her features. Kyrah saw the desperation in his eyes just before he bent to kiss her. When his lips subtly met hers, she felt his emotion pass into her. In the same moment that she became certain she loved him, she realized he was leaving, and tears welled up behind her eyes. She loved him far beyond the way she would care for a brother or a friend. And there was no denying the pain she felt in knowing this was good-bye.

He drew back to look at her, and she knew he'd noticed the mist in her eyes when his brow furrowed. His expression filled with compassion just before he kissed her again. His lips met hers with a tenderness that was characteristic of first kisses, then his mouth softened over hers, as if he could completely draw her into himself and take her with him. Kyrah held to him tightly, feeling as if they were moving together across a bridge with steps that could never be retraced. After eight years of holding hands, they were suddenly holding each other, caught up in a kiss both passionate and desperate, stirring something deep within.

"I must go," he said, reluctantly pulling away.

"I know," she replied breathlessly, sensing that he was forcing himself away from her for reasons she didn't completely understand. Ritcherd Buchanan was a man, likely very aware of matters that Kyrah was only becoming aware of in her youth.

"Kyrah," he whispered and looked right into her eyes, "I don't know how long I'll be gone, or what condition I'll return in, but I . . ." He paused and drew back his shoulders. "I want you to wait for me, Kyrah. I have to know that you'll be here for me when I come back."

The tears refused to be held back now. To know that Ritcherd wanted her in his future was the best thing she had ever known.

"I will," she said with fervor, and he sighed with relief at her promise.

"Don't cry, Kyrah," he said, forcing a smile as he wiped away her tears. "It always breaks my heart to see you cry."

"I'm sorry." She tried to laugh, hoping to push the tears back, but the forced chuckle turned into an irrepressible sob. Ritcherd pulled her close to him, holding her with that same desperation while she cried against his chest. He eased her back to the bench where they sat close together in silence until it became necessary to leave. The seconds ticked by mercilessly as he escorted her back to her home for their final good-byes, while their first precious kisses were still lingering on her lips.

They hesitated just outside the door, dreading the inevitable separation. The silence eventually became unbearable, and Kyrah was relieved when Ritcherd broke it.

"I don't want to go, Kyrah. If it were not a matter of honor . . ." He didn't finish, but she nodded to indicate that she understood. Their eyes met and she had to bite her lip to keep it from trembling. Her emotions began to get the better of her, and she turned her back to him and squeezed her eyes shut. A fresh surge of tears trickled down her face, but before she could lift a hand to wipe them away, Ritcherd took hold of her shoulders and turned her to face him. He gave her a sad smile and took her face into his hands, absently moving a thumb over her cheek to catch a tear. Then he pressed his lips to the other cheek to pull the tears away with his lips.

"I really must go," he whispered. "There are things I must see to, and I've got to leave at dawn."

She felt both relieved and terrified when he opened the door and followed her inside. Time was running out, and she knew he felt it as keenly as she did. They paused in the entryway where Ritcherd pulled her close to him again, closing his eyes as his lips came softly against her cheek. Kyrah felt an indescribable fear when he took his arms from around her, but she pushed the feelings away and led him into the drawing room.

"Ritcherd came to say good-bye," Kyrah said softly. Her parents both stood, looking dismayed.

"You're really leaving," Sarah said, moving toward him and taking his hand.

"I wish I weren't," he replied solemnly.

"Do take care, Ritcherd." She put her arms around him and went up on her toes to kiss his cheek. "We will miss you."

"And I'll miss you," he said, returning the kiss, "more than you can imagine."

"You keep your head down," Stephen said, giving Ritcherd a hearty handshake. "I've got plans for you when you get back."

Ritcherd chuckled. "And what might they be?"

Stephen glanced toward his daughter and smiled. "We'll talk about it when you return."

Stephen embraced Ritcherd, and Kyrah could see in Ritcherd's eyes the love he'd never felt for his own father. Then Sarah embraced him again. They followed him to the door as he held Kyrah's hand. Oblivious to spectators, he pulled Kyrah close to him, touched her chin with his finger and placed a warm kiss on her lips.

"Good-bye," he said, turning again to Stephen and Sarah. He squeezed Kyrah's hands and left.

Kyrah ran to the upstairs window and watched him ride toward Buckley Manor until he was out of sight. She rose the following morning before dawn to watch the distant lane until he rode past. She saw him pause at the crossroad and look toward her home. She knew he couldn't see her there, but somehow she knew he sensed her. Reluctantly he moved the stallion forward and disappeared over the moors.

Chapter Two

Too Long Apart

The pain and unbearable loneliness Kyrah dealt with daily in Ritcherd's absence was quickly added upon. The same fate that had delivered good fortune into her father's hands just as quickly took it away. The estate that Stephen Payne had won by careful stratagem in a game of cards was confiscated nine years later by the same methods.

Kyrah knew that to Stephen, being able to provide his wife and daughter with this elegant home was a dream come true. Sarah had grown up in a cottage on the estate, where Stephen had courted her and they'd fallen in love. Coming back had been a thrill for Sarah, and for this reason, the estate meant everything to Stephen.

There were no warnings, no gradual easing into the changes. It all happened in one day. When a knock sounded at the door, Kyrah happened to be nearby and went to answer it with her usual lack of enthusiasm. She knew it wasn't Ritcherd, but she was surprised to see two glum-looking men who introduced themselves as solicitors, solemnly asking if they might speak with her mother.

When she and Sarah were seated in the drawing room with their visitors, Kyrah felt suddenly tense.

"Mrs. Payne," the larger man said, "I'm afraid that, well . . ." He glanced toward his partner, as if for reassurance.

"You see," the other one took over, "it is regarding this estate. And I'm afraid, as far as you are concerned, it is not good news."

"We don't wish to be the bearer of bad tidings, Mrs. Payne," the large one said. Kyrah held her breath while she watched her mother closely. "But it's . . ."

"Perhaps you should discuss this with my husband," Sarah said when he paused too long. "He's out of town at the moment, but should return very soon and—"

"I'm certain your husband already knows about this," came the reply, and Sarah met Kyrah's eyes with a glance of fear.

"Please get to the point, sir," she insisted.

The large man took a deep breath, fingered the hat in his hands uneasily and said, "We are representing a Mr. Peter Westman." Sarah showed no recognition of the name. "And this estate, with all its properties and the like, is now under his rightful ownership."

Sarah laughed uneasily. "I don't understand. We've been here for years. I'm certain there's been a mistake."

"There is no mistake, Mrs. Payne," he said with a certain amount of compassion.

"But how . . ." she said breathlessly. "Why?"

Again the solicitors exchanged a rueful glance, then they both turned to Sarah. The one who wasn't so large cleared his throat and said, "Mr. Westman has come by this estate through, er . . . a game of cards."

"What!?" Sarah stood abruptly, but Kyrah thought she looked more hurt than angry. "Stephen wouldn't do that. I know it! This is a mistake."

Dazed and confused, Kyrah hardly took in the rest of their required discourse, which was stated quickly as the two men stood to leave. "We will have the papers sent out right away, and you can be assured that it is all very legal and proper. You must be out of the house in two weeks' time, and . . ."

"Two weeks!" Sarah exclaimed softly.

"And Mr. Westman will be happy to assist you in any way he can."

Sarah opened her mouth to speak again, but the solicitors donned their hats abruptly and left the room without waiting to be shown the way out.

Silently Kyrah watched her mother, waiting for a reaction. Kyrah herself could hardly think what to say. She felt numb and incapable of reacting.

Sarah's hand went to her heart as she sat down. She was obviously upset, but she did well in remaining unemotional. Kyrah could see that she was fighting to come to her senses and think reasonably, and then she was able to speak.

"Everything will be fine," she said with strength. "Your father would not have done it without good reason. If it's a mistake, he'll take care of it. If it's not, we'll move someplace else and manage just fine. There," she smiled toward Kyrah, "when your father gets back, he'll set things straight for us.

He's always taken very good care of us. Everything will be fine when he comes home."

The bit of assurance Kyrah felt from her mother's words was squelched only hours later, when the local constable came with news that made the earlier disclosure seem like good tidings. "Mrs. Payne," he said, standing in the entryway, fidgeting with a pencil, "I fear I've come with bad news. The very worst possible news."

Kyrah heard her heart pound audibly. She saw her mother turn pale as she waited silently to hear what the constable had to say. He cleared his throat and rocked on his heels. The tension in the air seemed unbearable. Drawing back his shoulders, he stopped rocking and said, "Your husband is dead."

Kyrah felt a painful sob catch in her throat, and she bit into the back of her hand to keep it from escaping. Her eyes went to her mother, and through the mist she could see her swallow hard as both hands went to her face, trembling.

The constable went on quickly, avoiding Sarah's weak gaze. "He was found in a London hotel room. The body and all of his belongings will be sent here right away."

With despair in her eyes, Sarah looked expectantly to the constable, waiting for an explanation. Kyrah was aware of what was said in those moments, but it wasn't until she was alone with her mother, who fell apart immediately, that the reality sank in.

Stephen Payne had died by suicide.

Kyrah cried. She cried sleeplessly through the night and far into the next day, while her mother murmured over and over that it couldn't be true. He couldn't be gone. He wouldn't have done it. It didn't make sense.

Kyrah was only able to get hold of herself when a fresh reality struck, and her grief was overshadowed by an ominous dread. Sarah showed little response when Kyrah told her they had received the official papers and needed to move. For the first time in her life, Kyrah felt completely alone.

The following days went by in a painful blur. Knowing that it had to be done, and needing to keep herself busy in order to avoid the pain, Kyrah began packing their things, with no idea of where to go or what to do. She was hardly aware that she reached the age of sixteen during the course of all this. And when her father's body arrived from London, the pain renewed itself.

It might have been difficult to believe that he was really gone, since the casket arrived sealed and remained that way, due to the irreparable gunshot damage. But the letter that accompanied Stephen on his final journey home made the reality undeniable.

Sarah insisted that Kyrah read it aloud to her, and it took all of her strength to complete the message without falling apart all over again.

My darling Sarah,

I will not ask you to forgive me, and I will not try to explain what has happened, for it makes no difference now. Instead I will ask you to remember, my darling, back to the time when we were young and our love was new. Try hard to recall the things I told you, the insignificant thoughts that were only a feeble effort to let you know how very much I cared. Look to the written evidence of my feelings, recall how we carved our love in the place where we came to return, and you will know that I did not leave you with nothing. Tell Kyrah that I love her, and know how very much I love you.

With all my heart,

Stephen

Sarah was so caught up in her emotion over the letter that she completely missed the hidden meaning Kyrah was certain he'd intended. She tried repeatedly to get her mother to figure out what he was trying to say, but Sarah insisted she didn't know. She accused Kyrah of grasping at something that wasn't there, but Kyrah tore the house apart, knowing that he'd left money hidden somewhere. He wouldn't leave them destitute. He *wouldn't,* just as he'd said. But she found nothing.

The cry of a bird startled Kyrah, and she looked up to see the flapping of wings as it flew away from one of the high windows of the church ruins. The present flooded back into her with a painful burst and she wrapped her arms around her middle, groaning at the reality. She'd lost all sense of time as she'd sat among the church ruins, lost in her memories. Now she felt suddenly very cold as she hurried quickly home, fearing that Sarah might have become distraught in her absence.

Kyrah found evidence that her mother had gotten something to eat and had returned to bed. It was becoming increasingly evident that Sarah would not be capable of solving their problems. Kyrah forced back a fresh tide of emotion and tried to focus on the future.

The days passed all too quickly. With a mounting sense of desperation, she kept her mother cared for, got all of their things packed and ready to go, and worried constantly over where they would go when their time ran out.

There were no relatives to speak of, and if there was money, Kyrah couldn't find it.

Three days before the two-week deadline, Mr. Westman's solicitors returned to see that the details were taken care of, and Kyrah stated her problem directly.

"You must tell this Mr. Westman that he has not given us adequate time. We have nowhere to go, and very little money to speak of, and—"

"I suspected that was the case," the large one said. "In fact, Miss Payne, we have taken this into consideration and have discussed it with Mr. Westman. There is a cottage on the estate, and he insists that this is where you must stay."

Kyrah didn't feel the least bit appreciative of Mr. Westman's apparent kindness, despite it taking a great deal of worry from her mind. She hadn't met the man, but already she hated him. He had taken everything from them.

Her next thought was that she would have to find work somewhere to support her and her mother. But as if her mind had been read, the solicitor added, "Mr. Westman also offers the suggestion that you might be able to work for him, as he will be needing to acquire servants. If this is agreeable to you, then everything should be taken care of."

Kyrah said nothing. It seemed that everything was well taken care of indeed. Two days later, she and her mother were residing in the small cottage where Sarah had grown up, and Mr. Peter Westman came personally to call. He sauntered into the tiny entry hall of the cottage to face her silent, expressionless stare. She was glad her mother was asleep.

"Good afternoon." He smiled, and Kyrah wanted to slap him as he glanced around easily and added, "This isn't such a bad little place."

He introduced himself arrogantly, then rambled on for a moment about how nice it was to have a home of his own. Kyrah scrutinized him closely, and thought that perhaps some might consider him handsome. But to her, his dark, slick hair and glassy eyes were revolting.

"State your business please," Kyrah said at last, interrupting his ongoing prattle.

He looked at her with a sharp smirk, then said in a tone to clearly indicate her new status, "I assume you're in need of work. If you want to stay here, you're going to have to earn your keep. I'll expect you at the big house early tomorrow."

"My mother is ill," Kyrah said quickly. Lifting her chin, she added, "But I will be there."

"Good," he said, and left Kyrah to her fate.

She quickly got their things in order and searched the cottage thoroughly, hoping to find what she was certain Stephen had left for them. Accepting at last that he'd been mistaken, or that it would simply never be found, Kyrah and her mother settled into a way of life that was utterly distasteful, simply because of the means that had brought it about and the emptiness that resulted.

Through the entire nightmare of dealing with her father's death, adjusting to life as a servant, and seeing her mother's health quickly deteriorate from the pain of the entire drama, Kyrah told herself over and over: *If only Ritcherd were here.*

Despite her constant anxieties, Ritcherd was always in her thoughts, and she ached for him. In order to cope, her mind became more and more preoccupied with the memories they had shared. As the months slipped by, she couldn't help recalling the countless times he had spared her from the harshness of the world. And Kyrah was certain that if he were not off in the colonies, this whole ordeal would not have gone so far. Ritcherd would have found a way to spare her and her mother from having to suffer through all of this humiliation and degradation.

She received letters from Ritcherd, usually in bunches and very rarely, since the passage of ships was infrequent. But Kyrah thrived on those letters and the tender things he had written, with vague references to their future. Although she wrote back, she couldn't be certain that he would receive all, if any, of her letters. Still, she wrote nothing about the circumstances she and her mother were enduring. She simply couldn't bring herself to write down the reality of what had happened in a letter that she doubted would ever make it to him. Besides, it would have been far too humiliating to tell Ritcherd that she was now spending several hours each day cleaning the home in which she had once lived so graciously. How could she tell him she had no choice but to cook and do laundry for this wretched man who had taken it all away from them, just to keep a roof over their heads and food on the table? How could she ever define in a letter the uneasiness she felt when Peter Westman was in a room with her? Ritcherd could do nothing about it from where he was, she reasoned, so there was no point in distressing him over it. When he came back, everything would be all right.

A loud knocking at the door aroused Kyrah from her typical train of thought, and she begrudgingly rose from her scrubbing to answer it, wiping her hands on her apron. She was pushing a stray wisp of hair away with the back of her hand when she pulled the door open to face the stern expression of Jeanette Buchanan. *What does she want?* Kyrah snarled inwardly.

She felt herself being smugly appraised from head to toe, then Ritcherd's mother curtly asked, "Is Mr. Westman in?"

"No," she stated. "He'll be gone until the end of the week."

"Will you tell him I called," she stated coldly. Jeanette surveyed Kyrah once more, then turned and walked back to the elegant carriage waiting in the drive, while Kyrah wondered what on earth would make this woman suddenly associate with Peter Westman. He'd lived in this house nearly two years, and she'd never come around before.

Kyrah closed the door and leaned against it, feeling almost weak. She had always hoped that time would allow Jeanette to accept her. But now the situation was far worse than Kyrah had ever imagined, and she knew it would never happen.

Knowing that daydreaming would not get the work done, Kyrah forced herself back to reality and kept far too busy to contemplate how much had changed in Ritcherd's absence, and how these changes would affect her when he *did* come home.

A familiar knot tightened in Ritcherd's stomach as he calmly reviewed battle plans with his officers. The sultry clouds gathering overhead well represented his mood. Despite the many times he'd lived through this, the dread never lessened. He knew that men—his men—would die. And he always wondered if this battle would be the one to cost him life or limb. But always foremost in his mind was Kyrah. Surrounded by death and dissolution, thoughts of Kyrah kept him sane. She had become his life's blood through the years they'd spent together, and no distance between them could keep her from his mind.

The years had made him well practiced at seeing from the inside out. He could stare at maps and battle plans and see nothing but Kyrah, the way he remembered last seeing her, blossoming into womanhood, her eyes full of innocent grief at his leaving. He could gaze over a littered battlefield and see only Kyrah, her dark curls wrestling with the Cornish wind, her timid purity that nearly left him breathless, even the first time he'd laid eyes on her. As young as he'd been, nothing since that day had left such a remarkable impression on him as Kyrah Payne.

"Letter for you, Captain Buchanan," a courier announced, startling Ritcherd from his thoughts. He sighed as he took it, wondering what new measure of bad news he might be receiving from his superior officers. But the knot inside him briefly dissipated into the first measure of happiness he'd felt in months as the courier added, "Looks like it's from a lady."

"Thank you," he barely managed to say, then nodded toward his men. "If you will excuse me." They smiled with understanding as he hurried away. Alone in his tent, he ran his fingers over the familiar scrawling of his name on the envelope, noting the tattered look about it. Just as the others, it had come into his hands with an obvious indication that the trek it had taken to find him had been difficult. This was only the fifth letter in two and a half years, and he wondered how many had not made it at all.

Her letters had always been lengthy and mostly filled with memories they had shared. He had read them each countless times, treasuring the evidence of their past together and the hope that they would share the future. But this letter already felt different, and he wondered why.

Carefully he broke the seal, and immediately felt something tug at him as he pulled out the single page and unfolded it to read:

Dearest Ritcherd,

I think of you often and hope this letter finds you well and safe. I am fearful when I think of the things you must be facing, and pray that you will return unharmed.

I received letters from you yesterday. There were four together with dates ranging over three months. I must thank you for them. They, as the others, are very dear to me. I hope that you are receiving my letters. I have sent several.

I should be going, for my time is brief. Mother and I are doing well and are anxiously awaiting your return. If you know when it will be, try to let us know. We need you.

God be with you, Captain Buchanan. May He keep you safe and return you to your homeland soon.

With much love,
Kyrah

Puzzled and disturbed by the letter, Ritcherd held the tattered page in his hand and closed his eyes. Trying hard to filter out the constant bustling noises outside his tent, he tried to imagine what she would look like if he could see her now. He was certain that time had changed her. She would be a woman now, and he hated the thought of having missed these years with her. He wondered if she had had a coming out. Surely Stephen and Sarah would have made it the finest, just as they did with everything for Kyrah. He realized the age difference that had put him and Kyrah in separate realms would no longer exist. He wanted to be with her, and his most fervent prayer was that she had not grown up to realize she could live without him.

Again he looked at the letter he'd just received, noting the date was several months earlier. That, combined with the subtle mood of desperation, left him feeling more helpless and frustrated than he ever had in his life. He wondered why there was no reference to Stephen, and why the letter's briefness made him feel like Kyrah was too busy to write more.

Sounds filtering from the camp forced him back to the present, and he grudgingly rose from his makeshift bed. Despite the uncertainty of a letter getting to Kyrah, he sat and wrote to her, if only to ease his own mind. He had it sent out right away, along with two others: another for Kyrah and one to his mother.

The night was sleepless and dawn came far too soon, accompanied by the threat of a storm. With Kyrah's letters tucked carefully in his breast pocket, Ritcherd stoically went into battle. The horror had barely begun when he turned to look into the eyes of a colonist soldier. The gun was aimed at his chest, but as Ritcherd lunged to avoid the shot, he felt his arm catch fire before he even heard the blast. Immediately he lost all sense of time. It felt like eternity before he finally passed out on the rain-worn battlefield, yet it seemed only moments later that he awoke in a makeshift hospital with the stench of war and death all around him. The pain in his arm was unbelievable. The fear that he might lose it to infection was worse.

His only method of coping was a conscious effort to become lost in memories that gave him some comfort. If he concentrated hard enough on the past, he could almost completely shut out the din of anguish surrounding him. When they gave him something to ease the pain, losing himself became all the easier, and he allowed his mind to drift back to the day he'd met Kyrah, the day that had changed his life more than he ever would have dreamed at the time.

When he'd first laid eyes on the beautiful little girl with dark, unruly hair, he'd wondered briefly if she could somehow ease the pain of recently losing his sister. By asking her questions, to which she'd nodded her replies, Ritcherd confirmed that Kyrah had just moved into the old Greene estate. It was the only house within walking distance of the old church that didn't have established residents. And he'd heard his mother make some derogatory comments at the breakfast table just that morning about the *nouveau riche* invading the area. Well, if the newly rich were a different breed from the old rich he'd grown up with, Ritcherd was all for getting to know them.

He immediately felt drawn to Kyrah for reasons he couldn't put a finger on. And when she took him home with her, his comfort only deepened. There was something about her and the surroundings in which she lived that fascinated him. He wondered if these were the kind of people he'd only heard of, people who didn't need money to be happy. He found a clue to support that theory when Sarah Payne first entered the room, dressed in a dark skirt and white blouse, with a scarf wrapped around her hair to protect it from the dust of renovation. She was as ordinary and beautiful as the moors. And Kyrah was very much like her.

When he inevitably had to introduce himself, he feared what the Paynes' reaction might be. He had truly hoped that his neighbors could have gotten to know him for what he was, without the prerequisite of having to be a Buchanan of Buckley Manor. But Stephen and Sarah's attitude quickly put him at ease. Their acceptance was immediate and true. In fact, he thrived on their acceptance so thoroughly that he often feared wearing out his welcome. But he wanted so badly to be with the Paynes that he made every effort to be perfectly polite and helpful.

Ritcherd's years of watching Kyrah grow from a child into a young woman were the happiest of his life. Right from the start, he could see that she had a sensitive perception of life that he knew he lacked. The day came when Ritcherd realized he was getting too old to play boy-hero to a little girl, and he began spending more of his time with other boys in the area. It didn't take long, however, to realize how much he preferred Kyrah's company to any available alternatives. The one friendship he maintained was with George Morley, who lived some miles north. George had a similar background, and he was fun to be with as they did the things that growing boys do. But his relationship with George simply wasn't enough on its own. Nowhere could he find the peace and perfect contentment he found with Kyrah. Instinctively he'd believed that the path to true happiness in his future could only be found by holding Kyrah's hand, even though he often felt unworthy of her.

Nearly six years Kyrah's elder, Ritcherd felt time begin to separate them more and more as they grew older. Of course, it was never difficult to conjure up the childishness to play their games and laugh and run, and inevitably she would raise herself to his level and spend hours talking about philosophies of life and the world in a way that left Ritcherd in awe. But gradually Ritcherd began to see Kyrah differently. It happened soon after he'd returned from a brief jaunt to Plymouth with George and a few of his friends. His experiences there were both disturbing and maturing. But the real growing up came when he'd returned to see Kyrah and he realized that in not so many years she would be a woman. The thought often brought on confusion or impatience, and at times it was difficult to be alone with her and not wonder what it would be like to hold her the way he dreamed about when he'd lie awake nights and ponder his relationship with a thirteen-year-old girl.

Knowing that Kyrah's parents were perceptive and sensitive to his moods, he felt certain they suspected the change in his feelings. And it wasn't a surprise when Stephen invited Ritcherd to go hunting and they ended up instead at the pub. It wasn't unusual for them to hunt or go into town, but the look in Stephen's eyes told Ritcherd there was something specific he wanted to say. He fully expected Stephen to bring up Kyrah, but his heart pounded as he wondered if Stephen would request that he and Kyrah not continue their relationship as it was. The thought seemed unbearable.

"There is something I'd like to talk to you about, my boy," Stephen said after ordering drinks and leaning across the table.

"Go on," Ritcherd replied, trying not to sound nervous.

"You'll soon be nineteen, and . . ." Stephen chuckled nervously. "You're already taller than I am."

Ritcherd gave a tense smile and glanced down at the drink he hadn't touched.

"You're a man now, Ritcherd. So I think you're old enough to understand something I want to tell you."

Stephen leaned back and pushed his fingers through the sandy red hair that reminded Ritcherd of a fox. "You know," he mused, "there are two things on this earth that are more precious to me than any measure of wealth. The first is Sarah." He sighed. "How can a man explain what a woman like that can mean in his life? I would die for her, Ritcherd. I've often wished that I was more than what I am—for her sake. She likely deserved better. But at least I'm good at what I do. Gambling may not be an admirable profession, but it's allowed me to give Sarah the kind of lifestyle she deserves."

Stephen paused to look at Ritcherd, who watched him attentively. This was not how he'd expected the conversation to go.

"And close to Sarah in worth to me is Kyrah. You can't imagine what it's like to love a woman so much, and then see her immortalized in such a way. I hope one day you will know what that's like." He smiled. "I believe you will."

Ritcherd glanced down again, feeling an indescribable emotion.

"You probably know Kyrah as well as I do—perhaps better. I don't need to tell you how wonderful she is. I can see how the two of you care for each other. And one day, some good things could come from the feelings you share."

Ritcherd held his breath. He could feel it coming.

"Kyrah is, in many ways, still a girl. But the separate realms you inhabit now, because of your age difference, will not exist one day."

Stephen paused and their eyes met. Ritcherd conveyed silently that he was listening, and Stephen continued with his natural ability to put the most sensitive subjects into the easiest words.

"I know how many years you and Kyrah have known each other, and I can well understand how you would want to express your affection for her—as any man would. But you must be patient, Ritcherd."

The intensity in Stephen's eyes deepened as he made certain Ritcherd was watching him. "You must remember," his tone was gentle despite the stern way he lifted his finger, "if you do anything to deny Kyrah the right to move from childhood into womanhood at a normal pace, and under the best possible circumstances, you will never cease to regret it. Do you understand what I'm saying, Ritcherd?"

"I understand," he answered directly, feeling immense relief. The man actually trusted him.

"It may not be easy for you, my boy. But I doubt there is any amount of desire, or gratification of that desire, that could ever compensate for what you'd be taking from her. If you're patient, Ritcherd, you will reap the rewards. She's a wonderful girl, much like her mother. And if it works out, well . . ." Stephen tipped his head and smiled widely. "The two of you could be very happy together." His expression turned speculative. "I hope I'm not making too much of a presumption by saying that . . . I mean . . ."

"No, sir," Ritcherd smiled, "you're not."

Stephen laughed and downed his drink. "We'd best do a little hunting before the day is through, don't you think?"

Hours later they returned to the house, and Sarah insisted that Ritcherd stay for supper, although he ate with the Paynes more than he did at home. After supper, while they were all seated in the drawing room, Ritcherd unobtrusively observed Kyrah, sitting close beside him, her feet tucked up beneath her. And he could see the wisdom in Stephen's advice. He knew the coming years could be difficult, feeling for her as he did. He longed for the day when she would be a woman, but he felt grateful for the privilege of knowing her as a child. Just looking into her eyes now, he was filled with a formless contentment. And it was easy to imagine the life they would share, raising children of their own.

The years brought them so close that Ritcherd often declared they could look into each other's eyes and know what the other was thinking or feeling. Kyrah's gentle perceptions taught Ritcherd that life was far more than the attaining of material possessions and the climbing of social ladders. And never once, with all the time he spent alone with Kyrah, did Stephen ever indicate a lack of trust in Ritcherd to keep Kyrah's best interests at heart. Stephen's attitude about this and so many other things made Ritcherd wonder why his own father had to be so stony and mistrusting. But knowing his father would never change, Ritcherd merely used the comparison to appreciate just how dear Stephen was to him.

"Stephen," he murmured, feeling a hand on his arm. He opened his eyes, and the present slapped him in the face with the sounds and smells of death and disease. "Stephen," he said again, trying to shut out the pain as the wound in his arm was cleansed and bandaged. How he longed to be with Stephen, to absorb his fatherly wisdom and caring. He drifted back into oblivion, imagining Stephen putting Kyrah's hand into his so they could be married.

Ritcherd nearly went mad through the weeks of recovery, wondering what was happening with Kyrah. At times he truly believed she was with him, then he became devastated to realize it was only a product of his fevered delirium. In the moments his mind was coherent, he filled his thoughts with her, and the one thing that kept him sane was the vision of returning home to Kyrah. He could almost feel her running into his arms, and everything would be all right again. With that, he swore that if he ever got out of this country alive, he would never come back. All he wanted was to go home. Home—to Kyrah.

Chapter Three

The Return of the Captain

The only bright spot in the drudgery of Kyrah's life was the rare opportunity to sit in the little garden by the cottage. An ivy-covered stone wall surrounded the garden, which could be entered through a wooden gate. A little stone bench and a huge broad-leafed tree were surrounded by little patches of wildflowers in no particular pattern. A little ditch of water ran under the wall, through the garden, and out again beneath the opposite wall. A carpet of little yellow buttercups grew on the banks of the ditch, and Kyrah loved the sound of water running past.

In her little snatches of free time, it was difficult to make a trek all the way to the church ruins and back. But she could come here to the garden and lose herself, if only briefly. And her thoughts were always with Ritcherd. If only he were here, she told herself, everything would be better. But he wasn't here, and life could not possibly be worse. Time had made Kyrah accept her circumstances, but it didn't make her burdens any easier to bear.

Each morning she would rise before the sun and see to her mother's needs before going to the big house to work. There were few other servants, and Kyrah found her responsibilities overwhelming. She was glad for the times when Peter Westman's business took him out of the area for long periods of time. But when he was home, he more than made up for his weeks away. Kyrah could never explain the subtle uneasiness she felt in his presence. There was something in the way he looked at her that made her feel cheap and dirty. His subtle comments and degrading glances continually belittled and humiliated her. When Peter Westman was around, he didn't let her forget for a moment that she was nothing more than a servant, the daughter of a foolish gambler. He seemed to take some kind of perverse

35

pride in having power over her, and she feared that one day he might want more out of her than cleaning and cooking.

Whether Peter was at home or abroad, Kyrah was continually reminded of his attitude simply by the work she was required to do on his behalf. It wasn't until she made certain the house was in order and the laundry gathered that she made it home to get her mother's lunch. She then washed the dirty clothes and linens, hung them to dry and went back to the big house, rarely returning home before dark. Just today Peter had returned from a particularly long jaunt to the continent, and Kyrah felt the increase in her workload by having to cook his meals and do his personal laundry.

Late that night, Kyrah stared into the dim reflection of her bedroom mirror as she brushed her hair down. Peter's insinuating glances catapulted through her mind, echoed by the childhood taunts that had mellowed to quiet whisperings each time she went into town. It was becoming more and more difficult to look at herself and comprehend the visions of a lady that Ritcherd Buchanan had often spoken of. Setting the brush down, Kyrah sighed as she turned her hands over to survey their worn appearance. They were not a lady's hands. Of that she was certain.

Exhausted, she attempted to push her thoughts away, knowing they were trite in comparison to her responsibilities. The days were long and hard, and the nights were too short to achieve the rest she needed. Habitually she sighed and pondered how it might be if only Ritcherd were here. But tonight something felt different. She looked into the mirror again and felt as if someone else was looking back at her. She'd changed. Perhaps it was one too many glares of smug disapproval from Jeanette Buchanan, or one too many times that Peter Westman had reminded her with a sneer of who and what she had become. Whatever the reason, something had changed in Kyrah, and she had to ask herself: what *if* Ritcherd were here?

If Ritcherd were here, she would be humiliated and torn to pieces by his feeling obligated to show interest in her when she was no longer of his social status, even though to many she never had been. The very idea was so devastating that she had to force it away in order to get some much-needed rest. But the spark in her thoughts needed little to kindle it into a consuming fire, and the following morning Jeanette Buchanan was quick to provide the fuel.

Fortunately for Kyrah, her path rarely crossed with Ritcherd's mother, and she fought to hide how the woman's very presence unnerved her as she waited in line at the post office for her mail. Kyrah knew that Jeanette could easily have her mail picked up by servants, but she seemed to enjoy opportunities to gossip, or at least to collect fodder for it. Jeanette, who had already received her own mail, stopped to chat with someone nearby, glaring several times toward Kyrah. Their eyes met only once, and Kyrah marveled at how thoroughly cold she could feel from a mere glance. Noticing the fineness of everything Jeanette was wearing, Kyrah couldn't help but feel intimidated when she compared it to her own humble attire. Trying hard to remain expressionless, Kyrah kept her eyes turned away, wishing she could ignore the conversation that was obviously being carried on for her benefit.

After Jeanette announced that she'd just received a letter from Ritcherd, she couldn't miss the opportunity to add that Miss Trenton, the daughter of a lord, had been writing to her son and was greatly anticipating his return, as was Miss Roscom, the sister of a baronet.

Kyrah was grateful to finally reach the window, and Mrs. Farrell, the postmistress, greeted her warmly. "I've got a surprise for you," she said, smiling. Kyrah could hear from behind that Jeanette had stopped talking. She couldn't help hoping that Mrs. Farrell was overheard as she added, "Five letters from Captain Buchanan. They sure come all at once, don't they?"

Kyrah thanked her and turned away, noting by her brief glance at Jeanette's expression that her hopes had not been in vain. Once outside, Kyrah shuffled through the bunch of letters, sighed, then went quickly to see to her other business. It would be hours yet before she would have time to read them.

Past midnight, in the loft of the cottage with a single lamp burning, Kyrah finally found herself alone with what Ritcherd had written. She sorted the letters in order of dates so that she could read them in sequence, then she read what she had come to recognize as an effort to tell her what he was doing without complaining about the circumstances, even though she knew he was miserable.

It was the last letter that struck her differently.

My dearest Kyrah,

I received a letter from you today, the first in a very long time. It was dated several months ago, and I feel so lost and isolated out here when I think of how separate our worlds are and the time that even communication takes to travel between us. I fear that perhaps things are not as they should be with you. I can't explain why. I only know that it adds to my frustration at being so far away.

There is little I can say, Kyrah, except that I pray constantly that this war will be over soon, and perhaps the gaps between our worlds can be bridged. I hope that time will have eased some of the differences between us, and fate will find us in the same realm at last.

Whatever it is, Kyrah, we will work it out. Give your parents my love. I hope it won't be much longer.

Forever yours,

Ritcherd

Kyrah wasn't certain why she felt suddenly angry, though she sensed her anger was directed more toward what fate had done to her than toward Ritcherd himself. She stuffed the letters in the bottom of a drawer with the others, then fell asleep quickly from exhaustion, knowing there was no bridge wide enough to bring her into the same realm as Ritcherd Buchanan.

Through the following days, she became certain that it would be best for everyone concerned if Ritcherd remained out of her life. She almost prayed that he had fallen in love in the months since he'd last written, so he could be spared having to graciously tell her that he couldn't associate with a servant girl.

She often thought of the little bird she had given freedom to so many years ago, and knew that the circumstances here were much the same. She had known then that despite how badly she had wanted to keep the little bird, it would have been selfish of her to expect it to stay. And now, she simply loved Ritcherd too much to see their relationship ruined by the change in circumstances that made it impossible for them to be together.

On a hot August afternoon, through the grapevine of servants she had unwillingly joined, Kyrah got word that Captain Buchanan was back in England and would soon be returning home. She felt tangibly ill. The wall she had built up to protect herself from any further pain or humiliation had wedged into her heart, leaving her with no desire to even see him. Little by little, she had convinced herself that they should not be together. And the attitude of the man she worked for only added to her conviction that she was not the woman for Ritcherd.

Nearly three years after Captain Buchanan left his home in Cornwall, word came that he would be arriving soon. Kyrah felt dismayed to realize that knowing he was nearby left her breathless, and she couldn't help wondering what he was doing. What did he look like? Was he still the same, or had he changed significantly?

She nearly hated herself for lying awake with thoughts of him, and told herself repeatedly that she must be strong and find a way to keep them apart—for his sake. It made her shudder to think of the degradation and humiliation he would suffer from his friends and acquaintances—not to mention his mother—if he were to associate with her after what had happened. She just couldn't let him face it. It was as simple as that.

Ritcherd leaned his head back against the plush interior of the carriage and thanked God for bringing him home at last. He had no idea how long he'd been hospitalized in the colonies, and the weeks on the ship returning to England had dragged incessantly. When they'd finally arrived in Portsmouth, he was hospitalized immediately because he was still having problems with his arm. The previous morning it had been decided that the arm was past the threat of infection, and that it would get no better and no worse. At last he was going home.

It was late when the carriage halted in front of Buckley Manor. Ritcherd stepped down, then he stood in the drive until it rolled away, looking up at the ominous structure before him, wondering why it filled him with dread. A maid he didn't recognize scurried into the hall when the door closed loudly. He eased her fearful look when he said, "Please tell Mrs. Buchanan that her son is home."

She curtsied and bustled up the stairs while Ritcherd set his bag down and absorbed the familiar surroundings that made him feel like a stranger. He pushed open the drawing room door and was not surprised to see that the room had been redecorated. He was just about to pour himself a drink when he heard someone enter the room and he turned to see his mother, who had obviously been about to go to bed. Her hair was down, and she wore an elaborate dressing gown that suited her well.

"Ritcherd," she smiled breathlessly, "I don't believe it."

Stepping forward to press a kiss to his cheek, she laughed slightly. Ritcherd returned the kiss and felt himself smile for the first time in months. He actually felt glad to see her.

"Oh," she said, touching his face, "you don't look so well. Sit down. I'm certain the journey was terrible for you."

"It was long," he stated, pouring a drink and sitting across the room from her.

"I was informed that you were in Portsmouth. And I got word just yesterday that you would be returning soon, but I had no idea when, or I would have been better prepared. You should have written."

"I couldn't," he said with no inflection in his voice, and Jeanette took obvious notice of his right arm in a sling.

"They told me you'd been wounded. Is it terribly serious?" she asked, wrinkling her nose in distaste.

"It could have been worse," he said.

"I've been dreadfully worried."

"Portsmouth isn't so very far. You could have inquired . . . or come yourself."

"I thought about it," she said apologetically, "but I've been so dreadfully busy and—"

"Yes, I see you've been redecorating again," he interrupted with a nonchalant glance about the room.

"Do you like it?" she asked with a lilt in her voice.

"It's not so bad."

"Well," she turned her attention back to him, "what will you do now that you're back? You look like you could use some rest."

"I'm sick to death of resting," he said and took a sip of brandy.

"I'm certain the Cornwall air will put some color back into you. You always thrived on it."

"I have to agree there."

"As soon as I heard you were in England, I set right to work planning a celebration." Ritcherd sighed. It was just like his mother to find any excuse for a social. "When I heard you were coming soon, I had the invitations sent right out. Everyone will be so pleased to see you again."

Ritcherd made a noise to indicate he'd heard. He couldn't think of anybody she might have invited that he had any desire to see.

"Beyond that," she went on, "do you have any plans?"

"The first thing I'm going to do is see Kyrah," he said with his first note of enthusiasm, but Jeanette's expression immediately lost all animation.

"Ritcherd! You can't be serious."

"Do I look serious?" he asked tensely, realizing it had been foolish to hope she might have changed her opinions of Kyrah.

"Surely you can't intend to maintain a relationship with her after all that's happened."

Ritcherd felt an uneasy prickle at the back of his neck. He knew his ignorance was evident when his mother added with an incredulous gasp, "Surely you've heard."

"Heard what?" His eyes narrowed.

"What's happened, of course. Obviously you haven't. I wondered if I should write and tell you myself, but I didn't figure it was any of my business. I'm surprised she didn't write and let you know. But then, I daresay she'd have been too humiliated to tell you herself. She should be. Although I expected something like this would happen. People like that never last long when they try to exist where they don't belong, and who's to say that—"

"Mother!" he interrupted impatiently, a nervous dread smoldering inside of him. "Get to the point."

"Why, they lost the estate, darling," she stated smugly, and Ritcherd felt a lump catch in his throat. When the shock left him unable to reply, Jeanette went on quickly, seeming to thrive on the conversation. "From what I hear, it happened just like that!" She snapped her fingers. "Of course, the man who has moved into the house is very nice. He's about your age, I believe. And I've—"

"Where are they?" he pressed, leaning forward.

"Most likely where they always should have been," she answered quickly.

"And where is that?" he asked, his impatience turning to anger.

"The cottage, of course . . . where Mrs. Payne lived years ago, with that . . . *school teacher.*"

Ritcherd sighed and looked toward the window. The formless concerns he'd felt throughout his time away came all too prominently to the surface. He wanted to know what had happened, but knew there was no need to ask. He only had to look pointedly at his mother for her to continue.

"You must know, Ritcherd, that things have changed a great deal in your absence." She seemed certain she could convince him that Kyrah was not the girl for him—and never had been. "She's working for Mr. Westman now and—"

"Doing what?" he shouted, moving to the edge of his chair.

"How should I know?"

"What *do* you know?"

"Miss Payne is working to keep herself and her mother fed, from what I hear. Thanks to Mr. Westman, they weren't thrown right out on the street."

Ritcherd felt sick inside already, but as certain aspects of Kyrah's letters came to mind, he had to ask, "Where is Stephen?" She looked at him bewildered, and he wondered what horrible thing had happened. Was he in prison? Had he become ill? His impatience rising, he clarified, "Stephen Payne. Kyrah's father."

"I thought you would have heard," Jeanette said in a tone that made Ritcherd's heart pound. "It's been years. It was quite a shock, though I daresay it shouldn't have been. After all, what would you expect from a gambler? It was his own fault that he lost everything he had in a game of cards. But that's the way people like that live, never knowing one day to the next if they'll have anything at all. If he'd been any kind of a man, he wouldn't have been a gambler in the first place. But it just proves my theory when you see how he took the cowardly way out and—"

"Mother!" Ritcherd shouted. "Where is he?"

Jeanette wore no expression at all. As if discussing the weather, she stated simply, "He's dead. He shot himself."

Ritcherd stood abruptly, and everything inside of him went cold. He threw his glass of brandy against the wall in a physical reaction to what his mind was still unable to comprehend.

"Naturally I assumed you knew," Jeanette stammered somewhere on the brink of his coherency, but he made no reply. His chest tightened and his palms began to sweat. A quick glance toward his mother showed only a dumb expression that he interpreted as disgust. Unable to bear her attitude any longer, he lumbered from the room and up the stairs, needing only to be alone. By the time he had his bedroom door closed behind him, the tightness in his chest had become painful and he struggled to fill his lungs with air. He went to his knees, suddenly weak as his mother's words catapulted through his mind over and over. *He's dead. He shot himself.*

"No!" Ritcherd groaned, losing his equilibrium as the blood rushed from his head. "Dear God, no!" he muttered, nearly pressing his head to the floor. "Please, no!"

What went wrong? he asked himself until his head throbbed. *What could have happened to cause such madness?* And as always, at the center of his thoughts was Kyrah. How had she coped with this? He groaned again to recall his mother's account. *Working to keep herself and her mother fed.* He couldn't believe it! Why hadn't Kyrah written and told him? He could have helped her. If he'd only known, he could have had his solicitor see that their needs were met.

He felt certain his mother's rendition of the story, in addition to being sordid, was most likely the product of gossip, and he had to wonder what really happened. There was so much that didn't make sense. It was all so horrible—so completely and utterly horrible.

Through a grief-stricken, sleepless night, the only comfort Ritcherd could find was his certainty that with morning, Kyrah would be in his arms. He knew that together they could overcome the pain of anything—even this.

The sun had barely appeared when Ritcherd hurried out to the stable, pleased to see his own stallion there and well cared for. He was grateful to be alone when saddling the horse with one hand made his struggle to get dressed seem easy. Mounting was not a problem, but he found it took him several minutes to be able to maneuver the reins with his left hand. Finally getting a feel for it, he rode quickly toward the cottage, inwardly cursing the damage this war had done to his life—and Kyrah's. His heart was racing when he knocked at the door, and Sarah's voice was the best sound he'd heard in years as she called for him to enter.

He stepped into the tiny, dimly lit entryway and closed the door behind him. He felt briefly uncertain until Sarah's voice came again. "I'm here in the parlor." He made no reply and she added, "Who's there?"

Quietly he stepped into the room, saying with an irrepressible smile, "Hello, Sarah."

Her eyes widened in disbelief from where she sat on the sofa with her feet up. Leaning forward expectantly, she whispered with a tremor in her voice, "Ritcherd? Oh! I can't believe it."

When his eyes adjusted to the light, the first testament of reality struck him. Sarah Payne was a shadow of the woman he'd left three years ago. She'd always been so vibrant, so youthful and full of life. But she had aged more than a decade in three years. Her eyes were sallow, and there was a weak, pained look about her.

"Oh, Ritcherd," she said, reaching her arms out for him and he moved quickly to her side, pulling her close to him with his good arm. She embraced him firmly, then pulled away to look into his eyes. "You're here." She touched his face gently and he saw tears glisten in her eyes. "We were so worried for you. I'm so grateful to see you here. Are you well?"

"Yes," he smiled, "I'm fine."

"You're hurt." Her eyes brimmed with compassion as they moved to his right arm, still cradled in a sling.

"I'm alive," he chuckled, and she smiled at him. "Where is Kyrah?" he asked expectantly.

"She's already left."

"This early?" he questioned in surprise.

"She'll be back around noon," she said. "If you come back then, you can see her."

The disappointment was consuming. Noon seemed so far away. But he smiled again at Sarah. "I'll do that."

Their eyes met, and he wanted to ask how she was doing. But it was so apparent that he knew it would be a stupid question.

"I didn't know," he said feebly, "what happened . . . until . . . just last night, and I . . ."

He stopped when he saw the grief come into her eyes. And she was obviously surprised that he hadn't known. He wanted to ask her what had happened. And even more, he wanted to be able to say something that could somehow make things better for her. It would have been natural to talk about the time they'd been separated, but there was nothing that had happened to either of them that could be discussed without adding to the sorrowful mood of their reunion.

Ritcherd chuckled tensely. "Three years, and I can't think of a blasted thing to say."

Sarah smiled but said nothing.

"I'll come back," he said, standing, "around noon. If she gets here before I do, don't tell her. I'd like . . ."

"Of course," she said easily when he faltered, "you'll want to surprise her."

Ritcherd nodded and bent naturally to kiss Sarah on the cheek. He left the cottage reluctantly, already counting down the minutes until noon.

Kyrah was at the big house earlier than usual, perhaps hoping to avoid the much-talked-about Captain Buchanan. She worked with extra vigor, hoping to push thoughts of him far into the back of her mind. As she walked to the cottage, carrying her usual load of laundry, she felt confident that she would eventually be able to rid him from her thoughts.

"Kyrah," her mother called as she came through the cottage door, "is that you, darling?"

"Yes, Mother," she replied.

"Come in here, darling," Sarah added from her usual spot in the parlor. Kyrah sighed, certain that her mother wanted to continue her speculations about Ritcherd. She had talked of him nonstop since word had come of his return to England. Kyrah didn't think she could bear it any longer.

"What is it, Mother?" she asked blandly, coming into the parlor.

"I believe I left my book in the garden. Would you mind getting it for me?"

Kyrah set the basket down and walked out the side door to the little walled garden behind the cottage. Not so long ago, she had spent every spare minute here, lost in her memories and dreams. But the way things had changed in her mind made the garden distasteful, and she had come to avoid it. The gate creaked as she opened it, and she moved toward the book on the bench.

Ritcherd held his breath as Kyrah walked into the garden, unaware of his presence. It took only a glance to realize that she was more lovely than he could have possibly remembered. But then, she had changed. The girl had become a woman. She was taller, more graceful, more curved. And clearly more beautiful. Her simple attire didn't detract from her natural elegance. The way her hair was pinned into an unruly knot at the back of her head only enhanced the fluid line of her neck and shoulders. It took only a moment to realize that his youthful fantasies of Kyrah becoming a woman had been shallow and incomplete. As difficult as their separation had been, he couldn't help wondering if being away from her had made it possible for him to fully appreciate this moment. He held his breath, counting the seconds until she would be in his arms. Then their lives would begin again, and everything—somehow—would be all right.

Kyrah sighed and picked up the book just as she heard a voice behind her. It was deeper than she'd remembered, yet all too familiar.

"Hello, Kyrah."

The book nearly hit her foot when she dropped it. Turning to face him, everything inside of her fell apart. Captain Ritcherd Buchanan was breathtaking. The fine red coat of his uniform was more striking than she'd remembered. The highly polished tall boots and stark white breeches accentuated the aristocratic air about him. The sling supporting his right arm looked conspicuously out of place. She wondered what had happened, but there was too much consuming her thoughts at the moment to question it. Her incredibly clear memories of the last time she'd seen him came nowhere close to the reality of the man standing before her. He looked more than three years older. It was evident that the time away had been difficult for him, and the hardships had left traces in his face. He appeared all the more dignified, with added character in his expression. But most captivating of all was the undeniable yearning in his eyes.

In Kyrah's resolve to change the circumstances between her and Ritcherd, she'd not counted on what the reality of his presence would do to her. It had become easy in his extended absence to believe that she could live without him. But as he stood directly in front of her, wearing an expectant smile, her resolve melted away. She didn't know what to say, or how to respond. Through an intolerable length of silence, she attempted to reassure herself that it was best to stop their relationship now, before it got started again. The sooner she ended it, the less opportunity he would have to humiliate her when he decided he didn't want her. But all she could think of was how it had felt when he'd kissed her. She had remembered his kiss, thrived on it, ached for it all these years. And now, here she was, facing him in awkward silence, telling herself she should not be his.

When he took a step toward her, Kyrah was startled back to the moment. Knowing she couldn't possibly find her voice even if she knew what to say, she turned away and quickly left the garden.

"Wait!" he called out and followed her, but she ignored him and ran toward the wooded area near the back of the cottage. Unshed tears scalded her eyes as she reached the trees and felt his arm come around her, bringing her to an abrupt halt. Despite his right arm's being useless, he turned her easily to face him. Kyrah felt something awaken inside of her at his touch. His very presence caused feelings she either didn't understand or didn't want to admit to.

Ritcherd couldn't believe it. He'd made it through three years of hell by imagining the joy of this reunion. He'd wanted only to hold her in his arms and cry with her over the death of her father. But the love and compassion he'd been banking on were nowhere to be seen. He wondered what he'd done to deserve such contempt from the one person on earth who meant more to him than any other.

"Where do you think you're going?" he asked, his tone betraying the hurt. "Three years and you can't even say hello?"

"Hello," she replied curtly.

"That's it?"

"What did you want me to say?"

"Say what you feel."

"I don't feel anything," she lied.

Ritcherd made no effort to hide the anguish in his eyes. "You can't mean it," he said hoarsely. Suddenly the months of lying in an army hospital seemed like sport compared to the desperation he was feeling now. She made no reply and he pleaded, "Will you not even give me a chance? I know a lot has changed, but . . . we need to talk about it. We have to try."

Kyrah broke away from his grasp and turned away, hoping to hide her emotion. "There's no need to try. There is not room in my life for you." She sensed more than saw the way his shoulders slumped as he stood behind her, and she wanted with everything she had to turn to him and tell him she didn't really mean it. She needed him. She wanted to be with him, to be a part of his life again.

"That's it, then," he stated flatly. His mind quickly flitted through the years he had invested in his relationship with her. Deeper feelings aside, she was the only true friend he'd ever had. "There's not room for me in your life." He paused and drew a deep breath. "Why?"

"The reasons don't matter," she replied quickly.

"Like hell they don't!" he shouted and grabbed her arm, turning her to face him. "You told me you'd wait for me. And if things have changed, so be it. I can accept that three years is a long time and a lot has happened, but I have a right to know why!"

Kyrah felt weak. She could hardly believe it. But it was true. Ritcherd Buchanan loved her. She could see it in his eyes, hear it in his voice. But that didn't change the circumstances.

"Tell me!" he shouted in response to her silent stare. "Tell me why!" She saw his chin quiver and moisture brim in his eyes. Only then did she realize that in all the years they'd shared, she'd never once seen him cry. She wondered what kinds of horrors he'd been witness to that would bring him back so utterly disheartened.

When Kyrah gave him nothing but a blank expression, he spoke through clenched teeth. "I want to know why you're throwing away everything we had together!"

Kyrah couldn't speak. She couldn't think of anything to say. The real reasons were too humiliating to discuss, if not too painful, so she just turned away while he continued to hold her arm in a firm grip.

"Look at me," he whispered hoarsely. Her eyes moved slowly toward his, but hesitated a moment on his wounded arm in its sling, and a wave of compassion swept through her. But before her gaze moved on, it became evident that she had been misunderstood. He nearly flung her out of his grip. "I would have given you more credit than that, Kyrah Payne."

"What are you talking about?" she asked, genuinely puzzled.

"Is it too much to take . . . to have a man who can't use his right arm?"

"Don't be ridiculous!" she said.

Ritcherd could see the sincerity in her eyes, and he became briefly mesmerized by them. Nobody had eyes like Kyrah—those wide, almost blue eyes, that in their very innocence held a natural provocative quality.

"If that's not it, then tell me what it is!" he pleaded.

"I can't, Ritcherd," she said softly, and his eyes widened in disbelief. "I just can't."

Kyrah ran toward home, unable to face him another second.

Ritcherd couldn't find the motivation to try and stop her.

Kyrah quickly grabbed her mother's book and took it into the cottage, tossing it onto the sofa beside her. "Why didn't you tell me he was out there?" she snarled.

Sarah's shock was evident. "He wanted to surprise you. I thought you'd be glad to see him." When Kyrah didn't respond, Sarah added, *"Why* aren't you glad to see him?" She didn't answer. "Kyrah! It's Ritcherd. He's home. How can you not—"

"I don't want to talk about it," Kyrah snapped and picked up the basket of laundry. Sarah followed her to the back of the house with more vigor than Kyrah had seen in months—maybe years.

"Kyrah," her mother's voice was stern, "tell me what's going on, and tell me now."

"There's nothing to tell," Kyrah insisted while she unwrapped the lunch she had brought from the big house for her mother.

"Then maybe you could tell me why Ritcherd never heard anything about what's happened. Stephen was practically a father to Ritcherd. How could you not let him know?"

"There's nothing he could have done about it."

"That is hardly the point. He had a right to know."

Kyrah sighed and closed her eyes, trying to block out the image of Ritcherd's blatant hurt. "Maybe he did," she admitted. "But it's in the past now. It's hardly worth dwelling on."

"And what about now?" Sarah asked, sitting at the kitchen table. "How can you be this way about seeing him? We're talking about *Ritcherd.*"

"Yes, mother. I know. Ritcherd Buchanan of Buckley Manor; Captain Buchanan, revered war hero. I know." Kyrah sighed again. "There is nothing good I can bring into his life. There's no point in seeing him for any reason."

Kyrah didn't know if her mother agreed, or if she was just too shocked to know what to say. Either way, she hurried outside to get water for the laundry before the conversation could go any further. And maybe, just maybe, if she worked long enough and hard enough, she could push Ritcherd's image out of her mind.

Chapter Four

The Abduction

Ritcherd looked hazily at the empty bottle in front of him, and couldn't believe the pain was still there. He wondered how one woman could make a man hurt so much. He'd been to hell and back in the last three years, only to come home and find that his world had turned upside down. But even having a ball shot through his arm hadn't hurt the way this did.

A tangible sickness enveloped him every time he thought about what had happened in his absence. Stephen dead. Sarah crumbling from a broken heart. Kyrah working night and day to make ends meet. *If only he had been here!* He probably couldn't have kept Stephen alive, but he could have kept the woman he loved from doing servant's work.

Ritcherd managed to make it to his bed late that evening, and awoke the following morning with his head pounding to match the lonely ache he felt. An ocean between him and Kyrah hadn't made him feel as lonely as this.

"You look awful. Have you been drinking?" Jeanette asked with disgust as Ritcherd seated himself at the breakfast table. He made no response and she continued, "That's not like you, Ritcherd. What did they do to you over there?"

"You wouldn't want to know," he stated.

"Whatever might be bothering you," she said while Ritcherd pushed his food around with a fork, "you'll get over it. After all, you're home now and—"

"There is nothing that will make me get over Kyrah," he said more to himself, still feeling half drunk. But Jeanette obviously overheard.

"Ritcherd! Don't tell me that you're acting this way because of *her!* I can understand your being disconcerted with all that's happened, but it should be more evident than ever that she's not the girl for you. Open your eyes and look around. There are plenty of young ladies who would—"

She stopped when Ritcherd's glare became fierce. Abruptly he stood from his chair and pointed a finger at his mother. "Let me make one thing clear. Nothing has changed the way I feel about Kyrah, and nothing is going to stand in my way. I intend to marry her."

Jeanette's shock was apparent, but Ritcherd's own words gave him the motivation he needed. Following a bath and a shave, he sat idly at the cross-road on a stallion when he knew Kyrah would be walking between the cottage and the big house.

He saw her glance in his direction and knew that she was aware of him. But she deliberately avoided looking at him. Coming to the conclusion that he would get nowhere just sitting there, he impulsively galloped the short distance, pulled up beside her, and dismounted as she neared the cottage.

"Good afternoon," he said casually.

"Good afternoon," she replied and continued to walk, but he moved quickly to block her way.

"I'd like to talk to you."

"What is there to say?"

"We could perhaps," he smiled mischievously, and Kyrah almost melted as his lips spread to show that wide, perfect smile, "pretend that we know each other and I could say, 'So how's the weather been the last three years?' and you could say, 'Not so good, really. How about you?'"

Kyrah found it difficult not to smile and felt proud of herself when she didn't. "I don't have time for this," she said, pushing her way around him. "I've got work to do."

"When won't you be working?" he called after her. "I'll make an appointment if I must."

"There are no appointments available," she said dryly, and continued walking toward the cottage.

"Kyrah." He took hold of her arm to stop her and turned her to face him. She noticed that his right arm was no longer in a sling, but he seemed uncomfortable with it, as if it had little use.

"What?" she asked impatiently, attempting to ignore what his touch did to her.

Ritcherd stood silently gazing at her, absorbing the wisps of dark hair blowing around her face that he'd missed so much. He looked hard into her eyes, wanting to ask so many things, but not knowing where to begin. In that moment he cursed the years away from her that had left him unable to predict her thoughts and feelings.

"Just answer one question," he said, fearing she would turn and run again if he didn't tread carefully.

"All right," she said, forcing herself to look down. She couldn't bear the eye contact.

"Why didn't you write and tell me? Or did you? Was the letter lost or—"

"I don't know what you mean," she said, as if she couldn't possibly imagine what he was talking about.

Ritcherd tightened his grip and eased closer. "Then let me clarify myself," he said, anger tainting his voice. "Did you write me a letter, telling me that your father was dead and you'd lost everything?"

Kyrah's breathing became sharp as he put a voice to the reality of her heartache—a heartache she'd never allowed herself to fully face.

"Is this problem between us partly due to poor delivery of the mail?" he pressed. "Or did you deliberately keep me ignorant of circumstances that I had every right to know?"

When Kyrah didn't answer, he pulled her even closer. She felt dizzy and weak from his nearness as much as from the questions he was posing that cut her to the very center.

"You didn't tell me, did you." It wasn't a question. Kyrah's dizziness increased as the anger in his voice became more defined. "He meant more to me than my own father, and you didn't even have the decency to let me know that he was dead. After everything we have shared, how could you leave me to discover such a thing through malicious gossip? Do you care so little for me? Are you so callous that you would—"

"You said one question," Kyrah snapped, unable to bear his tirade another second.

She attempted to squirm out of his grasp, but he held her tightly as he muttered, "I never got an answer."

Kyrah looked up at him with eyes so soft and genuine that Ritcherd was left momentarily speechless. Her eyes turned moist and her voice quivered with intensity as she stated firmly, "I was trying to protect you." The hardness returned to her eyes as she added, "I assumed you had enough to worry about without having to worry over something you could do nothing about."

"But I *could* have done something about it, Kyrah. It didn't have to be this way. There is no reason why you have to work like this. Just say the word, and—"

"I don't want your help, Ritcherd." She finally managed to jerk her arm free. "Go spend your aristocratic charity on someone who really needs it."

Once more, Ritcherd was left speechless as he watched her walk away. Confusion and heartache engulfed him all over again as he mounted his stallion and rode aimlessly over the moors. Eventually he found himself at the church ruins, where he sat for hours, pondering the events of the past three years and the way their world had turned upside down.

Kyrah quickly saw to her mother's needs and returned to the big house to continue her work through the afternoon. But her mind was riddled with confusion. One moment her insides would flutter violently at the thought of Ritcherd's having been so close to her. And the next she felt angry over the circumstances that had come between them, but determined to see that he was never put into a position where he could reject her. While a part of her wondered how she could ever bear living without Ritcherd Buchanan, an inner voice continually reminded her that she could never make him happy. She felt certain he was better off without her, and one day he would realize it.

Deep in thought, she didn't notice Peter Westman entering the room where she was dusting until he cleared his throat and startled her.

"What do you want?" she asked defiantly.

"You'd best tone down a bit, Kyrah Payne, and learn your place around here." He smiled as if his statement had been a kind suggestion. "One day, that attitude could get you into trouble."

Kyrah gave him a scornful glance and returned her attention to her work, trying to ignore his presence. She hated him with everything she had—for what he'd done to her family, for forcing her father to suicide, and for his constant belittling attitude toward her.

"Is there something you wanted?" she asked when he continued watching her.

"I'm glad you asked that," he smirked as he moved closer, and Kyrah felt suddenly afraid at the intensity in his eyes. "I just wanted to have a little chat."

"About what?" she demanded, watching him closely. She couldn't recall him ever wanting to *chat* before now. Simply put, she didn't trust him.

"Well, I understand your captain has returned from the colonies."

Kyrah's heart quickened for reasons she couldn't decipher. The last thing she wanted to discuss with Peter Westman was her relationship with Ritcherd. "He's not *my* captain," she retorted.

"Well, I'm terribly glad to hear that, Kyrah," he said, standing a little too close. "Although I've yet to meet the man personally, his reputation precedes him. I'm certain he's simply not your type."

"What reputation?" she asked, unable to curb her curiosity.

Peter laughed, as if her ignorance was terribly amusing. "He's pompous, arrogant, and full of himself. I've never heard his name come up without hearing that his only interest in women is . . . well . . ." Peter looked at her askance, as if he was too embarrassed to say what he was thinking. "Well, you know what I mean."

"I have no idea what you're talking about," she said, attempting to return to her work.

She gasped when Peter took hold of her arm with one hand and lifted her chin with the other. "Kyrah," he said in a gentle voice that didn't match the depraved glower in his eyes. "I just don't want to see you get hurt. He's not the man for you."

Kyrah jerked her chin away, only to have him touch her hair. She willed herself to stay calm, not wanting to make him angry. She'd seen his temper flare in the past, and she had no desire to tempt it. "Now, on the other hand, you and I are two of a kind."

Kyrah shot her eyes to meet his, wondering if he could possibly be serious. In the two and a half years she'd been working for him, she'd never once seen any hint of personal interest in her. The timing of Ritcherd's return made her wonder what he was up to. Could it be possible that he actually had some hidden romantic interest in her that the presence of another man had spurred to the surface? The thought was too incredulous to entertain. But whatever his motives might be, Kyrah wasn't interested.

"I don't know what kind of woman you think I am, Mr. Westman," she said, wrenching her arm from his grasp, "but it's not *your* kind."

He laughed with an edge of confidence that riled her. "Don't be too sure, Kyrah. One day you're going to have to forgive me for winning that card game. And you're going to have to accept that your father was a fool. And don't forget, my dear, if it weren't for me, you and your mother would be out in the street. A lot of good your darling captain's money did you when you really needed it."

"I told you before," she said, swallowing her anger, "he's not *my* captain."

"Let's hope it stays that way, for your sake." He said it like a threat, and Kyrah wondered what he was implying. "Get back to work," he uttered and left the room, pausing only to give Kyrah a demeaning glare before he left her gratefully alone.

It took several minutes for Kyrah to consciously push away the revulsion she always felt from her encounters with Peter Westman. Anger and fear and hatred all roiled together inside of her until she didn't know how to feel. The fact that he'd attempted to discredit Ritcherd only added to her confusion. Once her emotion had settled, she had to ask herself why her first impulse was to defend him, and to justify in her mind the reasons why she *was* the woman for him. Habit, she concluded and forced herself to finish her duties.

Kyrah's overactive emotions pushed her along more quickly than usual, and she left the big house early. Seeing that it wasn't dark yet, she knew her mother wouldn't be expecting her and she chose to take a long walk and clear her head before returning home. She felt compelled to go the church ruins, urged on by the reappearance of Ritcherd in her life. The memories felt tangible as she entered the stone structure, heaving a deep sigh. She yearned for the time when her life had been simple, and Ritcherd had been a natural part of it without the issues of war and death and poverty standing between them.

In the quiet loneliness of the church's structure, the events of the previous two days suddenly welled up with an unexpected surge of emotion and she sat on one of the stone pews and cried. When her emotion was drained and her tears spent, Kyrah curled up on the bench, too weary to even talk herself into returning home.

Ritcherd had been about to leave the church ruins when he noticed Kyrah approaching, and impulsively he moved into a dark corner and watched her enter. He felt hope in wondering if she had come here looking for him, but it quickly became evident that she was expecting to be alone. His broken heart threatened to crumble as he watched her fall apart in tears. He couldn't imagine what she had been through in his absence, and he cried silent tears while he allowed her to vent her emotion alone. When she finally quieted and curled up on the bench, he instinctively sensed that she needed him and moved stealthily out of the shadows, praying with everything he had that she wouldn't turn and run again.

Ritcherd hesitated, wondering what he could possibly say to bridge the chasm between them. He wished they could go back in time to that first day they'd met in this very place. The memory prompted his voice, and he impulsively repeated the first words he'd ever said to her. "This church was built in the fifteenth century."

Kyrah gasped and sat up straight. A familiar fluttering seized her as she saw Ritcherd silhouetted in the dusky light. The absence of his uniform made it easier to connect him to her childhood friend. His high boots and narrow breeches accentuated his lean, muscular form. The sleeves of his jacket were pushed up casually, and his cravat hung loosely around his neck, leaving the top buttons of his shirt undone and the hair on his chest teasing above it. She wondered briefly how to deal with the realization that she was relieved to see him here. She couldn't deny that her heart yearned to be close to him, to accept the love and support he was offering. But her head was overflowing with reasons why it wasn't right. At the moment, her head felt too weary to put up a fight, and her heart raced with anticipation as he approached and sat beside her.

"I just thought you'd like to know," he added, turning toward her.

Kyrah couldn't think of anything to say, but she found it impossible to tear her gaze away from him.

"You look frightened," he said softly. "Have I changed so much that I scare you?"

When Kyrah made no attempt to reply, Ritcherd cleared his throat and approached an idea that had come to him only a while ago. "There's something I need to clarify," he said. When she said nothing, he added, "Is that all right?"

"I'm listening," she said in a gentle voice that gave him hope.

"Well," he began then hesitated, trying to put the words together carefully. He took a deep breath, then cleared his throat again. "You know, Kyrah, from the day I met you, I always felt privileged and blessed to have you as my friend. And you were such a good friend to me. Your acceptance of me and my ideas was never conditional. I often wondered through these years away if I should have made a point to tell you that a long time ago. I spent time with you because it was where I wanted to be. You fulfilled something in me that I never found anywhere else. Perhaps I came to depend on it too much. Perhaps I took it for granted. At the time it didn't seem so, but living without you has made me appreciate what we shared."

Ritcherd blew out a long, slow breath, knowing he was approaching the difficult part. "The thing is, Kyrah, it wasn't until the day I left that . . . our relationship became something more, something deeper. In my heart I believed at the time that you felt for me . . . the way I felt for you. But we didn't have a chance to adjust to those feelings before I left, and now . . . well, I guess I'm trying to say that maybe I'm being presumptuous to think that you want what I want." He swallowed hard and got to the point. "Maybe we should go back to being friends, and . . . just let the rest . . . evolve . . . with time . . . depending on what *you* want."

Her silence began to unnerve him. He attempted to address some of the vulnerability he was feeling by adding, "Maybe I'm being presumptuous to think that you still want to be friends, but quite frankly, I don't know who else to turn to. You're all I've got that means anything to me, Kyrah, so please . . . if you . . ." He was surprised at the emotion that crept into his voice, and he quickly pressed a hand over his mouth to cover the quivering of his chin.

Kyrah turned away, suddenly feeling horrible at her lack of sensitivity. Whatever the outcome of their situation might be, she had obviously overlooked how all of this appeared to him. In her determination to sever their relationship, it was apparent that she had hurt him. He'd misunderstood her intentions, although she wasn't certain how to make him understand without opening up wounds that were too painful for her to even consider.

"Talk to me, Kyrah," he pleaded, his voice low.

Kyrah turned to look at him, feeling a degree of their comfortable childhood come back to her. She could barely see him as the little remaining light of day trickled out of the church. But his grief was evident. Finally she admitted, "I was wrong not to write and tell you. I can see that now. I apologize for that."

Ritcherd nodded and looked down. He felt like they were making progress, but he still felt as if a stone wall existed between them. He felt as if his heart and soul—even his very life—were on the line. But he couldn't think of anything to say.

He was surprised when she said, "You were not being presumptuous." And it took him a moment to orient his thoughts to her comment. He'd barely begun to make the connection when she added, "I loved you long before the day you left."

Ritcherd's sigh of relief came out sounding more like a sob. He hung his head forward and forced a chuckle in an attempt to cover his emotion. Looking at her again, he was overcome with so many emotions that he couldn't resist the urge to reach out and touch her face. Grateful that she didn't recoil, he eased subtly closer and put his arm around her, pressing his face into her hair. "Oh, Kyrah," he murmured, feeling her soften as she took hold of his shoulders. He eased back to look into her eyes, then meekly pressed a kiss to her cheek. When she didn't resist, he moved his lips close to hers. "My sweet Kyrah," he whispered and pressed his lips to hers. He felt her grip tighten at the same moment her mouth softened.

Kyrah's response brought feelings to the surface in Ritcherd that he'd struggled with through his three years without her. He'd spent countless hours thinking about the kiss they'd shared before he left. It had stirred something deep within him, and given him the hope he'd needed to make it home alive. But the relief of seeing her affection became quickly subdued by the fear and desperation he'd been fighting since the day he'd left her nearly three years earlier. He felt suddenly so afraid of losing her that he feared his emotions were making him overzealous. But Kyrah's response urged him on, and he kissed her the way he'd dreamed of night and day through their separation.

All the sensibility Kyrah felt pulsing into her mind, telling her that she should not be with this man, was banished by his soft words and gentle touch. She tried to tell herself she was leading him on, she was being unfair, she had no right to be allowing this. But oh, how it soothed her heartache and calmed her grief! She longed for it to go on and on. This was what she had dreamed of while she had yearned for him to come back. Then she felt a desperation seep into his kiss that frightened her. She couldn't explain the source of her fear, but it seemed to trigger a release of all the thoughts that she'd been trying to subdue. Once they were set free, they found their way to her heart, pushing all of her feelings for him out of the way.

"Please . . . don't, Ritcherd," she said, turning her face away.

"But . . . " he protested, "you just told me that you love me, and . . . "

"That was a long time ago. So much has changed, Ritcherd. You can't possibly expect everything to just pick up where it left off."

"I love you, Kyrah," he insisted.

"How can you when you don't even know me anymore?" she asked. He was ready to insist that he simply did, and he didn't have to justify his feelings. But she went on before he could speak. "You talk of being friends again, then you kiss me and speak of love as if . . ."

"As if what?" he demanded when she faltered.

"As if I should just fall into your arms and pretend that everything is the way it used to be."

"A lot has changed, Kyrah, but we're still the same two people. We still—"

"No, we're not," she insisted. "We're . . . just not right for each other, Ritcherd. You must trust me. It would be better if—"

"How can I trust something that goes against everything I feel and believe in . . . everything I've felt for you for so long that I can't even remember what it's like not to feel this way?"

"That's just it," she said, the coldness returning fully to her voice. "I'm a habit. But it's just not right."

"Why?" he demanded angrily. "Just tell me why!"

"Stop wallowing in the past, Ritcherd," she said with scorn. "And find someone else to share your aristocratic world with."

Before he could even begin to comprehend what she was implying, she turned and ran. Ritcherd reached out to grab her, but she eluded his grasp like a bird taking flight.

"Wait!" he called, running after her. "Blast you, Kyrah Payne! Don't you run out on me!"

From the doorway of the church he could barely make out her form as she ran over the moors toward home. He knew he could run after her; he knew he could get on his stallion and catch up to her in no time. But he felt drained and spent, and he figured he'd pushed enough against the wall she'd put up between them.

Ritcherd rode slowly toward home, wondering if it could be true that Kyrah hated him because he was an aristocrat. It wasn't his fault he had an old name and more money than he knew what to do with. Kyrah knew more than anyone how much he'd always avoided his aristocratic world. But perhaps it was a clue to the problem. Could this really be so simple as their difference in social status? To him it seemed preposterous. And if that was the problem, he didn't know what to do about it.

Kyrah's advice had been futile, he thought as he poured himself a drink in the privacy of his sitting room. He *would* wallow in the past until he found out why his dreams for the future were falling apart.

When Ritcherd woke up again with a hangover, he wondered once more what had happened to make his life such a mess. Of course, the war had been the beginning. He wondered how many relationships had been shattered through history as a result of war and its meaningless destruction. He wished that he'd been shot months sooner, or that he'd not had to go at all. He was beginning to see that the changes Kyrah had gone through in his absence were far more drastic than he'd first realized. But still he felt so utterly ignorant. He made up his mind that he needed more information, and there was only one place he could go.

Ritcherd paused hesitantly at the cottage door before knocking. He knew Kyrah was gone, but he wondered if his decision to discuss this with Sarah was right. He loved Sarah and had looked up to her as a mother. In turn, she had treated him as she would a son, both with love and discipline when she had felt it necessary. But he wasn't certain he wanted to draw Sarah into this mysterious estrangement between him and Kyrah. Making up his mind that he had nowhere else to turn for answers, he rapped lightly on the door and immediately heard her call for him to enter.

"Hello, Sarah," he said, moving into the parlor doorway.

"Ritcherd," she smiled with genuine pleasure, "I've not seen nearly as much of you as I might have expected since you've returned."

"That's what I wanted to discuss with you," he said soberly.

"Come in," she motioned with her hand, "sit down."

"Thank you," he said, moving to a chair opposite her.

"Now," she said, "what is it?"

"To put it bluntly," he began, "Kyrah doesn't want to have anything to do with me."

"Yes, I know," she said sadly. "I wish I could say I understood, but I don't. She won't talk to me about it at all. What has she said?"

"Very little," he replied. "She's told me she doesn't want me in her life, but won't give me an explanation." He blew out a long breath. "Perhaps I shouldn't have come to you. I don't want to put you in an awkward position, but I . . ." He looked directly at her. "I don't know where else to turn."

"I'm glad you came." She smiled gently. "I only wish I could help you. I could try and talk to her, but to be quite honest, she rather avoids you as a topic of conversation." Ritcherd tried to chuckle as he looked toward the ceiling.

"I've thought about it until my head hurts," he said, "but I just can't figure what I've done to make her so determined to be rid of me. I love her, Sarah. I have to know why she's changed."

"You always have loved her, I believe," she said and Ritcherd was surprised, though he shouldn't have been. He knew how perceptive Sarah was.

"Yes," he replied, "I always have."

"And now that the two of you are all grown up, you should be together."

"That's the way I see it," he said, "but Kyrah's got something else on her mind." He rubbed his fingers together nervously until the silence forced him to finally put words to a thought that kept nagging at him. "Is it another man?"

"She hasn't had time for another man," Sarah replied easily. "She's always working."

"What about him?"

"Who?"

"I don't know his name; that . . . man she . . . works for."

"That's ridiculous," Sarah chuckled. "She hates him."

"Is he married?"

"No."

"How does he feel about Kyrah?" he asked pointedly with a sick feeling rising in his chest.

"I don't know," she said quickly and Ritcherd gave her a deep, dubious look. "But I know how much Kyrah hates him. She's always . . . "

"She's always what?" he asked intently when she hesitated.

"Oh, Ritcherd," she gasped softly when she seemed to grasp what he was thinking, "you don't think that . . ."

"How should I know?" He stood in angry frustration. "I've been gone for three years!"

"Ritcherd! Calm down."

"Name one good reason why I should be calm! I thought I'd lived through hell twice over, then I come home to find my whole world has fallen apart. And I didn't even know anything was wrong. Do you have any idea how I felt when I heard that . . ." He turned toward her and his expression softened. "Yes, I'm sure you do. I'm sorry, Sarah. I . . . "

"Sit down, Ritcherd," she said calmly, and he did. "Your raging will not do any good. I can understand how all of this must be for you, but I learned a long time ago that no amount of anger or tears will bring Stephen back."

Ritcherd sighed and closed his eyes. Just hearing mention of Stephen's death tightened a knot inside of him. He'd been so consumed with Kyrah's attitude toward him that he'd hardly had a chance to digest the reality that Stephen was really gone.

"Now," Sarah continued, "I honestly don't believe he's harmed her, but I will find out. If there's anything wrong, I will tell you."

Ritcherd watched her silently a moment, then gave a subtle nod. Knowing there was nothing else to be done about it at the moment, he forced it to the back of his mind. "There's more, Sarah," he said. "I can sense it."

"Ritcherd," she said gently, and he met her gaze, "a lot has changed since you left here. Not only has Kyrah become a woman, but she has been through some terribly trying experiences. I don't understand why she wouldn't want to see you, but if I were to start looking for the answers, I would look to see what is different in her life. She is not the carefree child you left behind. You understand that, don't you?"

"All I know for certain is what I've heard through gossip. Kyrah said nothing about any of this in her letters."

"I know." Sarah sighed. "At least, I know now. I had assumed she'd written to tell you. I admit I've not been good for anything since I lost Stephen, or I would have written to you myself."

For a moment she seemed lost in her grief, then she turned thoughtful eyes toward him. "You're very much a part of this family," she said. "You have a right to know what happened in your absence." Ritcherd remained silent; sensing that she needed to unburden herself, he wondered if she'd talked to anyone about this. Did Sarah have any friends, anyone at all besides Kyrah? Or did she even want to talk about it? He could see the pain seeping into her expression and almost wished the subject hadn't come up.

"I assume," she said in a wispy tone, "that the gossip is probably quite true. All I know for certain is that Stephen lost everything in a card game. But that's not the tragedy."

He saw her bite her lip before she went on. "If only he'd have come home," she whispered, looking toward Stephen's portrait that dominated one of the walls in the parlor. "He wanted so badly to give us a good life, and when he learned that this estate had been purchased by one of his gambling acquaintances for a measly amount, he challenged him to a game and won.

"We were always happy there. But we had been happy before. He must have thought, somehow, that all of it meant more to me than it really did. If only he'd have come home . . . I'd have told him we could make it through. I didn't need the big house or the fancy things. I needed *him*, Ritcherd." She looked at him sadly. "If he'd have come home, I could have convinced him that it was not so terribly serious . . . but he didn't."

Sarah looked abruptly away and stared toward the floor. "He was found in a hotel room in London with the gun in his hand." She paused and her expression was blank. "What kind of desperation," she said, turning again toward Ritcherd, "does a man have to feel to put a gun to his head and pull the trigger?"

Ritcherd looked abruptly away as he felt the horror of Stephen's death strike him. Looking back toward Sarah, he noticed that her breathing seemed labored and her pallor had increased. But it was no physical ailment that had torn down Sarah's health. It was the pain of her loss. Stephen had been so much a part of her that he might as well have been half of her flesh and blood. And when he died, she'd lost so much of herself that she'd physically deteriorated.

He asked himself if he loved Kyrah that much, and the answer was easy. He did. He couldn't claim the years together that Sarah and Stephen had shared, but he knew how painful it was now to feel Kyrah tearing herself away from him. He had been drained of all strength since Kyrah had told him she didn't want him in her life. Although he couldn't comprehend Sarah's pain, he could perhaps understand what she was feeling. But he didn't know what to say. There was no way to console her pain. He couldn't tell her that Stephen had not died in vain, nor could he say that she would find happiness again. He knew himself that he could never find anything or anyone to replace Kyrah. Wanting to give her comfort, but unable to find the right words, he moved across the room and sat close beside her, taking her hand into his and squeezing it gently.

Sarah attempted a smile that quickly faded into despair. "What did I do . . . to make Stephen believe that the things he'd given me were more important than he was?"

Ritcherd swallowed hard. "I don't ever recall a time," he said gently, "when I was with the two of you and couldn't see plainly that you loved him for what he was. He must have seen that, too."

"I believe he knew that," Sarah said. "That's what puzzles me about his death."

"What do you mean?"

"Stephen was very good at what he did," she said carefully. "Although he wouldn't admit it, I believe he was one of the best. But he was not an impulsive gambler, nor was he reckless. He would not have risked so much if he hadn't been absolutely certain that he would win. It meant too much to him. He was not the kind to risk things that were dear to him in order to gain more. He was quite content with what he had.

"I believe it was his pride that killed him," she said solemnly. "But something about it doesn't seem right to me."

Not knowing what to say, Ritcherd tried to turn her thoughts to a more positive note. "Stephen Payne was a kind, decent man, and more of a father to me than my own ever was. I truly loved him."

"I know you did," she attempted a smile, "and he loved you. But that's not what you came to talk about."

"There's nowhere I need to be," he said kindly. "If you want to talk, please . . ."

"Some other time," she said, and he knew that even after the passing of years, it was still incredibly painful for her. But then she had nothing else in her life to compensate for the pain or to distract her from her loneliness.

"Ritcherd," she said, "you must know how it breaks my heart to see Kyrah having to work so hard just to keep us fed. I feel guilt and regret every time she goes out that door. But she's a proud girl and she won't have it any other way. I know Kyrah has been very unhappy the last three years. You must realize that in one day she lost everything she had, including her father. Before all of that happened, she had already become downhearted because of your absence. She couldn't speak without talking about you, and she spent hours every day sitting by the window, as if she was watching for you.

"Before Stephen left for London, he promised Kyrah that he would be back for her birthday. She was almost sixteen. And he was going to buy her the cloak she'd seen in town. It was beautiful: gray, lined with silver fox. She told me she hoped you would come back in the winter, so that she could wear it when she saw you again." Sarah paused and drew a barely detectable but sharp breath. "Stephen's body arrived from London on Kyrah's birthday."

Ritcherd's hand went unconsciously over his mouth. The pain he felt was deep, but he also felt something else—something strange that he couldn't quite put a finger on.

"She held up through it all," Sarah went on, bringing him away from his thoughts. "It was me who fell apart when Stephen died. Kyrah remained strong. She must have known she had to. But I wonder what kind of pain she's suppressing.

"For a long time she'd often say things to indicate that if you'd been here, things might not be so bad for us. She would sit in the walled garden whenever she'd find any bit of time for herself, and I knew she was missing you. Then one day she stopped going there—and she quit talking about you. She says very little about anything. She just comes and goes and keeps everything calmly under control.

"I'm very dependent on her," Sarah admitted. "But I know she's hurting. I was hoping your return would change that."

Ritcherd stood up quickly and clasped his hands behind his back. He understood more and more how difficult these years had been on Kyrah, but he still wondered why she would not let him be a part of her life and help her deal with all of this. He thought of her crying in the church ruins, and his heart ached for her.

"I'll find a way," he said with conviction, "to help her—and you . . . whether she loves me or not."

"Be careful, Ritcherd," she admonished. "Be careful of her pride. It is one of Kyrah's greatest strengths . . . and weaknesses. But right now, it's all she's got. And if you wound it, she might never be willing to face you the way she should."

"I'll be careful," he replied. "Perhaps I should go. She'll be returning soon, I believe. Thank you, Sarah." He bent to kiss her cheek and she returned the gesture. "Is there anything you need right now . . . anything I can do for you?"

"All we need from you is what I know you're already determined to do."

Ritcherd gave her a feeble smile and left the cottage, hoping her faith in him was warranted. He felt enlightened, but extremely depressed. Again, he cursed the war that had made it impossible for him to be here when he'd been needed so badly. He ached for Stephen's tragic death and for what Kyrah and Sarah had suffered as a result. Mounting his stallion, he told himself he would find a way to ease Kyrah's suffering—one way or another.

He was almost dismayed to see Kyrah walking toward the cottage. When she realized he was there, she stopped abruptly and shot him a scornful glare. As their eyes met, he wondered if she was blaming him for her pain, or just taking it out on him. His heart told him to pull her into the saddle with him, carry her away and force her to see things sensibly. But he knew that if Kyrah had somehow come to hate him, such actions would only cause more resentment and make it harder for him to find a way to help her.

Kyrah held her breath as Ritcherd gave her a penetrating gaze. She was expecting some kind of confrontation, but he simply nodded and rode quickly away, leaving her feeling somehow deflated. She entered the cottage expecting her mother to tell her why Ritcherd had been here, or at the very least, talk about him as she often did. But Sarah said nothing about him. And Kyrah was almost disappointed.

While Kyrah worked in the kitchen, her mind became absorbed with what Ritcherd might have been doing at their home. She wanted to demand that her mother tell her what they'd talked about, but she knew she wouldn't get an answer without an accompanying lecture on how unkind she was being to Ritcherd.

"What was that?" Kyrah asked when her mother mumbled something quietly.

"Oh, nothing important," she said in an unusually light tone. "I was just saying that your father was so sweet. A bit silly at times. I can hardly understand some of these. But he was sweet."

Kyrah glanced over her shoulder to see that Sarah was reading through a stack of little notes her father had written through the years. Sarah had kept them all, but Kyrah couldn't recall seeing her read them since soon after his death. And then she had cried helplessly over them. Seeing her mother smile, she couldn't help wondering what had suddenly made it possible for Sarah to reminisce about Stephen and feel happy. Could Ritcherd's visit somehow have made a difference? The thought only aroused her curiosity further regarding their visit. But by the way he'd left without a word, she had to wonder if he had finally seen things her way. If that was the case, she wondered why she felt so much pain in thinking that her wishes might be carried out.

Sarah drew her attention away from her collection of love notes and watched her daughter, feeling a growing concern. She wondered if it was Ritcherd's return that made her feel less inclined to ignore her worries and fears, and confront them instead. She knew Ritcherd would see that they were cared for. Perhaps that in itself made it easier to look at their circumstances realistically. And perhaps time had eased her loss enough to make living without Stephen not seem impossible. Whatever the reason, Sarah felt stronger than she had in a long time. And she knew that now was as good a time as any to ask Kyrah what she needed to know.

"Is something the matter, darling?" Sarah asked, noting the way her brow was furrowed.

"No, of course not," Kyrah insisted.

"There's something I need to ask you," she added, and Kyrah turned her attention away from her work. She could feel another scolding coming in regard to Ritcherd.

"How is it," Sarah asked carefully, "that Mr. Westman behaves toward you?"

Kyrah was taken aback. This wasn't where she'd expected this conversation to go. "He treats me like dirt," she said flatly.

That didn't surprise Sarah, but it wasn't what she wanted to know. "Has he ever done anything to . . . harm you?"

Kyrah looked sharply at her mother and wondered if her comment had anything to do with Ritcherd's visit. "Why do you ask?"

"You don't tell me things the way you used to. If there is something bothering you, I would like you to tell me."

"There's nothing to tell," Kyrah said blandly.

"Listen to me," Sarah said with more conviction in her voice than Kyrah had heard for years. But it got Kyrah's full attention. "I want the truth from you. If he's done anything that—"

"I think he'd like to," she stated, and Sarah felt both sick inside and relieved, "but I have no intention of giving him any opportunity."

Sarah watched Kyrah leave the room, feeling certain she'd told the truth. And she was grateful that her daughter hadn't been a victim of what she'd feared. Still, she hated having her work for that awful man, and she prayed that Ritcherd would find a way to get past Kyrah's pride—and soon.

Ritcherd rode slowly home, his mind consumed with prayer. In his youth, he'd not put much account in talking to God. But war had changed his priorities quickly. He never would have survived the experience with his sanity intact if he hadn't been able to pour out his fears to a supreme being. And his experiences, however difficult, had only strengthened his conviction that his prayers had been heard. He couldn't count the times that he'd prayed he would make it home alive in order to share his life with Kyrah. And now his prayers were focused on his desire to have things right with the woman he loved. He couldn't rest until they were.

He was dismayed to return home and realize he'd arrived in time to have lunch with his mother. Jeanette seemed delighted, and he indulged her if only for the sake of keeping peace. As long as Kyrah didn't come up, they could manage a civil conversation. But his mind kept wandering while his mother rambled on about all of the gossip he'd missed while he'd been away. He was nearly ready to excuse himself in order to be alone when Jeanette mentioned Mr. Peter Westman, who had won the estate from Stephen Payne in a gambling spree.

"He's invited us over for tea this afternoon," she said as if it was an invitation from the king himself. "He's been wanting to meet you, and I thought today would be perfect. You don't have plans, do you?"

Ritcherd's first reaction might have been to decline. But he suddenly felt that it was very important to accept. Perhaps it was just what he needed: to see the other side of Kyrah's world. And perhaps meeting the man she worked for would enlighten him.

"I'd love to," he said, and Jeanette looked genuinely pleased.

Ritcherd fought back the sickness that consumed him as they entered the house where Kyrah had once lived. But it only took a minute to realize that it was not the house that had once made him feel so welcome here. Now it seemed as cold and bleak as his own home.

Ritcherd managed to greet Peter Westman civilly when his mother introduced them as if they might become the best of friends. He had forgotten until now that his mother had mentioned they were near the same age. He tried to imagine how he might feel toward this man if he didn't have the prejudice of knowing what he'd done to Kyrah's family. But it didn't take long to realize that prejudice or no, he didn't like this man. He was blatantly arrogant, and just the type to give the new rich a bad name.

Jeanette and Peter dominated the conversation completely, but Ritcherd was content to sit quietly with his thoughts. He wondered, first of all, why his mother had never had anything good to say about Stephen Payne, who had been a good and decent man. But she was practically coddling this idiot who made his living in exactly the same manner, although he would daresay by less honorable means.

The sickness inside of him increased as he recalled a time when this had been Kyrah's drawing room, and his mind wandered through sporadic memories of the happy moments he'd spent here, feeling much like a part of her family. He remembered Sarah sitting prettily near the window doing needlework. And he had often tried to imagine Kyrah as she grew older, knowing she would be very much like her mother. Although Sarah was smaller in stature, since Kyrah had inherited her father's height, their coloring was much the same, and they both possessed an innate graceful quality that was difficult to describe. Ritcherd had quickly grown to love Kyrah's mother; she was everything that his own mother was not—cheerful, optimistic, kind. And she always laughed at his jokes, whether they were funny or not. She had often scolded him when she felt he was not behaving as he should. And he'd realized in his later years that many of his scruples had come from the gentle discipline he'd received from Sarah and Stephen, rather than the harsh tactics used by his own parents that had tended only to make him rebel.

Ritcherd's mind went to Stephen and his heart wrenched at the reality that he was dead. He remembered going hunting with Stephen many times, and the way they had talked and laughed together. Stephen's love for Ritcherd had been a careful balance of friendship and fatherhood. And Ritcherd couldn't ever remember his own father saying anything to him that was not in a stern, authoritative tone, and usually scolding in content.

Ritcherd was brought back to the present when his mother asked him some insignificant question, as if to make certain he felt included in the conversation. He grunted something to indicate he'd heard when he really hadn't, then he focused on their host. His dark hair was slicked back and cut short, which was unusual in this age of the fashionable ponytail. He dressed too sharply for good taste. And scrutinizing him carefully, Ritcherd decided this was not the kind of man he'd want to deal with in any matter. Instinctively, he didn't trust him. It was as simple as that.

Ritcherd thought of the circumstances that had brought Peter Westman to this house, and his distaste for the man smoldered into something more tangible. This was the man who had taken everything away from Kyrah's family in a card game. It didn't take much imagination to surmise that he probably cheated. And what Sarah had told him earlier only added to the theory. Was Mr. Westman the man who had driven Stephen to suicide?

Ritcherd was just contemplating a way to graciously make his exit when Kyrah came into the room to serve the tea. She nearly dropped the tray when she saw him, but she quickly recovered with dignity and went about her business as if nothing were out of the ordinary. *He* was the one falling apart inside. To see her doing servant's work under such circumstances made him want to carry her forcefully away from here this very minute. And he would have done it if he'd not remembered Sarah's warning about wounding Kyrah's pride.

The following five minutes were some of the worst he'd ever experienced. But the way they opened his eyes to the situation made them priceless. As soon as Kyrah entered the room, Ritcherd could see clearly that his mother was pleased with the situation. He thought of how Jeanette had accused Kyrah of everything from leading her son down a sinful path to being a freeloading lowlife who was out to catch herself a rich husband. At many times in his life Ritcherd had all but hated his mother, but now as he watched her attitude toward Kyrah's misfortune, he felt certain that his own mother was one of the lowest forms of life on earth. Perhaps second only to Mr. Westman, who seemed eager to mimic Jeanette's attitude.

"Thank you, Kyrah," Peter said. Then he added toward Jeanette, "She's priceless, you know." He turned and eyed Kyrah lewdly while she poured the tea.

Jeanette's smile made it evident that she thought Kyrah was exactly where she belonged. And Ritcherd had to wonder if her purpose in bringing him here was to somehow convince him of Kyrah's social status, which Jeanette deemed completely unworthy of her son. The thought sickened Ritcherd. But his sickness increased tenfold as Peter Westman watched Kyrah move across the room with a gaze that seemed to imply his ownership, as if she were no different to him than a prize mare or a hunting dog. He wondered what kind of cruelty Kyrah had been subjected to in being forced to work for this fiend. And he wondered if Sarah had gotten the truth out of Kyrah. If this man had so much as laid a hand on Kyrah, he'd kill him. It was downright pitiful that she should have to work for this degenerate who had put her in this position. Whether Kyrah still loved him or not, Ritcherd made up his mind then that he would find a way to get her out of this—a way that would let Kyrah save her pride.

"I don't know what I'd do without Kyrah," Mr. Westman went on, and Ritcherd sensed there was some playacting going on here. It all seemed so dramatic. When Kyrah moved within Mr. Westman's reach, he nonchalantly brushed his hand across her hip, and everything in Ritcherd became defensive. As soon as Kyrah moved away and gave Peter a cold glare, she shot a look at Ritcherd that pointedly indicated she would never forgive him if he so much as lifted a finger.

Jeanette seemed infinitely pleased with Mr. Westman's attention to Kyrah, but it was something else that now held Ritcherd's interest. He watched Kyrah closely, and felt something stab at him when she once again turned toward him, her eyes full of scorn and . . . what? Contempt? Hatred? *But why?*

Ritcherd didn't know the answer, but as she finished serving and left the room, he had to acknowledge that he had no reason to believe she felt any differently for him than she did this idiot she was working for.

"I hate tea," Ritcherd said suddenly as he set the cup down and stood. "I believe I'll run along and leave the two of you to chat."

Jeanette tried to sound disappointed that he was leaving, but Ritcherd knew she had done what she'd set out to do in bringing him here. And with him gone, she could now discuss whatever it was these two had cooking. He felt relatively certain that his mother was probably bribing this man to help keep him and Kyrah apart.

It was tempting to wander the house and try to find Kyrah, but he felt more inclined to be alone. He didn't know if he could take any more of her cold glares and hurtful silences. Since he'd arrived in the carriage with his mother, he decided to walk home the long way and ended up sitting in the church ruins. He lost track of the time as he considered the complete despair of his circumstances. He'd lost everything that mattered to him, and he didn't even know where to begin to put his life back together. He finally had to accept that maybe he really *did* have to learn to live without

Kyrah and get over her. The thought made him groan and double over. He couldn't even comprehend it.

"Please, God," he murmured. "Please, give me some hope. Show me the way."

In a conscious effort to open his mind to the answers, Ritcherd did his best to force away the darkness hovering over him. He took his mind, step by step, through every piece of information he'd acquired since his return, hoping to find something he'd missed that might help him know how to reach Kyrah. At the very least, he couldn't move on without understanding why she was behaving this way. If he had spurned her and done something to hurt her somewhere along the way, he could understand her attitude. He wondered if he'd inadvertently done such a thing. But no matter how intensely he thought it through, he couldn't find any obvious answer.

Again, he took his mind through everything his mother had said, Sarah had said, Kyrah had said. What had he missed? Instinctively he felt there was an answer buried somewhere in the conversations of the past few days. But the sun went down and Ritcherd still felt as ignorant as he had when he'd arrived at the church ruins hours ago. He began to pray that he could just be free of these feelings and move on with his life. Then a thought appeared in his mind that actually made him gasp.

"Kyrah's sixteenth birthday," he murmured aloud, wondering why it suddenly seemed so important. Frantically he thought it out. Sarah had said that Stephen's body arrived home on Kyrah's sixteenth birthday. But there was something else, something more personal for him. He just couldn't quite put his finger on it. He did remember, however, that when Sarah had brought it up, just this morning, he'd had a strange feeling pass over him—something beyond the surge of grief that had come with her report.

"Kyrah's sixteenth birthday," he repeated, as if it could clear his mind. And again he prayed. "Please, God! Show me what to do. Help me understand!

"Kyrah's sixteenth birthday!" he murmured once more, feeling suddenly weak. He pressed both hands over his heart, as if to steady its sudden pounding. He remembered now! He remembered recording it in his military journal. The first time he went into battle. The voice that warned him. The bullet that barely missed him. The realization that no one had been there but him. He'd passed it off with a logical explanation, but . . . that voice. *That voice!*

"Merciful heaven!" he muttered and slid off the bench to his knees. *"Stephen!"* He had thought the voice sounded like Stephen. But maybe . . . Was it possible? Could it have actually been Stephen? He'd convinced himself that Stephen had been an ocean away. But Stephen had been *dead*. And now some force he couldn't explain was verifying the truth to him with feelings more powerful than he'd ever experienced. As the reality settled in, everything changed. His entire perspective became very clear. He knew now. He couldn't explain how he knew. But he knew. He knew beyond any trace of a doubt. His life had been saved that day so that he could return home and care for the wife and daughter that Stephen Payne had left behind.

Filled with confidence and hope that more than matched his recent despair, Ritcherd turned his face heavenward and offered his deepest gratitude. He knew now what he had to do. And he had to start by making it perfectly clear to Kyrah where he stood and what he intended to do. What she chose to do had to be up to her. But it didn't change what *he* had to do. And he had to do it now!

Kyrah was on her way out of the house when her attention was caught by a conversation coming from the library. She was not one to eavesdrop, and certainly had no interest in Peter Westman's affairs. But the heated words filtered into the hallway with such volume that it was impossible to ignore what she heard.

"You are welcome to leave here," Peter's voice came clearly with a defensive tone, "if all you've brought are threats."

"Don't flatter yourself," a smooth voice replied, not quite as loudly as Peter's. "I just want you to know that I'm well aware of what you did to me, and sooner or later, justice will be met."

"Get out of here!" Peter demanded.

"I'm leaving," came the reply, "with pleasure."

"Good-night, Captain Garret," Peter added bitterly, and Kyrah ran quietly down the hall toward the door. She felt suddenly afraid of what Peter might do if he discovered that she'd overheard.

Walking slowly toward the cottage, Kyrah's thoughts didn't stay with the incident for long. Since she had seen Ritcherd that afternoon, visiting with Peter and his mother, her heart and her head had battled continually over what she should do. But she'd only come to one conclusion: she was confused. She hated the feeling creeping over her that she might have seen the last of Ritcherd Buchanan. He was a man who would only take so much, and she was certain he must have reached his limits. The scene in the drawing room flashed through her mind with fresh humiliation, and she thought of how much she hated Peter Westman. Then her mind darted to how it had felt to be kissed by Ritcherd Buchanan. Her heart made her wonder at times if she was doing the right thing. But logically she knew it would be best for both of them if she remained out of his life.

Kyrah actually felt relieved that her work had taken her longer than usual today. It was well past dark, and she knew her mother would be sleeping by now. She wanted nothing more than just to be alone with her thoughts and go to bed.

Not far from the cottage, Kyrah felt the hair on the back of her neck suddenly bristle. She hesitated and definitely heard something unusual behind her. Without turning around, she quickened her steps in time to her pounding heart. She had just decided to run when a hand was clamped over her mouth and she was dragged away from the road and into the shadows of a cluster of oak trees. The hand left her mouth only long enough to tie a scarf tightly there, and her protests were muffled. Another scarf went over her eyes, leaving her unable to see anything.

Kyrah had never been so frightened in her life as both her wrists were taken into a firm grip behind her back and tied. She was forced to walk ahead of her captor in the darkness. She wondered how much worse her life could get! Her mind went to the conversation she'd just overheard, and she wondered if Peter's visitor was going to use her to get even with him. Or perhaps he had somehow found out she'd been eavesdropping and feared what she knew.

Kyrah was lifted onto a horse despite her continued struggling. Her captor mounted in the saddle behind her and they rode for only a few minutes. The horse halted and she was pulled from its back and carried through a door that was kicked open. Her feet were set on the ground and she heard the door close—then it was latched. She was picked up again and set rather firmly into a pile of straw. She'd barely realized that she was in a barn when the cover was pulled from her eyes.

"Ritcherd!" she cried out, but the word was muffled by the scarf in her mouth.

"Now, little lady," he said firmly, "I have got some things to say to you, and this is obviously the only way I am going to get to say them. You are going to listen to me—and listen good. Do you understand?" She only stared blankly at him, not certain if she should be afraid of him or of her own feelings. "Do you understand?" he repeated adamantly, and she nodded.

"Good," he said and continued after he took a deep breath. "Now, Kyrah Payne, you and I have a problem, and I will not leave you in peace until we can work it out effectively. In order to keep things as simple as possible, let's just throw out any level of romantic involvement between us until we can get this sorted out. The bottom line is that you and I have been the best of friends since we were children, and I have done *nothing* to deserve the kind of treatment from you that I'm getting. At the very least, you should consider me as a brother to you . . . because I practically lived under your roof for eight years. And your parents are the only people who ever truly loved me and cared what happened to me—except for you. Are you following me so far?" he asked. When she didn't move, he raised his voice. "Well?"

Kyrah nodded and he went on. "All right. So, you can think of me what you want, and your feelings for me are certainly beyond my control. But I will *not* stand by and allow you and your mother to go on living this way. And if that wounds your sweet pride, so be it. There is no place for pride in this relationship. Because I know that . . ." He hesitated, feeling a sudden surge of emotion that verified all over again what he was trying to tell her. "I *know*," he repeated and his voice cracked, "that your father wanted me to see you and your mother cared for, and as God is my witness I will do that, with or without your approval. If you must be so proud as to work for a living, then I will help you find a suitable, respectable position in some other part of the country, away from my mother and that *idiot* you're working for now. Is that clear?"

Ritcherd watched her closely and had no doubt she wanted to give him a piece of her mind. But that didn't lessen his conviction. She would have her chance to speak, but for now, he was grateful she couldn't. Again he took a deep breath and forged ahead. "Now," he said more gently, "there is something that needs to be made perfectly clear, so that you don't have room to misconstrue how I feel. I love you, Kyrah. Let me repeat it: I love you. Read my lips, Kyrah." He mouthed it, *I love you.* "Three years away from you, nearly losing half my arm, my mother's scheming, and all the horrors you went through while I was away have not changed how I feel. *I love you!* I always have and I always will. And because I love you, your happiness is more important to me than anything else. You have the freedom to make your choices. I know I can't force you into feeling something for me that you don't feel. But if that's the case, I deserve to be told—straight out."

Ritcherd saw that recently familiar scorn appear in her eyes, and he wondered why *this* would raise her ire more than what he'd said so far. He pulled himself away from the distraction of futilely pondering her motives and forced himself to finish what he had to say.

"So, this is the way it's going to be, Kyrah Payne. You and I are going to talk; we're going to talk like two mature adults—because that's what we are, although it's difficult to tell. Quite frankly, I believe you acted more like an adult when you were seven years old than you have since I came home. I've said it before, and I'm saying it again: I have too much invested in you to be thrown out like an old pair of shoes because you've suddenly changed your mind about what *you* think is best for *me*. Well, I won't stand for it. I want to hear how you feel and what you want and what you need. Let me repeat those three items: how you feel, what you want, what you need. And when you can tell me those things *honestly,* then we will work all of this out accordingly. So consider me your brother, your friend, your husband, or all of the above. But I will not walk away from you until my responsibilities are taken care of, and I know exactly where I stand with you and why. And remember," he lifted a stern finger, "I said *honestly*. Maybe if you start being honest with yourself, you can manage to be honest with me and we can get past this, once and for all."

Ritcherd suddenly ran out of words and figured he'd said all he needed to say. But the growing contempt in Kyrah's eyes let him know that this was far from over. Of course, he'd known in bringing her here that he could force her to listen to him, but he couldn't force her to be reasonable. Hoping to soften her feelings, he lowered his voice to a gentle plea and added, "All I ask is that you talk to me, Kyrah . . . that you remember everything we've shared together. Help me understand what you've been through. We can work this out."

Her expression didn't change, but he figured he'd done everything he could. Blowing out a long breath, he knelt behind her to untie her wrists. He'd practiced tying the knots enough to do it efficiently in spite of his disabled hand. But untying it took more time, and he felt awkward and uncertain. When she was finally free, she jerked away from him and wrestled the scarf out of her mouth, leaving it to hang around her neck.

"You pompous, arrogant brute!" she growled. "You have no right to treat me this way, and I won't stand for it!" Kyrah had expected him to throw anger back at her. When he just stood as he was, looking sad if anything, she was stunned into silence.

When she turned toward the door, Ritcherd said in a tone that emphasized his sadness, "You can run, Kyrah, but you will never be free of whatever it is you're hiding from. And I will not rest until I do what your father wanted me to do."

She glanced over her shoulder, unlatched the door, and was gone. Ritcherd followed her home at a cautious distance to be certain she made it safely. Then he went home and crawled into bed, praying that she would somehow come to understand how deeply he cared for her.

Chapter Five

Disdain

*K*yrah hurried home and climbed quickly beneath the covers, as if the security of her own bed might somehow save her from the feelings Ritcherd had confronted. But as his words echoed over and over through her head, it soon became evident that he'd been absolutely right. *You can run, Kyrah, but you will never be free of whatever it is you're hiding from.* She finally managed to force that out of her mind, only to have it replaced with: *Maybe if you start being honest with yourself . . .*

When hours of darkness passed with the memory of all he'd said only becoming more prominent, Kyrah wrapped her arms over her head and groaned, wondering if she was going mad. Unable to bear the confusion another minute, she turned her mind to prayer. Uttering a desperate plea for strength and guidance, she realized that she couldn't recall the last time she'd even thought to turn to God. As subtle inklings of peace began to trickle into her, she wondered if her lack of prayer had contributed to the problem.

When morning came, Kyrah knew exactly what she needed to do. And she knew she had to do it before she lost her courage. She scribbled a quick note for Sarah, who was still sleeping, and left the cottage to find the early morning sun blocked by intermittent clouds. Going through the woods near the back of the cottage, Kyrah followed a trail that she had once used frequently. It was a significant walk, but she came out of the trees just behind the gardens of Buckley Manor. She recalled many times through her youth when she had taken this path and sneaked into the house to find Ritcherd when she had needed to talk to him and it couldn't wait until their usual daily meeting at the crossroad. By following a carefully thought-out series of steps, she managed to stay mostly hidden by shrubberies and fences until she came to a little-used side door of the house. Taking a deep breath, she almost hoped that it was locked. But the knob turned easily in her hand, and she slipped inside to be met only by silence. She knew this part of the house was rarely used, and the servants would be busy elsewhere. Quietly she traversed long hallways and narrow staircases that were intended only for the servants to use. She was surprised how easily she found her way, when she'd not come here for so long.

Entering the final stretch of hallway, where Ritcherd's rooms were, she hesitated, looking both ways to be certain she was alone. For a moment she nearly backed down and turned to leave. But she knew she could never live with herself if she didn't face this here and now. Taking a deep breath, she knocked softly at his bedroom door, wondering what she would do if he were still asleep—or already gone.

"Yes?" he called immediately with a terse voice.

Kyrah opened the door and peered in to see him sitting at the writing desk, wearing a long dressing gown. His back was to her, and she wondered how to approach him. Her heart was pounding so hard that she found it difficult to even speak.

"What is it?" he snapped, turning toward her.

His countenance changed abruptly, and he shot to his feet. "Kyrah," he muttered as if he'd seen a ghost.

"You should be kinder to the servants," she scolded and stepped in, closing the door behind her. "What have they done to deserve your disdain?"

"Forgive me," he said. "I thought . . ."

"I know." She hardly gave him a chance to continue. "You thought I was just one of the servants. Well," she leaned against the door, "it could have happened. Your mother actually offered me a job."

Ritcherd swallowed hard and bit his tongue. She was here and she was talking. He wasn't about to express his anger over *anything* right now.

"I bet you didn't know that, did you," Kyrah went on. "But she did. She sent a message, kindly expressing her condolences over our change in circumstances—with no mention of my father's death. She graciously offered me a job in the kitchen, saying she'd be happy to help us out in this way. Now, wouldn't that have been something? War hero Captain Ritcherd Buchanan comes home to a warm welcome from his community, to find the woman he loves scrubbing pots in his very own kitchen."

Ritcherd stared with no expression, and she forced herself to keep talking, if only to avoid the agonizing silence. "And I bet you didn't know that most of our childhood peers have grown up to be more petty and judgmental than they ever were as children. From your perspective, I bet it would be difficult to fully understand how ugly and evil some people become with titles and money at their disposal. And I bet you didn't know that one of the biggest things these people hold against me is not my change in status, or even the fact that I was once financially well off. No, what these people hate about me is the fact that *you* associated with me."

Ritcherd briefly squeezed his eyes shut as a new level of understanding filtered into him.

"I bet you didn't know any of that," she repeated, and he shook his head. "But then, I *am* a betting person—daughter of a foolish gambler, living the life I've been deemed to deserve by the mighty and all-powerful aristocracy of north Cornwall."

When Ritcherd said nothing, Kyrah felt suddenly unsure of how to continue. Needing a few minutes to compose herself, she suggested, "Why don't you get dressed, and we can talk. I'll wait in the sitting room."

Ritcherd nodded. "You won't run away, will you?"

"No," she said, moving toward the opposite door, "I'll be right here."

Ritcherd stood for a moment, staring at the door she'd just gone through, hardly daring to believe that she was actually here. He prayed silently while he quickly got into his clothes, not wanting to give her time to change her mind.

Kyrah was grateful for a few minutes to gather her thoughts, but she hated being in this house. She would be glad to have this over with for many reasons.

Ritcherd took much longer than she'd expected, and it occurred to her that with his wounded arm, he likely had difficulty fastening buttons and such. He finally came into the room, wearing the typical narrow breeches, high boots, and white shirt. But she'd never seen the brocade waistcoat before. His appearance momentarily took her breath away. In response to his expectant expression, she glanced around and asked, "Will we be disturbed here?"

"No, of course not, but . . ." He hesitated, and their eyes met briefly. "Would you like to go somewhere else?" he asked, and she felt warmed by the evidence that he could still almost second-guess her thoughts.

Kyrah nodded. Ritcherd opened the door and followed her into the hall, attempting to quell the trembling in his stomach. He impulsively reached out a hand toward her, fully expecting her to reject it and walk ahead of him. But she hesitated only a moment before she put her hand into his.

Hope surged through him as they walked together down the back stairs and out to the stables. "Or would you rather walk?" he asked as they entered. Kyrah shook her head and he added, "The church?" She nodded.

When Ritcherd had his stallion saddled and ready, he glanced toward her and asked, "Would you prefer your own mount?"

Again she shook her head and he added, "If I hadn't heard you speaking in my bedroom, I would think—"

"It's been so long, I'm not sure I can remember how to ride."

"Sure you can," he said. Knowing how uncomfortable she had been around him, and his less-than-conventional methods the previous evening, he wanted to give her every opportunity to keep her distance. "Do you want me to get you a—"

"We managed well enough last night," she said, climbing into the saddle without any help.

Kyrah held her breath as Ritcherd got into the saddle behind her. His nearness, combined with her more recent thoughts, ignited something inside of her that she'd almost believed was dead. She noticed how he took the reins into his left hand, and his right hand rested against his thigh.

Ritcherd hurried the stallion toward the church ruins, not wanting to appear that he was dragging this out—even though he wanted to. Having her so near was almost intoxicating, and he prayed that this was a new beginning for them—not an end. He dismounted outside the church ruins, and Kyrah slid out of the saddle before he had the reins tied off.

"All right," he said after they'd ambled inside. "We're here." She seemed hesitant, and he feared that her willingness to talk might have lessened with the time it had taken them to get here. After hearing what she'd said already, there was so much he wanted to say in return. But he felt that it was important to allow her to have her say first.

He was beginning to wonder if she'd ever get started again when she said, "Please sit down, Captain Buchanan. There's something I need to say, and I expect your undivided attention." Ritcherd sat on one of the stone pews and motioned for her to continue.

Kyrah glanced skyward, as if divine intervention might prevent her from having to do this. She reminded herself that in a few minutes it would be over. She just had to say it and be done with it. She wrung her hands nervously and began to pace, then she forced herself to face Ritcherd and stand still.

"I . . . have three things I need to tell you," she said, and Ritcherd's heart quickened a little. She was taking his request of last evening literally.

He hoped that was a good sign. "I need . . ." Her hesitance was so pronounced that Ritcherd could almost literally feel the courage she was gathering. He held his breath, as if he could somehow infuse his strength into her. When she squeezed her eyes shut and tears streaked down her face, Ritcherd unconsciously pressed a hand over his mouth to hold back his own emotion. "I need . . ." she repeated, her voice breaking, "your help."

Kyrah swallowed hard, realizing she'd just gotten past one obstacle. She cleared her throat and forced her eyes open as she went on. "You're right when you say that there is no place for pride between us, and I apologize for putting it there. You've never done anything to hurt me, Ritcherd. *Never!* The problem here is . . . circumstances. Yours. Mine. But . . . I realized last night that I can't live this way anymore. These circumstances will destroy me eventually. And I won't see my mother suffer any longer. I'm willing to lower my pride and ask for your help, not only for her sake, but for mine as well. So . . . later, can we talk about . . . what we could do so that . . ." again her voice broke, "so that I never have to set foot in that house again?"

"Of course," he said. "It's not a problem."

"Thank you," she said and drew a deep breath. "The second thing I need to tell you is . . . well . . . I feel . . . afraid. More than anything, Ritcherd, I feel afraid." Where her first confession had come with great emotion, this one came with only a distant, glazed stare. "I feel afraid every time I have to go into town, and I have to pass people on the streets who snub me and look down at me. I feel afraid every time I go into that awful house, that house where I spent much of my childhood. I'm afraid of what he might do to me—if not physically, I fear the way he looks at me, the way he makes me feel. I'm afraid every day that I'm going to lose my mother, too. And I'm afraid that if something else goes wrong, I could end up selling myself on the streets in order to stay alive."

"I would never let that happen, Kyrah," he interjected, finding the thought too unbearable to even ponder.

"Well, you weren't here to do anything about it, and I didn't even know if you'd ever come home at all . . . or if you'd want anything to do with me. It could have happened, and I've had to live with such thoughts for two and a half years."

Ritcherd swallowed any further comment and settled for saying, "I hear what you're saying, Kyrah. Go on."

"But more than anything," she said, finally turning to look at him, "I'm afraid that you will eventually become fed up with the ridicule and degradation that would come from associating with me. And I would far prefer to keep perfect memories in my heart of what we once shared, than to see it become tainted by the reality of what lies between us."

It took all of Ritcherd's self-restraint to keep from telling her exactly what he thought about *that*. He knew his anger was not appropriate—especially now. And he doubted that she would appreciate the language that came to mind in describing such people and circumstances. So he bit his tongue and motioned for her to continue. He could speak his piece when she was finished.

"And finally," she said, "I want . . ." The tears came again, this time gaining fervor. "I want . . . more than anything, Ritcherd, to be . . . to be a part of your life . . . for the rest of my life."

Ritcherd heard his breathing become raspy. He pressed a hand over his heart as it quickened. Could it be possible that his deepest hopes would come to pass? He waited for her to go on, not daring to believe it until her point was clarified.

"I love you, Ritcherd," she murmured through her tears, her hands trembling. "And I know in my heart that my feelings will never change. When I push away all of the fears and the doubts and the ugly realities of life, my feelings are very clear. I want to be with you forever, Ritcherd, but . . ."

When she hesitated too long, Ritcherd's racing heart came to a dead stop. "But?" he questioned. Still she hesitated, and he jumped to his feet, taking her shoulders into his hands. "But?" he growled, looking into her eyes.

"Your anger won't solve this problem, Ritcherd," she growled back. "I have to know beyond any doubt that it will *never* come between us, that your love and acceptance of me is complete and without condition. I have to know that you won't one day become disenchanted with me and regret the choices you're putting before me. I have to know that I'm not just a habit, a convenience, a comfortable extension of the security of your youth. *I have to know!*"

"You are *not* the security of my youth, Kyrah. You are the security of my *life*. You are my heart and soul. I can't promise you that difficulties won't come up. I can't promise you that it will always be easy, or that I'll always be agreeable. But I can promise you this: I will never, ever forsake you. I will never, ever be ashamed or embarrassed to have you by my side. I will be committed to you as long as there is breath in me. I would sacrifice all that I have to make and keep you happy and safe. And I would do it with joy in my heart."

He looked into her eyes, wondering what else he could possibly say to convince her. He hated this desperation that had become a constant companion for him. Watching her expression closely, he realized she was searching his eyes for sincerity. He'd seen that look dozens of times in their youth. He held his breath and tightened his grip on her shoulders. When she seemed to come to some kind of conclusion, she sighed and said, "In that case, the answer is yes."

"Answer?" he repeated, confused. "Was there a question?"

"In a roundabout way, yes, I believe there was."

"So, the answer is yes, as in . . ."

"As in, I want you to be my brother, my friend . . . and my husband."

Kyrah held her breath, waiting for a reaction. She heard a one-syllable sound erupt from his mouth, but she couldn't tell if it was a laugh or a sob. Perhaps both. Studying his expression, she felt suddenly overflowing with relief and delight. She felt as if a huge burden had been lifted from her shoulders, and somehow she knew that everything would be all right, in spite of her few remaining doubts. She only wished she hadn't been such a fool in taking so long to make this step. But everything fell perfectly into place when Ritcherd fell to his knees, pressing his hands to her back and his face into the folds of her dress. He sobbed like a lost child come home, while her own tears ran down her face.

Suddenly weak herself, Kyrah went to her knees as well, where they held each other and cried. Ritcherd finally pulled back just enough to touch her face, her hair, her face again, as if he had to reassure himself that she was real. Kyrah eagerly did the same, finally willing to accept that he had truly come home to her at last. Their tears turned to laughter, then to tears again as he pressed her face to his shoulder and held her there as if he could protect her from the harshest storm.

When their emotion finally quieted, Ritcherd put a voice to the thoughts that kept hovering in his mind. "Kyrah," he murmured, touching her face again, "those things you said . . . about the way people look down at you . . . because of me . . . You must know that I . . ."

"Ritcherd," she interrupted, "it's no fault of yours or mine. It's simply a matter of circumstances. But you have to know that it's there and it's real. It's as if I have leprosy and you're exposing yourself to it, which leaves the entire aristocratic community exposed, as well. And if you choose to marry me, it will not be taken well by most of the people in this community—most especially your mother. It will always be a part of who and what we are, and the only way to stay strong against it is to be strong together. Am I making any sense?"

Ritcherd nodded firmly, freshly amazed at her insight—a quality he'd always loved in her.

"I don't want you to one day regret bringing me into your life when people look at you askance one too many times."

"That day will never come, Kyrah. If anything, time will make people forget there was ever any distance between us. We will prove to the world that love is not born of old names and old money."

"I hope you're right, Ritcherd. But I wonder if you can accept that you're going to have to lower yourself to my social level, because I'm not capable of raising myself to yours."

Ritcherd felt briefly speechless. How could he ever explain to her this gut feeling he had that she was capable of that and so much more? He believed that in her present state of mind, she could never comprehend her own potential. And any effort on his part to convince her would only make her believe that he was trying to turn her into something she wasn't. He believed that time would prove his theory, but in the meantime, he admitted freely, "I will gladly be at any level, Kyrah, as long as you're there with me. Maybe we should just . . . move away from here; we could just pack up your mother and find a new place to live, where every person we pass in the streets isn't aware of every difficulty in our lives."

Kyrah thought about that a minute. "Perhaps," she finally said, "but . . . I love it here. The moors, the sea, the old church. They're like a part of me. If these people force me away from the things I love, then I've allowed them to have power over me. But . . . it's something to consider."

Ritcherd nodded and embraced her, silently thanking God for bringing this miracle into his life. Tears came to the surface again, and he marveled that they hadn't run dry. He'd hardly shed a tear in his youth, once Kyrah came into his life. And he'd forced them back time and time again through his years at war. Now he couldn't stop. But he felt a cleansing with his tears, as if their bathing effect could give him the chance to start his life again from this moment. Looking into Kyrah's eyes, he knew she felt much the same.

"How is your arm?" she asked quietly for lack of something better to say.

"Not so bad," he replied, displaying it with mock pride, as if it were humorous to have a battle wound—or rather that was all it was good for.

"I felt strength in that hand when I was being held captive." She smiled at him.

"Only here," he said and showed her how he could move his thumb and one finger, despite their being partially numb, which enabled him to do some things with his right hand. He demonstrated how easily he could hold her delicate wrist between them, but told her that the other three fingers were completely numb and useless.

"How did it happen?" she asked him.

"I was shot through the arm," he stated, "at close range. It's taken months to be able to use it at all." He rolled up his sleeve to show her the scar, and she couldn't help gasping. Just below his elbow, there was a wide depression where the muscle was sunken with matted scars all around it, and a scar on the opposite side of his arm where the ball had come through. It was obvious he'd lost a great deal of skin and muscle, and it must have been doctored quickly on the battlefield; the sight of it was atrocious.

Ritcherd quickly pulled the sleeve back down. "I'm lucky, really. He was aiming to kill me, but I managed to move quickly enough for my arm to take the shot. And I could have easily lost my arm. Many men weren't so lucky."

He became briefly distant, and Kyrah wondered what horrible things he'd witnessed during their time apart. She felt a surge of compassion as it became evident that he too had suffered greatly these past few years. She had heard that war aged men quickly, and she could see signs of hardship in Ritcherd's face. Instinctively she touched his wounded arm, rubbing gently where the sleeve covered his scars. He seemed surprised by the gesture, but smiled warmly.

"Does it hurt much?" she asked tenderly.

"Not really," he replied, and their eyes met again. "Not anymore."

"It must have been dreadful for you." Her gentle voice and intense eyes were almost hypnotic to Ritcherd. But her attention to his wound, which was something he resented, made him uncomfortable. He glanced away, but Kyrah's hand went down his arm and around his fingers. And he became intrigued by watching her touch him without being able to feel it.

Suddenly overwhelmed with exhaustion, he lay back on the grass, guiding Kyrah's head to his shoulder, where his discomfort gradually melted into perfect peace. While he watched numerous clouds floating overhead, with an occasional hole of sunshine, he was reminded of the countless times in their youth when they had done this very thing. He began to wonder if Kyrah was sleeping, but she lifted her head to look at him.

"There's something I need to ask you," she said. He nodded and touched her face, still hardly daring to believe that she was real. "Last night . . . somewhere in the middle of the night . . . I remembered something you'd said and . . . I have to know . . ." Her voice quivered slightly, and he realized she was having difficulty saying whatever she had on her mind. She took a deep breath and said, "How did you know, Ritcherd? How did you know that my father wanted you to take care of us? Did he . . ."

She stopped when Ritcherd abruptly turned his head away and squeezed his eyes shut. He wondered how to put words to an experience that was so illogical. How could he explain it when it was so difficult to understand? How could he let her know the full breadth of how this had affected his entire perspective of life—and death?

Kyrah's heart quickened as she perceived from Ritcherd's expression that this was difficult for him. She wondered if her father had said something to him before he'd left for the colonies. Could it give them a clue to his reasons for doing what he'd done? She held her breath when he finally turned to look at her, his eyes more intense than she'd ever seen them. His severity took her breath away.

"I think," he began in a pensive voice, "that deep inside I always believed God existed, that there was more to this life than what we see and feel around us. During my years away, my beliefs became more real. I started praying more, and truly believed my prayers were being heard, but . . ." Kyrah tightened her gaze on him. This was not at all what she'd expected. "But I had an experience that has changed me in that regard. I know now that this life is so much bigger than we could possibly comprehend. You see . . . just yesterday I realized that . . . well, let me go back." He paused to gather his thoughts. "The first time we went into battle, I came into this wooded area where I realized that I could possibly get a vantage point to see what the enemy was about. I was completely alone, moving through the trees, when I heard a voice say, 'Get your head down, boy. There's one coming right at you!'"

Ritcherd felt a shiver run through him at the thought. "That was it. Word for word. Anyway, I immediately ducked and heard a bullet whistle past. I knew I would have been dead if not for that warning. When I turned around, no one was there. Of course, I figured whoever it was had run for it. But looking back, I know that there was no sound there beyond my own breathing. I've gone over and over it in my mind, Kyrah. From where I was, it would have been impossible to see whoever was shooting at me. There is no way that someone behind me could have possibly seen him."

Kyrah wondered where this was leading, what it had to do with her father, and why it had changed his belief in God. Then the intensity in his eyes deepened as he said, "It sounded like your father's voice, Kyrah—plain as day." She held her breath as he continued. "Of course, at the time I disregarded it as ridiculous. I figured there had to be a logical explanation, that someone had a similar voice and a light step. I passed it off. But I remember the date clearly because as I was recording my account of that day, I realized it was your sixteenth birthday."

Kyrah heard her own breathing become labored as his implication sank in fully. "Just yesterday," he continued, "I was praying like I never had before, and eventually, well . . . I can't explain what happened. I just know that when I recalled that incident, I knew beyond any ghost of a doubt . . ." One corner of his mouth twitched upward as he added, "Pardon the pun." Then his entire countenance sobered, and fresh moisture appeared in his eyes. "I *know*, Kyrah. My life was saved that day because Stephen needed me to come home and take care of you and your mother. I can't explain how I know. I can't describe the way it makes me feel. I only . . . know that it's true."

Kyrah studied him for a long moment, his eyes, the air about him, and the message he'd just given her. She finally murmured in a cracking voice, "I think I know what you mean."

He gave her a serene smile, and she believed she felt closer to him in that moment than she ever had. She stared into his eyes long and hard, then she put her head back on his shoulder, holding tightly to him, wanting this spell hovering around them to never be broken.

A few minutes later, Ritcherd said in a gentle voice, "Kyrah. Tell me what happened. I know it's . . . hard, but . . . I have to know. I have to hear it from you."

It took Kyrah several minutes to gather her thoughts and find the fortitude to tell Ritcherd about her father's misfortune and subsequent suicide. She cried more than she had since the initial news had come more than two and a half years earlier. She hadn't had the time to cry; or perhaps she'd purposely kept herself too busy to fully feel the grief. But being in Ritcherd's arms made it suddenly easy to open up her heart and pour out the buried heartache and sorrow.

Ritcherd couldn't keep from crying himself as he listened to Kyrah's rendition of all that had gone wrong in his absence. From the intensity of her emotion, he wondered if she'd even allowed herself to feel the reality of her father's death prior to this day. He could well imagine how easy it would have been for her to hold it all inside in order to keep going for the sake of their survival. He was only glad that he was here now. Inwardly he vowed that Kyrah and her mother would never suffer again, so long as there was breath in him.

Once Kyrah's emotions were released, she was left thoroughly exhausted and completely drained of strength. By the way Ritcherd lay on his back, staring toward the sky with nothing to say, she knew he felt much the same way. The sun rose high in the sky, but they couldn't find the motivation to go home. The growling of her stomach reminded Kyrah that she'd not eaten anything today, and she doubted that Ritcherd had either. That, along with a sudden concern for her mother, prompted her to come to her feet and urge Ritcherd to do the same. Without a word between them, they mounted his stallion and rode toward the cottage. But after he took hold of her waist and helped her dismount, he pulled her into his arms and just held her for a seemingly endless moment.

They entered the cottage to hear Sarah call immediately, "Kyrah! Where have you been?" The tone of her voice made it evident that something was wrong. "Have you—"

"What is it?" Kyrah insisted, hurrying into the parlor. "Didn't you find my note?"

"Of course, but . . . it's been hours and—"

"Mother, calm down," Kyrah said, kneeling beside where Sarah sat, her hands trembling, her face more pale than usual. "Tell me what's happened."

"Mr. Westman was here," she said. "He wanted to know why you weren't working. He made all kinds of threats. He said if you weren't there by noon he would . . ." Sarah stopped when she noticed Ritcherd entering the room.

With anger barely disguised in his voice, he said, "Kyrah will *never* be working for him again."

Sarah glanced at Kyrah as if to verify what he'd said. When she nodded, Sarah sighed with visible relief and reached her hands out toward Ritcherd as if he had saved her from death itself.

"What is it, Sarah?" he asked, sitting close beside her. "What did he say to upset you so badly?"

"It doesn't matter now," she said. Then she smiled. "He'll just have to find someone else to do the work."

"Someone else to intimidate and belittle, you mean."

Kyrah's words seemed to bring back a degree of Sarah's anxiety, and Kyrah exchanged a concerned glance with Ritcherd. The glance melted into a heartfelt gaze as she paused to absorb the reality that he was here to share her burdens. The unspoken threat Peter Westman held over her suddenly seemed trite, even before Ritcherd said, "Don't you ever let him in that door again. I'll see that the rent on the cottage is paid. There is no reason for either of you to ever have to speak to him again."

Sarah nodded, but didn't seem completely convinced. Kyrah said, "I have to talk to him. I have to tell him that I've quit."

"No, you don't," Ritcherd said. "I'll do it."

"I'm perfectly capable of talking to Peter Westman," she said.

"I didn't say you weren't, but he—"

"Ritcherd," Kyrah interrupted, "I appreciate your help, more than you could possibly know. But that doesn't mean you have to take over my life. I'm not a child anymore." While Ritcherd was attempting to come up with a response, she glanced toward her mother and added, "I'm going to talk to him right now and have it over with. Then I'll get us some lunch." She said to Ritcherd, "You will stay for lunch, won't you?"

"Yes, I'd love to," he said, realizing the changes in Kyrah would still take some getting used to.

"Fine," Kyrah said. "I won't be long." She hurried to the door and pulled it open to see Peter with his hand lifted to knock.

"So, you finally came back," he growled. "I don't think you've got time to be roaming the countryside for a leisurely stroll when there's work to be done."

Kyrah took a deep breath and steeled herself against his attempts at intimidation. "I'm glad you're here," she said, ignoring his previous comment. "It will save me the trouble of having to come and find you. I won't be working for you anymore. You'll have to hire somebody else."

Peter's astonishment was evident. While he was apparently trying to gather his retort, she added, "Was there something else?"

"Only that you'd better be certain about what you're doing. If you can't pay the rent, you and your mother will be out on the street. And don't think that I won't do it."

"Oh, I have no doubt you'd do it. But I can assure you that you'll get your rent. Now, if you will excuse me, I have other things to attend to."

Peter put his hand on the door and his glare deepened. "I don't know what you think you're going to do, Kyrah, but you can't possibly—"

"Mr. Westman," she interrupted, "I have said all I have to say. You may leave now."

"Well, I haven't said what I have to say," he retorted in a way that made Kyrah wonder what interest he had in her beyond cheap labor. "You cannot expect me to find help at a moment's notice and—"

"I believe," Ritcherd's voice came from behind Kyrah, startling her as much as it did Peter, "that you've been asked to leave."

Peter glared at Ritcherd, then at Kyrah. Then he smiled. "Oh, I see," he said more to Ritcherd. "You pay the rent and keep her set up in return for—"

"Kyrah and I are getting married," Ritcherd interrupted angrily. He wasn't about to let this imbecile think anything but the best of her.

Peter raised his brows toward Kyrah, as if to say he was impressed. "Congratulations are in order then," he said. Then he leaned close to Kyrah and whispered, "Remember what I said. You're a fool if you think this is how it appears. Whether he puts a ring on your finger or not, he'll use you and leave you to suffer in the end." He lifted a finger. "Mark my words."

"You may leave now," Ritcherd said, stepping closer. He didn't know what had been said, but he didn't like what he saw in Kyrah's eyes when she turned toward him.

Peter's final comment was aimed at Ritcherd, with something subtly mocking in his eyes. "I'll be looking for that rent."

Once the door was closed, Kyrah leaned against it and sighed. Ritcherd folded his arms and said, "I cannot believe you've had to put up with *that* for two and half years."

"Neither can I," she admitted with an edge to her voice that made him realize it would take time to put the effects of all this behind them. But he believed that together they could overcome anything. And they could start now.

"I'll have my solicitor take care of the rent. There is no reason to ever have to talk to him again."

"Thank you," Kyrah said, finding it easier to swallow her pride now that she could feel the relief of having Peter Westman out of her life—once and for all. She took a deep breath, as if she could inhale the freedom Ritcherd had just given her. Then she reached for his hand, saying, "Come along. Let's find something to eat."

Ritcherd followed her to a relatively small kitchen with large windows. Just as with the rest of the house, the furnishings were minimal and old. But the feel of the room made him want to just bask in all that it represented. He'd come home. The tidiness and homey touches were evidence of the love and caring these two women had given to make the most of what they had. He could never put into words the value of these surroundings in comparison to the emptiness he felt within the walls of Buckley Manor.

"Have a seat," Kyrah said, the warmth of her voice adding to his serenity.

"Can I help?" he asked.

"No, thank you," she said. "There isn't much to do, really. I'm afraid we don't have much to choose from, but it should be adequate. I need to go into town and pick up a few things." She smiled toward him while she sliced a loaf of dark bread. "Perhaps you could come with me . . . if you're not too busy."

"I'd love to," he said.

He watched her as she set the bread on the table, along with some butter and cheese. She rinsed some fresh radishes and carrots in water that she poured from a bucket. He knew she must have carried the water from the well, and he suspected she had recently dug the vegetables herself as he recalled seeing neat rows of plants on the opposite side of the cottage from the walled garden. He was almost moved to tears at the thought of how hard she'd been working. He wanted to tell her how he respected her for her ability and willingness to work. He wondered how to tell her without hurting her feelings, that while he loathed the thought of her doing servant's work—and he would see that she never did it again—he loved the way she had been raised by people who weren't afraid to work. He thought of the endless hours he'd spent in his youth helping Stephen personally renovate and maintain their home, caring for their horses and the grounds surrounding the house. He thought of how he'd never seen his father lift anything beyond a pen or a newspaper. And his mother was only capable of ordering others about. He could never tell Kyrah how he loved her more for the very fact that she could, and would, work to survive—even though he would see that it never came to that. As she set the vegetables on the table, he took hold of her hand, pressing his lips into her palm, inhaling the scent of the earth, the food, and the water still lingering there. He looked up to meet the question in her eyes and simply said, "You have beautiful hands."

"They're ghastly," she said, knowing the hands of an aristocratic lady would be soft and white, with perfectly rounded nails.

Ritcherd shook his head and pressed her knuckles to his lips. "They're beautiful."

Kyrah felt so moved by the sincerity in his eyes that she couldn't resist the impulse to bend over and kiss him. Then she pressed her forehead to his, as if she could somehow draw his presence into her. "Thank you," she murmured.

"For what?" he asked, reaching up to touch her face.

"For coming home alive . . . for loving me in spite of myself."

Ritcherd smiled. "My pleasure."

Kyrah eased away and finished setting out their simple meal before she called Sarah into the kitchen, and the three of them sat together to eat. Sarah offered a simple blessing over their food, including an expression of gratitude for Ritcherd's safe return.

Only a few minutes into the meal, Ritcherd said, "I have a proposition for you, Sarah."

"Yes?" she asked expectantly.

"Would you be my mother?" he asked, and Sarah laughed. Kyrah wondered how long it had been since she'd heard her mother laugh. "What I mean is," he went on, "it's really good to hear you laugh, and . . . well, my mother never laughs. And I've always thought I'd rather have you for a mother, anyway. So I think it's about time I made my intentions known." Without warning he moved around the table and went to his knee in front of her, taking both her hands into his. "Please, Sarah. Tell me you'll be my mother."

"Just how did you propose to go about that?" Sarah giggled like a child.

"I'm glad you asked me that," he said as he stood and put his hands on his hips, looking at her pointedly. "What I had in mind was . . ." He glanced around. "Well, I like this little place. Not only is it cozy, but the mood here with you ladies is remarkable. Don't you agree this place is cozy, Sarah?"

"I agree," she said easily. "I rather like it myself."

"Well then, it makes sense that I'll just move in here when Kyrah and I get married. Then you can be my mother."

Sarah threw back her head and laughed. Kyrah could hardly believe her eyes as her sickly mother, who rarely had the energy to do more than walk from one room to another, jumped from her chair and threw herself into Ritcherd's arms. He picked her up off the floor and whirled her around the kitchen while they all laughed. Ritcherd Buchanan was like an angel sent from heaven. He had made Kyrah believe for the first time that her mother could survive without Stephen Payne.

"I take it you like that idea," Ritcherd smirked as he set her down and held her steady until she got her balance.

"Like it?" she said, pulling Kyrah into her arms and embracing her warmly. "It's by far the best idea I've heard in years."

Ritcherd embraced them both, then they all sat back down and finished their simple meal. When the table had been cleared, Ritcherd said, "I'm going home to freshen up a bit. I'll be back to get you within the hour."

"I'll be ready," Kyrah said.

The minute he was gone, she flew into a panic. "Mother, you've got to help me . . . quickly."

"What?" Sarah appeared in the doorway of the spare bedroom, which was mostly used for storing odds and ends. "What is it?" she asked, watching Kyrah rummage through a trunk.

"I'm going into town with Ritcherd Buchanan, and I refuse to go looking like I've just been scrubbing floors."

Kyrah found a dress that she'd only worn once—the day she had told Ritcherd good-bye nearly three years earlier. She had added some length to it soon afterward when she'd hit a sudden growth spurt, then her life had changed and she'd never had occasion to wear it again. Many of her finer clothes had been sold out of necessity, but she had kept this dress for sentimental reasons. With Sarah's help, she quickly fluffed it out then pressed it, grateful that it had simple lines. While Sarah gave it the finishing touches, Kyrah washed up and brushed through her hair, twisting it into the usual knot. She only owned one hat, a wide-brimmed straw that she wore any time she worked outside or went into town. But she dressed it up by adding a silk scarf from the same trunk where the dress had been stored. She pinned the hat into place and tied the scarf behind her head, leaving it to hang down her back in a fashionable manner. She was barely ready to go when Ritcherd knocked at the door. She hugged her mother and went to answer it. All her efforts were worthwhile when she saw the admiration in his eyes.

"I missed you," he said.

"It's only been an hour." She stepped outside and closed the door behind her.

Ritcherd chuckled. "I meant through the last three years, but . . . I must admit the last hour was awfully lonely."

Kyrah realized now that part of his purpose for returning home was to exchange his stallion for the trap. As he took her hand to help her step in, he commented warmly, "I remember this dress. You wore it . . . the first time I kissed you."

"The day you left me," she said as she was seated. Their eyes met as they shared the irony in silence, then he leaned forward to kiss her, as if to complete the bridge from their separation to their reunion.

Ritcherd drove the trap toward town with the reins in his left hand and his right arm around Kyrah's shoulders. Following Kyrah's comment on what a beautiful day it was, Ritcherd said, "The next item of business is a formal engagement." While Kyrah attempted to accept the reality of what he was talking about, he added, "My mother is throwing the biggest party of the year as a welcome home for her only son. You will be my guest of honor. And at that party, my dear, we will announce our engagement."

Kyrah tried to swallow her apprehension as she glanced away. "Is all of that really necessary?"

"What?" he asked.

"A formal engagement, and—"

"You did say you would marry me, didn't you?"

"Yes, of course, but . . ." She hesitated, wondering how to tell him that the very thought of attending a formal social at Buckley Manor put her stomach in knots.

"But?" he pressed.

"When is this party?" she asked.

"Three or four days; I don't remember exactly. Does it matter?" When she didn't answer he added, "Kyrah, we will never work out the differences between us if we can't talk. You're obviously not comfortable with this. You need to tell me why."

"I just . . . feel so . . . unprepared. I've never been to any such social in my entire life. I was always too young . . . before. I wouldn't know how to act. I've got nothing to wear. I'd feel so out of place."

"Kyrah," he said gently, "you're not talking like the girl I left three years ago. You are very capable of being a lady. I've seen it in you as long as I can remember. Think of all that dancing we did in the old church. It will all come back to you. And as for something to wear, I just figured we'd make a stop at Mrs. Harker's Boutique while we're in town."

Kyrah met his eyes and bit back the protest at the tip of her tongue. Instead she said, "This really means a lot to you, doesn't it."

"Yes, but . . ."

"But?"

"But not more than you do. If you really don't want to go, then . . . I'll make an appearance and . . . we'll do something else."

Kyrah sighed but said nothing for several minutes. After mulling it around in her mind, she had to admit, "I suppose if I'm going to marry a Buchanan, I had better get used to it."

Ritcherd smiled. "Not necessarily," he said. "All this social stuff isn't important to me, Kyrah."

Kyrah smiled back. But as they arrived in town, she immediately felt a new reality settle in. She would be courting—and marrying—Ritcherd Buchanan. She'd told him he would have to lower himself to her social level, and in many ways that was true. People who knew them would see his marriage as a descent on the social ladder. Still, she wanted him to be proud of her, and she had to lower her pride enough to accommodate herself to his lifestyle as much as possible. Glancing down at her three-year-old dress, one of the few things she had to wear that didn't look like servants' garb, she wondered what she might wear the next time she went into town with him—and the next. Realistically, she had no way to afford getting new clothes. Her only choice was to ask Ritcherd, but the thought was disconcerting at the very least. Thinking it quickly through, however, she realized that asking him would be far less humiliating in the long run than having him become embarrassed by having her wear the same old dresses over and over. As he halted the trap and tied off the reins, she swallowed her pride and forced herself to just say it.

"Ritcherd. There's something I need to ask you."

"I'm listening," he said, turning toward her. When she glanced down and wrung her hands, Ritcherd knew she was nervous. "What is it?" he pressed when she hesitated.

"Well . . . my wardrobe is extremely limited. I had to sell most of my clothes to . . . well, you know. And I . . . don't want you to be ashamed of me, so . . ."

"Kyrah," Ritcherd touched her chin to lift her face to his view, "listen to me, and pay close attention. There is nothing you could ever do that would bring me embarrassment or shame. *Nothing!* If anything, I feel like it's the other way around. There are times when I hate being a Buchanan; I hate the reputation that goes along with it, and the way everyone seems to know everything about me, as if my money made me some kind of public paragon. If anyone should feel ashamed, it ought to be you—for having to put up with such nonsense."

Kyrah's eyes widened in disbelief as she realized he was serious. Had he always felt that way? She never would have dreamed! And she could never tell him how much hearing such a confession helped assuage her doubts.

"Now," he continued, "I am absolutely delighted to buy you anything you need or want. If having new clothes will make you happy, or less uncomfortable, then by all means, get them. But don't do it because you think it will make any difference in how I see you, or how I feel about you." He smiled and touched her face. "You would look beautiful no matter what, Kyrah. In fact, you look more beautiful now than I've ever seen you."

"I love you, Ritcherd," she said, touching his face in return.

He laughed and kissed her quickly, oblivious to passersby regarding them oddly. "And I love you," he said, stepping down and holding out his hand to help her. As she stood beside him, he asked, "Was there anything else?"

"No," she said, smiling.

"Good. I'm going to let you go along to Mrs. Harker's while I see my solicitor for just a few minutes. I'll meet you there. Order whatever you like."

Kyrah smiled. "Don't be long. I'll be needing your opinion."

"I'll hurry," he promised, and they went opposite directions.

Kyrah quickly became aware of the typical skeptical glances from those who knew her. But today even that couldn't dampen her mood. Ritcherd Buchanan loved her, and everything was going to be all right.

Kyrah stepped into Mrs. Harker's boutique, and the little bell that tinkled above the door reminded her of many previous visits in the years preceding her father's death. She knew that Mrs. Harker had a thriving business, with a number of seamstresses and assistants, but the shop was extremely quiet today, and she was dismayed to be approached by Mrs. Harker personally. She'd only encountered the woman once or twice on the streets in the past few years, but she had no doubt as to her attitude concerning Kyrah's circumstances. Even now, her eyes clearly said that she felt Kyrah had no business being there. She was barely polite as she asked, "May I help you?"

Feeling inclined to keep their interaction as minimal as possible, Kyrah simply said, "I'm needing an evening gown for a social later this week."

"And what social would that be?" she asked, and Kyrah could almost imagine her eliciting fodder for gossip.

"Is that relevant?" Kyrah asked.

Mrs. Harker gave a bristly little smile as she said, "You wouldn't want to show up in a gown too much like one of the other young ladies, now would you? The only social I'm aware of in the area this week would be for the Buchanans. Would that be the very same?"

"Yes," Kyrah said, and there was no mistaking the meaning in Mrs. Harker's eyes. She might as well have come right out and said: *You're some kind of fool to think that getting a pretty dress and sneaking into that party uninvited is going to do you any good.*

Following a minute of insinuating silence, Mrs. Harker finally said, "I'm afraid I don't have time to make something by then. There have been so many orders for new gowns since the captain returned. I've got my seamstresses all extremely busy. It seems there are many young ladies wanting to impress him."

Kyrah swallowed carefully, reminding herself that nothing this woman said or thought made any difference. She knew Ritcherd loved her. His behavior toward her since his return was stark evidence of that. Still, she couldn't help thinking of the throng of beautiful young ladies in their expensive gowns and jewelry, flaunting themselves before Ritcherd as if he were some great prize to be contested for. She was nearly ready to thank Mrs. Harker and leave, when she said, "However, if one of my ready-made gowns appeals to you," she motioned toward a rack of gowns, "I could have it fitted for the social. They are all one of a kind."

Kyrah glanced at the varied colors of silk, satin, and taffeta, and felt somehow unworthy. But she swallowed her concerns and simply said, "Let's see what you have, then."

"That would be fine, but . . . unless you have an established account, I'll need to know how you'll be paying for your purchase."

Kyrah knew her alarm was evident by the obvious disgust on Mrs. Harker's face. Did she think that Kyrah had come in here intending to get a gown on credit and somehow worm her way out of paying for it? Did she see her as some kind of thief . . . or just the destitute daughter of a reckless gambler? She felt grateful for the anger that quickly covered her distress. With a terse voice she answered, "I believe money is the customary method."

Mrs. Harker sighed impatiently. "Of course, but . . . I'll need to have it up front. There's no point wasting my time or yours if you won't be able to pay."

For a moment Kyrah wished she'd never agreed to attend that blasted social. For a moment she wondered what kind of insanity had made her believe she could fit into a world completely foreign to her. For a moment she wanted to just slither out of the shop and never show her face in public. Then the little bell above the door tinkled. Mrs. Harker looked past Kyrah's shoulder to see who it might be. Her face lit up as she said with a syrupy falseness in her voice, "Captain Buchanan. What a delight this is. I'd heard that you'd returned. We're all so glad to see you safe and well."

"Thank you, Mrs. Harker," he said. Kyrah kept her back turned to him, hoping to gain control of her anger before he had the opportunity to see any evidence of it in her face.

"That social to celebrate your return is all anybody's talking about these days," Mrs. Harker prattled on while Kyrah discreetly moved closer to the rack of ready-made gowns, pretending to browse. "I've had many a young lady in here ordering the finest."

"Is that so?" he said, his tone bored.

"You must be here to get your mother's gown," Mrs. Harker said with confidence, apparently picking up on his indifference to the conversation.

"Actually, no," he said, and Kyrah could tell by the tone of his voice that he'd become aware of her discomfort, even though she'd managed to avoid looking at him. Kyrah momentarily closed her eyes, feeling all over again the countless times he had rescued her from the taunts and criticism of others. A part of her hated it; she hated this feeling of dependence on him. But how could she deny how thoroughly loved and protected he made her feel? How could she not be grateful to have him back in her life, and to know that he still loved her enough to keep protecting her? She reminded herself that his love was all that mattered. She reminded herself, just as he'd said last night, that there was no place for pride in their relationship. She lifted her eyes to meet his gaze just as he asked, "Is there a problem here?" When he talked like that, she could well imagine the military officer. And she was suddenly overflowing with pleasure and gratitude at being the one who had claimed his heart.

She forced back the threat of tears and smiled at him, saying firmly, "Mrs. Harker was just about to help me decide which of these would suit me best. Then she can have one fitted in time."

Kyrah absorbed his penetrating gaze, knowing that he was trying to read the undertones of what might be taking place. Then he smiled almost imperceptibly, and she knew that he hadn't lost his ability to read her. With perfect finesse, he turned to Mrs. Harker, who looked somehow alarmed. "As I was saying," he said, "I'm not here to pick up my mother's gown. I assume she is capable of taking care of that. I *am* here, however, to offer an opinion, and of course, to see that anything Miss Payne desires be put on my account. In spite of the short amount of time we have before Miss Payne's gown will be needed, it's important that it be just right. After all, this is a special occasion for her."

Mrs. Harker glanced at Kyrah, then back to Ritcherd, as if she didn't understand—or perhaps she couldn't quite believe the implication. Ritcherd took a step toward her and lowered his voice, as if to tell her a secret, even though Kyrah was the only other person in the shop, and she could plainly hear him. "You see, Mrs. Harker, in about twenty years, I intend to pull this gown out and show it to my daughter when I tell her that this is what her mother wore the night we announced our engagement."

"Of course," Mrs. Harker said, following a moment of stunned silence. Without further delay she began to bustle around like a mother hen, willing to see to Kyrah's every wish. She now declared that she could manage to make something to order for her, but Kyrah insisted that there were a few gowns that appealed to her, and she would like to try them on.

Ritcherd sat down and made himself comfortable, stretching out his legs and crossing his booted ankles. His response to the first gown Kyrah tried on was a subtle wrinkle of his nose and a simple, "I don't think yellow is your color." The next one provoked a contemplative, "I like you in green, but the style isn't quite right."

Kyrah wondered as she slipped into the third one if maybe the problem was her. Perhaps she just wasn't suited for evening gowns. But when she stepped out of the dressing room, noting that the fit would only need minor adjustments, Ritcherd's face lit up. "That's the one," he said firmly, his eyes glowing with admiration.

Kyrah turned to survey herself in the long mirror and was actually surprised to see that he was right. The gown was a deep turquoise blue with dropped shoulders and a graceful waistline, and though it bagged a little here and there, Mrs. Harker pinned and tucked and assured her that by the day after tomorrow it would be perfect. Just before Kyrah returned to the dressing room to remove it, Ritcherd said, "Mrs. Harker, I would like you to meet the future Mrs. Ritcherd Buchanan."

Mrs. Harker said nothing, but her expression clearly stated that she thought he was crazy, in spite of her plastered-on smile. Ritcherd just laughed, and Kyrah couldn't help laughing with him.

Chapter Six

Diamonds Round Her Throat

*R*itcherd kindly informed Mrs. Harker that Kyrah would be back soon to order more clothes to be made. They left the dress shop together and went hand in hand to get all of the groceries they needed and much more. As they started toward home, Kyrah closed her eyes and relished the abundance surrounding her in the trap. She inhaled deeply, attempting to grasp the reality that she would never have to worry about the next meal or the next month's rent. Her thoughts went to her father as it occurred to her that his absence was now the only real deterrent to her happiness.

Impulsively she said, "Before we go back, I want to go to Father's grave. I've not been there yet this week."

Ritcherd looked at her sadly. It was still only sinking in that Stephen was really dead. "All right," he said, and halted the trap near the church at the edge of town, where the graveyard was located. After helping Kyrah down, he followed her silently with his hands behind his back. She made her way between the gravestones to a spot where she had obviously come often. When she finally stopped, Ritcherd hesitated to come beside her. Reading the stone, reality struck him deeply—and it hurt.

"Mother wanted a finer stone," Kyrah said softly, "but it was all we could afford."

"I think it's nice," he said noting the simple yet tasteful marker that read:

Beloved Husband and Father
Stephen Payne
1734–1777

"I would suspect," he went on, "that the majority of people lying beneath ornate markers are rarely visited or remembered the way your father is."

"That's what I told Mother," Kyrah said without moving her eyes from the stone. Reverently she knelt before it, meticulously brushing it clean with her hands. Ritcherd went to his knees beside her. Putting his arm around her, he could see his own emotions reflected in her expression. He took her hand and squeezed it, wondering how he could possibly offer her reassurance when he felt so much pain himself over Stephen's death.

"You know," she said quietly, "we were very fortunate to have him buried here." Ritcherd's surprise went unnoticed. "Even though the official verdict was suicide, the vicar allowed us to pretend otherwise, so that he could be buried in the churchyard."

"Maybe it *was* otherwise," Ritcherd said, hoping to offer a positive note. But Kyrah looked at him sharply.

Her eyes quickly turned distant again as she looked back at the stone. "He sent a letter," she whispered. "He said that he wouldn't ask us to forgive him, nor would he try to explain . . . because none of it mattered anymore."

Ritcherd felt her squeeze his hand, and her eyes closed briefly as she gave a heavy sigh. "We didn't see him," she said blandly. "The casket was sealed because he had . . ." She stopped abruptly, sighed again, then finished by saying, "He was right. None of that matters anymore."

There was a long reign of silence while Kyrah tried to recall a pleasurable memory of her father. The wind picked up, and she removed her hat to be free of the way it grabbed at the pin holding it in place.

Ritcherd watched her closely while the Cornish wind pulled at her hair, tugging it out of the pins that held it in place. He was about to ask where her mind was when she began speaking as though he weren't present. He was surprised at first, but it soon became evident that she had made a habit of coming here and talking to her father.

"Papa," she began, "you'll be pleased to know that things are going much better now. Ritcherd is back, Papa, and you'll probably be glad to know that I was wrong. I was being foolish, but he made me see things more clearly. He is a good man, Papa. But I think you knew that all along. We're

100

to be married soon, and we wish you could be there. Perhaps you will be, in a way.

"Mother is doing much better, I believe. She was so happy this morning when Ritcherd told her we would be getting married. I know he'll take good care of us. I guess Mother knows that, too. She still misses you. She was reading your letters just . . ." Kyrah bit her lip and Ritcherd expected her to cry, but she only took a sharp breath and laid her head against his shoulder. He pulled her closer and a painful knot formed in his throat. He looked skyward while tears ran down his face.

"Why?" he cried as if the heavens might answer him. "Why?"

"Take me home," Kyrah said, coming to her feet. She walked away and Ritcherd followed, wiping his face with his sleeve.

The ride home passed in silence, but Kyrah knew that Ritcherd shared her grief. She took his hand and squeezed it, hoping he understood how good it felt not to be alone.

Ritcherd helped carry her purchases into the cottage, then he left with the promise that he'd come back in the evening. Kyrah put the kitchen in order and put some soup on to simmer while she told her mother of all that had happened since they'd last been able to talk. While her mother rested, Kyrah took the opportunity to prepare herself a hot bath. She couldn't remember the last time she'd been able to indulge in such a luxury. It was rare that she found the time to do more than clean up quickly with a basin of water, and she usually washed her hair the same way. But today she immersed herself, hair and all, in water that seemed to bathe away much of the horror she had endured in Ritcherd's absence. She finally emerged, feeling cleaner than she had in years. And the thought of becoming Ritcherd's wife was most prominent on her mind.

After putting everything in order and sharing supper with her mother, she wondered when Ritcherd might return. She pulled out the only other dress she owned besides the clothes she'd worked in and pressed it so it would be ready whenever she might need it. Unable to find anything else to occupy her time, she began to feel tense. She was so accustomed to being busy every waking moment that she hardly knew what to do with herself. Gradually the tension settled in more deeply, reminding her all too easily of the constant anxiety she had felt in his absence. When he finally knocked at the door, she actually gasped, then wondered what was happening to her. She took a deep breath and reminded herself that Ritcherd was never leaving her again. Everything would be all right.

"Is something wrong?" he asked when she opened the door, and she marveled at his insight when she had made such an effort to cover her anxiety.

"Of course not," she said, urging him inside. He greeted her with a kiss, and she basked in his presence as they sat in the parlor with her mother, teasing her in a way that brought memories of their youth rushing back. Following a brief visit, he comically asked Sarah's permission to take Kyrah on a long walk, and she waved them off with a smile.

They walked hand in hand over the moors while the sun moved gracefully toward the western horizon. Recalling her walk to Buckley Manor just this morning as the sun was coming up, she felt as if she'd lived three days in one. So much had happened. So much had changed. Ritcherd had come home.

They talked of trivial matters, sharing memories and hopes for the future, avoiding any topic that touched on their years apart. It seemed there was nothing to say about them that didn't encourage dismal thoughts. By way of habit, they arrived at the church ruins to find them appearing almost unreal, surrounded by dusk. They walked aimlessly among them, while Ritcherd occasionally moved his hand over one of the pews or a stone archway, as if to reacquaint himself with an old friend.

When nothing was said for several minutes, Ritcherd turned to Kyrah and looked into her eyes. Emotion tinged his voice as he touched her face, murmuring, "I missed you, Kyrah . . . so very much."

He kissed her meekly and she pushed her arms around his waist, holding to him tightly. "And I missed you," she said, looking into his eyes as if she had found the answer to every mystery of life. Her emotions consumed her entirely, and she felt an unfamiliar desire rising inside her. As his nearness began to affect her in a way it never had before, she became both thrilled at the prospect of becoming his wife and terrified at what these feelings might tempt her to in the meantime.

Ritcherd pressed his hands down her arms and back up again, while he closed his eyes and nuzzled his face into her hair, inhaling its sweet, clean fragrance. He drew back just enough to look into her eyes, marveling at the enormity of his feelings.

"Kyrah," he murmured, pushing his arms around her, "do you have any idea how many years I have wanted to hold you this way?"

"No," she said in a voice that sounded dreamy and distant. "Tell me."

"Forever," he said and kissed her. "It seems like forever." He kissed her again.

Feeling suddenly overpowered by his emotions and drawn into sensations that were both unfamiliar and exciting, he was startled by Kyrah's abruptly easing away. "We must be careful," she said without looking at him.

It took Ritcherd a moment to grasp her implication, and another full minute to comprehend the bridge they had crossed. She was a woman now. The age difference that had kept them in separate realms of one kind or another for as long as he'd known her no longer existed. Through the silence that followed, he found himself watching her as if he'd never seen her before. *She was so beautiful. He loved her so much.*

Her expectant expression startled him back to the moment, and he fumbled to say, "Yes, of course . . . we must be careful." But he felt somehow guilty for the thoughts parading through his mind that directly contradicted his words. He didn't want to be careful. He wanted only to take her in his arms with no heed to propriety or moral judgment. And even knowing how wrong it would be, he couldn't help indulging in a momentary fantasy. His state of mind was only fueled when Kyrah looked up at him with his own longing mirrored innocently in her eyes.

"You know," she said, turning her back to him, as if she had somehow sensed the need to break the spell between them before he lost complete control of his senses, "I always wondered why . . . you never kissed me . . . when we were younger."

As the reasons came into Ritcherd's mind, his guilt magnified. Stephen would not have appreciated Ritcherd's having such thoughts about his daughter before he'd put a wedding ring on her finger. Freshly determined to get that ring on her finger as quickly as possible, he simply said, "You were so young. I didn't want to take advantage of your innocence."

"Then you must have made a conscious decision."

"I did," he admitted. "It was mostly due to something your father told me."

"What?" Kyrah asked, thinking how good it felt to talk to someone who had known him as well as she had.

"Oh," he chuckled, "it doesn't really matter what he said. I'm just grateful that he did."

After a long moment of silence, Kyrah said quite seriously, "And I thought it was because I was too skinny."

Ritcherd laughed out loud, hugging her tightly from behind. The mood quickly sobered again as he admitted, "I . . . was always afraid that . . . if I kissed you, I'd never be able to stop. I was . . . afraid you would end up having to marry me before you hardly had a chance to grow up. I didn't want you to resent me for stealing your childhood." He chuckled tensely. "I must confess, the only reason I kissed you when I did was . . . well, I knew I would be gone . . . and you wouldn't be there to tempt me."

Kyrah turned back to look at him, wishing she could tell him how comforting his explanation was. Her respect for him deepened, and she had to admit, "I doubt I would have had the sense to . . . well, keep such things from getting out of hand." She looked into his eyes. "I was so hopelessly in love with you."

Ritcherd cleared his throat, but his voice was still raspy as he said, "I know."

"How did you know?" she asked, laughter trickling into her voice.

He chuckled. "I just knew," he said.

"I wanted desperately for you to kiss me . . . long before you did."

"I know," he repeated.

"But I don't think I had any comprehension of what else it might have led to . . . when we spent so much time together."

"I know," he said again.

"Did you know me so well?" she asked.

And it was easy for him to admit, "Yes."

She smiled. "Yes, I believe you did. And I want you to know how much I . . . respect you for the way you . . . well . . . waited. It makes me love you all the more, to know that you put your love for me above your own desires."

Ritcherd swallowed his longing, along with a dose of self-recrimination. He reminded himself that he had no business entertaining such ideas in the present state of their relationship. He moved away and sat down, making a mental note to post the banns this coming Sunday. Whatever formalities needed to be seen to in order to be married, he would see that they were taken care of as quickly as possible. Kyrah sat beside him and took his hand into hers. It was his right hand, and he could feel very little of her touch, but he was grateful to at least have a right hand—and to have Kyrah holding it. He was surprised when she unbuttoned the cuff of his sleeve and bared his scarred lower arm. With purpose, she explored the matted scars and sunken muscle with her fingers. Feeling tense, he wondered why her attention to it would bother him.

"Does it hurt?" she asked when he flinched slightly.

"No," he admitted. "I mean . . . it's a little tender here and there, but . . ."

"Then what's wrong?" she asked, looking into his eyes while her fingers continued their exploration.

"It's just so . . . hideous. I would have thought you'd find it . . . repulsive . . . distasteful."

"Is this why you came home?" she asked.

"Yes," he admitted. "They don't want a man who can't use a weapon."

"Then perhaps it was this that prevented you from going into another battle that might have found you dead. Therefore, it is not so distasteful."

"I've tried to look at it that way," he said, "but there are times when I feel like I've lost something. A part of me will never be the same, and that can tend to make me feel sorry for myself. On the other hand," he opened his eyes and looked directly at her, "I would have given much more to be able to come home to you when I did. I only wish it could have been sooner."

"You're here now. That's what matters."

"Yes," he smiled and kissed her quickly, "I'm here now. And I'm not going to let you get away from me again."

She smiled and rested her head on his shoulder. The church became completely dark as they sat together in silence. Only the rustling of the breeze could be heard until Kyrah said, "I do love you, Ritcherd."

"And I love you." He tightened his arm around her. "I always have, you know."

"You have?"

"I believe something inside of me loved you the first time I saw you . . . not in the way I love you now, of course. But still . . . I think there was something special between us—right from the start."

"I believe you're right," she agreed, and her next awareness was Ritcherd nudging her awake.

"Come along," he said, urging her to her feet. "Let's get you home to bed. It's late."

Kyrah felt her lack of sleep the previous night as she walked blindly over the moors toward home, supported and guided by Ritcherd's arm about her.

When they arrived at the cottage, Ritcherd went inside with her to make certain all was well. Kyrah slipped into her mother's bedroom and returned a moment later to report that she was sleeping soundly.

"I wouldn't want her to be angry with me for keeping you out so late," Ritcherd said. "She's been a better mother to me than my own ever was."

Kyrah smiled at him through a yawn. "I wish you could stay," she admitted.

Ritcherd cleared his throat tensely, unwilling to admit his own thoughts on the matter. He did say, however, "I don't think you should be thinking that way, my dear. Until we're married, you should—"

"Not like that, silly," she said with a laugh that made her lack of sleep all the more evident. "I mean . . . we have a spare bedroom. It's a little crowded, but . . . then you wouldn't have to go home and . . . you would be here in the morning . . . and I wouldn't have to wonder if this day had just been a dream and—"

"I get the idea," he interrupted. "I'd love to stay. My mother won't be worried. Just show me to this room so you can get some sleep."

Kyrah made certain he had what he needed before she kissed him good night and went up the small stairway that more resembled a ladder, which led to the loft where she slept. She barely managed to put on a nightgown before she crawled between the covers and fell immediately to sleep.

She woke with sun streaking over the bed and sat up abruptly, thinking she was late for work. Memories of the previous day washed over her, and she lay back down with a contented sigh. Recalling that Ritcherd had spent the night, she hurriedly got dressed and pinned up her hair. Peeking into the room where she'd left him, she sighed to see him still sleeping. Quietly she closed the door and went to the kitchen to start cooking breakfast.

A short while later Sarah appeared, looking bright and almost vibrant. "Good morning, darling," she said, pressing a kiss to Kyrah's cheek.

"Good morning, Mother," she replied. "You must be feeling better."

"Oh, I am!" she said with enthusiasm as she sat near the window and smiled toward the sun streaming through the glass. "You were out rather late. Is everything all right?"

"Of course," Kyrah said. "We just . . . had a lot to talk about, I suppose."

"That's understandable." Sarah laughed as if she couldn't suppress her happiness. "I'm just so grateful he's returned—for many reasons. He's like the son we never had, and I don't know what we would ever do without him."

"It's my pleasure, actually," Ritcherd said, startling them both. They turned to see him leaning in the kitchen doorway, his arms folded casually.

"I didn't hear you knock," Sarah said as Ritcherd greeted Kyrah with a kiss.

"Well, you wouldn't have," Ritcherd said, sitting across the table from Sarah, "since I spent the night here." Sarah's eyes widened and he added, "In the spare room, of course."

"Of course," Sarah said with obvious relief.

When nothing more was said, he asked, "What's for breakfast? I'm starved."

Kyrah gave him a sideways smile. "You'll get breakfast a lot faster if you get over here and help me, Captain Buchanan."

"As you wish, my lady," he said and sidled up next to her at the stove.

A few minutes later the three of them sat together to eat breakfast. Ritcherd told Sarah about the party the day after tomorrow, and how they were going to announce their engagement. He also told her that he thought she should come to the party as well. But she insisted that without Stephen, she wouldn't know what to do.

"Are you certain?" he asked, taking her hand. "I don't want to put you in a situation where you would be uncomfortable. But I would like to show you off."

"Perhaps another time," Sarah said, and seemed relieved when they changed the subject.

They began making plans for the wedding, while Ritcherd held Kyrah's hand across the table. She still couldn't believe this was happening—and so quickly. It seemed too good to be true. But each time Ritcherd squeezed her hand, or glanced at her with that undeniable sparkle in his eyes, the reality sank in a little further.

Ritcherd insisted on helping clean the dishes while he reminisced about the many times he'd done so in his youth. Sarah sat at the table, reading a little, but mostly enjoying their display of happiness. She was amazed that the dishes got clean at all with the way they were laughing and playing in the water like a couple of children. With her attention briefly on her book, Sarah noticed that it became suddenly silent. She glanced up to see Ritcherd kissing Kyrah as if they were alone. She felt both emotional and a bit embarrassed. But she cleared her throat dramatically and they both turned toward her in surprise. Kyrah blushed in response to her mother's warm smile, but Ritcherd simply said, "Isn't she beautiful, Sarah?"

"Yes, Ritcherd, she is."

Kyrah returned her attention to the dishes in an effort to avoid the compliments, and Ritcherd laughed as he went back to helping her.

Later that morning Ritcherd and Kyrah returned to town, this time taking Sarah with them. Ritcherd couldn't believe that Sarah had not once been beyond the yard of the cottage since they had moved there following Stephen's death. He left them at the dress shop with Mrs. Harker fussing over Kyrah and helping her order an appropriate wardrobe. He returned two hours later to find them just finishing up. Mrs. Harker promised that the evening gown would be ready first thing the following morning, and she would get right on the other things once the social was over.

Ritcherd took the ladies to an inn called the Golden Lion, where he had often gone with Stephen. They dined together on roast beef, hot bread, and cider while they talked more about the plans for the wedding. After seeing Sarah safely home, Ritcherd told her he wanted to take Kyrah for a little ride and they'd return in time for supper. Halting the trap near the church ruins, he tied off the reins and helped Kyrah down.

As they wandered between the stone pews, holding hands, Ritcherd said, "I love this place—perhaps more than any other place on earth. There's a quality to it that's difficult to describe. And in all the years we've come here, I've hardly ever seen anyone else around. Sometimes I feel as if it belongs to us."

"Perhaps the way we feel about this place has more to do with the memories we share here."

Ritcherd looked into her eyes. "My thoughts exactly. Which brings me to my point."

"Were you making a point?"

"No, but I'm about to."

"All right. I'm listening."

"Do you remember the day we met?"

"Of course."

"Yes, but . . . do you remember what I said when you told me your name?"

"Something about it sounding like a lady's name."

"That's right," he said. "An elegant lady . . . with diamonds round her throat."

"And I thought you were rather silly."

"Did you?" He chuckled softly. "Well, the thing that's strange about that is . . . when you told me your name, that image appeared in my mind— an elegant lady, wearing diamonds." He sighed and looked briefly at the ground, putting his hands behind his back. "I've often tried to imagine how you might look all grown up, but when I saw you for the first time after I returned home, I couldn't believe how beautiful you had become."

When he looked up again, Kyrah became breathless. His expression made it evident that he was telling her something close to his heart. He glanced away again, and she knew he was nervous.

"What I'm trying to say is . . . I'm grateful for having known you as a child. And even more grateful to know you as a woman. And now that we've come this far, I feel it's time for me to complete a circle that, in my opinion, began the first time I saw you here, when you were seven years old." He took her hand into his and went down on one knee. "I know it's already been established, but I wanted to make it official . . . to do it right." He took a deep breath. "Kyrah, will you do me the honor of becoming my wife?"

Kyrah was so touched by his chivalry that she couldn't keep her voice from breaking when she answered, "Yes, Ritcherd. Of course." He smiled and she added, "Now get up off the ground and kiss me."

Ritcherd laughed and did as she'd asked, but he had to remind himself they weren't married yet when it quickly became so enjoyable. Forcing himself to step back, he cleared his throat and said, "I have something for you." He drew a velvet box from his coat pocket, and Kyrah held her breath as he opened it to reveal an exquisite diamond necklace and earrings. "To go with the dress," he added easily.

"Oh, Ritcherd," she gasped. "They're so beautiful, but . . . how can I?"

"Don't you even dare ask such a question! I've got more money than I'll ever know what to do with. And the best thing I could possibly do is spend it on you."

"But I don't need things like this to know you love me."

"I know," he said with a smile. "That's why I like giving them to you. If I thought you couldn't live without things like this, I wouldn't love you the way I do. But there's no reason why you shouldn't have them."

She still seemed hesitant to take them, so he set the box down to take out the necklace and fasten it around her throat. When he turned her around to see how she looked, the necklace was overlapping her brooch.

"Well," he smiled, "it will go better with the gown, but . . . let's just see if . . ." For a full minute he attempted to undo the tiny clasp of the brooch, then he looked at his right hand scornfully. His voice betrayed the extent of his humility as he admitted, "I can't do it. It's too small. I could do the necklace, but I . . ."

Kyrah smiled warmly and unfastened the brooch, tossing it to the ground. "I won't wear it anymore."

Ritcherd glanced to where it had landed, then turned toward her, a trace of shame showing in his eyes. Kyrah took his right hand into both of hers and pressed her fingers around it affectionately. "I love you, Ritcherd," she whispered. "It makes no difference to me." She kissed his hand and brought it to her face. "I love you more for what you have suffered."

Ritcherd pulled her into his arms and pressed a kiss to her brow, unable to express what her acceptance meant to him. To men who had lost so much more, his injury might seem trifling. But it was still a loss that would be with him for the rest of his life. He doubted that many of the eligible young ladies in the area, the same ones his mother had always tried to steer his way, would accept the injury so easily. Of course, his money could compensate for a great deal to women like that.

Kyrah eased back and touched the necklace reverently. "Thank you," she said. "You treat me like a queen."

"As I should," he said. Inhaling deeply, as if to more fully absorb her appearance, he had to admit, "We've come full circle, Kyrah. And wherever we go from here will always bring us back to this place."

Kyrah nodded in agreement, wondering if her life was really going to be as good as it seemed. She fingered the diamonds round her throat, realizing that it was easy to forget just how wealthy Ritcherd Buchanan really was. But her reasons for marrying him had nothing to do with money.

While they stood facing each other she became lost in the intensity in his eyes, marveling once again at the love coming to light between them. The reality that he shared her feelings glowed in his eyes just before he closed them and bent to kiss her. The momentary anticipation sent her heart racing as if it were their first kiss all over again. When his lips came over hers, she felt at first as if she could fly, and then as if she might melt into the ground. He pulled her completely into his arms while his mouth softened over hers. She moaned when their kiss became warm and moist, stirring sensations in her that she'd never imagined she could feel. She pressed her hands over his back and moved impossibly closer. Just when she feared she could bear no more without collapsing in his embrace, he eased back to look into her eyes. The evidence of his desires quickened her heart further, but she was equally warmed by his obvious effort to maintain an appropriate boundary between them. He stepped back and touched her face with an unspoken promise of all they would share as husband and wife.

"I love you," he murmured, and she smiled in surprise when he led her into a dance, keeping a silent rhythm. And despite the years since they had done this, she followed his lead easily while they practiced them all, adding to Kyrah's confidence that she would be able to get through this grand social without embarrassing herself—or him.

When she was too tired to dance anymore, she returned the necklace to its box and asked Ritcherd to keep it in his pocket until she could put it safely away. They returned to find Sarah sitting in the walled garden, reading.

"Hello, Mother," Ritcherd said as he opened the gate and led Kyrah by the hand, sitting on the grass near Sarah and pulling Kyrah onto his lap.

"Well, hello," she smiled, and Kyrah noticed color in her mother's cheeks. "Did you have a good time?"

"Oh, yes," Kyrah said.

"Where's your brooch, darling?" Sarah asked. "You had it on when you left."

"I must have lost it," Kyrah said with indifference. "I've got something much better now anyway." She smiled at Ritcherd. "I'll show you later."

"I'll look forward to it," Sarah said, noticing how Ritcherd lifted his eyebrows playfully. "Perhaps you left it at the dress shop," Sarah said.

"What?"

"The brooch."

"Oh, of course," Kyrah replied. "Perhaps."

"What are you reading?" Ritcherd asked, and Sarah handed him the book. "Looks dull," he said with a smile as he thumbed casually through the pages. Kyrah stood and walked listlessly about the garden, and Sarah followed her, pointing out the progress of some odd flower growing in the corner.

"I should be going," Ritcherd said as he stood and brushed off the back of his breeches. "It's getting late. If I don't make an appearance at home once in a while, my mother gets . . . well, you know." He mimicked a visible shudder that made Kyrah laugh. "But I might be back for breakfast."

Kyrah walked him to the front of the cottage and watched him drive away. She couldn't help thinking that she'd not been this happy since her youth, before she'd learned that he was going off to war. Now that he was back, they could put the past behind them once and for all, and find the happiness she had always dreamed of.

Ritcherd entered the dining room to find his mother just starting her supper. "Looks like I'm just in time," he said, noting the place set for him at the opposite end of the table.

"You've missed most of the meals since you returned. I didn't necessarily expect you for this one."

Ritcherd tried to ignore her tone, which was more caustic than usual. With a smile he said, "But you had a place set for me. You must have been hopeful."

Her scowl deepened and her voice tightened as she said, "I would have hoped that you'd *want* to spend a little time with me, now that you're back."

Ritcherd sighed and leaned back in his chair. He wondered why he would want to be here any more than he absolutely had to when her attitude was so thoroughly repulsive. He had hoped that his years away would have eased the estrangements between them, but it was easy to see that his mother was still too caught up in her elaborate lifestyle. And her preoccupations revolved even more around the latest gossip and her pursuit of having the best of everything. He could tell she had something on her mind, and he would have no peace until he'd heard whatever it was. But he waited until the soup had been served and the maid left the room before he continued the conversation. Doing his best to remain civil, he stated, "So, I'm here. What would you like to talk about?"

"George Morley is looking for you," she said in a tone to indicate that his friend's visit was not the most prominent thing on her mind.

"I didn't even know he was in the country."

"He hasn't been, as far as I know, for quite some time. Perhaps he heard you were back."

"Perhaps," Ritcherd said. "I hope you invited him to the party."

"I did."

"Good. I'll talk to him then. Did he say what he wanted?"

"No. But he's been here three times. He says you're never home. I tend to agree."

"What does George know?" Ritcherd chuckled, hoping to keep the mood light. But his mother didn't change her expression in the slightest.

"I want to speak with you," Jeanette said sternly, and he could feel it coming. She practically slammed her spoon down on the table, but he had learned to ignore her dramatics.

"What is it, Mother?" he asked blandly, certain that his nonchalant attitude made her even angrier—which in turn made him try all the harder to be nonchalant.

"You've been seeing that tramp again." She spat the words like venom.

Ritcherd tensed but reminded himself to stay calm. "She is no tramp," he said easily, and took an abundant swallow from his glass of wine.

"You don't see her the way I do. I know from a mother's wisdom that she is no good for you. How many times do I have to tell you?"

"You might as well stop telling me, Mother. You should know by now that it won't do any good."

"So I've heard," she said bitterly.

"What *have* you heard?" he asked with an expectant smile.

"Tell me the rumors aren't true." She put her hands at the edge of the table and leaned forward. "Please, my son, tell me you're not going to marry her."

Ritcherd knew she'd either been talking to Peter Westman or Mrs. Harker—perhaps both. But he had expected this—even wanted it. He wanted her to know, but he'd had no desire to tell her himself. Remaining collected he said, "You wouldn't want me to lie to my own mother, would you?"

"But why, Ritcherd?" she asked with disgust. "Why?"

"Because I love her," he replied with confidence.

"She's a servant girl. Don't you see what this means for your future?"

"I only know that I have no future without Kyrah," he stated with conviction.

"You must be mad. It only takes one look to see she's no lady."

Ritcherd glared at her but answered coolly, "You don't see her the way I do."

"She's got you wrapped around her finger. Can't you see a money-hungry tramp when she's right under your nose?"

"Yes, Mother." He finished his drink and set the glass down abruptly. "I believe I can see a money-hungry tramp."

His gibe was totally lost on Jeanette. Her mind was obviously absorbed with this situation. Ritcherd scrutinized his mother closely and wondered if she knew that the angry contortion she commonly wore was becoming permanent, distorting her otherwise youthful appearance of dark hair and a slender figure.

"Don't you realize," she said at last, "that there are other young ladies in the valley who would make a much more suitable wife for you than . . . Miss Payne?"

"I think I can judge what is suitable for me," he said adamantly.

"And you really intend to marry . . . *her?*" she added distastefully.

"I do." He smiled at his own pun.

"And what if I said you would lose your inheritance if you did?"

"I'd say you can't pull that one on me. I inherited everything when Father died. It's all legal and proper, and you know it. And you're a fool to even think that I wouldn't know it. I have more right to this estate than you do. That's why I don't understand why you want me to marry some greedy snob who will spend it all."

Jeanette made no response. She obviously couldn't dispute his reasoning. The conversation came temporarily to a halt as the servants entered to serve the main course. Ritcherd's thoughts became lost in the simple meals he'd shared recently with Kyrah and her mother. It was little wonder that he far preferred the simplicity of Kyrah's life—and the lack of contention and anger that went along with it.

"Ritcherd," she finally said, "I'm pleading with you. Don't do this!"

"I've made arrangements to post the banns on Sunday. And you have no justifiable cause to stop this marriage that you would dare admit to in public. Your snobbery regarding social classes would hardly stand up with the vicar, the way you claim to be a Christian and all." He could see her seething but he didn't care. "Let me make something clear, Mother," he went on, "I am not going to let you bully me out of marrying Kyrah Payne because you're too narrow-minded and self-centered to see her for what she really is. You've never even given her a chance. I don't need your approval or your blessing. I *will* make her my wife. And soon. I'm announcing the engagement tomorrow night."

"Here?" she shrieked. "You're bringing her here?"

"However unfortunate for her, I am. But it will probably be the last time. I'm not about to sentence her to spend the rest of her life in this miserable place. You can live here until you die and then I'll sell it. I hate this place!"

"And I suppose you'll move into that quaint little cottage with your wife and her mother," she said with sarcasm.

"That's what I had in mind, as a matter of fact." His mother truly looked shocked, and he wondered if she had any idea about the source of true happiness. Obviously not, or they wouldn't be having this conversation. "Of course when children come along I'll have to buy a bigger place," he added. "But I'm not certain where I want to live yet, so for now, I'm quite content with that quaint little cottage."

"You must be mad!" she sneered.

"Quite mad," he replied. "I've lived under the same roof with you for the better part of my life. That's enough to make any man go mad."

"Is there anything I can say to make you change your mind?"

"Nothing!" he said adamantly as he stood and threw his napkin to the table.

"Not even if you knew you were breaking your mother's heart?"

"I believe that would only make my cause more pleasurable," he said through clenched teeth. "If for no other reason, I will marry Kyrah just to prove my point."

He turned to leave the room and was almost to the door when she said, "I can't allow this marriage to take place, Ritcherd. I'll do whatever I have to." Through all the years of arguing with his mother, he had never heard her use that tone of voice. It was completely devoid of her usual histrionics, cold and sinister in a way that made the hair bristle at the back of his neck.

Ritcherd turned slowly to see her expression harden with a determination that was only intensified by something almost evil in her eyes. He wondered what kind of monster had given birth to him as he struggled to find his voice enough to say, "Are you threatening me?"

"It's up to you to determine if you're going to put yourself—and Kyrah—in a position where such drastic measures would be necessary."

"Drastic measures?" he echoed in disbelief. "You *are* threatening me."

"You can think what you like," she said. "But if I were you, I would seriously reconsider what you're willing to do with your life—for her sake, if not your own. No girl is worth the kind of trouble she could bring to you. One day you'll realize that—one way or another."

She left the room before he could even come up with a reply. He was so stunned that he could hardly see straight. He didn't know how long he stood there, attempting to digest what had just happened. But once the reality settled in, he had only one tangible thought.

It only took a few minutes to ride to the cottage once he had the horse saddled. But it was long enough for anger to consume him so completely that he was hard-pressed to even speak calmly when Kyrah answered the door.

"What's wrong?" she asked as soon as she saw his face.

"We need to talk," he said. "Tell your mother we're going out."

"All right. Just a minute."

Ritcherd was already in the saddle when Kyrah came out the door. Without a word he held out a hand toward her and she mounted behind him. She barely had a chance to take hold of his waist before he heeled the stallion to a gallop. She wondered what had gone wrong; something to do with his mother, no doubt. She wasn't surprised that he rode to the church ruins, but when they'd been there for several minutes and he'd done nothing but pace back and forth, her nerves became raw.

"What is it, Ritcherd?" she finally demanded. When he said nothing, she added with confidence, "It's your mother, isn't it." He gave her a brief, sharp glance that told her she was right. "Let me guess," she said. "Your mother's gotten wind that we're getting married, and she's furious."

"Oh, she's well beyond furious." He finally stopped walking and stood to face her. "She actually *threatened* me."

Kyrah couldn't suppress a little gasp. "With what?"

"She didn't say *what*. She just made it perfectly clear that if I went through with this, we would . . ." Ritcherd stopped when he saw the horror in Kyrah's eyes. He scolded himself for not thinking this through before he'd said anything. Kyrah had always been frightened and intimidated by his mother. She didn't need this new turn of events to add to her concerns.

"We would what?" she demanded when he didn't finish.

"It doesn't matter," he said more calmly.

"It *does* matter. What did she say?"

"She was vague, Kyrah. But it was still a threat."

When nothing was said for several minutes, Kyrah's thoughts wandered into territory she had no desire to dwell on. But she wasn't about to wonder. Drawing a deep breath, she said, "Maybe it would be better for everyone if we just . . ."

"What?" he demanded, the anger in his eyes deepening.

"You could help me . . . find work somewhere. We could still be friends." Ritcherd was so stunned he couldn't come up with any kind of response before she added, "Maybe it just isn't worth it."

Consumed with unreasonable fury, he grasped her shoulders and almost shook her. "Don't you *ever* say anything like that to me again. I would walk through hell in bare feet to have you in my life. We *will* be married, Kyrah. There is nothing she can do to stop it."

"I'm not so sure," Kyrah said, moving away from him.

Ritcherd watched her for a moment and had to ask, "Is it worth it to you, Kyrah? Is it worth what you would have to go through to be my wife?"

Kyrah's eyes mirrored his anger. "I would do *anything* for you, Ritcherd. *Anything!* But you have to learn that your anger will not solve this problem. You can't battle it out with your mother like she's some colonist battalion. And I have to know that you're in this for the right reasons."

Ritcherd did his best to keep his anger from showing, but his voice still grated when he said, "I love you, Kyrah. There is no other reason."

Kyrah knew that he did, but she instinctively believed there was much more to this situation than she could ever understand. She could only pray that the bitterness he felt toward his mother wouldn't end up coming between them. Beyond that, she couldn't deny that she was afraid of what Jeanette Buchanan was capable of doing. Until they were married, the thought of being anywhere in the vicinity of that woman suddenly terrified her.

"Let's leave here, Ritcherd, tonight. We could be packed in no time. We'll go to Scotland, or the continent, and get married right away. She'll never be able to find us."

"I'm not going to let her intimidate me like that. I'm not going to run away like some frightened animal when she says boo."

"That's pride talking, Ritcherd. You told me there was no place for pride in this relationship."

"And you told me that if people force you away from the things you love, you're allowing them to have power over you."

"I was talking about gossip and cold stares. You're talking about being threatened by a woman who has too much power for anyone's good. She has too much time on her hands, and too much money at her disposal."

"She's just a big bully, Kyrah. That's all. She's become obsessed with this, but it will pass. There's nothing she can do to keep us apart, Kyrah, because I won't let her." He took hold of her shoulders again. "I won't let her, Kyrah. I won't!" She wondered who he was trying to convince as his grip tightened and his voice became more intense. "She wouldn't do the kind of thing she's implying. I know she wouldn't."

"If you really believed that," Kyrah said, "you wouldn't be so upset."

"I won't let her!" he repeated and immediately kissed her, as if that could convince her of what his words couldn't. "I won't!" he murmured and kissed her again.

Kyrah could feel his anger and fear coming through in his kiss. And she eagerly accepted it, if only as an avenue to calm him down and help him think more reasonably. But before she had a chance to even grasp what was happening, she realized his passion was being fed by everything else he was feeling. She couldn't help getting caught up in it. She loved him so much. How could she not want to be close to him this way? By the time she realized his affection was getting out of control, she was caught up in feelings so dizzying that she could hardly think straight herself.

"Heaven help me," he murmured and lifted her into his arms. He carried her only a few steps before he went to his knees in the grass and shifted his hold on her until she knelt to face him. He kissed her over and over, leaving her breathless with excitement one moment and clouded with trepidation the next.

"Ritcherd," she muttered, clutching his shoulders while his lips devoured her throat, "we mustn't."

"I know," he whispered and lowered her back onto the cool grass.

Her desire to protest weakened with the increasing passion. She told herself that he surely wouldn't allow this to happen—not here, not now. Not like this! He loved her. He respected her. Surely he would measure his concern for her above whatever madness was consuming him! Putting her trust in him, she became lost in the sensations of the moment. Nothing existed beyond Ritcherd's kiss, his touch, his overwhelming presence.

Ritcherd was overtaken by the sensation that he was drowning, slipping helplessly downward into a torrent of passion unlike anything he'd ever experienced. While a tiny measure of logic reminded him that he had no right to be touching her this way, holding her as if she were already his, he couldn't find the strength to curb this unfathomable excitement swirling around him. His logic died a quick and easy death as passion consumed him completely. Oh, how he wanted her! He loved her. He *needed* her. And it was evident that she needed him, as well. He marveled at her ardent response, and when he reached a moment of incomprehensible ecstasy, she held to him as if he had become her air to breathe.

Everything became so still so suddenly that it was almost eerie. Even the air was still. Kyrah felt herself gasp and realized that she'd momentarily stopped breathing. She felt Ritcherd take a deep breath close to her ear, and the reality of what had just happened began to descend. She tightened her hold on him and squeezed her eyes shut, wanting to hold on to the perfect contentment of the moment forever. She tried to imagine that everything was as it should be, and all was well. But a deep foreboding crept into her. She'd never been prone to superstition, but she couldn't deny the sudden fear that seized her every nerve, as if they had somehow cursed their future by acting so impulsively. As the shock began to settle, Kyrah fought back the sob that rushed to her throat, but it escaped as a sharp whimper.

Kyrah's cry startled Ritcherd to the realization of what he'd just done. The brief elation of the experience was quickly squelched by regret. He wondered at what moment he had lost control of his senses enough to allow himself to do this to her. Her lack of protest in the matter didn't change his knowing that he was responsible. He squeezed his eyes shut in self-recrimination as Kyrah turned away from him, and he knew she was crying. He eased close to her back in an effort to offer some form of comfort. He thought of his promise to Stephen and groaned. He'd waited for her to grow up, but he'd still taken something from her that he was not entitled to have until he had given her his name. He pressed his face into her hair, wondering where to begin to make something like this right—if such a thing was even possible.

"Kyrah," he murmured, and she immediately turned toward him, clutching his shirt into her fists. "I'm so sorry, Kyrah. I . . . don't know what happened. I just . . . Oh, Kyrah. What have I done?"

Knowing she would never calm down until he did, Ritcherd forced himself to relax and urged her head to his shoulder, whispering gentle words. "It's all right, Kyrah. We'll make it right. I'll post the banns on Sunday. We'll be married before you know it." When she didn't respond, he rambled on. "I don't know what came over me, Kyrah. I guess I've just spent so much of the last three years afraid I'd never see you again. And nothing frightens me more than the thought of ever being without you again. I just felt so . . . desperate all of a sudden. But I should have been stronger than that. I should have—"

"Hush," she whispered. "It's done and we can't undo it. Just promise me you'll always be here. Promise me you'll never leave me, Ritcherd, never! Promise me, and everything will be all right."

"I promise," he murmured. "Oh, Kyrah, I swear to you, we will never be apart again. You will never go without again. I swear it by all I hold dear."

Kyrah sighed and rested her head on his shoulder, willing herself to believe him.

Hardly a word was spoken as Ritcherd took her back to the cottage before he returned home. His night was restless as the reality of what he'd done haunted him. The pleasure and intrigue of the experience made him long to be with her again. But he knew that some measure of trust and respect had been lost between them, and he could only pray that one day she would forgive him.

Ritcherd finally slept before dawn, and didn't awaken until late morning. He freshened up and hurried to the cottage. Sarah answered the door, looking concerned.

"Kyrah's not here," she reported. He couldn't help noticing the blue evening gown hanging in the hall.

"Where is she?" he asked, wishing it hadn't sounded so terse.

"She told me she needed some fresh air. That was over an hour ago." Her voice softened as she asked, "Ritcherd, what's wrong? She just didn't seem like herself this morning."

Ritcherd bit his lip and attempted to swallow his guilt. He wondered what he could say. "I . . . uh . . . had a little trouble with my mother, and we were both pretty upset. I fear she has cause to be unhappy with me, but . . . everything will be all right, Sarah. I promise."

She showed a faint smile and motioned him toward the door. "You'd do well to go and find her, I think. It's not long before she'll be needing to get ready for that party. Hurry along now."

Ritcherd wasn't surprised to find Kyrah at the church ruins, and mingled with the sorrow in her eyes was a blatant desire. He had little doubt that she was remembering, as he was, all that had transpired between them. Blended with the regret was an intense longing to take her in his arms and explore the experience all over again. But he knew that such madness would only deepen the heartache hovering between them, and he forced his eyes away in order to clear his head. Giving in to temptation and allowing his emotions to rule him had already brought more grief into their lives than he ever could have comprehended. He thought how ironic it was that their concerns over his mother's threats had become swallowed up in their indiscretion.

Ritcherd sat beside her and touched her chin, turning her face to his view. Tears cascaded from beneath her closed eyelids. He kissed them away and murmured close to her ear, "I love you, Kyrah. You must believe me when I tell you that I was wrong. And I am so . . ." his voice broke with emotion, "so . . . incredibly sorry. You must forgive me. We must go on . . . because . . . my life is nothing without you. I love you."

Kyrah opened her eyes and found his face close to hers. His sincerity was evident. She bit her tongue to avoid asking the question that had haunted her through the night. Would he have taken such a step with her if she had been the daughter of an aristocrat? And what made her believe that if it happened again, she might somehow be reassured of his love for her? Knowing that such speculations would never change the circumstances, she took a deep breath and said, "I know I could have stopped it, but . . ." Her lip quivered. "I . . . didn't think you would . . . really do it."

"And I shouldn't have," he murmured.

"I can't say that everything's all right, because it isn't. But . . . with time . . . I know it will be. It just has to be." She managed a smile and touched his face. "I love you too, Ritcherd."

Ritcherd relished her embrace and silently thanked God for her understanding. He knew, just as she'd said, that it would take time. But they would be married in less than a month, and he would make it up to her. If it took the rest of his life, he would make it up to her.

Chapter Seven

Criminal Accusations

*S*arah was pleased to see Kyrah return in better spirits. While she was heating water for a bath, Sarah asked her, "Have you seen the book I was reading?"

"The last time I saw it, Ritcherd was holding it in the garden. Have you had it since then?"

"No," she said, "I don't believe I have. I'll go out and get it. I'm glad it hasn't rained."

Sarah found the book on the bench and sat down there to read. She opened it to find an envelope tucked between the pages. Opening it, tears came to her eyes as she found an immense amount of money, along with a note. The handwriting appeared almost like a child's, then Sarah recalled that Ritcherd would be learning to write with his left hand.

For my room and board. And don't be unbearably proud like your daughter. I want you to take this so you'll know there will be food on the table, and next time I come to breakfast, I'll help cook. And remember, there's always more where this came from. All you have to do is ask.

All my love,

your son

Sarah held the note tightly, thanking God for Ritcherd Buchanan's presence in their lives.

Ritcherd fought to push away his disturbing thoughts as he dressed for the party. He did his best to convince himself that he could not undo what had happened between him and Kyrah. He could only be certain that she was cared for and make it right as quickly as possible.

When he drew his mind away from that, it inevitably went to the ugly conversation he'd had with his mother the previous day. He wanted to believe that she was just attempting to bully him, that in spite of her harsh personality, she wouldn't really do something underhanded to keep him and Kyrah apart. Not certain what to do—or if there was even any reason for concern—he pushed it out of his mind. Once this social thing was over with, he would sit down with Kyrah and they would decide what to do—without pride or anger.

Riding in the carriage to pick her up, he felt assured that if he kept her beside him every minute, he would make certain she had a good time at the party. And then, just as he'd told his mother, he would never take her there again. Once he was married, he didn't care if he ever went back to Buckley Manor—which made him all the more determined to have this wedding take place just as soon as possible.

All dismal thoughts fled when he entered the cottage parlor and Kyrah turned to face him. He couldn't believe how beautiful she was. When he finally managed to propel himself forward, he took her hand to kiss it, keeping his eyes locked with hers, oblivious to Sarah, who stood close by, beaming with pride.

"This," he said, "is the way I imagined you the first time I saw you."

"But I was only seven," she said, her full lips spreading with a lustrous smile that lit her eyes.

"I had a vivid imagination," he added, lifting his brows.

"You look nice," Kyrah smiled, admiring his appearance in the uniform. The red coat enhanced his coloring well, she thought. "You must be the most handsome captain of the king's armies."

"I didn't want to wear it, actually," he said with a humble smile. "But my mother suggested . . . since it is my welcome home party . . . and I thought, well, why not?"

"That was very thoughtful of you," Sarah said as she smoothed the shoulders of Ritcherd's coat. He thought of how she had always encouraged him to try to have a good relationship with his mother.

Before they left, Sarah took Ritcherd into the kitchen for a private word and went up on her toes to kiss his cheek. "Thank you," she whispered. "I don't know what to say. I don't want to take the money from you, but we need it so desperately."

"I won't miss it," he said. "I consider it a privilege to see that you're cared for, Sarah. Whether I married Kyrah or not, I would consider you family, and I would always see that your needs were met."

Sarah smiled humbly. "There is something I want you to have," she added and pushed a tiny object into his hand. "Stephen gave this to me the day he married me." Ritcherd opened his hand to see a narrow gold band. "I couldn't bear to wear it after he died, but it's very special to me. It was one of the few things that Stephen didn't acquire from a card game." She smiled sadly.

"Stephen was a good man, Sarah," he said with conviction.

"I know that," she said firmly, then her voice lowered to a sincere whisper. "Marry Kyrah with this ring. It's all I have to give the two of you—beyond my love and my blessings. But this ring has always been a token of perfect love. It would only be right that you have it."

"Thank you, Sarah," he said and put his arms around her, hugging her tightly. "This means a great deal to me."

She smiled and touched his face. "Now you two get along to that party. You're already fashionably late enough."

"Yes, Mother," he said, offering his arm, and they walked together back to the parlor. "By the way," he added with a smile, "you're looking much better. I assume you're feeling as such."

"I am, thank you," she said as they entered the room where Kyrah sat waiting patiently.

"Shall we go?" he said and helped her into her cloak.

"Have a good time," Sarah called.

Ritcherd winked at her and closed the door behind him.

"You look so beautiful," he whispered close to her face while they rode in the carriage holding hands. "This is like a dream come true for me."

"Then why do I feel so nervous?"

"Let me clarify something," he said. "Having you in my life is a dream come true for me. As for tonight, well . . . I'm just glad for the opportunity to show you off."

She glanced at him skeptically and turned toward the window. "I'm scared, Ritcherd," she admitted. "I can't help thinking about what your mother said, and—"

"Everything will be all right, Kyrah. I understand that this is difficult for you. My home has never represented anything pleasant for either of us. But it's just one evening. I'll stay with you every second."

Kyrah nodded, trying to tell herself that she was just caught up in the habit of feeling ashamed and intimidated. And if she was going to be Mrs. Ritcherd Buchanan, she was going to have to get over it.

Ritcherd felt Kyrah's fingers tense against his hand as they stepped down from the carriage and walked up the steps to the main entry. But when she entered the ballroom on his arm, there was a sudden hush in the air beyond the continuing music. All eyes turned toward them, and Kyrah froze beside him.

"Everyone is staring," she whispered, trying to appear dignified. "They're horrified that you would dare show your face with me."

"Oh no, Kyrah," he said, tilting her chin to look at him, if only to distract her from their surroundings, "they're dazzled by your beauty. They don't know what they were thinking all these years." He smiled and touched her face. "It doesn't matter what they're thinking, Miss Payne, because I am dazzled by your beauty. I am in awe that you would love me in spite of me. And I am grateful to have you in my life."

"I love you," she said, realizing that she actually felt better.

"Let's mingle and get it over with," he whispered and moved her into the crowd.

Kyrah kept her hand on his arm while he introduced her to his guests. They all smiled politely, though she didn't miss the skepticism and disdain in many eyes. But all she had to do was look into Ritcherd's eyes and everything fell into perspective. Even the way his mother blatantly ignored her didn't seem quite so ominous with his hand in hers.

She noticed several other young ladies present. And by the way some of them were glaring at her, she felt certain Jeanette Buchanan had made a point of inviting them for Ritcherd's benefit. But she felt secure in the way Ritcherd skillfully steered away from them, and he hardly seemed to notice their presence.

She was hesitant at first to go onto the dance floor, but Ritcherd teased her about the dance lessons in the church, and it took little effort before she was dancing as gracefully as any lady present. And she had to admit she was enjoying herself.

Ritcherd realized as he watched her that this was her very first social experience. And he couldn't help thinking of what Kyrah had been cheated out of because of the unfair circumstances. He completely monopolized her on the dance floor and refused to let her dance with anyone else, until George Morley showed up. In fact, she showed her first genuine smile when George approached them, took her hand, and kissed it gallantly.

"It's no wonder you waited for her to grow up, Ritch," he said with an impish smile. "You must let me dance with her."

"I hear you've been gone a lot the last few years," Ritcherd said with a smile, avoiding the subject. "So, what brings you back now?"

"I heard that Kyrah Payne would be at this party, so I hurried back to get a dance."

Kyrah smiled and turned to Ritcherd, "It's all right."

"One dance," Ritcherd said, feigning a threat in his voice. "And I want her delivered right back into my arms. Just because I've known you all my life," he teased, "doesn't mean I trust you."

Ritcherd leaned against the wall and didn't take his eyes off them for a second. He smiled to himself when he saw her laugh, and he knew George was teasing her. When the set ended, George led her directly to Ritcherd, placing her hand elaborately into his. "Not to worry," he grinned, "I wouldn't dare take a lady away from the great Captain Buchanan."

"The day you settle for one woman, I'll buy you the most expensive bottle of brandy I can get my hands on."

"Don't bother making the investment just yet," he returned impishly, and Ritcherd laughed. As Kyrah's attention turned briefly elsewhere, George leaned closer to Ritcherd and whispered, "I need to talk with you about something."

His seriousness caught Ritcherd's attention. "So talk."

"I believe it warrants a little more time and privacy than what you're offering here, my friend. I've been trying to catch you home for days. It is important. Can you get away?"

"No." He smiled toward Kyrah. "Not now."

"When?" he asked pointedly, and Ritcherd couldn't help being curious. This wasn't like George.

"After I take Kyrah home," he said.

"Sounds good." George slapped Ritcherd lightly on the shoulder and disappeared into the crowd.

The dinner hour was announced, and Kyrah sat by Ritcherd's side at the table. Jeanette continued to ignore Kyrah, even when she proposed a toast to her son, who had at last returned from serving his call.

As Ritcherd observed Kyrah through the evening, he found it difficult to imagine why his mother couldn't look at her and see how perfectly she conducted herself as a lady. He felt so thoroughly proud of her, and he knew if his mother would take the shades from her eyes and look at Kyrah without prejudice, she couldn't help but see how wonderful a woman she really was. But there was no good in hoping for such a thing. His mother would never lower her bitter wall. And he wondered why the thought actually caused him pain. But Kyrah made up for it. She made up for every bit of pain his mother had ever caused him. He felt so happy having her near him like this that he thought he would burst.

Kyrah found it difficult to keep her eyes off Ritcherd. Her discomfort at being here was eased by his nearness, and she marveled at the reality of all that surrounded her. It was good to have him back and be with him—and he looked so very handsome tonight. How could she not be proud to be the woman who had claimed Captain Buchanan's heart?

The party wasn't making her as nervous as she had expected. But the icy glares from Ritcherd's mother unnerved her. Jeanette made no effort to hide that she'd noticed the elaborate diamonds Kyrah was wearing. She gazed at them often with contempt in her eyes. Ritcherd did well at ignoring his mother's insinuating silence, but Kyrah found it difficult. She was grateful to have dessert served, knowing that she could soon be away from Jeanette's gaze.

"Here goes," Ritcherd whispered to Kyrah and squeezed her hand. He stood and made it clear he had something to say. Her heart began to pound. A quick glance told her that his mother was visibly tense. Would she be so low as to make a public scene?

"Ladies and gentlemen," he said. "I want to thank you all for coming tonight. But before we move back to the ballroom, I have a formal announcement to make." He glanced affectionately toward Kyrah. "Well," he chuckled slightly, "how else is there to say it? Kyrah Payne is going to honor me by becoming my wife."

Kyrah was amazed to realize that many of the people present seemed genuinely pleased. But it was easy to lose perspective given the obvious disdain of others. A quick glance around the room made the differentiation very clear. Amidst cheers and applause, Ritcherd took her arm and urged her to stand next to him. A toast was offered to their happiness before they sat back down and finished the meal, enjoying an array of congratulations and lighthearted comments that made it easier to avoid looking at Ritcherd's mother. And when she did, she wished she hadn't. All enjoyment crashed down around her. Jeanette's expression wasn't angry or horrified. She looked subtly smug, almost complacent.

"There," Ritcherd whispered when the people nearby stood to leave the table, "it's done. Now let's get out of here."

"I couldn't agree more," she said, wishing her voice hadn't betrayed her sudden change of mood.

"What's wrong?" he asked.

"Your mother," she said discreetly, and Ritcherd glanced her way.

He needed no further explanation. Something in his mother's eyes suddenly made him wish he'd never come tonight. "You were right, Kyrah," he admitted. "We should have been halfway to Scotland by now."

"It's not too late. We could leave tonight."

Ritcherd looked at her long and hard. "I just need to pack a few things. It will only take five minutes. Then I'll take you home to pack. We can be gone before midnight. Do you think your mother will be all right with that?"

"Yes. Hurry up. I have to get out of here."

Moving out of the dining room, Kyrah went around a corner with Ritcherd right behind her. She gasped as she nearly bumped into Peter Westman.

"Kyrah," he said with a sneer and she felt Ritcherd go tense beside her, "you look lovely. And you, Captain Buchanan. How good to see you."

Ritcherd nodded curtly.

"Looks like I've missed all the fun," he said, looking over Ritcherd's shoulder into the empty dining room.

"You have indeed," Ritcherd said. "The announcement's official now."

"Really?" Peter laughed. "I'll believe this marriage when I see it."

"You won't see it," Kyrah said. "You won't be invited."

Peter seemed amused, and Ritcherd nodded again. "If you'll excuse us, Mr. Westman. I believe you could find company more suitable to your taste."

"Indeed," Peter smiled, lifting his glass to them as they walked past. Kyrah sensed a smugness about him that only added to her discomfort. She could never put it to words, but she knew she had to get out of here. Something wasn't right.

Kyrah lost her bearings as she followed Ritcherd to his rooms. Her visits there had always been from a different part of the house. She was amazed at how quickly he packed some clothes and a few essentials. When he was finished, he peered into the hallway to make certain it was clear. Taking Kyrah by the hand, he led her toward the stairs. They'd not reached them, however, before they were approached by Ritcherd's mother and an official-looking man, obviously not a guest. The uneasiness she had felt all evening blew into full-fledged fear when she saw that Jeanette was holding her cloak.

"Does this belong to Miss Payne?" Jeanette asked Ritcherd, totally ignoring Kyrah except for a cool glance toward her necklace.

"Yes, it does," Ritcherd said, taking it from her abruptly. "Thank you. I was just going to take her away from this wretched place."

"Not just yet," the man said.

"Who is he?" Ritcherd asked, hating the way he was wishing they'd never come here tonight.

"This is Constable Killeen," his mother said. "Now Ritcherd, I want to keep this as quiet as possible."

"What are you talking about?"

"I'm certain Miss Payne knows what I'm talking about."

A quick glance told Ritcherd that Kyrah was as ignorant as he. "Explain yourself, Mother."

"These!" she said, opening her hand to reveal several small pieces of expensive jewelry. "I'm certain Miss Payne has seen these before." Jeanette glared at her, and Kyrah couldn't begin to hide her horror as the implication began to set in.

"Get to the point!" Ritcherd demanded.

"These are mine!" she shouted, then lowered her voice. "The maid discovered they were missing before dinner. And when the house was searched, they were found in the pocket of Miss Payne's cloak."

Ritcherd actually laughed. Was that the best she could come up with? Was this her attempt to keep them apart? "That's ridiculous," he said. "If they were in Kyrah's pocket, then they were planted there, and you know it."

"I know no such thing." His mother was adamant.

"She has not been out of my sight for a minute since we arrived."

"Of course you'd stick up for her." Jeanette's voice was caustic. "She's had the wool pulled over your eyes for years. You can't trust poor people when they get around all of this wealth."

Ritcherd felt Kyrah grab his arm tightly with both hands. The constable, who had observed this family quibble with no expression, suddenly said, "You'll need to come with me, Miss Payne." Kyrah moved directly behind Ritcherd and her grip tightened.

"She'll do no such thing," Ritcherd said angrily, then turned to his mother. "How much did you pay him to arrest an innocent woman?"

"I'm just doing my job, Captain Buchanan," he stated, as if this bored him terribly.

"Well, she's innocent. She was set up. I was with her every minute. You've got your jewels back. Let's drop it."

"I will do no such thing," Jeanette said hoarsely. "I'll not tolerate thieves in my home."

"Well, we're leaving." Ritcherd moved quickly past them, pulling Kyrah by the hand. But the constable moved close behind them and reached out to take Kyrah's other arm.

"You are under arrest, Miss Payne," he said. "Running will only get you into more trouble."

Kyrah was so stunned, so thoroughly frightened, that she couldn't even respond. Ritcherd put himself between her and the constable, saying firmly, "Arrest me. I'll take full responsibility."

"Don't be ridiculous, Ritcherd!" his mother said with disgust.

"This entire thing is ridiculous," Ritcherd retorted. "Just drop the charges and let us—"

"Captain Buchanan," the constable interrupted, his irritation evident, "I am under obligation of the law to take Miss Payne into custody." He almost seemed compassionate as he added, "She simply needs to come down to the station for the night. We'll get all of this straightened out tomorrow."

Ritcherd glared long and hard at his mother, then he eased Kyrah beside him, keeping his arm protectively around her. "Well, she can't go dressed like this," he said. "Let me take her home to change and pack a few things."

Kyrah's heart pounded even faster. What was he saying? How could he possibly turn her over to this man under such circumstances?

The constable exchanged a studied glance with Jeanette, as if they had some private form of communication. Then he nodded. "That would be fine. But if you don't mind, Captain, I'll be following you there."

"Fine," he said and hurried down the hall with Kyrah's arm in his hand.

"What are you thinking?" she whispered in astonishment when they were out of the constable's earshot.

"I'm thinking that once you change and pack a few things, we're heading out through the woods. We'll get out of the country by any means possible and just let all of this die down."

Kyrah took a deep breath of relief. She'd much rather spend the rest of her life as a fugitive than allow herself to be left alone in a jail cell, knowing that Jeanette Buchanan was holding some sick power over her.

Little was said as the carriage drove them to the cottage. They were both well aware of the constable waiting in the drive as they went inside. "Don't be trying anything funny, Captain," he called after them. Ritcherd just waved and closed the door. While Kyrah went to change her clothes, Ritcherd sat down to explain to Sarah what had happened.

Kyrah almost tore off the beautiful gown and threw it scornfully to the bed. She felt angry and confused. And most of all, scared. But she concentrated on getting away with Ritcherd. She got dressed and threw two changes of clothes, a nightgown, and a few essentials into a bag. She put the necklace and earrings into the box that housed them, then wrapped it carefully in some of her clothes. Impulsively she tossed in her book on birds, if only because it represented some measure of comfort. Returning to the parlor, she wondered what Ritcherd's plan was exactly. She didn't see sneaking out the back way and losing the constable to be terribly difficult. But she wondered how long they would be on the run. She wondered what her mother might do. Would they send for her? Come back for her? Would she go with them now?

All her plans came crashing around her when she entered the room to hear Sarah saying, "You can't get away with it and you know it."

"What choice do we have?" Ritcherd retorted, oblivious to Kyrah standing in the doorway.

"You can stay here and face up to the consequences, whatever they may be. I will not allow my daughter to become some kind of fugitive when she hasn't done anything wrong. She's innocent. They'll prove she's innocent, and it will be over."

"That woman will never allow me to be innocent," Kyrah insisted, startling them both. "It's her word against mine, and it's not difficult to see that my word will mean nothing."

"You're talking like a child," Sarah said. "Now, we will work this out like adults. You can't run away from this, Kyrah. We know you're innocent. We'll find a way to prove it."

Kyrah quickly searched her feelings and had to admit, "I don't believe that's possible. We have to leave, Mother. We have to." She looked to Ritcherd for support and was relieved when he took over.

"Sarah, listen to me. I'll take good care of Kyrah. We'll get settled somewhere and send for you. Kyrah's right. My mother is too powerful. She's—"

Kyrah gasped when a loud knock sounded at the door. "It's now or never," she said to Ritcherd.

He reached for her hand and headed toward the hall, but Sarah rushed to the front door, saying quietly, "I can't let you do it."

"Mother, no," Kyrah pleaded, but the door came open and Constable Killeen was standing in its frame, looking impatient.

"You'll take good care of her, now won't you," Sarah said to the constable.

"Of course," he replied. But Kyrah felt a chill run down her spine. She met Ritcherd's eyes and saw her own fears mirrored there. She wanted to be angry with him, but knew this wasn't his fault. "We should be able to get this sorted out tomorrow," the constable added. "One night ought to be enough to appease Mrs. Buchanan. Let's get it over with."

When it became evident that their options were gone, Ritcherd said to the constable, "Just give us a minute, please."

He motioned with his hand as if to grant it, then leaned against the doorframe. Ritcherd eased Kyrah out of earshot, but where they could still be seen. It was evident from the constable's expression that he wouldn't let them out of his sight. The pistol he carried limited their options considerably.

"I'm so afraid," she admitted.

"I know," he said. "So am I, but . . . maybe it's not as bad as it seems." He took her face into his hands and looked into her eyes. "Our love is strong enough to make it through this, Kyrah. Whatever happens, we'll get through it together. Are you hearing me?"

She nodded and bit her lip, fighting off the desperation rising in her.

"I'll find a way to get my mother to drop the charges," he said. "I'll threaten to kick her out of the house if I have to. One way or another, we'll get it taken care of. I promise." Feeling an unexplainable urgency to make his point very clear, he deepened his gaze, as well as his voice. "I would walk through hell in bare feet for you, Kyrah. I will see us through this. No matter how long it takes, don't you forget that. Do you hear me?"

Again Kyrah nodded, unable to speak.

"I'll be there first thing in the morning," he promised. "And I'll have my solicitor right on it." He pulled her into his arms, holding her as if he might never have the chance again. "I'm so sorry for all of this, Kyrah. I'll make it up to you. I promise."

He could feel her trembling in his arms and had to suppress the urge to knock the constable out cold and drag Kyrah away. He told himself there was no reason to feel like his heart was breaking. He would see her again in the morning.

Ritcherd embraced her once more, then it became evident that the constable had used up his patience. Kyrah embraced her mother, trying not to feel angry with her for preventing them from leaving when they'd had the chance. Walking out the door with the constable, she felt as if she was being led to the gallows. She glanced back over her shoulder just once, wishing she could believe this would be taken care of as easily as Ritcherd had tried to convince her. Somehow, she knew this was just the beginning of a nightmare. She couldn't even fathom what Jeanette Buchanan might be capable of. That in itself frightened her most of all.

When she arrived at the station, very little seemed to happen. Constable Killeen discussed something with another man out of her hearing range, then she was taken to a room that more resembled a bedroom than a cell. Once she was left alone, she curled up on the bed and tried in vain to relax. In her heart she knew this was not what it appeared to be. She only prayed that Ritcherd's love for her was as strong and true as he claimed it to be.

"Please, Ritcherd," she murmured into the dark silence. And then she cried.

Ritcherd arrived home to find a few guests still lingering. He had no desire to even see his mother. He probably would have killed her if he did. He managed to avoid having to speak to anyone as he went up to his room and went to bed, doubting that he'd be able to sleep at all. Every time he closed his eyes, he could only see the fear in Kyrah's expression. He felt sick inside at the reality of something like this happening, and wondered how so much could go wrong in so little time. When he forced his mind away from the current situation, he could only recall his intimacy with Kyrah the previous evening, and guilt and regret threatened to choke him. How could he be such a blasted *fool?*

He'd not been in bed long when George opened the door and stuck his head in without any warning. "Hey, Buchanan!"

"You scared the hell out of me," Ritcherd snarled.

"Wouldn't hurt." George chuckled, then added, "Can we talk?"

Ritcherd had forgotten all about his promise to give George some undivided time. But he knew his mind was far too wound up over the situation to even be able to think straight. "Listen, Morley," he said. "I'm really sorry, but this isn't—"

"It's not a good time," George interrupted with sarcasm.

"No," Ritcherd said tersely, "this is not a good time."

"When?" George asked.

"Tomorrow afternoon."

"Say three?" George asked.

"Fine," Ritcherd agreed, praying he would remember.

"I'll be here," George said adamantly and pulled the door closed. But it came open again only seconds later, startling Ritcherd once more. "By the way," George added, "congratulations. She's a beauty."

"Yes," Ritcherd tried to smile as he thought of his beauty sitting in a cell tonight, "she is."

George left the room and Ritcherd wondered again what he could possibly want to talk to him about. What could be so important? Then he decided he didn't really care. His heart, his soul, and his mind were all concentrating on Kyrah. And he would rot in hell before he let this stupid drama tear them apart.

George hadn't been gone long when a knock came at the door. He knew it wasn't George; he'd just been reminded that George never knocked. It had to be his mother.

"What?" he called angrily.

He was surprised when one of the maids came in, gave a light curtsy, and looked embarrassed to see him sitting in bed.

"What is it?" he asked, trying to be kind as he recalled Kyrah's scolding him for his sharpness with the servants.

"Mrs. Buchanan asked me to bring you this." The maid set a cup of hot cocoa on the bedside table and curtsied again. Ritcherd would have laughed if the evening had not been such a nightmare.

"Thank you," he said and she quickly left the room.

It had been years since his mother had sent hot cocoa to his room at bedtime. And he wondered if she really believed that this tiny gesture would actually make up for what he knew she had done. But he had to admit that it smelled good. Savoring the aroma, he realized that hot cocoa at bedtime was one of the rare good memories he had of his childhood. Setting the empty cup back on the table, he extinguished the lamp and settled into the bed. Despite the tremendous anxiety weighing on his mind, he fell quickly to sleep.

Chapter Eight

The Nightmare

As the night wore on, Kyrah stared aimlessly toward the ceiling and couldn't help fearing the worst—whatever that might be. The very uncertainty of her circumstances was perhaps the most frightening of all. What would they do to her? Would they ever believe she was innocent? And perhaps worst of all, she wondered if Ritcherd's mother would ever cease trying to destroy her.

The cell-like room was still completely dark when a key turned loudly in the lock and light filtered in from the hallway. Kyrah sat up quickly, knowing something was terribly wrong.

"Come along, little lady," the constable said sternly.

"Where are we going?" she asked, unable to disguise the panic in her voice. She clutched her bag tightly, grateful that she'd not undressed for bed.

"Just come along," he insisted and took her arm far too firmly. As he ushered her outside, Kyrah hoped for a fleeting moment that the charges had been dropped and she would be allowed to go home. But the constable pushed her into a carriage that rolled the wrong direction as soon as he was seated beside her. Across from them was a foul-smelling man with eyes that chilled her through the dim glow of the carriage lantern. His build was husky, and his entire aura was menacing. The way he was dressed reminded her of the men she'd seen on her visits to the pier. *He was a sailor!*

Kyrah couldn't suppress a gasp when the likelihood of what was happening struck her. The man sitting across from her smiled, showing a number of missing teeth.

"Where are you taking me?" she demanded, forcing her voice to remain steady.

"Where every criminal ought to go," the constable mumbled under his breath, as if her objection was merely a slight inconvenience.

"I'm not a criminal!" Kyrah protested. "I demand a trial! This is not right!"

When the constable ignored her and the burly sailor grinned, Kyrah panicked. She lunged toward the door, clutching her bag tightly, heedless of the speed of the carriage. She screamed as strong arms dragged her back onto the seat. She became dizzy with fear and felt suddenly nauseous from the odor of her captor as he slapped a hand over her mouth.

"You'd better shut her up," the constable said, "or we'll never get her on that ship without causing a scene. And we don't need a scene."

Kyrah squirmed and fought with every ounce of strength she possessed. She felt a sharp pain at the back of her head only an instant before everything went black.

Ritcherd woke with his head pounding like his worst hangovers. It only took a minute to recall that he'd had nothing extra to drink last night, and he knew something was terribly wrong. A quick glance at the clock proved it. Almost eleven.

"Damn!" he muttered, ignoring the throbbing in his head as he pulled on his breeches and boots. He put on a shirt as he ran down the hall, fighting the pain and dizziness. An ominous dread tightened his chest and put knots in his stomach as he rode without a saddle toward the station. The man seated behind the desk stared blankly at Ritcherd, as if his request to see Kyrah made no sense whatsoever.

"Well?" Ritcherd demanded.

"I'm sorry, sir. I'm afraid she's gone."

"Gone home, you mean?" Ritcherd said as an inkling of hope replaced his fears.

"The charges were dropped early this morning, and she—"

"I'll handle this," Constable Killeen said as he appeared and motioned for Ritcherd to come into his office. Ritcherd was offered a seat but he refused to take it. The dread he'd felt culminating inside him since his mother had threatened to keep him and Kyrah apart blew into a roiling nightmare as the constable closed the door and sat behind his cluttered desk.

"Where is she?" Ritcherd demanded.

"As you've already heard, she's gone."

"Gone where? What do you mean, *she's gone?*"

He saw the constable's eyes shift and intensify. He knew before he heard it that the news would be devastating. But he never would have dreamed . . .

"Captain Buchanan," he began in a voice that was smooth and cool, "Miss Payne was deported early this morning."

That dizzying, pounding sensation he'd awakened with suddenly increased tenfold. He felt as if the floor had turned into a whirlpool that would suck him helplessly downward. He gripped the edge of the desk, so consumed with rage and pain that he could hardly tell which way was up. In the brief moment it took him to digest what he'd just been told, his rage erupted into the open. His voice seethed as he leaned over the desk and pulled the constable out of his chair by his shirt collar. "Deported?" he growled. "What do you mean, *deported?*"

The constable's voice remained steady. "She was put on a ship going out of the country, just as many common criminals are. If you'll let go of me, Captain, we'll discuss this like civilized adults."

Ritcherd forced himself to let go and step back, fighting with everything inside of him to stay calm. As the anger briefly relented, the pain rushed forward in its place. He wanted to collapse on the floor and cry like a baby. He felt as if his heart had been ripped out of him in little pieces. He couldn't believe it! *He just couldn't believe it!*

Wrenching himself back to the moment, he said sharply, "She was not a common criminal."

"She's a thief." The constable said it as if he'd done Ritcherd some huge favor.

"I was just told the charges were dropped," he argued, as if he could convince this man to undo what had been done.

"You were misinformed," he drawled. "She was found guilty."

"She had no trial."

"You must have slept late, Captain," the officer said smugly, and Ritcherd felt an indiscernible piece of a complicated puzzle fall into place in his mind. But he was too focused on the moment to think it through.

"People don't get accused, convicted, and deported in one morning."

"They do when it's necessary."

"What was the big rush?" Ritcherd pressed.

"Really, Captain," the constable said as if to avoid the question, "she was just a servant girl. Surely you can find another."

"She was going to be my wife!" Ritcherd shouted and swept his arm across the constable's desktop, sending all of its contents flying. In one swift movement he sailed over the desk and pulled the constable out of his chair. He couldn't believe the strength in his left hand that more than compensated for the lack of it in his right. Holding the constable by the throat, he slammed him against the wall and hissed in his face, "You filthy, lying coward. How much did she pay you?" When he got no response, he slammed him again. "How much?"

"I don't know what you're talking about," the constable squeaked.

"You do, and I know you do. My mother gravitates to people like you—you slimy, two-faced imbecile. So what's the going price for getting rid of an innocent young woman?" The constable said nothing and Ritcherd slammed him again, shouting, "Tell me!"

"Captain Buchanan!" the constable shouted back, exerting a burst of energy that pushed Ritcherd away. "Miss Payne was put on a ship this morning. I saw to it personally, and there is nothing I can do about it now."

"Where was it going?" Ritcherd demanded. "What ship was it?" The constable didn't respond and Ritcherd shouted, "Tell me!"

"I don't have to tell you anything," he retorted. "She's gone. That's all I know. And your behavior will land you in a similar position if you're not careful."

"That's exactly where I want to be!"

"Get out of here!" he demanded.

"Gladly," Ritcherd retorted. "But this is not over yet. Jeanette Buchanan is not the only one around here with power and money to throw around. You will be undone by this, I swear it."

"Get out," he repeated, "and take your threats with you."

Ritcherd turned to leave the room, then turned back and threw his left fist into the constable's jaw. The man reeled back against the wall and Ritcherd pointed a threatening finger. "This is not over yet, Constable. You have not seen the last of what I am capable of doing to you."

The constable touched his bloodied lip as he steadied himself, eyeing Ritcherd with contempt. "Get out," he repeated.

"Gladly," Ritcherd snarled and trudged back outside. The unreasonable strength that had fed his anger toward the constable drained out of him with each step he took. The moment he was alone, he leaned against the wall of the building and had to bend over to keep his equilibrium. He groaned and pressed a hand over his chest, fearing his heart would pound right out of it. He couldn't believe it! This had to be a nightmare. Any minute he would wake up and find Kyrah home with her mother, where she belonged. But the truth had to be faced. This was *real!* And the reality was so thoroughly horrible that Ritcherd couldn't even think beyond taking his next breath. He groaned again as the reality seemed to take hold with fresh constrictions of his chest. He turned and threw his fist into the wall, oblivious to the pain that reverberated up his arm.

"No," he murmured and pressed his face to the wall, wondering where to begin to undo what had been done. He looked down at his bleeding knuckles and told himself he had to come to his senses. There were questions that needed to be answered. Action had to be taken. And he had to start *now!* Every minute wasted was taking them farther apart. Fueled by the determination to find Kyrah and bring her home, Ritcherd mounted his stallion and quickly put miles behind him.

At the pier he found very few people and little activity. He spent better than two hours talking to every person he saw, but no one knew anything that helped him. Finally he started home, knowing nothing beyond the fact that Kyrah Payne had been put on the only ship that had left dock in the past twenty-four hours. But no one seemed to have any idea whose ship it was, or where it was headed. The only definitive answer he'd gotten was from a bartender who rambled about the effect of the war on trade and deportations. His theory was that she had probably been sent to Australia. *Australia?* He wondered how long it would take him to get to Australia. And how would he ever begin to find her once he got there?

As the horse beneath him plodded slowly homeward, Ritcherd played it all over and over in his mind. He couldn't believe it. *Kyrah was gone.* Kyrah—the woman who was part of him. He loved her, he needed her. And she needed him. He had fought so hard to have her. And she was gone. He had failed her completely. He had promised her he'd always be there, always care for her. And now he didn't even know where to begin to find her. What kind of horrors would she be subjected to? The very idea made him physically ill. He would move heaven and earth to find her—if only he knew where to look. He'd told her he'd walk through hell in bare feet for her. And he would! If only he knew where to find the door. Where could he turn? Where would he possibly begin?

"Please God," he murmured, hoping his prayer would penetrate beyond the numb horror that consumed him. "I know I've been a fool, and I can only hope that you will forgive me for being so stupid . . . for hurting her the way I did. But . . . I need you, God. Please . . . guide me. Show me the way. And keep her safe and strong. Please," he howled toward the sky. Then he had to stop as emotion overtook him so completely that he couldn't see where he was going. He slid to the ground and went to his knees, while the pain of losing Kyrah was accompanied into the open by the pain of losing her father. And the burning knowledge deep inside that he had disappointed and betrayed them both was perhaps most painful of all.

When his tears ran dry and his emotion subsided again into a dull, aching shock, Ritcherd tried once more to sort out the chain of events that had led to this, hoping for a place to start. Then it hit him. And the sensation reminded him of being shot in the arm. The pain of his loss exploded into anger, and the anger was fed by years of resentment and bitterness. The anger fed his determination, pressing him blindly back onto the stallion. The speed fueled his anger into a glaring rage as Buckley Manor loomed up before him. He intended to have a little chat with his mother.

Kyrah merged slowly into an awareness of the horrible ache at the back of her head. She drifted in and out of consciousness, vaguely mindful of the mooring of the ship, which only added to the dizziness that stifled any effort to open her eyes. As the memories came together in her mind, the reality of her surroundings began to sink in. The tangible evidence that she had not been dreaming made her gasp as the horror of her circumstances consumed her. She was being deported for reasons that had nothing to do with the law.

She forced her eyes open and gradually took in her surroundings. The tiny cabin held only a narrow bunk where she lay. The glass of the little porthole was thick and mottled, making it impossible to see anything. Only the vague light coming through the glass let her know it was daylight.

The desperation of her circumstances forced her to sit up. She groaned from the pain in her head and reached back to find dried blood in her hair. Stumbling to the door, she wasn't surprised to find it locked, but she beat her fists against the hard wood, calling, pleading for someone—anyone—to let her out. Pacing the tiny cabin between bouts of screaming at the door, she became more keenly aware of the sea rolling beneath her. She wondered how long they'd been sailing while she tried to think of ways to escape this cabin cell and swim back to shore.

A thought occurred to her that deepened her panic. She frantically searched for her bag and was relieved to find it beneath a large burlap sack on the floor. The size of the sack made her wonder if she had been brought aboard inside of it. Looking closer at her clothing, she found remnants of the burlap clinging to the fabric. As another question struck her, she tore through the contents of her bag, fearing she might have been robbed as well. Her relief was indescribable when she found the diamond necklace and earrings right where she'd left them. Fearing some future search of her belongings, she carefully removed the thread of a small section of wide hem around one of her skirts. She slipped the box into the hem and slid it far beyond the opening. Then she folded it, along with her other clothing, making it all appear very ordinary. As an added precaution, she slid the bag beneath the bunk, into the corner as far as it would go. When that was seen to, she made another attempt at getting someone's attention.

Kyrah's heart quickened with a combination of hope and fear when, at last, a key turned in the lock. The fear overruled as two burly sailors, who didn't smell any better than they looked, entered the room. She recalled one of them being in the carriage with the constable. She backed into a corner as he said to the other, "You grab 'er an' I'll give 'er some o' this stuff afore she gets the cap'n down 'ere t' really keep 'er quiet."

Kyrah stepped onto her bed and lunged for the open door, but one of the sailors quickly blocked it with his broad body. She tried to scream, but a dirty hand clapped over her mouth until they had her down on the bed, pouring something between her lips. Kyrah bit a finger then tried to spit the bitter liquid out, but that hand came back over her mouth and nose, and she had no choice but to swallow. Almost immediately her vision became hazy, and her limbs went weak as she attempted once more to stand up and get away. She was thrown back onto the narrow bed, and her last coherent thought was the hope that this was some kind of poison, capable of taking her eternally away from all this misery.

"Jeanette Buchanan!" Ritcherd shouted and slammed the front door loudly enough that the echo penetrated the hallways. Servants scurried quickly from his view. Then there was silence. "Jeanette!" he repeated, not moving from where he stood.

A moment later she appeared, looking as if she had no idea in the world why he might be so angry. "What is it, dear?" she asked. "Is something wrong?"

For a long moment he just watched her, trying to comprehend the kind of woman she was. He reminded himself that he needed to stay calm if there was any hope of getting workable information out of her.

"That was quite a cup of hot chocolate you sent up to my room last night."

"Don't blame me for your hangovers," she said without looking at him.

He reminded himself to stick to the point. "I want to know what is going on, and I want to know now!"

"Whatever are you talking about?" she asked with easy innocence as she sauntered carelessly toward him.

"You will never convince me that you don't know what's going on." He looked at her closely as she stood near him. He wanted to see her eyes when he asked her this question. "How much bribery did it take to have Kyrah deported before I woke up this morning?"

"Don't be absurd," she said, but something in her eyes blatantly contradicted the innocence in her voice.

Ritcherd moved closer. "How can you stand there and lie to me like that, after you have looked me in the eye and threatened me? You told me you couldn't allow this marriage to take place. You told me you would do whatever you had to. So, is this what it comes to?" She said nothing. Her expression remained stone-like. The very fact that she didn't respond to his accusations only added to the verity of her guilt. "Listen to me, Jeanette," he said through clenched teeth, taking her arm in a firm grip, "I want some answers and I want them now!"

"Let go of me," she cried, pulling her arm free. "I dropped the charges this morning."

"Then why was she deported?"

"How should I know?" she snapped with a determination that only urged his anger closer to the surface.

"Tell me!" he growled. "Tell me what ship it was! Where was it going? Tell me!" he shouted, even though she was only inches away.

"I don't know," she retorted. "And even if I did, I wouldn't tell you."

"What you have done, Jeanette, is evil. You think because you gave birth to me that you can toss me around like some toy to see where I land? You think you can manipulate who I care for and what I do with my life just because of your whims and fancies? Well, it's *evil!* You had the nerve to come up with a false crime as a feeble excuse to discredit her. You will never make me believe that Kyrah would even want your jewelry, when every piece you were holding last night didn't come near the value of the necklace she was wearing. Even if she was dishonest—which she is not—she had no reason to steal. I was with her every minute last night. I know she's innocent. And so do you."

"Of course you'd stick up for the little tramp," she spat. "That's the best way to keep her in your bed."

Ritcherd slapped his mother without hesitation. Feeling no regret, he wondered what kind of man she had molded him into. Jeanette cried out as her hand went over her face. She glared at Ritcherd with bitterness in her eyes as she sneered, "You son of a . . ."

"Go ahead and say it," Ritcherd said when she hesitated, then he gave a humorless chuckle. "You know what that makes you."

Jeanette looked distressed at her poor choice of words, but she recovered quickly. "Can't you see you're better off without her?" she said. "She's ruined you! Nothing's ever been the same since she came into your life. I'm glad she's gone! And someday when you realize that she's nothing more than a comfortable habit for you, you'll thank me for sending her away."

She looked briefly startled at what had come out of her mouth, but it quickly disappeared behind a bitter determination that gave Ritcherd the excuse to do what he'd wanted to for years. Taking another hard look at his mother, he almost wanted to kill her. Instead he strode abruptly past her, grabbing her arm to bring her along.

"What are you doing?" she demanded as they entered a room that resembled a museum. The focal point of one wall was a huge, elaborate china closet with framed glass doors.

"Do you see this, Jeanette?" he said, motioning absently toward it.

"Why do you keep calling me that? I'm your mother."

"I will *never* call you mother again," he said calmly. Hearing the composure in his own voice, he felt somehow detached from himself in a way that made him wonder if he was going mad. From the fear in his mother's eyes, he felt certain she was wondering the same.

Ignoring anything but his purpose, he pointed at the china closet and spoke bitterly. "I hate these dishes," he began. "This set of china that you ordered custom made, with enough service for a hundred people. These gaudy, despicable-looking dishes that you treasure more than anything else completely represent everything you stand for. See how elaborately each piece has been hand-painted with the Buchanan family crest. You know, Jeanette, you got these dishes the same week my sister was taken away. Quite an exchange, don't you think? And when I came home and found my sister gone, all you could talk about was your blasted new china. I realized then that it had always been that way—with everything.

"I loathe the aristocratic system that allows people with money to get so caught up in greed that they are only concerned with whether or not they have the best of everything, and they can't even stop long enough to see life. I resent being raised by parents who were so concerned with social status and public demeanor that they could never find the good in me—or in the people I care for. I hate these dishes, Jeanette Buchanan, and for what little time I am going to remain in this house, I will not look at them again."

Ritcherd reached out calmly to open the huge china closet and found the door locked. Jeanette looked smug as if she'd outdone him, but Ritcherd just smiled satirically.

"It figures that you'd lock it. Let the thief take anything—even your children if they must. But don't let them get their hands on that china."

"Ritcherd! No!" she screamed when he picked up the fire poker and sent it crashing through the glass doors.

"You might think it's childish of me to be throwing a fit like this and breaking your china." He spoke in heated, breathless spurts as he raged his way through the china closet. "Well it is! But I'll tell you something, *Jeanette!*" He threw every individual piece crashing to the floor, except for the few that he hurled across the room where they shattered against the wall. "You have torn my world apart!" He raged with no control. "You're a narrow-minded, self-centered snob, and you have taken from me the only thing that ever mattered to me. And I'm not going to let you get away with it. You are going to pay for this! You will pay for sending her away! I love her and she's gone! I hope you *rot* in everlasting hell!" He shouted and raged until the closet was completely empty, then he picked up broken pieces and broke them again. When he couldn't possibly find a piece big enough to pick up, he unwillingly tensed every muscle in his body as he looked toward the ceiling and screamed, "How could you do this to me?"

In the stillness that followed, Ritcherd turned to look at his mother. She was sitting on the floor as if she'd wilted into the carpet. Her face was pale, and the regret in her eyes penetrated through the shock in her expression. But he felt relatively certain that she felt a lot more regret for the loss of her china than for the way she had torn his world into little pieces—not unlike the innumerable pieces of broken glass that crunched beneath his boots when he left the room. Walking back out the front door, he wondered where to start searching for those pieces. And if he found them, would he ever be able to put them back together?

Ritcherd stood outside the cottage door for several minutes before he found the courage to knock. He couldn't help thinking that just yesterday he had been here with Kyrah. Now she was gone. And how could he possibly tell Sarah?

He wasn't surprised at the shadow that fell over her face when she opened the door to see his countenance. "What's happened?" she said, pressing a hand over her heart. Ritcherd stepped inside and she closed the door. But he couldn't put the words together. "What? Tell me!"

"She's gone," Ritcherd said, his voice hoarse.

Sarah gasped. It took a moment for her stunned expression to turn to alarm. "Gone?" she echoed. "You mean . . . You can't mean . . ." Her voice quivered and her hands began to shake. "Please, Ritcherd, don't tell me she's dead. What could—"

"No," he interrupted, taking hold of her shoulders, "of course not." She sighed with visible relief while her eyes bored into his, demanding an explanation. Ritcherd hung his head, unable to look at her. "But it might be better if she were . . . for her sake."

"What are you saying?" Sarah's voice rasped and she clutched onto his arms. "What's happened?"

Ritcherd swallowed hard and just said it. "She's been deported, Sarah." He felt her hands tighten around his arms, while the rest of her drooped like a rag doll. Now that he'd said it, the explanation bubbled out. "I . . . woke up late . . . and realized that something had been put into my drink last night and . . . when I got there . . . she was gone. The constable told me she'd been found guilty . . . and deported . . . but he wouldn't tell me anything else. I went to the pier . . . but nobody knows anything." His tears began to flow with the hopelessness of his report. "I . . . I don't know where to even begin . . . to look for her. I don't know . . . where to go . . . or what to do." Drained of strength, he slid down the wall until he sat on the floor. Sarah crumbled in his arms and wept with him.

Ritcherd felt Sarah's thoughts change when she straightened abruptly and moved away from him. "I should have let you leave last night," she murmured and pressed both hands to her face. "I should have listened to what she was telling me . . . what you were telling me . . . I should have let you take her . . . Oh, Ritcherd! What have I done? *What have I done?*"

"Sarah, listen to me." He took hold of her shoulders and forced her to face him. "You couldn't have known. You were doing what you thought was best. This is not your fault, Sarah. Are you hearing me? My mother did this to us, Sarah. She manipulated this to keep me and Kyrah apart. But I'm not going to stand for it. I *will* find her, Sarah. I don't know where to start, but I'll find a way—and somehow I'll find her and bring her safely back to you. I swear it by all I hold dear. I will not rest until she's found. Do you hear me?"

Sarah nodded feebly and fell apart in tears all over again. Ritcherd held her and let her cry while determination whirled helplessly inside of him. He *had* to find her. If only he knew where to begin. *Please God,* he prayed silently, *show me the way.*

Long after Sarah's tears dried up, they sat together on the floor, holding hands, lost in silence. Ritcherd finally spoke, fearing he'd go mad otherwise. "I don't want you to worry, Sarah. I'll see that all of your needs are met. I won't leave any room for you to go without."

She looked alarmed, as if she'd just recalled something that troubled her.

"What?" he asked.

"Mr. Westman was here last night . . . after you left. He said that he wanted to talk to Kyrah, but then he didn't really seem surprised when I said she wasn't here."

"Did you tell him what happened?"

"No, of course not. But he . . . threatened me about the rent . . . the way he always does. You took care of that, didn't you?"

"Yes, my solicitor saw that it was paid for several months."

"Will you talk to him?" she asked. "Do whatever you have to to make him leave us in peace."

"I will," he promised, wondering if Peter Westman knew something that could give Ritcherd some direction. Instinctively he knew, at the very least, the man had to be aware of what his mother was up to. He recalled Peter's comment just last night at the party. *I'll believe this marriage when I see it.*

"In fact," Ritcherd added, "I'll go and talk to him right now." He stood up and helped her to her feet. "Is there anything you need?" he asked.

"No. Just . . . find Kyrah."

"I will," he said, feeling hypocritical as he realized she'd not lost her faith in him. "Do you have enough food in the house?"

"Yes."

"And you still have some money?"

"Yes, of course."

"I'll check back with you as soon as I have any news," he said and embraced her, pressing a kiss to her brow. "Thank you for being here for me, Sarah; for loving me in spite of everything."

She nodded, too overcome with emotion to speak.

When Ritcherd arrived at the big house, his nightmare intensified. No one answered after he knocked loudly several times, so he cautiously went inside. A quick peek into the main rooms along the hall showed all of the furnishings covered. He found an older woman working in the kitchen, and once she recovered from his startling her, she stated simply that Mr. Westman had left for an indeterminable length of time.

Every nerve in Ritcherd's body bristled as he asked skeptically, "He's left?"

"All I know, sir," the old woman said blandly, "is that he left very early this morning, which leaves me without a job. But I suppose that's just as well. He wasn't payin' me anyhow. He woke me before dawn and ran out o' here with his bags, sayin' he had a ship to catch and he wanted me to—"

Ritcherd didn't wait for her to finish. He lumbered back outside, feeling a whole new level of shock settle in. Wherever Kyrah was going, Peter Westman had gone with her. She might as well have been sentenced to serve time in hell, with the devil himself as her warden. He felt so tangibly ill that he was hard-pressed to keep from throwing up. If he'd had the strength, he would have returned to Buckley Manor and started in on his mother's crystal collection.

Ritcherd found himself back at the pier, looking westward out to sea as the sun sank against the far horizon. Consumed with despair and void of strength, he sat down at the water's edge where he spent half the night, praying with everything inside of him that he would be able to find Kyrah before the results of this nightmare set in too deeply. He finally returned home, convinced that he was likely not worthy to have such prayers answered. His only hope was that God would intervene on Kyrah's behalf and use him as the means to bring her home. Otherwise, the future was bleak.

Chapter Nine

The Proposition

Ritcherd managed to focus his eyes, only to see the top of a table very close to his face. He lifted his head and immediately regretted it as the pounding made him moan audibly. He didn't ever remember a time he'd been so drunk that he'd not made it to bed. He didn't know for certain why he decided in that moment not to get drunk anymore, but it was likely a combination of hating these headaches and knowing he would never find Kyrah if he didn't stay sober.

Kyrah. He felt sick inside wondering what she might be going through right now. He could easily imagine her fear and wished desperately that he was with her. She had already suffered so much. She didn't deserve this. *Why,* he kept asking himself over and over. *Why did this have to happen?* Ritcherd moaned again as his thoughts seemed to intensify the pounding in his head.

"The dead do come back to life," a light-hearted voice said from behind him, making his ears ring. Ritcherd turned carefully to see George sitting casually with his feet up—smiling. "I've been waiting to talk to you, my friend."

"This isn't a good time," Ritcherd said, feeling as though his mouth was full of cotton. Then he put his head back down on the table, moaning again.

"I've been trying to find you alone for several days. It wasn't a good time the night of the party, and I stopped by yesterday and heard you rampaging. I knew that wasn't a good time. I've been here half a dozen times since and found you gone. So, good time or not, I'm going to talk to you."

"Get on with it then," Ritcherd said without lifting his head.

"A little attention please," George said. "I'd at least like to know you're not asleep."

Ritcherd lifted his head and turned in his chair, looking at George through dazed eyes. "I'm attentive."

"How do you feel about the revolution in the colonies?" he began, and immediately Ritcherd was puzzled. This was not the usual brand of conversation between them.

"I nearly lost my arm fighting for England," he said, feeling more alert.

"And was it worth it?"

"Why?" Ritcherd looked intently at George, whose demeanor was casual, but his eyes were severe.

"What were you fighting for?" George asked cautiously.

"England."

Dissatisfied with the answer, George sighed, wondering how to get the hardheaded, cursory Ritcherd Buchanan to get beyond this surface conversation. He cleared his throat and reworded the question. "What is this war all about?"

"There is no reason for me to tell you that."

"Well then, I'll tell you . . . my theory at least." George stood and began walking with purpose about the room, glancing occasionally at his friend. "There are people—many of them from recent English ancestry—who have decided they don't want to live under the king's reign any longer. They want a place where there is freedom from the king's taxation, freedom of religion, and of course, freedom from social barriers."

Ritcherd sat up straighter. George seemed to have expected it.

"These people have been less than affectionately called rebels and traitors, and our king has armies over there trying to stop them from gaining the independence they need in order to establish such freedom."

"What is your point, George?"

"I'm a traitor."

Ritcherd truly looked surprised, but George would have been disappointed if he hadn't. At least he had his attention—which was definitely progress.

Ritcherd found it difficult to comprehend that this man, who had never seemed to care about anything more than living life to its fullest—with as many women and parties as he could possibly fit in—was now fighting for a cause. Recalling that George had left the country nearly a year before Ritcherd had gone to war, he had to wonder if there was a connection. "Why?" Ritcherd asked pointedly.

"Because I believe in it."

"I can give you credit for that. And I certainly wouldn't turn you in."

"I know that, or I wouldn't have told you."

"Why *are* you telling me?"

"Because I need help."

"Help?" Ritcherd laughed, then regretted it when his head rebelled. Absorbed with what was facing him right now, he retorted, "I don't think I'm in a position to help anybody."

"I don't need *you,*" George said forthrightly. "I need money."

"Money?" Ritcherd laughed again. "What happened to yours? Your family's not so bad off."

"You have to remember I'm not the oldest son like you are. I didn't inherit the whole lot. I've used everything I can get my hands on for this cause. Now my resources have gone dry."

"So you intend to drain me as well?"

"I wouldn't ask if I didn't already know that you've got enough to spend foolishly for a lifetime, and still not know what to do with the rest."

"What do you need this money for?" he asked, and George felt hopeful. At least he was interested enough to ask.

"A ship."

"A ship?"

"Must you repeat everything I say?"

"What would you do with a ship?" Ritcherd asked.

"The same thing I've been doing with one for the past three years. But the ship we had was shot down. It sank."

"Shot down?"

"There you go again."

"Well, what do you mean *shot down?*" Ritcherd leaned toward George. He was beginning to see this was no game.

George looked down solemnly and cleared his throat. "We were fired upon by a British Letter of Marque."

Ritcherd's brows went up. He knew there were many private vessels with written permission from the king to fight on his behalf at sea. But he wondered what George had been involved in to come up against one of them. "And?" he urged.

"And what?"

"What happened?"

"I told you. It sank."

"Listen to me, George. Like it or not, I'm a captain in the king's army with more experience than I care to admit to. If you're asking what I think you're asking, I have a right to know what's happening here. And I want to know *everything*."

George sighed and sat back down. He had hoped to accomplish this without having to get into the details so deeply. But he was determined to see it through, and knowing he had to work on Ritcherd's terms, he cleared his throat again and went on. "Fine, then I'll start at the beginning. You know, of course, that our fathers were very good friends."

"Yes," Ritcherd drawled. This was the last place he'd expected this explanation to begin.

"You know they went regularly to London together, where they spent a great deal of time. And you also know they shared a number of business investments."

"Yes," Ritcherd said again, although he'd remained relatively ignorant of his father's interests. William Buchanan had never seemed to want his son involved in anything that required interaction between them.

"Well, one of their major investments had to do with shipping. Now, I'm almost as ignorant of the details as you are. However, our fathers also had a mutual friend, who was very much into shipping. And through circumstances I won't bore you with, I became good friends with this man's grandson. It was through this friend I became involved in my present endeavors."

"Which would be . . . precisely?"

"The ship was called the *Falcon Star* . . . a privateer."

Ritcherd swallowed his reaction and simply said, "You've been sinking British ships?" He thought of the one he'd sailed home on, not so long ago.

"We've done our best to avoid the actual fighting—although sometimes it's unavoidable. We concentrate most of our efforts on smuggling arms, ammunition, and supplies to the colonists."

"Good heavens, man," Ritcherd said, standing at last. He clasped his hands behind his back. "It's amazing you're still alive."

"More amazing than you'd believe," he said with a severity that made Ritcherd wonder what else he'd been up to.

"So what happened when this *Falcon Star* went down?" Ritcherd pressed.

"Just as I said. We were fired upon. We fought back but they did us in. The ship went down with full cargo."

"Which was?"

"Arms and ammunition," George said tersely. "Now you're making *me* repeat everything."

"How bad was the loss?"

George looked to the side quickly and folded his arms. "We had invested everything we could get our hands on for that run. We were hoping to get enough profit from it to be able to make another." George paused and looked directly at Ritcherd. "We lost twenty-three men." His expression betrayed how deep the loss had been. Having faced battlefronts himself, he knew exactly what George was feeling.

A long silence preceded Ritcherd's stating, "And now you're going to try again."

"That's right."

"And you want my help."

"That's right." When Ritcherd remained silent, George got to the point. "Will you do it?"

"What exactly do you want me to do?" he asked, facing him directly.

"Finance a ship. But this is no loan I'm asking for. I'm asking you to give it to me."

Ritcherd chuckled without humor. "And what do I get out of it?"

"Not a blasted thing."

"Well, at least you're honest," Ritcherd said with sarcasm. "I spent three of the worst years of my life fighting those colonists. Do you suppose it was one of the guns you smuggled in that nearly got my arm blown off?"

George sighed. "I've thought about that," he said, and Ritcherd saw a flash of confusion in his eyes.

"Why are you doing this?" Ritcherd went on. "What is it that gives you the conviction to risk so much, and to continue taking risks when you've lost so much?"

"I'd like to turn that around if I may," George replied with purpose in his expression. "What is it that this country has given you that makes you defend it? What kind of system is it that lets people like your mother run people like the Paynes into the ground?"

Ritcherd shot George an angry glare. He'd struck a sensitive nerve and he knew it. But it was evident that George didn't know about the latest event in the ongoing drama. And how could Ritcherd argue? He knew George was right. He hated this aristocratic system. He believed that people should be treated equally regardless of money or social status. And he knew that the American colonists didn't believe in titles, nor did they judge people by family names or background. Wasn't it the very reason he had made such an immature display just yesterday with his mother's china? Still, Ritcherd loved his homeland. In the years he'd been gone he'd come to miss this beautiful place where he'd grown up, and he had fought very hard for his king.

George knew he needed to give Ritcherd time to think, but he began to feel impatient with the continuing silence. Attempting to lighten the mood with some small talk, he asked, "Where were you last night anyway? I tried late. And I didn't see your horse at Kyrah's place."

"I was at the pier," he answered blandly.

"Really? Was there any action?"

"None," he replied, "I was all alone."

"That's where I was the night before," George said easily. "It was pretty dull then, too."

Ritcherd turned to look at George as if he'd never seen him before. "You were *what?*" he asked, wondering if he'd heard correctly.

"I was at the pier . . . night before last," George repeated, wondering why it seemed so important.

Ritcherd came to his feet, ignoring the pain in his head. "How long were you there?"

"All night, actually," George answered. "It was unfortunate for me that I wasn't able to leave until the sun came up."

"And this was the night of the party?"

"Yes."

"Did any ships leave?"

"Just one."

"Tell me what you know," Ritcherd said, sitting near his friend and leaning forward expectantly.

George was baffled, but he was willing to discuss just about anything if it might bring out Ritcherd's sympathy toward his cause. "I was watching to see if a certain man got on that ship—as a favor to a friend. I waited all night. As it was, he came running down the pier just as the ship was lifting anchor. He got on board and the ship left."

"Whose ship was it?"

"It's a privateer vessel." He smirked. "But that's a secret, of course. It's a barque called the *Libertatia,* and was supposedly going to Jamaica. But I know different."

Ritcherd glanced heavenward and briefly squeezed his eyes shut. Perhaps God had heard his prayers after all. "What do you know?" he demanded, returning his focus to George.

"It was going to the colonies—with smuggled goods."

"Oh, help," Ritcherd murmured. Now he knew. Kyrah was on her way to a country at war—with privateers, no less. But he *knew!* Instead of feeling as if he'd be swallowed up by a dark cloud of hopelessness and ignorance, he knew where she was going. He had a place to start.

"What?!" George asked, throwing his hands in the air.

Ritcherd was silent a long moment before he asked, "Did you recognize anyone else who boarded?"

"Just a bunch of scruffy-looking sailors. Nobody you'd know. Why?"

"Did any women board?"

"If a woman got on board, she was either awfully ugly, or she was carried on disguised as cargo." He'd meant it facetiously, but Ritcherd's expression intensified.

"What do you mean?"

"I mean . . . all I saw was a bunch of ugly sailors loading supplies. They took all kinds of crates and sacks aboard. What are you trying to get at?"

Again Ritcherd was silent. When he spoke at last, George was surprised by the zeal and determination in his voice. "Exactly what are your plans at this point . . . if you had a ship?"

"Well, right now we've got a stable full of arms and ammunition. We got a good price and came up with some credit. When we get a ship, we'll load it up. We sail to the colonies, dock the ship at night in an inconspicuous place, and take the goods ashore once we find a suitable buyer. When the ship's empty, we claim to be on whoever's side we need to be in order to dock and get supplies, then we come back."

"It sounds dangerous."

"It is. But we've learned the ropes. These men are good. The captain doesn't press for men or drag them out of a local tavern. The size of our crew has diminished somewhat, but he far prefers quality over quantity, and that usually means less risk of betrayal. We can trust these men, and if we're careful, we usually don't have any trouble. You'd be surprised what a big business this is. But we're not in it for the profit like many people are. The point is, however, that there are a lot of other people, if you'll pardon the pun, who are in the same boat, and are willing to help us if we'll help them. We've been doing it long enough to know who those people are."

Ritcherd became thoughtful again and George waited expectantly, sensing something deep, even emotional in Ritcherd's expression. He was surprised, nevertheless, that Ritcherd's answer had such conviction. "I'll do it," he said with enthusiasm.

"You will?"

"Yes," he smiled, "but . . ."

"But what?" George asked, afraid of what conditions he might put on the deal.

"Well, it will be my ship, right? What I mean is . . . I don't have to give it to you. I could just buy it and let you use it. Right?"

"I suppose," George said. "But what would you want with a ship?"

"A good investment, don't you think? Let's go buy a ship."

George stood and glared at Ritcherd. "You said there was a but."

"There is."

"Tell me. I want to know before we go through with this."

"I'm going with you."

"You're *what?*"

"Would you like me to repeat it?" Ritcherd asked.

George's brow furrowed with confusion. "I thought you were getting married."

Ritcherd looked away solemnly and answered, "Not just yet."

"May I ask wh—"

"No," Ritcherd cut him off.

"Fine," George said, holding his hands up. "I'm not about to intrude when it comes to women."

"How long will it take?" Ritcherd asked. "To get the ship, I mean."

"There's one in the harbor just waiting to be purchased. And it's exactly what we need. Apparently it's practically new. It was custom built, then the buyer didn't come through. Once the transaction takes place, it's just a matter of some necessary maintenance and loading it up. I can notify the captain and he can be here from Falmouth in no time to get things underway. He's already seen the ship, so it's up to you."

"How long before we can sail?" he asked with obvious impatience.

"Five days . . . say four if we push it. The captain is anxious to get the goods out of the country."

Ritcherd smiled. "Perfect."

Again George felt puzzled, but he knew that whatever was behind Ritcherd's motivations, he was in no mood to talk about it. So George just changed the subject. "What are you going to name it?" he asked.

"What?"

"Your ship. It has to have a name."

"I don't know," he said, "but I'll come up with something before we sail—something with a good omen. This ship of mine is going to bring about good things."

"Aye, Cap'n," George said, mimicking a pirate smirk.

Ritcherd laughed. He actually felt hope.

"Give me ten minutes to clean up," Ritcherd said, "and we'll take care of it now."

Ritcherd went with George to the Golden Lion, where he said the owner of the ship could be found every afternoon. He wasn't there when they arrived, but since it was just past noon, they sat together to eat. George was certain he would be there before long.

Ritcherd found it difficult to keep his thoughts from Kyrah. The last time he had eaten here, it had been with her. The whole thing was so awful. He hated every minute that ticked by, knowing it was taking her farther from him. But at least he had the knowledge and the means to find her. He had to keep his thoughts focused on the positive, or he would go mad.

The owner of the ship appeared before their meal was finished. George made introductions that Ritcherd barely heard before the three of them went together to the pier, where the ship was docked. Ritcherd was pleased immediately with the sight of it, and realized now that it had been there along with a few others last night when he'd been at the pier.

The owner called the vessel a barquentine, then went on to explain to Ritcherd that of the three masts, only the foremost was square-rigged. The other two were fore and aft. From the detailed description this man was giving him, Ritcherd wondered if it was so obvious that he knew absolutely nothing about ships. As they were taken aboard and given a tour, he explained a great deal about the ship's structure, most of which was totally lost on Ritcherd. But he couldn't help being impressed with the vessel, and he could see that George was as well.

Following the tour, Ritcherd confirmed that he would buy the ship, and they settled on an amount as well as a time to meet later that day. George laughed out loud as they left the pier together. Ritcherd went with George to send word with a courier to Falmouth, where the captain and crew were waiting.

"Tell them to hurry," Ritcherd said while George was writing the message.

George just smiled. "Don't fret, Ritch. They'll hurry."

When that was seen to, George went with Ritcherd to get the money at the bank. They met the owner at the office of Ritcherd's solicitor, where the transaction was completed. Ritcherd stayed behind when the others left, needing a private word with his solicitor. James Hatfield was a man Ritcherd had counted on long before his father's death. He was honest, efficient, reliable, and discreet. In a voice completely void of emotion, Ritcherd explained to Mr. Hatfield the occurrences of the last few days. He told him of his plans, and made full arrangements to see that Sarah's needs were taken care of. Mr. Hatfield offered some sound advice and assured Ritcherd that he would keep the matter quiet. Ritcherd didn't want *anyone* to know where he was going—especially anyone who might tell his mother.

It was late when Ritcherd returned to Buckley Manor, entering through a seldom-used side door in order to avoid being seen. He was both exhausted and satisfied with the day's accomplishments. He had made some very big steps in setting his feet upon the road that would lead to Kyrah. He prayed the road would not be too long or too hard—for either of them.

Ritcherd worked quickly to prepare for his journey to the colonies, his first concern being for Sarah. Following a suggestion from his solicitor, he hired a young girl to stay with her, as much for companionship as to help her. He reassured her that the rent had been paid for eighteen months, and he gave her copies of the papers to prove it. She was overflowing with relief when he told her that he had uncovered some information and he was going to find Kyrah. But she started to cry when he told her he'd set up an open account for her at the bank that she could draw on when necessary, because he didn't know when he was coming back. He also told her where to find Mr. Hatfield's office, assuring her that he would help her with any problem that might arise.

"I'm truly going to miss you, Sarah," he said as she walked him to the door, "just as I did before."

"And I you. But when you come back with Kyrah, everything will be as it should be."

"Yes." He forced a smile, pressed a kiss to her cheek, and left.

Ritcherd didn't see his own mother again before he left. He packed what he was taking with him in a valise and put everything else of his that was of any value in a trunk that wasn't much bigger. Sarah had gladly consented to let him leave it in Kyrah's room.

He left a note to his mother in the library that simply stated: *Jeanette, I'm leaving the country. Ritcherd.*

He stopped at the cottage to see Sarah one more time, then rode toward the pier, stopping for a short time at the church ruins. They wouldn't be sailing for two more days, but George had suggested that Ritcherd get settled in and acquaint himself with the situation for a day or two before they set out. And Ritcherd was only too eager to have everything in order so they could leave. Perhaps he could hurry them along.

Wandering through the church ruins, his heart ached for Kyrah in a way he'd hardly allowed himself to feel since he'd become distracted with the hope of setting out after her. Absorbing the familiarity of every stone, he wondered if Kyrah had come here alone when he'd been away. He prayed that she was well. His thoughts were constantly filled with worry for her. Where was she? What was happening to her? Oh, how he longed to be with her now!

Deep in thought, he sat on one of the stone pews and leaned forward against his hands where they gripped the pew in front of him. He felt no sense of time while he prayed that he would be able to find Kyrah. He knew already that there had been an unseen hand in this. The timely knowledge that she had gone to the colonies was uncanny, along with the opportunity to go himself. Even if he had previously known her destination, there was a war going on. It was difficult, if not impossible, to get passage to America. But the pieces had come together in a way that seemed like a miracle. Still, he needed more miracles. The colonies were big, with a lot of ports and cities, and there was indeed a war going on.

As he became absorbed with what lay ahead, a combination of despair and expectation flooded through him. His neck began to ache and he leaned back, spreading his arms over the top of the pew. With his eyes closed, he felt more than saw the sun's rays sweep over his face as it moved westward, coming through one of the high church windows. Warmth bathed him as he opened his eyes. Before they adjusted to the light, a large bird flew in and lighted in the window. He squinted but couldn't discern what type it was; only the outline of large wings with the sun at its back. The bird flew away almost as quickly as it had come, but the impression it left in Ritcherd's mind was unforgettable. He thought of the Egyptian legend of the phoenix: a large bird that had consumed itself by fire, then had risen after five hundred years, renewed of its own ashes. Knowing Kyrah's fascination with birds, he imagined some kind of symbolism in the one he'd just seen. He decided that his ship would be called the *Phoenix*. It seemed a good omen.

As he stood to leave, Ritcherd glanced around the old church once more to absorb the memories. He had seen Kyrah here for the first time. They had played here as children, laughed and talked through endless hours. He remembered them dancing here, their first kiss, and . . .

His memories caught him off guard as he recalled the intimacy that had occurred between them not so many days ago. To have her torn away from him after such a thing had occurred made him physically ill. The idea was so unbearable that he had to push it away. He couldn't even ponder how she might be feeling toward him in that respect. He forced his mind to better memories. Their first kiss. And their reconciliation after he'd returned from the colonies and they'd finally talked through all of their feelings. It seemed that he'd lived a lifetime since then. And, oh how he ached for her! Then he remembered the brooch. She'd lost it here. He recalled how she'd thrown it to the ground, and it took him only a minute to find it. Fingering it carefully, Ritcherd found comfort in this tangible assurance that his memories were real. He tucked it into the pocket of his waistcoat and mounted the horse he'd left tethered near the church.

It was easy to leave now. He'd received what he'd come for. Memories that had given him comfort. A vision that had given him hope. And a talisman to carry as a reminder of all they had shared. As he rode at a full gallop to the pier, he wished that he could be like that great bird he had seen. It would be easy to find her if he could soar over the ocean, seeing everything below him from the sky's perspective. He knew that he couldn't fly, but the image of the great bird emblazoned in his memory reminded him that God knew where Kyrah was. Putting his trust into divine guidance, he knew in his heart that he *would* find her. He just had to!

Ritcherd stopped at a local livery stable and made a deal on the horse he'd ridden into town. He'd left his stallion in the stables at Buckley Manor, knowing it would be well cared for, just as it had been through his years at war. But this horse had no sentimental value to him, and he knew he wouldn't be needing it for a long time. When that was seen to, he went to an inn to get something to eat. The growling of his stomach reminded him he'd hardly eaten at all today. When his meal was finished, he walked the short distance to the pier where his ship was proudly docked. He just had to look at it for several minutes in the moonlight, thinking of the name he would give it and the places it would take him. When he stood there another few minutes and realized there was absolutely no one around, he wondered where this captain and crew that George talked about had all gone. He wandered around for a short while, and still saw no one. Answering his fatigue, he got a room at a nearby inn and slept better than he'd expected. Following a bath and a hearty breakfast, he went back to the pier and found an entirely different picture. He could hardly see the hull of the ship for all the crates and sacks stacked around it on the dock. A number of rather colorful-looking men he'd never seen before were systematically loading the goods onto the ship. Their laughter and conversation filled Ritcherd with added anticipation. He hoped it wouldn't be too long before they set sail.

He was just wondering where George might be when he was startled by a hearty slap on the shoulder. "Yo ho ho," George said, then he laughed. Ritcherd figured it must be some kind of sea humor.

He was taken aback by George's appearance, until he concluded that he was dressed to fit in with the men they'd be sailing with. His clothes were old and worn, unlike anything Ritcherd had ever seen him wear. His hair was tied back in the usual ponytail, but it looked almost sloppy, as if he'd not taken the time to actually put a comb to it. But most startling of all was the gold ring that hung in a pierced earlobe. He smirked at George but chose not to comment. Instead he stated, "I was here last night, but nobody was around."

"We all turned in early," George explained. "It was a long day."

"I see." Ritcherd glanced around again at the bustle of activity. "Exactly how much food do we need?" he asked, noting the markings on most of the crates.

George leaned closer and whispered, "Most of this *food* is explosive."

"I see," Ritcherd said again, glancing around as if they might all be immediately arrested. He wondered what kind of connections they had with legal authorities to let something like this go unnoticed.

"Hey," George changed his tone, "I've got a painter on hold. We've got to get a name on this ship before we sail. You got any ideas yet? 'Cause if you start asking these guys for ideas, it'll be—"

"Yes, I do, actually," Ritcherd said.

"Great." George seemed pleased. "Let's go talk to him. Then you can get settled in."

Ritcherd saw George smile as he explained to the painter what he wanted on the ship. "Can you do it?" Ritcherd asked, ignoring George for the moment.

"O' course I can do it," the man insisted.

"Today?"

"Aye. I'll have m' boys 'elpin' me."

Ritcherd pulled out some money to pay him, and George intervened. "We'll pay you when it's finished," he said to the painter.

As they walked back to the pier together, George told Ritcherd, "If you paid him now, he'd be too drunk to show up and get the job done."

Ritcherd didn't say anything, but he was glad George knew what he was doing. He felt vulnerable and out of place already. Then George took him aboard the ship while the sailors all eyed him skeptically. He felt chilled at the thought of Kyrah sailing with men like this—or worse.

Ritcherd followed George below deck and down the long hallway between the crew's cabins. He knew from his brief tour that the captain's cabin was at the back of the ship, and it was huge in comparison to the others. George knocked at the door and heard a gravelly "Yeah?" in response.

"So you *do* knock," Ritcherd whispered.

"Occasionally," George smirked and opened the door, motioning for Ritcherd to enter. A quick glance told him the room was in shambles. His eye was drawn to a burly sailor with his hair hanging over his eyes in a way that made Ritcherd wonder how he could see what he was doing as he gathered up several rolls of paper.

"Put the charts there . . . in that . . . No, not there!" The man giving the orders was obviously the captain, but his back was turned and Ritcherd couldn't get a good look at him beyond the dark hair that was worn in a longer-than-normal ponytail. His voice was deep, and that gravelly quality came into it with an increase in volume. "Very good," he drawled as the sailor apparently found the right compartment. "Thank you, Patrick," he added. "That will be all for the moment." The sailor left the room with a suspicious glance toward Ritcherd.

"Captain Buchanan," George said with a histrionic wave of his arm, "I'd like you to meet the man who'll be sailing your ship—Captain Garret."

Ritcherd tried not to feel unnerved when Captain Garret turned around and their eyes met. He was close to Ritcherd's size and build, and he guessed they weren't too far apart in age. A neatly trimmed beard framed his face, where deep-set eyes peered from beneath brows that were dark and thick. A gold earring hung from his left ear. Combined with his manner of dress, he looked downright treacherous. He wore doeskin breeches and high boots; a wool shirt, belted around the waist with the sleeves rolled up almost to the shoulder, and black leather gloves, leaving his muscular arms showing prominently in between. With a pistol and straight-bladed cutlass at his side, it was immediately evident that this man was not to be crossed, although the message came more from his eyes than the weapons he sported. As Ritcherd felt Captain Garret surveying him, he could almost believe the man was seeing into his soul.

"So this is Captain Buchanan," he said. His voice came across more smooth and mellow than when he'd been giving orders just a minute ago. "I must thank you for giving us the means to continue our work."

"It's my pleasure, actually."

Garret folded his arms over his chest. "So, you're coming with us, I hear."

"That's right."

Garret looked Ritcherd up and down, clucking his tongue as if what he saw was pitiful. "Not looking like that, you're not."

Ritcherd glanced down at himself, then back at Garret, certain he wasn't going to like this man. "Is there something wrong with the way I look?" he asked in a voice tinged with anger.

Garret leaned against the large table that was bolted to the floor. "You look an awfully lot like an aristocrat."

Ritcherd gave George a sidelong glance, as if to say *is this guy crazy?* Ritcherd wondered what exactly he'd expected. Before he had a chance to retort, Garret added, "Most of the men I know in this business would shoot an aristocrat for sport." Ritcherd felt his defenses heighten, but he could hardly protest when Garret explained, "I will not risk my crew, and the people we're trying to help, with you standing out as conspicuous as a full moon on a black night." He walked around Ritcherd as if he was somehow sizing him up. "I'll admit," he said more to George, "at least he's got a rugged look about him. Some of the clothes might work. At least he's not all fluff and frills like most of those aristo imbeciles."

"That's true," George said, and Ritcherd shot him a harsh glare. George just shrugged his shoulders and smirked, as if he was actually enjoying this.

While Ritcherd was trying to decide if he felt humbled or humiliated, Garret's voice picked up that gravelly quality that seemed to come with giving orders. "Take him to that secondhand shop down the pier, Morley. Then take him to Sam."

"Who's Sam?" Ritcherd asked, not liking the glance that passed between Garret and George.

"Sam will get your ear pierced for a fair price. And he actually cleans the needle first."

"What?" Ritcherd retorted. "If you think that—"

"Captain Buchanan," Garret interrupted. "Poor sailors and pirates wear gold in their ear, as an insurance policy, so to speak. That piece of gold guarantees that if you die, I will be able to afford seeing that your body is properly cared for, and your loved ones are notified. You're not sailing without it." He leaned forward slightly, and there was a subtle bite to his voice as he added, "I assume you can afford it."

While Ritcherd was contemplating a retaliation worthy of his growing anger, he felt George's hand on his arm, as if to warn him. Recalling his purpose for doing this, he swallowed his anger and simply stated, "Yes, Captain, I can afford it."

"Good," Garret said. "See to it. Then we can talk." With that he motioned them toward the door like a king dismissing his servants.

Ritcherd followed George out of the cabin, pausing to give Garret a long, hard glare. Having served in the military, he knew how to take orders from his superiors when necessary. But as an officer, he was also accustomed to being in charge when he needed to be. He didn't like this guy's attitude, and he feared the journey could be far more of a challenge than he'd anticipated.

Garret didn't seem the least bit ruffled by the disdain in Ritcherd's expression. In fact, his brows went up in a way that implied he found the situation humorous. Ritcherd turned and left the room, hating his mother all over again for putting him in a position where he had to deal with such circumstances.

"You can put your things in here," George said, distracting Ritcherd as he opened the door to one of the cabins. Ritcherd tossed his bag on the narrow bed and closed the door again.

"Ah, lighten up," George said as they returned to the deck. Ritcherd hadn't said anything for fear of erupting. "Consider it a form of playacting. And as for Garret, you'll get used to him."

"Looks like I don't have much choice," Ritcherd said.

"You don't have to come with us," George suggested.

"Yes, I do." Ritcherd's voice came softer as he recalled again his motivation for doing this. George looked curious over his reasons, but he didn't ask. And that was fine with Ritcherd. He figured that eventually George would learn the whole story. But for the time being, he preferred to keep it to himself.

Ritcherd did manage to lighten up a bit as George helped him pick out a number of pieces of secondhand clothing. It was evident that everything had been well cleaned and put in good repair. And the shopkeeper's comical flair took the edge off Ritcherd's mood. While they were finishing up, Ritcherd picked up a black tricorne and patted it onto his head, mostly hoping to provoke some laughter out of George. But his friend only smiled and lifted one eyebrow, which prompted Ritcherd to look in the mirror. He actually felt startled by his own reflection. The man looking back at him seemed so unfamiliar, but in a way that intrigued and inspired him. While he was assessing that the hat was a perfect fit, the shopkeeper said, "Got that from a redcoat for a fair price. He took it off o' one o' them rebel colonists after he'd shot him."

"Really." Ritcherd removed the hat and rubbed his fingers over the fine texture while he contemplated how that made him feel. He thought of the colonists he'd shot personally. He'd never felt good about doing it, but a new level of regret settled over him. Now, he had to wonder how he might feel if he were American, wanting only to live in peace without social barriers, ridiculous taxation, and the threat of tyranny. He recalled all too well the faces of the men he'd killed. They had been typical of the soldiers they'd come up against—if they could even be called soldiers. They were unruly, undisciplined, and most of them had been dressed as if they'd just walked away from their farms and shops. And that's what struck Ritcherd as he held the hat in his hands. That was the reality he had overlooked. They *had* just walked away from their farms and shops, taking up any weapon they could get their hands on to defend what they had worked so hard for.

Ritcherd put the hat back on and looked at himself again in the mirror. He saw anger and determination. He *felt* like a rebel. He felt like spitting at the society that created such social injustice, the same way colonists—men and women alike—had spat at him when he'd led his troops through the villages of New England. And if that made him a traitor, so be it.

"I'll take it," he said and saw George smile.

Ritcherd came away not feeling too out of sorts with the clothes he was wearing, and his own clothes tucked into a bundle with his other purchases. George declared that he liked the changes, and Ritcherd had to admit that he didn't necessarily dislike them. At least now he wouldn't stick out like an aristocratic sore thumb. And at the moment, becoming inconspicuous was awfully appealing. He kept that in mind as they paid a visit to Sam.

The ear piercing hurt more than he'd thought it would, but George informed him that in a day or two he wouldn't notice it at all. Before they left Sam's place, George roughed up Ritcherd's hair a little. And the satin ribbon holding his ponytail was replaced with a thin leather strap. Walking along the pier, Ritcherd liked the lack of skeptical and suspicious glances. Feeling a little more prepared to face the journey, his determination to sail increased.

They returned to the ship to find the painter they'd hired sitting in a harness attached to ropes that hung over the bow of the ship. He was hard at work, with a rough outline of the image already taking shape. He waved at George and took a second glance at Ritcherd, obviously wondering if it was the same person. All of the cargo that had been stacked about earlier was completely gone, but Ritcherd noticed the ship was sitting lower in the water with the weight that had been taken on board. Approaching the stairs to go below deck, they met Patrick, who had just come up. He pushed his hair out of his face long enough to survey Ritcherd's appearance.

"Cap'n had your stuff moved," he said. "Don't want ye t' panic when it ain't where ye left it."

"Thank you," Ritcherd said, wondering why one cabin was any different from another. Perhaps Captain Garret wanted to demote him to the cargo hold in order to humble him completely.

"'E's waitin' for ye," Patrick added and moved past them.

"Great," Ritcherd said with sarcasm as he followed George below. "Perhaps he's wanting me to do a little kitchen duty."

"Nah," George said with no trace of humor, "he's already got that covered."

Ritcherd's first surprise upon entering the captain's cabin was to find it immaculate. Obviously he'd gotten settled in. Captain Garret was seated at the desk, absorbed in whatever he was writing in a large book.

"Just a minute," he said, motioning absently with his free hand. "Have a seat."

George plopped into one of the chairs that surrounded the table, where the captain's cutlass and pistol were now lying. Ritcherd set his bundle down but stayed on his feet, feeling too tense to sit. When Captain Garret was apparently finished, he turned in his chair and folded his arms over his chest. With harsh eyes he surveyed Ritcherd from head to toe, then back again. While Ritcherd was struggling to come up with some terse remark that might express his disdain for this situation, Captain Garret broke into a broad grin that completely destroyed any previous effort he'd made to appear menacing.

"Very nice," he drawled. Nodding toward George, he added, "You do good work, Morley. Remind me to promote you."

George laughed. "There's no place to be promoted to around here."

"Exactly," Garret said and laughed as well. He motioned toward the larger of the two beds in the cabin as he said to Ritcherd, "I had your things moved here. I don't know what possessed you to think you'd be sentenced to sleep in one of those rabbit holes."

"*I* have to sleep in one of those rabbit holes," George said.

"You get the accommodations you pay for," Garret said with a smirk that made it evident he was mostly teasing. "Besides, I'm not rooming with you. You'd drive me crazy . . . as if you don't already."

"How do you know Ritch here won't drive you crazy?"

Garret met Ritcherd's eyes. "I guess we'll have to see." Then to George, "Get out of here, Morley. You've got work to do."

George came to his feet and gave Garret a mocking salute. "Aye, Cap'n," he said with comical sarcasm and left the room.

"Sit down, Captain Buchanan," Garret said. Ritcherd hesitated a moment, still caught up in his mental reevaluation of this man. He gave himself a quick scolding in regard to judging on first impressions, then took a seat, feeling an instinctive desire to get to know this man better.

"Ritcherd," he requested.

"Fine, Ritcherd." Captain Garret held out his left hand, as if he'd previously noticed Ritcherd's hesitation in using his right, although Ritcherd couldn't recall him paying any attention to it. Ritcherd took the proffered hand and gave it a hearty shake. "Call me Garret. It's the only name I've got. Would you like a drink?" he asked, pouring one for himself.

"No, thank you," Ritcherd said and Garret looked surprised. He quickly explained, "The last time I got drunk, the hangover reformed me."

Garret chuckled. "I'm not suggesting you get drunk," he said, pouring a cautious amount into two glasses. "This is the only bottle on the ship, and I'll be hiding it soon. There will be no drinking once we set sail." Ritcherd lifted his brows in question and Garret explained, "It's tempting to get drunk when you're at sea for so long. But when you're in a dangerous business, drunk men become dead men."

"Very poetic," Ritcherd said. Taking the glass from Garret, he took a long swallow.

Garret took a sip and sat down, lifting his booted legs onto the table. He motioned absently toward Ritcherd with his glass. "You transformed well," he said.

"Thank you," Ritcherd said, glancing down at himself. "I think," he added with a chuckle. "I suppose I'll get used to it."

"You'll have to if you're sailing on my ship."

Ritcherd met his eyes and, once again, felt as if Garret could somehow see into his soul. But he met his gaze without flinching as he said, "But it's my ship."

"Can you sail it?" Garret asked lightly, though his eyes remained intense.

"Did you buy it?" Ritcherd replied.

Garret's brows went up. Then he laughed, and Ritcherd joined him.

"Captain Buchanan," Garret leaned forward and held up his glass, "I think a partnership is in order here."

"Fair enough," Ritcherd smiled, "Captain Garret." He lifted his glass to touch Garret's before they both emptied them.

"I really don't need to sleep . . . there." Ritcherd motioned toward the bed where his bag was sitting. The cabin was obviously set up for a first mate or assistant to sleep in the same room, but Garret had made it clear that Ritcherd should take the more comfortable bed. "The cabin I had was fine. You have a great deal of responsibility here. It's evident you need the space to do your work . . . and you need to sleep well when you have the chance."

"I can sleep just about anywhere," Garret said. "But if we're going to be partners, the crew will see us as equals."

Ritcherd couldn't believe what he was hearing. He had been ready to denounce the man as arrogant and rude, but before Ritcherd had even returned to the ship, Garret had moved his things here with the intention of putting equality between them. "Why are you doing this?" he asked, wondering if he should be suspicious.

"Doing what?" Garret asked, lifting his brows.

"This . . . partnership thing. You have no idea what kind of man I am. Maybe I *will* drive you crazy."

Garret's smile was gone as quickly as it came. "I know you're the kind of man who would let me use his ship with no apparent concern over financial return."

"I have my motives," Ritcherd said.

Garret chuckled. "There isn't a man alive who doesn't have motives." Ritcherd wondered for a moment if he might demand to know what they were, but he only said, "For what it's worth, I just want you to know that I'm grateful, Ritcherd. This cause means a great deal to me. And being at sea is about the only thing in this life that gives me any pleasure. At the risk of gushing, I would like to say that your gesture has restored something for us that we'd lost."

"We?"

"The crew. Me."

"And what is that?"

"Hope."

Ritcherd swallowed carefully, feeling suddenly very humbled. He wondered if he would have supported this cause if not for his motives. His humility deepened when Garret added, "And also one more piece of evidence that there is a greater hand in this work."

"I don't understand," Ritcherd said.

"I don't know whether or not you're a God-fearing man, Ritcherd. But I'm not ashamed to admit that I am. And I *know* that God wants those Americans to succeed. They *will* succeed. And we have the opportunity to make a small contribution to that success—thanks to you."

Ritcherd had to say, "I'm a redcoat, you know."

"Not anymore," Garret said. "Now you're a turncoat." Ritcherd straightened his back and felt his heart quicken. He removed his hat and fingered it carefully. His thoughts when buying it returned and he couldn't deny the unrest he was feeling.

"Whatever your motives might be, Captain Buchanan, you have now aided a cause that is far greater than you or me."

"And if God is on the side of the colonists, do you think He'll forgive me for fighting on the wrong side for three years?"

"You did what you had to do. I can respect that. As for the other . . . well, I suppose that's between you and God."

Ritcherd was thoughtful a moment before he said, "Well, at the risk of gushing, I would like to say that I am humbled and also . . . grateful . . . to be given this opportunity." Hearing the words come back to him, he couldn't believe what he was saying. He had to clarify in his mind that he was glad to be able to help their cause, but would have far preferred to do it without having these horrible circumstances that had come between him and Kyrah. He glanced at Garret and marveled that they were having this conversation. They had been complete strangers only hours ago. This was the kind of philosophical conversation he recalled having so many times with Kyrah. He felt comfortable, and somehow . . . comforted. But he could almost feel Garret wondering over his reasons for being here. And he just wasn't ready to delve into that . . . not yet. He was relieved when Garret changed the subject and lightened the mood.

"Now, to the business at hand. It's best if you don't get involved with illegal activities using your real name. George and I will be the only ones to know who you really are. Let's keep it simple. Shorten the first name."

"Ritch?" he suggested and George entered the room—without knocking.

"Perfect!" Garret said with a quick glance toward George. "And the last?"

"Buckley," George said as if he'd given this matter great thought.

"Buckley," Garret repeated. "Captain Ritch Buckley."

"I like it," George said.

"Now we just have to work on the voice."

"The voice?" Ritcherd echoed.

"Aye," Garret drawled, "the voice'll give ye away every time, Cap'n."

Ritcherd laughed at the drastic transformation. It might not have occurred to him if he hadn't heard the difference, but it was evident now that Garret was a man of refined speech and manners. Yet his sailor's drawl came naturally and fluently. His curiosity over this man only continued to increase.

"Well," George said, using the same drawl just as naturally, "I came t' tell ye it's time t' be 'avin' supper. Let's be about it. The men won't be eatin' without the cap'n."

"Don't worry," Garret said in his normal voice as they moved toward the door. "You'll catch on. With a little time at sea, you'll be able to actually open your mouth in a tavern without getting yourself shot. If we keep up the proper appearances when we're on board, then it comes more naturally when we come in contact with others."

Ritcherd nodded and followed Captain Garret and George to the galley where the rest of the crew was seated at a long table. As they entered, Garret spoke loudly with his phony drawl, "Might I introduce the man responsible for providin' us with this lovely vessel t' further our endeavors." He motioned toward Ritcherd. "Cap'n Ritch Buckley."

The men all came to their feet with whoops and hollers of approval. Ritcherd didn't know whether to feel humbled or terrified at the reality of what lay ahead. But he was pleased as the meal progressed to realize that the food was good. He decided that almost anything could be endured if the food was good.

Before the sun went down, Garret walked onto the pier with Ritcherd to survey the results of the painter's work before he was paid. In spite of the hasty job, Ritcherd liked the way he had depicted the huge bird with sunlight behind its wings on the hull of the ship, with *The Phoenix* standing out boldly above it. *The Phoenix* was also painted across the stern.

"I like it," Garret said, tipping his head as he gazed at the image for a long minute. "But it's a little eerie."

"Eerie?" Ritcherd repeated.

Garret hesitated, as if he was wondering whether or not to tell Ritcherd what he was thinking. He finally said, "The ship we lost was the *Falcon Star*."

"Yes, I recall George mentioning that."

"But did he mention that we had a bird painted on the hull?"

"No," Ritcherd said, meeting Garret's eyes. "He didn't mention that."

"Eerie," Garret repeated, turning back to look at the painting of the phoenix. "In a good way, of course. I think it's a good omen."

"That's what I thought," Ritcherd said, and they went back on board together.

Entering the cabin to turn in after a long day, Ritcherd picked up his bag and tossed it onto the smaller bed. "I'm sleeping here, *Cap'n*." He dramatically imitated Garret's drawl. "Like it or not, if you're sailing *my* ship, you're going to have to live with it."

"Aye, Cap'n," Garret said with an exaggerated salute. They laughed together and called it a day.

Ritcherd came out of a deep sleep with a hearty nudge in the ribs. "Hey, Buckley," George's voice broke the stillness. "We're setting sail. I don't think you want to miss this."

Ritcherd bolted out of his bed and into his breeches and boots. He grabbed his shirt and coat, holding the coat in his teeth as he put his shirt on, following George toward the stairwell. George hurried ahead and quickly disappeared. Ritcherd stepped onto the deck and anticipation rippled through him. The sky was lit in brilliant hues of pink, waiting for the sun to peer over the horizon at any moment. Captain Garret stood at the helm, shouting orders to the men, which were seen to with precision and expertise. Ritcherd caught his breath as one sail went up, then another, and another. The ropes were manned so efficiently that the sails seemed to read Garret's mind as he maneuvered the *Phoenix* carefully toward the sea. Once they had cleared the dock, Garret shouted some indecipherable phrase. The ropes were all shifted. The sails drew full and blossomed, and the *Phoenix* soared. Captain Garret let out a loud whoop, followed by a stretch of laughter. It was evident he couldn't suppress the joy he found in the experience. Garret's laughter spread throughout the crew. And Ritcherd couldn't help but appreciate the thrill as he moved toward the bow. He closed his eyes and listened to the sound of the wind whipping at the billowing sheets above him, and the water pushing around the vessel below. Gazing westward as the sun came up at his back, he contemplated his reasons for going to a place where he had once sworn he'd never return.

The thrill of leaving port quickly dwindled into the relentless miles of ocean that had to be crossed. The days dragged by slowly for Ritcherd. Since he'd learned of the opportunity to go and find Kyrah, he'd been completely preoccupied with his preparations to sail. But now there was nothing to do with his time. And the waiting seemed unbearable.

He was impressed with the efficient way the ship was run. Despite the crew being small in number, they were all hardworking and knew their jobs well. And the respect they had for each other was apparent. Captain Garret with his phony accent was a good captain, and his word was heeded without question. Ritcherd appreciated the comfortable relationship they'd fallen into so quickly, but he didn't know how to tell Garret he felt useless. Having the money to pay for this ship didn't seem to have much meaning when he was the only one on board who was idle.

One of Ritcherd's few pastimes was his observation of Garret as he attempted to figure him out. He gradually came to see that Garret was a deep thinker, and much of what he did seemed to have significance. Even the way Garret dressed seemed to make some kind of statement. While he commonly wore the rugged sailor's garb that suited his work and position, he made a habit of changing his clothes when the majority of the work was done for the day. Evenings would often find him wearing an elegant white shirt, topped by a variety of fine waistcoats. The rich fabrics were such a stark contrast to his rugged appearance that they clearly made a statement. But it took Ritcherd several days to figure out what that statement was. It came to him when Garret appeared at supper wearing a high-necked white waistcoat over a shirt of the same color. It looked familiar to Ritcherd, because he owned more than one just like it; it was part of the uniform of a British officer. But Garret's waistcoat had a neatly mended, but conspicuous, tear over the right ribs. When Garret wore that waistcoat, he might as well have been shouting at the top of his lungs: *I killed a British officer!* And wearing that officer's clothes was Garret's way of declaring some kind of triumph. It was the same with his other fine clothes; they looked as if they'd been stolen from aristocrats—probably dead ones. And Garret's wearing them was a mocking declaration that he loathed everything they stood for. But what surprised Ritcherd the most about Garret's silent insinuations was the way he agreed with them. He felt some kind of willful pride as he dug out his own clothes that so much resembled Garret's "triumphant wardrobe." And he started wearing them for the same reasons. The first time he did it, Garret looked him up and down before their eyes met with volumes of silent understanding. Then he smiled.

Life aboard the *Phoenix* quickly fell into a routine, and Ritcherd's fascination with the ship and the sea—and even Garret—soon dwindled. His heart was held captive somewhere in the colonies, and his mind continually concentrated on that destination. For hours every day he stood at the bow, gazing westward, praying with all his heart and soul that he would be guided to her as quickly as possible, and that she would remain safe and strong until they could be together again.

Chapter Ten

Captive Hearts

*K*yrah lost all sense of time, drifting in and out of consciousness. At times it felt as if she had been home only moments ago. At others it seemed forever since she had been with Ritcherd. *Ritcherd!* She cried his name out over and over, as if he might hear her and come flying over the ocean to save her from this nightmare. She was vaguely aware of being repeatedly forced to drink more of the bitter liquid that lured her back into oblivion, where her dreams merged with her memories until nothing seemed real anymore.

When Kyrah finally became wholly conscious, she felt disoriented and afraid. The total absence of light through the little porthole told her it was dark out. Instinctively she wanted nothing more than to resume her shouting and banging on the door, even though she felt certain it would only bring on another visit from the smelly sailors with another dose of obscurity. But she felt so completely weak that she had to wonder how many days she'd been drugged. How long had she gone without food? A deep ache in her stomach suggested it had been far too long.

Hours passed with only silence surrounding her, and the mooring of the ship reminding her continually that she was far from home—and getting farther. Soon after some measure of light appeared through the mottled glass of the porthole, a key turned in the lock and she looked up to see a scruffy boy, not more than twelve, she guessed.

"'Ello," he said. "The cap'n thought ye might o' finally come around. I brought ye somethin' t' eat. But ye'd do well t' take it slow. 'Tis been a while."

Kyrah sat up slowly, fighting to keep her equilibrium. The tray of food he set on the bed beside her smelled good and her stomach growled in response. But she turned her attention to the boy first. "How long . . . have we been at sea?"

"A week t'morrow," he said. He looked hesitant and nervous as he added, "The cap'n said t' tell ye that ye'd best stay quiet, and if ye do, 'e'll see no need to be givin' ye any more o' that stuff. I'd be doin' what 'e says."

Kyrah nodded, not willing to protest. After nearly a week with nothing to eat, they'd made certain she was too weak to cause any trouble. The boy left the cabin, promising to check on her later and bring some water for her to wash up. Kyrah stared at the door long after he left, feeling hopelessness and despair settle around her. There was no way out of this. There was no way back. She was being torn away from her home and the people she loved—perhaps forever.

The smell of the food brought her back to her senses. She forced herself to eat slowly, not wanting to make herself ill. But she was so hungry that she devoured every morsel and wondered how long it would be until they brought her some lunch.

With her hunger eased, the despair settled in more fully. She cried helplessly against the bunk, wondering if she would ever be able to return home. Would she ever see her mother again? And Ritcherd? The very idea provoked tangible pain, and she curled around her arms and sobbed without restraint. When she became too exhausted to cry, she stared toward the little porthole, wondering what Ritcherd might be feeling now. What was he doing? Would he be able to find her? She didn't know herself where she was going. Would he even *try* to find her? Perhaps his mother had somehow convinced him by now that things were better this way. No, she couldn't think that way. She knew he loved her. She knew his heart would be broken by this, just as hers was. But perhaps no matter how much he loved her, he couldn't do anything about it.

Realizing that without hope she would never get through this, Kyrah squeezed her eyes shut and concentrated on an image of Ritcherd in her mind. Just as when he'd been at war, she focused on the memories they had shared, and the strength of the love between them. She prayed that wherever this ship might take her, she would be able to find her way back home.

Days passed while Kyrah drifted in and out of a dazed shock. Her only diversion was the boy bringing her meals and seeing to her needs, with hardly a word spoken between them. In an effort to maintain her sanity, she began playing a game in her mind, where she would repeatedly go over every detail of her home, going through each room. And she did the same with the church ruins. Then she returned again to detailed memories of her childhood, and all of the things she and Ritcherd had done together. Rather than going over the bad times, she would stop when Ritcherd had left for the colonies and start over again with the day they met. She often contemplated the few days they had shared before this horror had begun. Recalling the intimacy that had taken place between them, she could hardly believe it had really happened. It had been so brief and unexpected that it now seemed hazy and dreamlike. The corresponding regret made her force that memory out of her mind. Instead, she concentrated on Ritcherd's declarations of love, his proposal of marriage. He had promised that they would never be apart again, that she would never go without. Tears leaked into her hairline as she wondered if his inability to keep those promises was causing him as much grief as it was her. She thought of her mother and wondered what Sarah would do without her there.

Freshly consumed with despair, she squeezed her eyes shut and prayed with all her heart and soul . . . for peace, for strength, for hope. After praying the better part of one day and into the next, she was overcome with the feeling that Ritcherd *would* do everything in his power to keep his promises. She knew he would see that her mother was cared for. And he would move heaven and earth to find her. She couldn't explain how she knew. She just knew. She thought of Ritcherd telling her that he knew her father had wanted him to take care of her and her mother. Recalling how she'd felt then, the warmth inside her increased. She knew they would be together again. And with her knowledge came tangible hope.

Her hope increased on the rare occasion when she took the diamond jewelry from its hiding place. It was tangible evidence of Ritcherd's love, and having it now gave her the security of knowing that wherever she ended up, she would not be destitute. Even in Ritcherd's absence, the security he offered was still with her. The necklace and earrings were worth a great deal of money—perhaps even enough to get her passage back home. She never dared keep them out for long, fearing she might get unexpected visitors, or she might fall asleep without having them properly concealed.

She was glad that she'd packed her book on birds. But she quickly became tired of it when there were no real birds to look at. Setting it aside, she turned to look at the wall next to her bunk where she had scratched a mark for each meal she had eaten. Kyrah multiplied three meals a day and added the days she had been unconscious before that. Realizing she'd been at sea for more than three weeks, she was surprised to think that she hadn't gone insane. But then if she had, would she know?

Kyrah sat up abruptly when she heard the key in the door. It hadn't been so long since she'd eaten, and no one had ever come in except to bring meals. Her eyes widened in horror when Peter Westman entered the cabin, closing the door behind him. While she had expected to be threatened by smelly sailors, she thought she might have preferred their company. She couldn't imagine what he was doing here, but she felt certain he had something to do with her being in this mess. His alliance with Jeanette Buchanan suddenly made perfect sense.

"Don't look so frightened, my dear," he said with a warm smile that actually seemed genuine. "You should be amazed, as I was, to discover that we ended up on the same ship. Why, I only just discovered this morning that you were aboard. Imagine them keeping you a secret like this."

He stepped toward her and she backed away. "Take this," he said, holding out his hand. Kyrah only stared at his closed fist apprehensively. "Come on, take it," he insisted, then took her hand and pressed a key into it.

"What is it?" she asked.

"It's your freedom, my dear." He smiled again. "It wasn't easy, but when I found out you were here . . . and why, well I—"

"Why am I here?" she asked.

He looked truly surprised. "You mean you don't know?"

"No one's told me anything."

"Well, my dear, it appears there was a misunderstanding concerning your being accused of a theft at Buckley Manor. I spoke with Mrs. Buchanan that night and coerced her into dropping the charges. I couldn't bear to see you involved in such a scandal—whether you'd done it or not."

"I didn't do it."

"That doesn't matter now," he said with a trace of compassion. "The charges were dropped, but apparently someone got their information wrong."

"You mean I was torn away from my home because of a stupid mistake?"

"That's right. But it's all straightened out now. It took a lot of talking, but I've convinced the captain that you are no criminal, and he's allowing you to go free—provided you don't cause any trouble. And you'd best not do that. It could look bad for me after I worked so hard on your behalf."

Kyrah didn't know what to think. There was no reason on earth why she should trust Peter. He had done so much to discredit himself. Yet if what he said was true, she couldn't help being grateful. After being alone for three weeks, even Peter Westman was welcome company—as kind as he was being.

"Would you like some fresh air?" he asked in response to her silence.

"Yes," she said quickly, "I would."

"It's a beautiful day," he smiled and offered her his arm. "Shall we?"

There was a surge of hesitance in Kyrah as she reached out to take Peter's arm. But her desperate need for what he was offering at the moment over-ruled all other emotions. It felt strange to move outside of the cabin. She had lost all comprehension that a world existed past the realms of that tiny room. When fresh air struck her face, she almost laughed out loud. She noticed that Peter smiled, as if her happiness touched him.

They walked the decks of the ship while Peter told her what little he knew about it, and she found it difficult to believe he was the same man she had worked for. Kyrah told herself it was because she'd gone insane in the past three weeks. It was her desperation that made her enjoy his company.

She couldn't help noticing the glances she received from members of the crew as they passed by. They all reminded her of the men who had drugged her. And there was no denying the suggestive implications in their eyes as they took notice of her. She wondered if there were any other women on board.

"Why are *you* aboard this ship?" she asked Peter, keeping her focus on him.

"I own a share of the *Libertatia*," he said proudly, "and I occasionally sail with her—for lack of anything better to do. I'd been planning for quite some time on taking this voyage."

"Where are we going?" she asked timidly, afraid of the answer.

"The colonies," he stated.

"But isn't there a war?" she asked, wishing she hadn't sounded so frightened.

"There is indeed," he told her with a sober expression. "This ship is loaded with supplies to aid the colonists."

Kyrah didn't care why the ship was going there—only that it was. And the prospect frightened her. She understood nothing about wars or being deported for crimes. She only knew, as she looked in every direction and saw nothing but the sea, that she was going to a place completely foreign to her and had no idea how she would ever get home.

"Will this ship be returning to England?" she asked with a hopeful note in her voice.

Peter's inquisitive glance made it evident that he sensed her purpose. He turned away and cleared his throat. "Eventually," he said, "but I believe it will be going to Jamaica and on to South America first."

Kyrah looked out to sea and sighed, knowing that she would have to find another way. Standing against the rail, she thought it strange that she felt a surge of nausea. After weeks of being at sea, she would have thought the fresh air would make her feel better rather than worse. This was the first sign of seasickness she'd had yet.

"Is something wrong?" Peter asked when her hand went to her stomach.

"Just feeling a little queasy," she replied.

"The sea will do it to you," he said with an easy smile.

"Perhaps I should go lie down," she told him and he graciously escorted her back to her cabin, telling her she could come and go as she liked. But he suggested that she keep the cabin locked from the inside—since she was the only woman on board. Peter kissed her hand gallantly, saying, "I'll check on you, my dear. If there's anything you need, I'll do what I can to get it."

"Thank you," she said and watched him leave. After locking the door behind him, she almost wanted to call him back. She *had* lost her mind.

The days passed more quickly with the new diversion that had freed her from her cabin cell. Kyrah was dismayed that the nausea became almost constant, and beyond brief walks to the deck, she spent the majority of her time in bed. She saw Peter two or three times each day. He would occasionally escort her around the deck, or share a meal with her. He was compassionate to her illness, seeming eager to do anything he could to make her comfortable. Kyrah's misery didn't allow her to think too hard on why he was being so kind. She simply had to be grateful that he was. Her humble position left her needing his companionship and assistance greatly. And for the time being, she wasn't going to question it.

Kyrah stopped scratching marks in the wall. Now that she could go on deck each day, there was no need. Lying on her bunk to rest one afternoon, she noticed the marks there and realized it had been more than two weeks since she'd stopped putting them there. Over five weeks at sea, she thought. It seemed like forever. Then it struck her—like a splash of cold water against her face. She asked herself the obvious questions, and came up with one very real answer.

"Ritcherd," she whispered aloud in the privacy of her cabin. She pressed her hand over her belly that was already beginning to swell slightly. "Oh, Ritcherd, my love," she took a sharp breath, "I'm going to have your baby."

While this connection to Ritcherd provoked a surge of joy, the memory of its conception seemed dreamlike and unreal. The timing and circumstances had been all wrong. And now the results would make her situation doubly difficult. If the circumstances were different, if they had been married, nothing could have made her happier than the prospect of having Ritcherd's baby. But as it was, she could only feel afraid.

What would she do? How would she manage alone in a strange country—unmarried and pregnant? In her entire life, she had only known of one woman who gave birth to an illegitimate child. She recalled hearing her parents talking about her, and the tragedy that had befallen her when she'd ended up selling herself on the streets to keep the child fed because her family had disowned her and society had shunned her completely. She had eventually died from some horrible disease, and the child had gone to an orphanage.

Kyrah became preoccupied with the possibilities of horrible things that might happen to her as a result of this. Fear consumed her until she could hardly breathe without feeling the strain. Knowing she would never make it through this if she didn't get hold of herself, she turned her mind to prayer. She had to believe that in spite of the sin she'd committed in the conception of this child, God would be merciful and guide her back into Ritcherd's life. He would see her and the baby cared for, no matter the circumstances. Of that she was certain.

Concentrating on an eventual reunion with Ritcherd, Kyrah tried to remain positive. But an extreme sadness enveloped her as she went to the deck and stood at the stern, looking in the direction where Ritcherd had been left, with many weeks of sea between them. Her heart ached for him: the man she loved, the father of her child. They should have been together. They should have been married by now. It could be months before he found her—if he ever found her. She had no idea how long it would take to arrive in the colonies, and then to return to England—if she could return at all. There was a war going on. As fear overtook her, she squeezed her eyes shut and prayed with everything inside of her that Ritcherd would find her before it was too late. Hope gradually trickled into her mind as she felt the fear relent. Perhaps God was with her after all.

"You look sad, my dear," Peter said as he stood beside her. Kyrah made no reply. "Are you homesick?" he asked.

"I've been homesick since I came aboard," she stated.

"Then it must be something else."

Again Kyrah was silent, biting her lip to avoid becoming emotional. When that didn't work, she pressed a hand over her mouth and turned away. She was startled to feel Peter's hands at her shoulders, but she didn't feel the repulsion that she might have expected. She had to wonder if she had somehow misjudged him as she found herself crying in his arms.

"There, there, my dear. Everything will be fine. I'll not let anything happen to you."

She wondered what he would think if he knew the truth. She was certain he'd not be so compassionate. He lifted her chin and smiled pleasantly at her, leaving her bewildered by the different sides she had seen of him.

"Come, my dear," he said kindly, "let's take a little walk. I'm certain you'll feel better."

Kyrah put her hand over his arm, wondering where the *Libertatia* would take her life—and the life of Ritcherd's child.

Days continued to pass while Kyrah spent more time on deck, finding that the fresh air eased her symptoms. Preoccupied with her dilemma, Kyrah had learned to ignore the men on board. Their brash conversations and lewd glances disgusted her, but she did her best to avoid them, and she never went out of her cabin alone after dark.

One particular evening she went below deck just as the sun was going down, so tired that she only wanted to crawl into bed and sleep through the remainder of the journey. Moving slowly down the narrow hallway to her cabin, she was distracted by her thoughts until she came face to face with a despicable-looking man with foul breath, greasy hair, and a huge gold ring in his ear.

"Excuse me," she said and pushed her way past him, repulsed by the way she was forced to brush against him because the hall was so narrow. Without looking back, she went quickly to her cabin and turned the key in the door to open it. She cried out when a large hand, connected to the man she'd just passed, came beside her and pushed it open. Kyrah tried to scream, but the same hand abruptly clamped over her mouth and the door was kicked shut.

"Ye're a pretty one," he rasped, and she could feel his foul breath against her face. "But then, I don't care much whether ye are or not."

He laughed deep in his throat and Kyrah squirmed helplessly, almost wishing that she were dead. Her fighting seemed futile and she almost gave up. Squeezing her eyes shut, Ritcherd's image came clearly to her mind, and her thoughts went to the child she carried. Praying for strength, she moved enough to bite the hand over her mouth, then she screamed and took advantage of the distraction to send her knee into his groin. He moaned and began cursing, but he didn't give her time to get away. Kyrah began praying for the strength to endure this and survive—for the sake of the baby. She screamed again in startled relief when the door flew open. A gunshot rang out, and the filthy sailor landed face down on the floor of her cabin.

Peter entered the room and threw the gun on the bed. He murmured something under his breath as he rolled the dead man over with a hefty kick, and Kyrah's stomach lurched.

"Are you all right?" Peter asked, moving quickly to her side.

Kyrah nodded adamantly but closed her eyes, trying to shut out the horrifying image of the dead man in front of her. Peter's arm came comfortingly around her shoulders and he whispered with reassurance, "It's all over now. I can assure you it won't happen again. There's nothing like a dead man to set an example for these brutes. Did he hurt you?"

Kyrah shook her head. Without opening her eyes, she uncovered her mouth enough to say, "I'm fine. Just get him out of here. I want to be alone."

When the body had been removed and the blood mopped off the floor, Kyrah found herself alone with frightening images that accompanied her into sleep. She awoke in the night, cold and frightened, calling out Ritcherd's name, certain that her life couldn't possibly get any worse. She was convinced she would go mad before she ever found the opportunity to put all of this behind her. But thoughts of her child made her determined to remain sane and healthy.

She would survive this. She just had to! She only prayed that if she couldn't find her way back to Ritcherd, he would somehow be able to find her. Without him, she couldn't even fathom how horrible her life could be.

"We'll be arriving in just a few days," Peter said to Kyrah the following morning as they took their usual stroll. She hadn't wanted to leave the security of her cabin, but he'd insisted. And now she was glad for the fresh air.

"How long have we been at sea?" she asked.

"Nearly six weeks," he said. "We've made good time."

Kyrah was glad to know so that she could estimate the expected arrival of the baby.

"There is something we should perhaps discuss," Peter said with caution.

"What?" Kyrah asked blandly.

"I'm not certain you realize how difficult it will be when we arrive, for a girl of your . . . inexperience. This is a harsh new world we're going to."

"What are you getting at?" she asked, not liking the way he'd pegged her own fears so accurately.

"I'm concerned for you, my dear," he said kindly. "You are free, but I wonder what kind of trouble your freedom might get you into."

"Are you trying to tell me something, Peter?" She had a feeling he was trying to say something she didn't want to hear.

He took a deep breath and looked down almost nervously, but Kyrah sensed something slightly phony about it. Or perhaps he was simply nervous. "I would like you to marry me," he said quickly.

Kyrah couldn't believe it. She was caught so off-guard that all she could do was turn and walk away.

"Wait," he said, taking hold of her arm. "You've got to think practically, my dear," he said. "A lone woman in a new country. What will you do?"

"I'll manage," she stated without looking at him.

"With what? You have no money. And worse, you have no idea what kind of lowlife you'll be coming up against."

"Perhaps I do," she said, looking directly at him.

"Kyrah," his tone was scolding, "if it's Ritcherd Buchanan that keeps you from consenting, you'd better think again."

"Why?" she asked, feeling her heart race at the mere mention of his name.

"Can't you see that you're better off without him? He's as pompous and arrogant as his mother."

"That's not true," she insisted.

"I think you've seen it all from a very distorted perspective," he said. "And I hate to be the one to set you straight. I don't want to see you hurting, but you've got to face the truth."

"Ritcherd loves me."

Peter laughed as if her statement was terribly amusing. "I'm certain he's told you that many times," he said, "but did he also tell you the real reason he was going to marry you?"

Kyrah waited, silently daring him to discredit Ritcherd. "I know for a fact," he began, "that he told his mother he would marry you just to prove his point."

Kyrah turned away quickly, convincing herself it wasn't true. "You can hide from it if you want, but one day you'll realize it's the truth. You know how bitter he is against Jeanette. He'd do anything just to spite her, and there was nothing that got to her more than his attention to you. He could have had any woman in the county, and you know that as well as I do. Face the facts, Kyrah. However painful, you've got to know. He was using you to prove his point. I don't doubt that he would have married you, but I wonder how loyal he might have remained. I also doubt he'd go to the trouble of trying to find you, considering the circumstances. There were many young ladies in Cornwall that would be much more suitable to his lifestyle."

"It's all a lie," Kyrah said, her back still turned. "I've known Ritcherd for years. I know he loves me."

"How long have you been around him since your station in life was so dramatically lowered?"

"We know whose fault that was," she spat.

"Now don't go blaming me for your problems, Kyrah. Like it or not, one day you're going to have to accept that your father put your security on the table in a card game. And when he lost that, he took the cowardly way out and left you to fend for yourself. And now you're avoiding the truth about Ritcherd because you don't want to face it. You and I are alike, Kyrah. You don't belong in their aristocratic world. You belong with me. We come from the same background. I've known it ever since I first saw you. Admittedly, I'm not very good at expressing such things, and I know I was difficult at times . . . but I'm sorry about that. I wish we could just start over and . . ." His nervousness increased and she turned to look at him, amazed at the apparent sincerity in his eyes. "I know your feelings for Ritcherd are really none of my business, but . . . what I'm trying to say is . . ." He paused a long moment and added, "I love you, Kyrah."

Kyrah was so stunned she couldn't even speak. Could he possibly be genuine? Whether or not he was, it didn't change where she stood. "I don't love you," she said flatly.

He didn't appear too distressed or surprised. "Love can grow with time," he said. "But whether you ever love me or not, I know one thing for certain. One day you will realize that what I say is true, and you will want to be my wife. I'll be patient. We'll see what being alone in a port town will do to your pride."

Peter left Kyrah standing on the deck, feeling lost and alone—and afraid. However much she didn't want to admit it, she feared Peter might be right. She felt certain enough that Ritcherd loved her. But the rest was true. She didn't belong in his world. She was only a servant girl. And being pregnant and unmarried didn't help her situation any. She wondered how many servants had been taken advantage of by aristocratic men, then left to bear their illegitimate children on the premise of good intentions. She rubbed the chill from her arms as she recalled Peter once saying: *He'll use you and leave you to suffer in the end.* She tried to tell herself that Ritcherd's love would be there for her when all was said and done, but her present situation made it difficult to feel confident in that respect.

Trying to weigh her feelings on the same scale as the facts, Kyrah's confusion only deepened. But one thing was certain: if Ritcherd didn't find her soon, she would be forced to make some very difficult decisions.

She finally convinced herself that she could do nothing more than take one day at a time and do the best she could—keeping the child's well-being foremost in importance. Forcing all else to the back of her mind, she began watching for the colonies to come into view.

Ritcherd became frustrated and increasingly tense with his preoccupation of finding Kyrah. Unable to do anything more about it for the time being, he made up his mind to find something to keep him occupied—for the sake of his sanity. He tried to find a way to help with the work, but everything was run so efficiently, he felt hardly needed. Still, he did his best to help here and there, in spite of his awkwardness with the limited use of his right hand. The men were cordial for the most part, but seemed hesitant to say too much.

He began to enjoy the time of day when the work was completed. The men gathered in groups where they'd talk and laugh, while Ritcherd remained a silent observer. He found every one of them to be colorful and unique, and began to enjoy their sailor's chatter and exchange of stories. He watched for hours while they played dice or cards, betting only with seashells or insignificant paraphernalia, which left the games purely for entertainment and to pass the time. He wasn't surprised to note that George was usually the center of the fun. He was always joking and teasing, and he seemed to know each of the sailors well as individuals.

While Ritcherd was trying to pick up the names of the men he was sailing with, he noticed that Patrick was something of an assistant to Captain Garret, though it seemed more like they were closer as friends than anyone else in the group, rather than Patrick's having any distinction of rank or knowledge of sailing. Patrick was quiet and a bit intimidating by his stature, and his hair was usually hanging in his eyes. But often during their relaxation time, he would perform little magic tricks. He had no props, but used everyday items that were handy. As casually as breathing, Patrick would often make eating utensils, money, scarves, or other odd things disappear or turn into something else. Ritcherd knew it was just illusion and sleight of hand, but he was fascinated by the ease with which he did it, making it seem almost real. He noted too how it helped to keep the men's spirits high. This group was far happier than he would have expected from men at sea. Ritcherd's previous journeys to and from the colonies had been difficult and discouraging for him. He'd mostly kept to himself, but he'd been keenly aware of discontentment and contention. On the *Phoenix*, however, these men had no apparent animosities between them. Ritcherd figured that for whatever reason each of them was involved in this cause, they were making the most of it. He wondered if the majority of them were simply patriots, or if they were doing it for sport. Observing them more closely, he began to wonder how many of them might be aristocrats in disguise, as he and George were. Or were they from as diverse backgrounds as they seemed to be?

Captain Garret was heavily involved with social life aboard the *Phoenix*. And the more Ritcherd observed him, the more he liked him. He was amazed at the way Garret could appear so menacing and intimidating—unless he smiled. His smile always gave him away immediately. But the men did what he asked of them without question, and he doubted that their homage had anything to do with the fear he was capable of instilling in others. Their respect for him was evident. And no matter how Ritcherd looked at Garret, he had to admire him. He had a straightforward, light-hearted way of dealing with every situation that came up. Garret could be confronted with any problem, however large or small, and calmly take it for what it was worth and solve it.

The only thing Garret didn't take in stride was the way George Morley frequently burst into the captain's cabin to get his attention. Garret would rarely, if ever, show that he was startled. But he would inevitably get angry and tell George if he did that again, he was going to have him walk the plank. With Ritcherd sharing the captain's cabin, he was usually around when the unexpected appearances occurred. But it had taken several days before he realized it was all a joke. Garret never cracked a smile while George was still in the room. But gradually Ritcherd learned how to read Garret's silent amusement in the situation, and he could see that Garret and George knew each other well.

Gradually Ritcherd became more comfortable around the men, but he still felt very much on the outside. In spite of his changed appearance and his efforts to learn to speak as they did, he wondered if he simply didn't fit in. Or perhaps it was his solemn mood that kept him severed from the group. Whatever it was, for the first time in his life, Ritcherd felt unaccepted. But his humility caused him introspection rather than any kind of resentment. He wondered if he might have gained some minor insight as to how Kyrah might have felt in facing her struggles all alone.

Ritcherd spent a great deal of time holding Kyrah's brooch, fingering the clasp. It challenged him. He remembered well his humility when he'd had to admit he couldn't unfasten the simple clasp, and he wanted to be able to use his right hand. He worked on it each day until he became frustrated and stuffed it back into his pocket. But the following day would find him at it again.

"What happened to that arm?" Garret asked in his normal voice while Ritcherd toyed with the brooch one afternoon. It was only when they were alone together that he didn't use the sailor's drawl. Besides himself, it seemed that only George and Patrick were aware that he could talk any other way.

Ritcherd glanced at Garret, who sat casually across the table in the cabin. He was surprised by the question. Although they'd been at sea for weeks and had gotten along well, there had been little conversation beyond necessary exchanges.

"I was shot," Ritcherd replied simply.

"War?" Garret asked.

"Yes."

"You must feel a little vulnerable without full use of a right arm," Garret added.

Ritcherd fired a defensive glare toward Garret. But he was apparently unaffected as he added, "What I mean is, could you shoot a gun or use a sword if you had to?"

"I doubt it," Ritcherd replied, his tone bitter.

"It's not very smart to be traveling on a ship carrying illegal goods, and not be able to defend yourself."

Ritcherd watched Garret closely for a long moment. He was so matter-of-fact that Ritcherd couldn't possibly disagree or get angry. He wondered now if their former lack of conversation beyond the day they'd met had been to allow Ritcherd to become comfortable enough around him that sensitive issues could be broached. Whatever his motives might be, Ritcherd had no choice but to say, "There's not a lot to be done about that, now is there."

"That all depends on how you look at it," Garret smiled in a familiarly devious way. "I'm left-handed, you know."

Ritcherd hadn't even noticed. But as he absorbed what Garret was saying, he felt something flicker inside of him. Still, he said nothing.

Garret continued. "I've got several left-handed firearms. I had them custom made. You're welcome to use them. And . . . we could have you fencing like a pro before we hit the colonies—if you're willing."

Ritcherd didn't even have to think about it. The thought of regaining some of the confidence he'd lost in that respect seemed like an answer to a prayer that he'd never even cared to voice. On top of that, the prospect of having something to fill his time and give purpose to his empty hours made Garret's offer doubly inviting.

"I'm willing," he said. "The question is, are you—"

"Yo ho ho," George shouted as the door of the cabin flew open without warning. It closed just as quickly and he was gone.

"I'll 'ave yer 'ead for that one!" Garret shouted.

"Aye, Cap'n," George called back as his voice trailed down the hallway.

"Wretched sailors," Garret mumbled under his breath, but Ritcherd could see the subtle smirk teasing at the corners of his mouth. "You were saying?"

"I was just wondering if you're up to the task."

Garret grinned. "It would be more of a pleasure than you could possibly imagine."

Ritcherd chuckled. "You're in one of those humble-the-aristocrat moods."

Garret came to his feet. "At least I don't shoot them—not the ones who are on my side, at least."

Together they laughed and Ritcherd thought that beyond the continual heartache he felt in longing for Kyrah, things were looking up.

Chapter Eleven

Captain, Captain

 itcherd felt awkward with the pistol in his left hand, but Garret was patient and had a way of making Ritcherd be more patient with himself. The rifle was awkward as well, but Garret gave him plenty of time to just get a feel for holding the firearms and maneuvering them.

"And when you're up to it," Garret said, "we'll do a little target throwing over the water."

"Really?" Ritcherd said, sliding his right hand over the stock of a rifle with craftsmanship more beautiful than he'd ever seen. He wished that he could feel the intricate carvings with the fingers of his right hand.

As if Garret sensed his discouragement, he said, "You learned to eat with your left hand, didn't you?"

"Enough to keep from starving."

"And you learned to write as well?"

"Not that anyone can read it," Ritcherd replied.

"Give it time," Garret answered matter-of-factly. "You were forced to learn how to do the things you needed to survive. You need to know how to fight to survive. Give it time."

Garret proved to be right. In just a few days Ritcherd gained a certain amount of confidence in using both the pistol and the rifle. When his work was done, Garret took Ritcherd to the rail of the ship, where Patrick was waiting with a crate full of pieces of broken dishes and pots. Ritcherd was a little unsettled by the memory they provoked regarding his mother's china. He was glad for Garret's explanation, which distracted him.

"I get them from a potter in Jamaica," he said. "He appreciates getting a fair price for his failures and accidents. And I make good use of them."

Ritcherd watched in amazement as Patrick tossed the pieces of clay into the air and Garret hit nine out of ten with the pistol, and ten out of ten with the rifle. He then handed the rifle over to Ritcherd. In response to his hesitance, Garret said in a voice that only he could hear, "A ship is always safe in the harbor, but that's not what a ship is made for."

"What?" Ritcherd asked, not catching the connection.

Garret leaned closer and added, "If you don't try, you'll never learn." He motioned with his head to indicate the small crowd that had gathered. As if he'd read Ritcherd's mind, he said, "They all know you were wounded. Just get on with it."

Ritcherd scowled. "And do they also know I'm a turncoat?"

"Of course," Garret said. "But they like you anyway. Get on with it."

Ritcherd missed the first five shots. But he hit the sixth and marveled at how it made him feel when the men cheered. He missed the next three, then hit four in a row.

"Now the pistol," Garret said, trading Ritcherd firearms. When he'd missed more than ten times, he was ready to give it up. But Garret wouldn't let him. "Ye're not eatin' until ye 'it at least one."

"It's a good thing I'm not shootin' what we'll 'ave for supper, eh?" Ritcherd said and the men laughed.

"Blast it t' bits, Buckley!" one of them shouted and the rest echoed his cheer. Ritcherd hit the next three shots.

"Very good," Garret drawled, then he motioned the other men forward and gave them each a turn. Ritcherd could see that this was a typical exercise to keep their skills honed. He was amazed at the proficiency of these men and recalled George saying the crew was not many in number, but they were quality.

That evening while Ritcherd was sitting at the table in the cabin, playing with Kyrah's brooch, Garret tossed a leather-bound book down in front of him.

"What is this?" Ritcherd asked.

"It's a journal," Garret said. "Take a look."

Ritcherd opened the book and thumbed through it, stating the obvious. "The pages are blank."

"That's because you haven't written anything on them yet." Ritcherd lifted his brows. Garret just set a pen and inkwell in front of him. "You should be recording your experiences at sea. It keeps the head clear. And if you don't feel like writing, do it anyway. It'll improve your penmanship and strengthen the muscles in that hand. And you're going to need all the strength you can get if you intend to use a sword with any skill whatsoever." He sat down and added, "You've made some progress with shooting, although some daily practice would be to our benefit."

The way he said it made Ritcherd wonder if Garret considered his inability to fight a hazard to himself and his crew. If for no other reason, Ritcherd was determined to prove that he could master this.

"Fencing, however, will not be so easy," Garret added. "Now start writing, and we'll get at it tomorrow."

Garret left the room. Ritcherd stared at the first blank page of his journal for more than an hour before he found words in his head that he felt prone to put on paper. And it was another twenty minutes before he worked up the courage to dip the pen and begin. What little handwriting he had done since his injury had looked worse than the scrawling of a four-year-old. And the first few pages that Ritcherd wrote were no better. But as days passed, Ritcherd could see a gradual improvement in the appearance of his written words. And he was beginning to understand what Garret had meant when he said it cleared the head. As he became more comfortable with his journal, he began to pour his feelings into it—feelings he couldn't express to a bunch of hard-nosed sailors.

In correlation with his writing skills, Ritcherd gained skill with the firearms a little every day. And each day Garret had him working with a sword in his left hand. Ritcherd appreciated the way Garret could remind him to be humble when it was necessary without forcing him to lose his pride or become defensive.

"After using your right hand all your life," he said when Ritcherd hit a particularly discouraging moment, "it's going to take perseverance to use your left with any kind of skill. Were you any good with your right hand?"

"Good enough," Ritcherd admitted. "I could hold my own."

"Well, that's a start," Garret said, and they got back to work.

The long, straight-bladed cutlass Garret had given him was heavier than what he'd been used to, but Garret told him that was what pirates fought with.

"Are we pirates?" Ritcherd asked.

"In a way, I suppose," Garret said as if the thought amused him. "Although pirates are a dying breed. Still, we'll pretend to be whatever we need to be to get the job done."

Ritcherd gradually became accustomed to the weapon and found that he was gaining the strength to maneuver it rather well. Garret had told him it carried more threat if one learned to handle it to its best advantage. And with time, Ritcherd could see what he meant.

When maneuvering around the furniture in the captain's cabin became difficult, Garret had a place cleared in one of the holds below deck where Ritcherd could practice to his heart's content, away from the crew's curiosity. He spent time there on his own every day while Garret was busy at other things, and Garret also spent a couple of hours with him each day, coaching him through his skills. Ritcherd was amazed at how quickly the days flew now that he had purpose to fill his time. He began to look forward to writing in his journal each day, where he poured out his love for Kyrah and his determination to make right all that he had wronged on her behalf.

After several days of hard work below deck with the sword, Garret decided it was time for some action. He cleverly muted the ends of two swords, but Ritcherd was disconcerted when Garret made it clear that their little fencing match would take place on deck. The men's interest was roused immediately, and they all gathered around, apparently enjoying this opportunity to see the two captains engaged in this lighthearted match.

At first Ritcherd knew that Garret was going easy. But as Ritcherd began to maneuver the sword with more confidence, Garret gradually pushed more skill into his offense. Ritcherd was impressed with the sleek way that Garret fenced with his right hand casually behind his back, moving his feet with natural fluency. He felt good as he started to loosen up, and it occurred to him that he had lost a great deal more confidence than he'd wanted to admit when he'd lost use of his right arm. Not only in fighting, but in every aspect of his life. As he felt that confidence surging back into him, he started to enjoy the playful match. He actually laughed as he momentarily caught Garret off guard and almost gained the advantage.

Ritcherd knew immediately when Garret let his full strength and skill come forward. He concentrated with everything he had on staying in control, and he felt sweat rising. But still he enjoyed it. Even when Garret's sword came against Ritcherd's neck, he laughed out loud as Garret shouted, "This cap'n wins round one, eh?"

They each stepped back to catch their breath before they lifted their swords in a unified gesture to begin a new match. The men moved back to create more room as the footwork increased, and they circled around each other, while Garret occasionally let out a whoop to indicate that he was thoroughly enjoying himself. Ritcherd's sword was swept strategically from his hand, and Captain Garret won round two—and round three. But he kept his lighthearted attitude that left no room for Ritcherd to become defensive.

They both took a few minutes to stretch their arms and breathe deeply before round four began. Ritcherd felt fresh life surging through him and realized that even having lost three rounds, he felt like more of a man than he had since he'd awakened in a hospital bed with his arm half gone. The fourth round became intense with a match of skill, and it seemed to go on forever. When Ritcherd turned quickly then lunged forward, Garret landed on the ground with a sword against his chest. He looked completely surprised but laughed boisterously as he relaxed on the deck. Ritcherd threw down the sword and joined in the laughter as he reached out his hand to help the captain back to his feet. George joined in with a "Yo ho ho!" And the sailors all broke into laughter.

"Well," Garret said, removing his glove to wipe the sweat from his face, "I think we've accomplished what we set out t' do."

"'Ave we?" Ritcherd asked. "I was killed three times before I got ye down."

Garret looked thoughtful then shouted, "Patrick!"

"Aye, sir." The magician stepped forward.

Garret picked up his sword and fingered it thoughtfully for a moment before he handed it to Patrick, who was near Garret's height, but much more muscular.

"Th' cap'n needs t' fight a right 'anded man," Garret said and stepped back, holding out his arms elaborately to indicate that they proceed.

Ritcherd sensed a seriousness come over Garret, and he looked skeptically at his new opponent, who was tying his hair back to keep it from inhibiting him.

When Patrick was ready, his sword was returned to him. Ritcherd was about to bend and retrieve his own when Patrick lifted it skillfully with his toe and it sailed through the air, right into Ritcherd's hand. By the time Ritcherd got the sword into position, Patrick was *en garde,* facing him with an amused intensity in his eyes. Ritcherd took his stance, and a hush fell over the men as they began.

It took only seconds for Ritcherd to realize that this was completely different. Fencing a man who used the same hand left him working opposite his maneuvers as he faced him. But now his opponent was fighting on the same side, with the opposite hand, leaving Ritcherd at a great disadvantage. He knew Patrick was going easy on him, and Ritcherd wondered what maneuvers he could pull to even the odds a bit before Patrick brought forth a skill that Ritcherd already sensed was remarkable. He moved with eloquent ease into each lunge and thrust, fencing with intensity and striking rhythm. It took almost no time for Ritcherd to be defeated.

"I believe we've 'ad enough fun t'day," Garret said immediately. "If none o' ye can find anythin' t' do, then swab th' decks."

The men all laughed as they dispersed, and Ritcherd assumed it was a joke among them. He stood solemnly watching Garret, sensing expectancy in him, while Patrick pulled the string from his hair and shook it down, giving the sword back to Garret.

"I'm impressed with your skill," Ritcherd said to Patrick, who smiled humbly.

"Cap'n Garret taught me t' fence," he said. "I never 'eld a sword afore I started sailin' with 'im."

"But it didn't take long for the student t' outdo the teacher," Garret grinned. "This man's a natural."

"So I see," Ritcherd replied, and there was a moment of silence. "Will ye teach me?" Ritcherd asked Patrick, who exchanged a glance with Garret.

"Aye," he smiled wryly. "I'd be 'appy t' 'elp ye what I can."

"T'morrow," Garret said, slapping Patrick on the shoulder. "We'll start t'morrow."

"Aye, Cap'n," Patrick replied, then nodded toward Ritcherd and went below deck.

"He's good," Ritcherd said.

"Yes, he is," Garret replied. "And he's a good man. You'll like him."

The two captains walked along the rail while the men went about their duties. Ritcherd sensed there was something Garret wanted to say to him by the way he stuck close by as Ritcherd came to his comfortable spot at the bow. He leaned his forearms on the rail and looked westward. Garret stood near him in the same manner, but when they remained in comfortable silence, Ritcherd just gazed out over the water, enjoying the company of this man that he admired more and more.

Garret finally broke the silence by saying, "How would you describe the sea, Captain Buckley?"

"Is this a trick question?"

"No," Garret laughed. "It's just . . . food for thought."

"How would *you* describe the sea?" Ritcherd countered.

"No, that's not fair. My answer might influence yours. I want to know how *you* would describe the sea."

Ritcherd gazed out over the endless stretch of blue and contemplated his answer carefully. Through their weeks at sea he had seen the water take on many different moods, and he searched for words that would summarize his feelings. Garret didn't seem impatient. He seemed to expect his question to be taken seriously.

"Provocative," he finally said and ventured to explain. "It has an alluring quality that . . . you want to get hold of but you can't quite grasp."

"Very good," Garret said. "And I must say that I agree on that point. What else?"

Ritcherd inhaled the salt air deeply and said, "It's breathtaking. Every time you turn around, you see something about it that takes your breath away all over again."

"Well said." Garret turned his back to the rail and leaned his elbows behind him.

"This isn't my first time at sea, you know," Ritcherd said.

"I know. I would assume, your being a *redcoat* and all, that you were shipped to the colonies and put on the battlefront, then you were probably shipped back when you became a liability."

"That's right. On the voyage out I didn't pay much attention to anything. I was too depressed; oblivious, I guess. And on the way home, I was holed up in my cabin, too full of infection to get out of bed. So," he added, taking another deep breath, "this is the first time I've really . . . felt the sea."

"And what do you think?" Garret asked.

"I already told you."

"Tell me more."

"Well," Ritcherd chuckled, "I don't think it's in my blood the way it's obviously in yours. But . . . I feel like it's trying to teach me something. It's . . . challenging! That's the word. It would never let a man get bored for too long, because it would continually put a challenge before him."

"How right you are," Garret said. "And again, I agree. In fact," he pointed north, "you see those clouds?" Ritcherd nodded. "We're in for a storm. You find new meaning in the word 'challenging' when you ride a storm at sea."

Ritcherd felt momentarily afraid from the intensity in Garret's eyes. He glanced away, wondering how Kyrah might whether the storm if the ship she was sailing on had less than a week's headway.

"It's interesting," Garret said, "I've asked a lot of people to describe the sea. No one's ever echoed my feelings the way you just did."

Ritcherd turned back to meet his eyes. "Is that supposed to mean something?"

"I don't know, Ritcherd," he said. "What do you think it means?"

Ritcherd chuckled. "I'm afraid I'm not the philosopher that you are."

"Am I?" Garret snorted dubiously. "Not likely. I just . . ."

"Think very deep," Ritcherd said. "But that's all right. I like it. It reminds me of . . ." Ritcherd stopped himself from saying Kyrah's name. It wasn't that he didn't feel he could tell Garret about her. Perhaps he was more afraid that he couldn't talk about it without falling apart. The pain associated with thoughts of her was too deep and too fresh.

"You know," Garret said, turning back to look over the water, "I got into this describing the sea thing many years ago. My grandfather asked me to do that very thing when I was approaching adulthood. He was one of the few people in my life who really knew me. He told me that my views of the sea might change through the years, as I matured and learned to understand myself more fully. And now I know he was right. He also told me that . . . when I found a woman who made me feel the way the sea made me feel, I should take hold of her and never let go—even if it meant giving up the sea."

Ritcherd watched Garret closely, wondering if the man knew more about him than he was letting on. Or were Garret's words just stirring something in him that he found too poignant and ironic to think about too deeply? Garret went on to say, "If you turn that around a bit, you'll find that the way you just described the sea would perfectly describe the woman that could make you happy."

Garret sighed and looked away. His voice picked up that gravelly quality as he added, "Is that the way she is, Ritcherd?"

"Who?" Ritcherd retorted, wishing it hadn't sounded so defensive.

"The woman who is at this very moment somewhere west of the *Phoenix*. Is she provocative, breathtaking, challenging? Does she have an alluring quality that you want to get hold of but can't quite grasp? Every time you turn around, do you see something about her that takes your breath away all over again? Is she capable of keeping you from getting bored because she continually puts a challenge before you?"

A knot gathered in Ritcherd's throat that made it impossible for him to speak. Garret tossed one more quick glance his direction before he walked away. But his words echoed over and over in Ritcherd's mind. Tears coursed down his face and dried quickly as the salt-tinged wind blew them away. How had Garret managed to so perfectly describe Kyrah, and everything he loved about her? But he hadn't. He'd only repeated what Ritcherd had said. But how had he known there was a woman? Ritcherd hadn't said a word—not even to George. Was he so transparent? Gazing out to sea in a way that had become habitual, he wondered if his longing and heartache were so readily evident.

Not willing to wonder, he answered the unspoken challenge that Garret had left hanging in the air. He found Garret in the cabin, bent over his book work. He glanced up and seemed to sense that Ritcherd had something to say. Ritcherd tossed his gloves to the table. His voice came firm and steady. "Yes. She is. She's all that and so much more. And next time you want to know something, just ask me. Don't lure it out of me like some fisherman with a baited hook."

Garret stretched out his legs and crossed his booted ankles. He folded his arms over his chest and sighed. "I think you misunderstand me, Ritch. When I need information that concerns me or my crew, I ask. When I am concerned about a friend, I might not know how to ask. I have no reason to believe that you know me well enough to trust me when it comes to personal matters. I just wanted to let you know that it's not necessary to carry your burden alone—whatever that burden may be. But of course, that's up to you. Forgive me if I was out of line."

Ritcherd sighed and sat down. "There's nothing to forgive," he said more humbly. He contemplated a way to tell Garret that his concern was appreciated—and perhaps needed. But the supper bell rang and he followed Garret silently to the galley. When the meal was finished, Garret was called away to deal with some matter concerning supplies. Ritcherd found himself again at the rail, pondering the things he was learning on this journey that he'd never considered possible.

He was startled from his thoughts when George came up beside him. "That was quite a match," he said.

"Yes it was," Ritcherd half-smiled.

"Whose idea was it . . . to do all this left-handed stuff?"

"Garret brought it up."

"He's a good man, you know."

Ritcherd looked him in the eye and had to ask, "Have you been talking to him in the last few hours?"

"No, but the tension between the two of you at supper was a bit obvious. Now, don't change the subject. As I said, he's a good man."

"Yes, I know," Ritcherd admitted. "I've gained a great deal of respect for him since we've been on board."

"Why is it that you share a cabin when there are several others empty?"

"That was his idea, too. He said the captain's cabin was huge compared to the others, and if one of us slept elsewhere, the men would see a differentiation of authority. I told him that he was the captain who needed the authority, but he insisted we were partners and the men would see it that way."

George chuckled. "Garret knows human nature well. Once you look past his brusque exterior, you can't help but find a man worth knowing."

"Why are we talking like this when we've hardly talked at all since we set sail . . . and about Garret?"

"We haven't talked for two reasons," George said in his light way. "Either I've been busy," he smirked and added, "I'm just one o' th' mates. Or," he went on in his normal voice, "as the men say, 'Captain Buckley looks like he'd rather be left alone. He's got something on his mind.'"

Ritcherd looked seaward. So, he *was* transparent. "All right, we're talking now. Why about Garret?"

"You and Garret are partners," he said, "but I wonder if you've really thought about what that means. I wonder if you know anything about him. I doubt he'd tell you himself."

"He seems to know a great deal about me, and I didn't tell him."

"Well, I told him very little, if that's what you're implying. Garret is a perceptive man. He puts pieces together. That's why he's good at what he does."

Ritcherd sighed. "I'm sorry, George. I need to learn to not take my anger out on you—or Garret."

"Apology accepted. Now stop changing the subject. I think it's time you knew what kind of man Garret really is."

"What is there to know that matters? I like him for what he is."

"He's a baronet."

Ritcherd tried not to look surprised, but it truly took him off guard. He'd noticed right off his refined speech and manner. But a title? Suddenly the entire situation became terribly amusing. He laughed as he said, "He's an *aristocrat?*"

"Hush!" George insisted. "It's a secret. He doesn't like people to know."

"Then why did you tell me?"

"Because this partnership he's making such a point to clarify needs to be understood. You need to know that he is, in every sense of the word, your equal—and very much like you. Things like that are important to know when life-and-death situations come up."

Ritcherd looked into George's eyes and felt another layer of reality settle into place. What they were about was no game. While George had his attention, he added, "Let me just make a suggestion, Buckley. You don't need to tell me what's going on, but if you're smart, you'll tell Garret. You need him. And he needs you. That's all I have to say."

George slapped Ritcherd on the shoulder, as he had come to realize was a common gesture among these men. He walked casually away, leaving Ritcherd with more food for thought than he knew what to do with.

"Hey, Buckley," George called back suddenly, startling Ritcherd. "Yo ho ho!"

Ritcherd gave him a sarcastic salute and George walked lightly away.

By the time Ritcherd figured out that he should likely take George's advice and have a good, long talk with Garret, storm clouds were gathering and the wind had picked up considerably. The crew bustled around, obviously well versed on their preparations. They all seemed confident enough. But Ritcherd couldn't help feeling unnerved by the dark threat in the deepening clouds.

He found Garret near the main mast, pointing upward and giving instructions to one of the men. Ritcherd waited for him to finish before he asked, "Is there something I can do?"

"Everything's under control," he said as if the previous exchange between them had never occurred. "The best thing to do is stay in the cabin, hold on tight, and let the storm ride. When it's over I'll put you to work. I'm certain we'll have a mess then."

At first Ritcherd did as he was told, not wanting to admit that this situation was unnerving. He was reminded of his feelings going into battle, knowing that danger was imminent—and beyond his control. But as the storm dragged on, he began to wonder what Garret was doing through all of this. He managed to make his way down the hall and up the stairs, feeling like a weed being tossed on the wind as the ship lurched back and forth. He emerged onto the deck only to be slapped with an onslaught of water, a combination of pelting rain and salt spray. Captain Garret was at the helm with Patrick at his side. As always, he appeared calm and in control, doing his best to guide the *Phoenix* safely over the violent waves.

Ritcherd knew absolutely nothing about getting a ship through a storm, but it was evident that the members of the crew each had a position and a job to do. Ritcherd wasn't going to bother asking Garret what he might do. But he wasn't going to be the only one below deck while everyone else risked their lives to keep *his* ship above water. He noticed one of the older men gripping a rope for dear life. He didn't know the rope's purpose, but he sidled up next to the man and took hold of the same rope, wishing he had enough strength in his right hand to make more of a difference.

The man nodded in appreciation and they were soon pelted with a fresh wave that rose over the deck. He realized that he didn't have a clue what this man's name was, and he made up his mind that if they survived this, he was going to find out.

When the storm subsided at last, Garret left Patrick at the helm and wandered the ship to assess the damages in the pre-dawn light. When he saw Ritcherd sitting on the deck, leaning against the mast, he snapped, "What are you doing up here? I thought I told you to—"

Ritcherd saluted tersely and retorted, "Just attempting to pull my weight, *sir.*"

Garret walked away looking angry, and Ritcherd wondered if the sarcastic use of his title had prickled a nerve—even if he believed that Ritcherd had no idea of the connection.

Through the day the men took turns catching some sleep and working to clean up the mess. And there was indeed a mess. Ritcherd worked side by side with the others, talking with them in a way he'd never broached before. He found out that the man he'd shared the rope with was called Mort. He was amazed at how asking a few simple questions could get a man to talk. When Ritcherd asked how he'd ended up at sea, Mort said in a matter-of-fact tone, "Watched m' wife and four kids take th' fever an' die. Couldn't stay there."

Ritcherd felt a little queasy. He thought of the love he felt for Kyrah and tried to comprehend what this man had been through, then he realized that he couldn't. He could not possibly imagine. "I'm so sorry," Ritcherd said when the silence became uncomfortable.

"We all got our grief," Mort said, then he smiled as if to say that he knew Ritcherd had his own burdens.

Ritcherd worked his way around to different parts of the ship to help with the repairs and cleaning. He talked with Joe, who had run away from a workhouse where he'd been put at the age of seven, working sixteen hours a day for barely enough to feed himself. He'd run away at twelve and gotten work on a ship. He'd been sailing ever since.

Ritcherd met Willard, who was not yet sixteen. He'd been sailing since he was eleven, and all he remembered of his life before that was stealing to eat and staying out of the way of those who would gladly beat him to death to take what he'd stolen.

Ritcherd forewent his turn to sleep. He was enticed by the opportunity to talk with Eugene and Lou. They were brothers whose father had regularly beaten them—and their mother. They'd been at sea for more than twenty years—since their mother's death.

Charlie grew up as a servant in a manor where his parents had both worked from their youth. But Charlie had been beaten up and left for dead after he'd confronted the lord of the manor, who had gotten his thirteen-year-old sister pregnant. After his sister died in childbirth, he left and never went back.

Albert had grown up in an orphanage where food and a blanket had been his most prized possessions. Reed was the son of a merchant who got deeply in debt when business went bad. Both of Reed's parents had died in debtor's prison. Fred's parents had been killed in an accident when he was young. He'd been passed around from one relative to another, never feeling wanted or cared for. And then there were the men who wanted to be known only as Curly, Botch, Sonny, and Greenie. They had all grown up in port towns, where going to sea was the only way they had to make a living. The remaining members of the crew seemed prone to keep more to themselves, and Ritcherd didn't bother approaching them.

It was evening before Ritcherd finally realized he'd gotten all the confessions he was going to get. Suddenly exhausted, he trudged down the hallway to the cabin, grateful to find himself there alone. Unwillingly he sank to his knees and pressed his head into his hands. He felt the burden of each sad tale on his shoulders, a burden that opened up a perspective of life he'd never bothered to contemplate. He marveled at the horrors of this world, the atrocities of hunger and abuse and disease. And he realized that he had no idea how it felt to really be hungry, or unwanted, or alone. If not for his years at war, his comprehension would have been even further removed from the reality of life. He contemplated his own upbringing, and the injustice of aristocracy settled into him in a way it never had before. He thought of people like his mother, hoarding their money and their possessions, looking down their noses at those less fortunate, as if they had made some ill choice that had deemed them worthy to live lives of misery.

Ritcherd groaned and wrapped his arms around his middle, feeling his burden deepen. He crawled onto his bunk and actually found it difficult to sleep, in spite of his exhaustion. But as he pondered again the stories he had heard, he recalled the contentment and happiness he had observed with these men through their many weeks at sea. A new perspective settled into him, and he marveled at the resiliency of mankind. Each of these men had risen above their circumstances to find some level of happiness and peace, and they were doing it without getting drunk and groveling in the gutters of the world. They had a cause, and they were willing to risk their lives to fight for the freedom of people who likely meant nothing to them.

And then, for no apparent reason, he heard Kyrah's words in his memory, as clearly as if she had spoken them just today. *I wonder if you can accept that you're going to have to lower yourself to my social level, because I'm not capable of raising myself to yours.*

He had thought that she believed she wasn't capable of being a lady, of fitting into his life. But he knew now that wasn't what she'd meant at all. Of course, he knew that people would regard his marrying her as lowering himself socially. But he didn't care about that. And he knew that Kyrah hadn't been talking about that, either. Had she been able to see what he couldn't? Through her struggles to survive her father's death, and to keep her and her mother fed, Kyrah had experienced a level of life that Ritcherd had never comprehended. But he understood now. He'd been given a glimpse into *real* life, not the aristocratic veil that shielded those of noble blood from having to view the trenches of reality. Yes, he understood. But he didn't feel as if he'd been *lowered* to anything. He felt lifted up, enlightened, and grateful to have the shades removed from his eyes that had, in spite of all his efforts, kept him in the same realm as people like his mother.

"Thank you, Lord," he murmured and drifted immediately to sleep.

Ritcherd awoke to find it still dark, and Garret absent. Since he'd fallen asleep in his clothes, it took little effort to wander to the deck. He found Garret leaning his back against the rail at the stern, gazing upward.

"Isn't it past your bedtime?" Ritcherd said, startling him.

"Nah," Garret said, looking upward again. "This is when I do some of my best work."

Ritcherd moved beside him and imitated his stance, looking at the stars as if he'd never seen them before. Garret was obviously concentrating, and he allowed him to do so. After several minutes of silence, Garret said, "Now that the clouds have cleared, I know where we are."

"And where would that be?" Ritcherd asked, not liking the tone of his voice. When Garret hesitated, he said, "Please don't tell me we're lost."

Garret chuckled. "No, Ritch. We're not lost. As long as I can see the stars, we'll never be lost. But we're way off course—even worse than I'd suspected."

Ritcherd's heart dropped to the pit of his stomach. He couldn't even begin to express how that made him feel—especially when Garret had no idea of his own personal quest. He managed a steady voice as he asked, "What exactly does that mean?"

"It means we're going to Jamaica," he said firmly.

"I see."

"Do you want to know why?" Garret asked. In a light tone that Ritcherd realized was meant to subtly mimic him, he added, "If you want to know, all you have to do is ask. You don't have to lure it out of me."

"All right, Garret. Why are we going to Jamaica?"

"Our supplies of food and water are fine. I learned a long time ago to allow for plenty of extra. Of course, stocking up with more never hurts. Our cargo stayed dry. We can thank the good Lord for that. But the materials we need to repair the ship properly will not be readily available in the colonies. We've used a lot of our backup materials to make repairs, and I will not return to England without two of everything. We're a lot closer to Jamaica than any American port that would do us any good anyway." He turned to look at Ritcherd. "There. I have given a full report to the owner of the *Phoenix*. Does it meet your approval, Captain Buchanan?"

Ritcherd swallowed his inclination to get angry. The subtle terseness in Garret's voice was not enough to get angry over. And perhaps Garret had cause to be angry. He wondered how to rebuild the trust they had been building. But not knowing the answer, he stuck to the matter at hand. "Yes, Captain Garret. I don't especially want to go to Jamaica, but I'm more grateful than you can imagine to know that the captain of my vessel knows what he's doing and takes his responsibility to his crew and his cause very seriously." Since he had Garret's attention, he added for good measure, "On a more personal note, I'd like you to know that I have a great deal of respect for you—philosophies and all." Deciding he didn't really want a response to that, he walked away saying, "Now if you'll excuse me, I'm going to get some sleep."

Ritcherd was almost to the stairs when he heard Garret holler, "I'm goin' t' bed. Stay awake up there."

"Aye, Cap'n," a voice hollered back from the crow's nest high atop the main mast.

"Good night, Mort," Ritcherd hollered upward, recognizing his voice.

"'Tis almost good mornin', Cap'n," Mort hollered back.

"Aye, so it is," Ritcherd replied. "Good mornin', then."

"Good mornin', Cap'n Buckley. Rest well, eh?"

"As long as I know ye're up there, I'll rest just fine."

Garret slapped Ritcherd's shoulder as he caught up to him. "The feeling is mutual," he said and went down the stairs. Ritcherd followed, wondering how Garret managed to become more likable every day—when he could be so difficult to understand. Then it occurred to him that perhaps Garret considered *him* difficult to understand. That wasn't too hard to believe. As they both crawled into their beds and settled down, Ritcherd had a feeling that he was in the process of uncovering a friendship here that would last far beyond the delivering of smuggled goods to the colonists.

The following morning at breakfast, Captain Garret announced the change in plans. "We're goin' t' Jamaicer," he said simply and the men all groaned, perfectly expressing the ache in Ritcherd's heart. "We've been blown way off course. We'll be there in less than a week. Then we'll proceed with th' original plan."

When the meal was finished, the men returned to their work and Ritcherd went below to spend some time with a sword in his hand. He worked up a healthy sweat in his effort to push thoughts of Kyrah out of his mind. When it simply wouldn't work, he pressed his head to the wall and groaned. Every day that passed seemed to draw him further away from Kyrah, and the possibility that he would find her before the circumstances changed too drastically. He couldn't even entertain thoughts of his fears on her behalf. And now, the time and miles between them were only becoming greater. *Please God,* he prayed for what seemed the millionth time. *Please keep her safe and strong.* Putting the matter in God's hands was the only way he could find any peace.

Chapter Twelve

Separate Realms

The final days of the voyage were long and restless for Kyrah. Peter was amiable, and seemed to have forgotten their distasteful conversation. But Kyrah had trouble forgetting the things he'd said, and she hated him all the more, simply for the doubt he had manipulated into her mind. In Peter's presence, it took all of her mental effort to remain focused on what she knew in her heart. Ritcherd did love her. And he would come for her. Somehow, she just knew!

At the very least, she had difficulty trusting Peter's motives, but she couldn't rid herself of the one point he'd made that was likely true. How would she manage on her own in a strange land? She couldn't answer that question, but she was determined to take it one step at a time. And with any luck, Ritcherd would find her before any further repercussions became a concern.

She awoke one morning to realize that they had arrived in the colonies during the night—and Peter had already left the ship. Her heart quickened with anticipation and fear as she gathered her belongings, all too grateful to leave the tiny cabin that had briefly become her only security. She spoke briefly with the captain, who told her in his brusque way that they'd arrived on the heels of a storm and had made good time. He made it clear that she was free to go, and he would most likely consider her absence a blessing. Considering the way he unnerved her, Kyrah was equally happy to leave the *Libertatia*.

It was raining hard when Kyrah made her way into a small port town called Hedgeton. Every face Kyrah met seemed either cruel or hard. She knew if she was going to survive here on her own, she would have to keep up that same stiff facade she'd practiced with the men on the *Libertatia*. Kyrah felt certain that if she acted timid and afraid, she would more likely be asking for trouble.

Kyrah was relieved when the rain eased a bit. But as people passing by became less preoccupied with the storm, they became more aware of her. She knew she looked out of place, which only increased her hope that she could leave soon. Formulating a plan, Kyrah knew the first thing she had to do was find a place to stay. Then she could start searching for a way to return home.

Once she mustered up the courage to stop someone and ask, it didn't take much effort to find a boardinghouse. Kyrah wasn't impressed with the owner or the other tenants that she saw, but the rooms were clean and it was near the pier. She found out how much it would be, then asked Mrs. Dodd, the owner, to hold the room and she would have the money before the end of the day.

Mrs. Dodd peered curiously at Kyrah over the rims of her glasses and gave a grunt that Kyrah interpreted as an agreement. Kyrah turned and left quickly, praying inside that she could get some money before nightfall. The thought of what might happen otherwise was too dreadful to contemplate. Each time she asked for guidance or directions, it took all the courage she could muster just to speak. And several attempts left her with no information that would help. But her desperation forced her to be persistent, and she finally learned of a man who owned a cobbler's shop, and also did buying and trading of precious gems. Though it broke Kyrah's heart to think of selling the earrings, she had no choice. She was penniless, and they were her only means of survival. Kyrah kept the necklace hidden, not wanting the merchant to even see it. She intended to save that to buy her passage home.

She found the cobbler shop easily enough, and knew immediately that this was the right man by his appearance. His hard, skeptical eyes were intimidating, but she approached him stoically, determined to barter if she must in order to get the most money possible.

"What can I do for ye?" he asked in a voice that grated on her nerves.

Forcing herself to appear tough, she stated, "I have some diamond earrings I need to sell. Are you interested?"

"Aye," he said. "Let's 'ave a look."

His eyes lit up when he saw them, and he took several minutes to examine them closely while Kyrah's palms grew moist with sweat. When he finally gave her an offer, it took her breath away. It was far more than she'd even hoped for. But she remained expressionless and told him that she knew they were worth more than that. She just had to have more.

"I must say," he scrutinized them again through his glass, "I've not seen gems s' perfect in a long time." He seemed reluctant to admit it, but for a moment Kyrah saw something almost warm in his eyes, as if he actually wanted to be fair. Kyrah forced herself not to become distracted by his report. It astounded her to think how much Ritcherd must have paid for them. She absorbed this reminder of his love for her, and the security he had unwittingly sent with her on this journey. Then she steeled herself to face this man appropriately.

"Of course they're perfect," she stated. "I'm certain you can give me more and still make a fair profit."

He quoted another offer, and again Kyrah talked him up. When he stated his third price with a tone that indicated he would go no higher, Kyrah consented graciously and left the cobbler's shop with more than twice the money she had hoped for. She tucked the money in a safe place and prayed that she would be spared from thieves or those who might do her harm. She stepped back into the storm, which had worsened. Then she hurried back in, wondering if he might be able to help her further.

"Excuse me," she said, and he lifted his head from examining his purchase. "Could you tell me where I might go to find passage to England?"

He chuckled satirically. "Lady, there's a war goin' on. That's one thing you ain't gonna find right now." His voice softened as if he'd sensed her discouragement. "Things change and you could keep tryin', but I wouldn't get yer hopes up."

Kyrah nodded politely and thanked him, but she felt sick inside as she went back onto the street. She wondered how long she would be stuck in this hole. She wondered if Ritcherd would be able to find out where the *Libertatia* had docked. And if there were no ships going out, there would be no way to get word to her mother. At least she knew that Ritcherd would have seen to her mother's needs. Walking briskly through the continuing rain, Kyrah made a firm decision to only concern herself with the present. Otherwise she would go mad.

Kyrah returned to the boarding house and found Mrs. Dodd to be far more amiable with money in her hands. Wanting to feel some sense of security, she paid for two months in advance, which included two meals a day. With that seen to, she went back into town to purchase some things she would be needing. After eating a good meal at an inn, she carefully chose a few simple skirts and bodices that would serve her increasing size, as well as underclothing, nightgowns, shoes and stockings, and a new burgundy-colored cloak. After her weeks on the ship with almost nothing, it was a pleasure to purchase a new hairbrush and mirror, bath items, needle, thread, and some dress lengths, as well as some fabric to begin making things for the baby. Last of all, she purchased a carpet bag large enough to hold all of her things in preparation to return to England—whenever that might be.

Kyrah was exhausted when she returned to the boardinghouse just before dark. But considering the circumstances, she felt satisfied to know that at least things were going as well as could be expected. After eating supper in the dining room, she went upstairs and built a fire to ward off the chill of the storm. She cleaned up and slipped into new underclothing and nightgown. Impulsively she burned the clothes that had seen her weeks at sea. She felt it was a good omen in putting the episode behind her.

Feeling cozy and secure, Kyrah surveyed her simple surroundings in the firelight. The only furnishings besides the bed were a couple of chairs, a small table, and a bureau with three drawers. But it was hers for the coming two months, and the security she felt gave her hope. She sat on the bed to count her money, and was pleased to find that she still had a fair amount left. With needle and thread she sewed the majority of it, along with the diamond necklace, beneath the lining of her bag. After putting her newly purchased items in their appropriate places, Kyrah went to bed feeling an ache of loneliness as her mind went inevitably to Ritcherd. She did her best to ward off her concerns for the future. Its uncertainty was perhaps the most frightening thing of all.

The following morning, Kyrah arose to sunny skies and some measure of hope. She was pleased to note that Mrs. Dodd's cooking was favorable, and the hearty breakfast eased the smoldering in her stomach. Almost unwillingly, she hurried to the pier. Even knowing that it was ridiculous to think Ritcherd could have set out so quickly behind her, she couldn't help hoping that he might arrive. The *Libertatia* was still there, and the only other ships docked had been there when she'd left the previous day. She asked around and discovered that no ship had come in since the *Libertatia*.

Kyrah quickly settled into a routine that included regular visits to the pier. She had only been in Hedgeton a few days when she saw a ship approaching, and her heart beat quickly as it slowly moved closer. Shading the sun from her eyes with her hand, Kyrah could see the seemingly tiny outline of sails against the horizon. She thought of Ritcherd, trying to imagine him on that ship. Picturing clearly what he might look like standing at the bow, her excitement increased as the ship drew nearer and the sails became more defined. By the time it finally came to shore, she felt weak with anticipation.

Watching the sailors on board busily lowering the sails and dropping the anchor, Kyrah convinced herself that Ritcherd would appear at any moment. When the gangway was lowered, she continued to watch as several colorful-looking men filed ashore. She moved back and was careful to stay out of the way, biting her lip tensely—hoping, praying that he would come. Kyrah noted that this ship was smaller than the *Libertatia*, with only two masts. But the sails looked much the same. On the hull was painted *Charming Sally*. She thought the name suited it well.

Gradually the activity on the pier subsided. When it seemed that everyone who was coming ashore had done so, Kyrah stared numbly at the docked ship for another hour, not wanting to let go of that last shred of hope that Ritcherd might disembark. When a rise of nausea reminded her that she had to return home and get something to eat, she approached one of the sailors from the *Charming Sally*.

"Excuse me, sir," she asked, gratified to realize that she didn't feel afraid to talk to him. She concluded that even in her few days here she had become more capable of taking care of herself.

He turned and gave her a curious glance, but his eyes were kind as he replied, "What might I do for ye?"

"Was there a Captain Ritcherd Buchanan on board your ship?"

"'Fraid not, ma'am," he said, shaking his head and showing a smile. "Never 'eard of 'im."

Kyrah only realized how his statement must have affected her when the sailor's voice startled her. "Is somethin' wrong, ma'am?" he asked.

"Uh . . . no. Thank you."

Kyrah hurried quickly back to the boarding house, deflated and lonely. She reminded herself that it would logically take Ritcherd time to make arrangements and find his way here. She had to be patient. Trying to be positive, she turned her thoughts toward the next ship that might come into Hedgeton.

The *Phoenix* arrived in Jamaica in the middle of the night. Immediately after breakfast, Garret made preparations to go ashore. Ritcherd watched as he adjusted his pistol and cutlass in his belt, then he motioned toward equivalent weapons laid out on the table. "You'd better take those," he said. "Wearing them generally means less chance of having to use them." Garret pulled on his gloves as Ritcherd picked up the pistol. "In fact, just keep them."

Ritcherd absorbed the craftsmanship of the weapons. He'd used them before, but he had to say, "I'd be happy to pay you for them. They're too fine—"

"They're not for sale," Garret said. "I'm giving them to you. Just because I want to," he added as if he knew Ritcherd's next question.

Ritcherd swallowed and reminded himself to be gracious. "Thank you, Garret," he said. "This means a great deal to me." Their eyes met, and Ritcherd thought of the hours Garret had invested in teaching Ritcherd to use the weapons. That in itself made the gift doubly meaningful.

"My pleasure," he said. "Now hurry up. We need to make good time here, and . . . oh, have you got any coins packed away? Odd trinkets? Anything like that?"

"I've got money. Why?"

"Take some with you. British coin has more value here than you can imagine. It'll be well worth it."

Garret left the cabin and Ritcherd dug out the coins he'd packed. He filled his pockets, adjusted the weapons in his belt, and hurried to the deck. Patrick and George were the only ones to accompany the captains ashore. There was no pier, so it was necessary to take one of the longboats in to the beach. It felt good to Ritcherd to feel the earth beneath his feet. He only wished it was American soil.

The recent broadening of Ritcherd's mind was aided as they wandered into a nearby village. The poverty of the natives was immediately evident. Their dress and culture was startling. But Ritcherd was most fascinated with the way dozens of dark-faced children flocked around them, chattering incessantly in an accented form of English. Garret laughed at the children's attention. He tickled them and growled at them, and they tugged at his coat until he brought out handfuls of candy that made them jump up and down with excitement.

The children stayed with them as they came to a spot in the center of the village where they sat next to some semblance of a tavern, beneath a huge awning made from some kind of enormous leaves. A woman served them drinks and food, and Garret gave her money. He spoke to her amiably, as if they were previously acquainted. The children gathered around with obvious expectancy, and many adults stood back to observe with pleasure. Through the following hour, Ritcherd watched as Garret told them stories, George told them jokes, and Patrick performed magic tricks. The children moaned when Garret told them they had business to be about. But he dug into his pockets again and pulled out a number of odd trinkets. There were strings of glass beads, satin ribbons, polished stones, and other odd paraphernalia. One by one each child received a gift with wide-eyed pleasure and gave Garret a hug. When he was nearly finished, he winked at Ritcherd and said, "I think Cap'n Buckley might 'ave somethin' for ye, as well."

Ritcherd dug into his pockets and brought out handfuls of gold coin. The children gasped and hovered around Ritcherd, who laughed as he placed one into each outstretched hand. When he realized he had plenty left, he gave each child a second one.

"You see," Garret said quietly near Ritcherd's ear, "what greater value can you get for your money than that? That will likely feed their families for a month."

Ritcherd swallowed, wishing he could find the words to tell Garret how he appreciated his insight, and the opportunity to experience such perspective.

With their socializing apparently completed, they made arrangements for supplies with little difficulty. But Ritcherd nearly went mad when they had to wait a number of days for new sails to be made. Ritcherd wanted to insist that they could manage—or get some elsewhere before sailing for England. But he knew Garret wouldn't bend. Some of the sails had been damaged beyond repair in the storm, and Garret wouldn't sail without more than a complete set of extras.

When the sails were finally delivered, they sailed with the evening tide. Ritcherd was glad to be one step closer to putting all of this behind him. He resumed his fencing lessons with Patrick, which helped to occupy the time. Patrick proved to be a good teacher and an amiable companion, although he was guarded about his background. But they came to be on good terms, and Ritcherd quite liked him.

The *Phoenix* was just a few days out of Jamaica when the albatross began trailing it. Garret pointed it out to Ritcherd, and he was immediately fascinated by the lone bird with the huge wingspan. As with any bird, it made him think of Kyrah. Had she been with him, she would have been fascinated, spending hours speculating over its past and future.

Ritcherd's interest in the albatross increased when Garret told him of the well-known adage among sailors that it was a symbol of luck. It would follow a ship to eat tidbits of food from the refuse thrown overboard. As long as it followed and was satisfied, good luck would abound. But if it were shot down by one of the sailors, they would all be doomed.

"Then luck is with us," Ritcherd said without taking his eyes from the bird as it soared and dipped into the water to feed.

"Aye, Cap'n," Garret said. "Luck is with us."

But in spite of the albatross, as the days passed Ritcherd found his mood turning steadily more sour. Time slipped by, and he felt subsequently helpless. He often became lost in deep thought, wondering what Kyrah might be doing. Had she arrived safely in the colonies? Did she have shelter? Food? Safety?

"Where are you?" Garret's voice interrupted Ritcherd's thoughts one evening. Ritcherd glanced up from where he sat at the table in the cabin to see Garret stretching his arms as he finished a session with his book work.

"Just thinking," Ritcherd said.

A minute later, Garret moved to a chair opposite Ritcherd and sat down. "You're doing very well with the old sword," he said, "don't you think?"

"Patrick's a good teacher," Ritcherd replied.

"Aye, he is."

"And as you said, a good man. I've come to think a great deal of him."

"One can't help it," Garret smiled and went on. "So, you are gaining some confidence with the sword, are you not?"

"I'm feeling good about it."

"Then what's eating at you?"

"What do you mean?"

Garret leaned closer and his eyes deepened. "Listen to me, Buckley, and listen well. I have done my best to let you know that I'm a man you can trust, that I respect you and what you're about. And I appreciate the respect you have given me. But respect is only half the quotient here. I keep expecting you to let me know exactly what you're doing here. And I have to wonder why you're so hesitant to talk about it."

Ritcherd kept his eyes focused on Garret, but he couldn't find words to respond.

"All right," Garret said, leaning back, "let me approach this from my perspective as the captain of this vessel. I tend to get suspicious of a man who goes to sea for no apparent reason—then sulks around and has nothing to say about himself or his purpose."

"Are you saying you don't trust me?" Ritcherd asked.

Garret chuckled. "I trust you enough, Captain. But we'll be reaching our destination soon. We've got serious business to be about. If we're truly going to be partners in this endeavor . . ." He hesitated. "Well, you know why I'm doing this, but I have no idea why you—"

"Tell me," Ritcherd interrupted, looking across the table at Garret with the lamplight accentuating his dark eyes. It was still difficult to envision this rugged man as a baronet. He knew Garret had a love for the sea and a certain patriotic zeal for the colonists, but the reasoning behind his motives was a mystery.

"I feel very strongly about what the colonists are fighting for. I admire it."

"Why?" Ritcherd persisted.

It was apparent that Garret didn't want to answer, and Ritcherd added, "If this conversation is about trust, you'd better be willing to give what you're asking."

Garret scowled slightly as he said, "England's done nothing for me."

"Are you speaking politically or personally?"

"Does it matter?" Garret asked pointedly.

Ritcherd remembered what George had said to him about understanding a partner completely, and the question was easy to answer. "It matters to me."

Garret shifted uneasily in his chair. "You might say that I've got a few resentments toward some of the social barriers I grew up with."

The statement surprised Ritcherd, only because he knew Garret was a baronet. But immediately he felt scenes from his own life fitting the same description. "I can relate to that," he stated.

"You can?" Garret asked, lifting his brows.

"Who is it that caused your resentment?" Ritcherd tried to keep the conversation steered toward Garret.

"Who is it that caused *your* resentment?" Garret returned with a slight smirk, and Ritcherd chuckled.

"It was mostly my mother," Ritcherd said at last, sensing that it would take confessions on his part to keep Garret talking.

Again, Garret lifted his brows. "In my case, it was my father."

Ritcherd remained silent, making it evident that he wanted to know more. "It wasn't until I was oh, thirteen or so," Garret continued, "that I realized my father's attitude toward me had made me think so little of myself that I . . . Well, I became an outcast, you might say—from family, friends. Until then I'd thought it was just me. But one day I woke up and realized that I wasn't such a bad guy, and I would find a life where none of what he said mattered."

"Is he still living?" Ritcherd asked, knowing that if Garret had inherited the title, his father would not be alive.

"No," Garret answered dryly. He drew a deep breath and leaned back in his chair. Ritcherd remained silent, waiting for him to go on. "He's gone now," Garret said at last, "and I don't miss him a bit."

Ritcherd related to that as well. He'd hardly felt anything when his own father died.

"But," Garret went on, "perhaps that's because he'd always made such a point of letting me know that he wasn't really my father." Ritcherd tried not to look surprised as he began to understand. "It was never brought up publicly," Garret said, watching his fingers drum against the table. "He was too concerned with social distinction to ever jeopardize his image. But it was well known whenever he—my mother's husband—was in the same room with me, that I was not his son."

Ritcherd hoped his tone of voice expressed that the confession had not affected his opinions one way or the other. "And that's why you're a privateer for the colonists?"

"That's a good part of it," he stated.

"Despite having fought for England," Ritcherd said for reassurance, "I have often felt bitter against the system that doesn't allow a man," or woman, he thought to himself, "to be judged for what they are, rather than the circumstances under which they're born—or are forced to live."

"Well then," Garret said, "I suppose that needs no more explanation."

"I suppose," Ritcherd repeated. When Garret said nothing more, Ritcherd took the opportunity to ask something he'd often wondered about. "So, might I presume that Garret is your given name, and you prefer not to use your legal surname?"

"Very good," Garret drawled with a subtle smile, as if to compliment Ritcherd on his perception. "Of course, I've long ago come to terms with my feelings toward my parents. I no longer have difficulty with using the name, but . . . well, in this business, people know me by the name I've been using. Perhaps one day when I settle down, I'll go back to using the name."

"Which would be . . ." Ritcherd pressed.

Garret chuckled. "Stick around, Ritch, and one day I just might tell you." He laughed and added, "Not that it's any great secret, but . . . well, one day."

Again Garret became silent, and Ritcherd figured that the conversation concerning his name had been ended.

"Now," Garret went on with his original purpose, "you know why I'm going. Why are you going? Why didn't you just buy this ship and let us take it?"

"This is a big investment." Ritcherd smirked slightly. "I want to keep an eye on it."

"Nice try," Garret nodded, "but there's more. Are you running from something? Someone?"

"No."

"Then what is it in the colonies that makes you stand at the bow, gazing westward with a desperate look in your eyes?"

Ritcherd stood up and turned away, clasping his hands behind his back.

"George told me it wasn't a week before we left port that you announced you were getting married," Garret went on in a cautious voice, and Ritcherd felt something wrench at his heart. Hearing his pain verbalized somehow freshened it. "Why would you leave the country when the woman you love is there?" he asked when Ritcherd remained silent. "I'm guessing it's because she's not there anymore. And I'd bet she—"

Ritcherd turned quickly and interrupted, feeling a need to even out the odds. "You know, something, Captain? George Morley is nothing but an old gossip. But maybe you don't realize that he gossips both ways, so I'm going to let it slide." Garret actually looked unnerved and Ritcherd chuckled, glad for the way it suppressed his rising emotions. "What? The great Captain Garret is worried that I might know *his* secrets?"

"Do you?" he asked with disgust.

"Yes, actually . . . *Sir* Garret." Ritcherd laughed when Garret's disgust increased. "Do you know how long I've been wanting to call you that . . . you scoundrel, you." He mimicked Garret rather unkindly. "Most of the men I know shoot aristocrats for sport."

Garret finally laughed, but his eyes betrayed that it was against his will.

"Admit it," Ritcherd said more seriously. "We're two of a kind and you know it. We're victims of a system we resent, and too arrogant and proud to admit that we can't always be in control."

"I have no trouble admitting that," Garret said. "But you're trying to change the subject. Our time is running out, and I need to know why you're here."

Ritcherd sighed and turned his back again. While it was difficult to voice, he couldn't deny a degree of relief in—as Garret had once suggested—sharing his burden. "She's not in England anymore."

"I was right then," Garret said with conviction. "It is a woman."

"That's right!" His voice picked up an edge as he turned to face Garret.

"Where is she?" Garret asked coolly.

"If I knew," Ritcherd nearly shouted, "I wouldn't be tearing myself apart wondering where to start looking for her."

"Now, Captain Buckley, there's no need to bring that raging temper to the surface, I was only—"

"What is it about you," Ritcherd said, leaning his hands against the table and looking into Garret's eyes, "that enables you to practically read my mind? You knew I needed to learn to fight. You know why I'm on this ship. You know I've got a temper."

"I'm perceptive," Garret said as he stood to lean across the table in exactly the same manner, meeting him eye to eye. "And the moment I met you, I knew you were a man I could relate to and understand, or I never would have agreed to be your partner. I don't really care what it is you're searching for, only that I know so I can understand what we're facing. I'm not going to have the lovesick Captain Buckley blow my operation all to hell because he suddenly finds what he wants and the rest doesn't matter anymore.

"Now, I'm willing to help you if you're willing to help me. But we can't do that without perfect trust between us. There's no reason we can't find a woman when you consider all the other impossible odds we've come up against. But we've got to deliver these guns, and our first law around here is that nothing is worth the life of one of these men—not even a woman.

"If you're honest with me, Ritcherd Buchanan, and do what you can to assist us in this, I will do everything in my power to help you find this woman. You're a good man and I could use you. I also think there are probably some things I know that could help you." He inhaled deeply as he stood up straight and tugged at his waistcoat. "Is that fair enough, Captain Buckley?"

Ritcherd leaned back and put his hands on his hips, chuckling slightly. This partner of his never ceased to amaze him. "That is more than fair enough," he stated and their eyes met, "Captain Garret."

Garret held out his left hand and Ritcherd took it. They gripped forearms strongly across the table. Garret laughed and went to the trunk at the foot of his bed. He dug deep into it and brought out a bottle of brandy. "This calls for a drink," he smiled slyly.

"So the captain breaks his own rules," Ritcherd smirked.

"One bottle can't get anybody too drunk. And I save it for special occasions. Being the captain should allow for certain privileges."

He poured out two moderate glassfuls and returned the bottle to its hiding place. "You're the only one who knows that's there," he smirked, "so if it disappears, I'll know who's to walk the plank."

Ritcherd laughed as their glasses rang together. They each downed their drink and set the glasses down in unison.

"Thank you, Ritcherd," Garret said.

"For what?"

"For trusting me, and even . . . for believing in me."

"The feeling is mutual," Ritcherd said, appreciating the lack of tension between them that had been there ever since Garret had implied his knowledge of Ritcherd's motives.

Ritcherd motioned toward Garret's fine waistcoat, which was typical of his attire, and chuckled. "Here all this time I thought you were wearing clothes you'd taken off dead aristocrats."

Garret smirked. "Maybe I am."

"But you're not, are you," Ritcherd said.

"*Most* of the clothes are mine," he said. "There are a few pieces, however, that . . . I came by through . . ." He laughed then said nothing more, as if he found pleasure in leaving Ritcherd guessing. Ritcherd figured that was his privilege, but he felt certain that Garret wasn't nearly as formidable as he'd once wanted Ritcherd to believe.

"So, how is it that you gained so much experience at sailing?" Ritcherd asked. He bit his tongue from saying that he was amazed to see a man under twenty-five years with such incredible knowledge, and a commanding presence that put his crew—most of them much older—in awe of him. That kind of finesse couldn't have been acquired with only a year or two at sea.

"Well, I owe that to my grandfather," Garret said. "My mother's father was likely the only person in my life who seemed to understand me—or care about what was really going on inside of me. He always had a fascination with sailing, and after my grandmother passed away, he invested nearly everything he had in shipping. He started going along on voyages—to get away from the loneliness, I suppose. During his visits through my childhood, I believe he sensed my unrest. I was twelve when he talked my mother into letting him take me. I never went home again more than a few weeks at a time. I watched. I asked questions. Sometimes he actually had a tutor sail with us so that I got my education. But it didn't take me long to learn where my real interests lay. When my grandfather died, he left me his prize vessel."

A thought occurred to Ritcherd and he had to ask, "The *Falcon Star?*"

Garret just nodded. The fact that it had been shot down became doubly poignant.

A loud knock at the door startled them. "Can't be George," Ritcherd said. "He never knocks."

"Yeah?" Garret called, and the door flew open.

"Cap'n!" Patrick said breathlessly.

"Yes?" they both said together.

"Land on th' 'orizon, Cap'n." He paused then added, "And Cap'n."

Garret let out a whoop of excitement and followed Patrick down the narrow hallway with Ritcherd right behind him. The deck was lit well by an almost full moon. Although they couldn't yet see any shoreline with the naked eye, the sailor manning the mast saw the captains emerge from the stairs and lifted his telescope high above his head, shouting, "Land 'o, Cap'ns!"

Captains Garret and Buckley saluted him casually. Charlie handed a telescope to Garret, who put it to his eye and adjusted it carefully before he laughed aloud. He handed it to Ritcherd, who laughed as well when he saw the evidence for himself. When the excitement had died down a bit, they walked together toward the bow. Ritcherd's heart beat quickly. He was almost on the same continent again as Kyrah.

"We'll find her," Garret said almost tenderly as they both leaned their elbows on the rail. Ritcherd made no reply and he went on lightly, "She must be a beauty, eh?"

"Aye, Cap'n," Ritcherd said, and Garret smiled.

"You're getting pretty good at that," Garret said.

"You think I can open my mouth in the taverns without getting shot?"

"Aye, Cap'n," Garret repeated. Then his voice turned serious. "I can't help being curious. Why is it that you were about to marry her, and now you don't know where she is?"

Ritcherd looked down and blew out a long breath. "She's in the colonies," he said, wanting to avoid the rest.

"I figured that much."

Ritcherd looked at him directly, figuring Garret had a right to know what they were dealing with. "She was deported."

If Garret looked surprised, he covered it quickly. His voice lightened as he turned to lean back against the rail, lifting one foot to press it up behind him. "Tell me about her," he said. "Tell me what I'll be looking for."

Ritcherd's voice became dreamy as he described Kyrah the way he remembered her. Barely realizing what he was doing, he went on to tell

Garret how they'd met and grown up together, and the problems he'd had with his parents concerning her. He told him that when his father had died, his mother's bitterness had more than made up for the absence of his father's criticism. With a strained voice he told Garret what he knew about Kyrah Payne's having been deported, and how he'd torn apart his mother's china closet. Then he suddenly had nothing more to say.

"Didn't I tell you that you had a nasty temper?" Garret said lightly. "But I daresay if I'd have been there," his voice became intense, "I'd not have stopped with the china."

"I'm not sure I know why I did," Ritcherd said, chuckling without any trace of humor. "So why is it that I feel some kind of guilt or regret or something, when I realize I never want to see my mother again? And even more so when I think about her never knowing what a good woman Kyrah is, or that she'll never even care to see our children."

"She's your mother," Garret stated. "You'd be no better than her if you felt no qualm in having such animosities toward the woman who brought you into this world."

"I suppose," Ritcherd said distantly.

"Perhaps," Garret added, "there's a reason for the way she acts about Kyrah—something you don't understand."

"Oh, I understand it," Ritcherd said. "Kyrah has nothing of value in my mother's eyes. No great family name. No old money. Questionable background."

"Well," Garret said, "it could be that. It could be more. What I mean is, well . . . for years I thought my father hated me because I wasn't his son, and . . . I suppose that was part of it. But one day I realized that I was an only child. Stopping to analyze the circumstances, I honestly believe that he would not have resented me so much if he could have had children of his own. It doesn't take away any of the pain he caused me, but it helps me understand why he behaved the way he did."

"You make it sound so simple."

"Sometimes it is," Garret said. "I believe there are times when people can't see the answers because the problem is too close to their face. If they'd step back a few paces and take on a different perspective, it usually is just as you said—simple."

Ritcherd wondered if Garret's philosophies had any merit in his own situation. But at the moment his mind was too preoccupied with finding Kyrah to analyze it any further.

"So, what's our first move," Ritcherd said easily, "now that there's *land ho?*"

"Before the sun comes up, we'll be in a nice, secluded cove. We'll send a few men ashore to check out the situation and go from there.

"I'm going to get some sleep," Garret added, slapping him on the shoulder. Ritcherd smiled and Garret left.

Alone at the bow, Ritcherd reached into his pocket and pulled out the gold band that Sarah had given him. Just as he had a hundred times before through the course of his journey, he thought of how Kyrah should have been wearing it by now. Fingering it carefully, he thought of the years Sarah had worn it as a symbol of her love for Stephen. He knew she had made a sacrifice in giving it to him. Every bit of his wealth could not have bought a wedding ring that meant more to him than this. And he would find a way to get it onto Kyrah's finger. He looked again to where he knew the colonies lay just out of sight, and whispered aloud, "I'll find you, Kyrah. Somehow I'll find you—if it's the last thing I do."

A meager hint of light showed in the predawn sky as the two longboats were lowered into the water. Captain Garret called off the orders and who was to go down, with himself on the list. But Captain Buckley was to stay with the ship. Ritcherd did Garret the courtesy of taking him to the cabin before his temper let loose.

"I can't find Kyrah if I stay with the ship," he said angrily.

"First things first, Buckley."

Ritcherd calmed down, realizing his anger would get him nowhere with Garret, who remained intently cool. "Is it really so bad that I just go ashore and make inquiries? I've got to start somewhere."

"I know what I'm doing, Ritch. This is not a good place for us to be showing up, so I'm taking the most experienced men to scout out the situation. I'll let you go ashore when I know the situation better. I had every intention of making inquiries for you."

Ritcherd shook his head humbly. "I'm sorry, Garret. I . . ."

"Don't worry about it. Just be patient," he added with conviction. "We'll not sail for England without Kyrah Payne . . . I promise." He slapped Ritcherd on the shoulder and left the cabin.

Ritcherd felt a surge of emotion to realize all that Garret had done for him. He had given Ritcherd more than any man ever had, with perhaps the exception of Stephen Payne. And he had to believe him when he said they would find Kyrah.

Setting his emotion in check, Ritcherd went to the deck and watched the longboats rowing to shore. He noticed the albatross flying overhead, as it had been since they'd left Jamaica. The crew had all been surprised that it had stayed with them. The albatross was supposedly never seen in Atlantic waters this far north—which convinced Ritcherd all the more that luck was with them. He wasn't one to be superstitious, but the sailor's adage of the albatross suited him. And he liked having the bird nearby.

It was long past dark that evening before the signal came from shore. Immediately Ritcherd knew something was wrong. The sailor at the mast shouted something he couldn't discern, and the men on deck moved like scurrying mice at the appearance of a cat. The sails were raised, the anchor lifted, and the *Phoenix* moved seaward. Shadows moved across the beach, and Ritcherd easily picked out Garret, even from the distance. The longboats moved out from the rushes where they were hidden, and skidded across the water with haste until they caught up with the ship. The *Phoenix* kept moving while the longboats were lifted. A sigh of relief fell over the crew when Captain Garret came over the rail with every man accounted for.

"What 'appened?" Ritcherd asked him.

"Th' war's gone mad. We had th' audacity t' land in th' 'eat of it. We're sailin' away from th' 'igh battle points, and we'll land where it's not so dangerous. It might take a dozen tries t' find a place where we can get rid o' the goods, but . . ." He looked around at his entire crew, all watching him expectantly. "Well," he grinned, "we've done it 'afore, ain't we? It took ten tries last time. Let's shoot for fourteen and go for th' record."

The men dispersed to their posts. Captain Garret walked to his cabin with Ritcherd following silently behind. When they were alone, Garret turned to him and said, "Kyrah Payne was never there. That's one down."

"How did you find out?"

"Connections," he stated. "If she was there, she walked in, walked out, and didn't eat or sleep while she was in town. I know she was never there."

Ritcherd's immediate reaction was a downhearted stare at the floor. But Garret with his unbending optimism was quick to rejuvenate his hope. "We'll find her." He grinned. "How about a late-night fencing match to keep the wits sharp?"

"After you." Ritcherd bowed and motioned toward the door, grateful for a distraction. If they didn't find Kyrah soon, he was going to lose his mind. He prayed that he wouldn't lose anything more than that.

The following morning, Garret tossed a small book onto Ritcherd's bed just after he'd gotten out of it and pulled on his breeches.

"What is this?" Ritcherd asked.

"Surely you've heard of Thomas Paine."

"It sounds familiar," Ritcherd said, "but . . ."

"Well, in my opinion, Thomas Paine is an inspired and valorous man. His writings are at the heart of everything the Americans are fighting for." He motioned toward the little book, and Ritcherd took note of its title: *Common Sense*.

When Garret sat down and leaned his forearms on his thighs, Ritcherd knew there was something important he wanted to say. Ritcherd picked up the book and sat on the edge of his bed, facing Garret.

"From what I understand," Garret said, "Thomas Paine was a poor Englishman who had more or less failed at every occupation he'd attempted. He came to America, and this book was soon filtering all over the country. It would seem the concepts in it were the missing ingredient in what the American continental congress was trying to accomplish. They all had good ideas, however . . ."

"Yes?" Ritcherd pressed when he hesitated.

"Well," Garret said, "in my opinion, the one concept the congress could not fully comprehend was that . . ." He hesitated again, as if to give emphasis to what he wanted to say. With deep fervor he finished, "That all men are created equal. You see, it takes a man who has seen the face of poverty, oppression, and . . . social imbalance . . ." Ritcherd sat up a little straighter, feeling a sensitive nerve prickled. "It takes a man like that to fully understand the need for equality . . . among all men. And that is something the wealthy representatives of the American colonies couldn't see . . . until Thomas Paine gave them this. You see, the Americans could never succeed without the belief that their fight was by the people, and for the people . . . *all* of the people."

He motioned toward the book and Ritcherd thumbed through it, feeling both intrigued and a little apprehensive.

"Read it," Garret said as if it were an order. "Then we'll talk."

Right after breakfast, Ritcherd started reading, expecting to find it a tedious endeavor that he might feel obligated to do in order to appease Garret. But he was quickly compelled by Paine's writing and found his concepts stirring. There was something formless about his ideas and the way he presented them that seemed to speak to Ritcherd's very soul—almost against his will. And by the time he finished reading *Common Sense* sometime the following day, he felt changed; irrevocably and wholly changed. Prior to this time, he'd been able to admit that he didn't fully agree with England's reasons for fighting the colonists. He'd been able to see that much of what the colonists were fighting for had merit. But he'd never imagined that what they believed in could be so . . . *awakening*. He couldn't help imagining how life might have been for him and Kyrah if they had been born and raised in a country where all men—and women—were considered to be created equal. He was suddenly grateful for the opening of his mind on such matters, and glad to be contributing in some small way. With an entirely different perspective, he was proud to be the owner of a privateer, and hoped that he and Garret could continue to work as partners to aid the cause of the colonists.

The evening after he'd finished the book, Ritcherd and Garret talked far into the night about its concepts. Ritcherd felt their friendship deepen as it became apparent that they were two men of the same mind in many matters. Once again, Ritcherd was glad for all he had learned and gained. If not for the horrible circumstances he knew Kyrah to be in, he could almost be glad he'd been forced to leave the narrow realm of his life, and to have found Garret's friendship, with his insight and perception that continually amazed Ritcherd.

But the full impact of Garret's influence didn't strike Ritcherd until his new friend brought forth a printed copy of a page that he slid across the table.

"What is this?" Ritcherd asked.

"It's the *Declaration of Independence,*" Garret said. He added severely, "*That* is why King George sent you—and thousands of others like you—to war."

Ritcherd's heart quickened at the irony even before Garret pointed to a paragraph near the beginning and said, "Read this; read it aloud."

Ritcherd cleared his throat and focused at the point of Garret's finger. "'We hold these Truths to be self-evident, that all Men are created equal, that they are endowed by their Creator with certain unalienable Rights, that among these are Life, Liberty, and the Pursuit of Happiness. — That to secure these Rights, Governments are instituted among Men, deriving their just Powers from the Consent of the Governed . . .'"

Ritcherd gasped aloud as the concept began to sink in, but it took a moment to absorb the full impact of what he'd just read. He met Garret's eyes and felt certain he understood, even before he said, "In my opinion, Captain Buchanan, your search for Kyrah Payne, and your fight to live with her in peace and happiness, are merely manifestations of everything America stands for."

Ritcherd felt an incredible warmth envelope him, as if to verify the truth of what Garret had just said. He was left completely speechless, but somehow he knew Garret understood. How could he not, when he had managed to so perfectly voice what he was feeling?

Ritcherd's new insight concerning Garret's cause made the weeks of carrying out their mission a little more bearable. The *Phoenix* landed and the longboats went ashore twelve times before they found the contacts and positioning that could see their goods delivered to the right people with the least risk. Each time Captain Buckley stayed with the ship, and Captain Garret returned with the same statement: *Kyrah Payne was never here.*

"Don't panic, my friend," Garret added after the final try. "When the ship is free of the goods, we'll go to a real port to get supplies, and you'll be able to find out a lot more from there. At least we're narrowing it down a bit, eh?"

Garret then went on to explain to Ritcherd their plan for getting the goods ashore and added, "I'd like you with me."

"Really?" Ritcherd was pleased. "Why?"

"Wouldn't you like to feel some earth beneath your feet for a change?"

"I would indeed. Is there another reason?"

"I need a good man by my side who knows how to fight—if the need arises. You're my first choice."

Their eyes met, and Ritcherd silently thanked God for sending a man like Garret into his life. If he had to be about this ridiculous business of finding the woman he loved, there was no man he'd rather have by his side.

Chapter Thirteen

She Couldn't Wait Another Day

Very few ships came into the little port town. But when they did, Kyrah watched carefully as everyone got off, hoping she might see Ritcherd. Instinctively she believed he would have gotten on a ship just as fast as he could to try and find her. She had discovered that this was a popular port for ships coming from England—mostly privateer vessels. It was a place strictly used by people who lived for any profit they could make off this war. And as yet, the British authorities had no holdings here. She felt that these facts increased the likelihood that if Ritcherd came looking for her, he would eventually come here.

At times she became filled with doubt, convinced that it was ridiculous to expect him to find her here. At other times she felt certain he would arrive any day. Despite her constant changes of heart, she waited patiently day after day, watching each ship carefully. From the window of her room she could see the tops of the docked ships' masts. She became accustomed to counting the number of masts each night and comparing them the following morning. Occasionally she would awaken to see that a ship had come in during the night. The first time it happened she panicked, thinking he might have come and she'd missed him. But by making inquiries about town and learning to assert herself more, she found methods of getting information. And her time at the pier made her rather proficient at knowing which men came and went from which ships.

To ease the wait, she often worked on sewing clothing for the baby. She wasn't as skilled with a needle as her mother, but she was grateful for the skill she'd been taught in her youth that allowed her to be prepared for the coming arrival. There were days when thoughts of her baby gave Kyrah great comfort and a sense of serenity and purpose. But just as with her hope for Ritcherd to find her, she was often swayed to feelings of doubt, even despair, in wondering what kind of life she would have to offer her child.

Kyrah remained persistent in her efforts to find an England-bound ship. Only one opportunity came up, but her hope was dashed when the captain of the vessel adamantly refused to take her aboard. It wasn't until after it had sailed that she wished she had at least sent a letter for her mother. Still, she refused to give up hope that eventually she would find a way home, or that Ritcherd would somehow find her.

The weather cooled as autumn deepened in its march toward winter, but Kyrah couldn't be discouraged from her vigil at the pier. She often wrapped her cloak tightly around her to ward off the continual breezes from the sea. Her days were all much the same. Each evening she would have dinner at the boardinghouse and go to bed with the hope that perhaps tomorrow would be the day Ritcherd found her. After eating breakfast she would walk to the pier, where she sewed a little and watched the seagulls and other shorebirds. She marveled at their simple displays, and enjoyed identifying each type according to her book. The sound of the birds' crying became familiar to her, along with the rush of waves against the shoreline. She would often close her eyes and listen, inhaling the salt in the air, absorbing the cool breeze from the sea. As her surroundings mingled with her emotions, she felt certain that being near the sea would always represent sadness to her. Looking out across the seemingly endless stretch of blue, it seemed to clearly mirror the feelings in her heart. She felt as if the ocean had somehow become her friend, even though at times she had been intensely angry with it for providing the means to tear her away from her home and all she loved. Still, with the endless hours she had spent mesmerized by the ebb and flow of the tide, she felt somehow compelled by the sea. It was as if the ocean itself somehow understood her, and in turn, she had come to understand it.

Kyrah pondered deeply her feelings for the sea, searching for the words that would describe it best. Of course, she found it captivating. She felt drawn to it in the same way she had felt drawn to Ritcherd from the first time she'd laid eyes on him. It was as if there was something inside of her that couldn't be complete without being close to him. But the emptiness she felt in his absence was somehow soothed by the ocean's continual whispering along the shoreline. Still, she knew that the captivating whispers were only one facet of the sea. It was powerful and intense in a way that sharply contrasted with its eloquence. And most amazing to her was the way it could be all of those things at the same time, always leaving her fascinated over what new aspect she might discover.

The only company Kyrah had, beyond the sailors who came and went, was a market vendor with a little cart that he pushed down the pier and back up again each day. He was a clever old man with a lot of beard and very little hair. He sold fruits, breads, and cheeses, and Kyrah often made little purchases from him. His company helped ease her boredom, and the food settled the nagging nausea caused by her condition.

The only break in Kyrah's routine came on Sundays when she visited a local church. She slipped in quietly after the meeting had started in order to avoid bringing any attention to herself. Then she slipped away as soon as the congregation was adjourned and she hurried to the pier.

Kyrah had been visiting the pier for nearly a month when a deep voice startled her from her reverie. "I've heard rumors about you." She turned to see Peter Westman, and had to admit she wasn't entirely disappointed. It was good to see a familiar face—even his.

"Really?" she said. "And what have you heard?"

"There's talk around town of a beautiful phantom woman who stands at the pier every day. And here you are."

Kyrah shrugged, certain he was teasing her. She turned her attention back to the gulls flying overhead. "I would have thought you'd be long gone by now."

"Nonsense," he chuckled. "I wouldn't leave here without you. How are you getting along?" he asked, seeming genuinely concerned.

"Fine, thank you," she replied. He smiled, but Kyrah could almost imagine that he was disappointed. He was congenial and stayed to talk with her until early evening. Kyrah appreciated his company, even though much of what he talked about held no interest for her. He walked her back to the boardinghouse, where she thanked him and left him standing at the door.

Peter began making a habit of seeing her daily at the pier; occasionally he would stay to walk her home, although she was careful never to let him into her room. He seemed puzzled over how she had managed to come up with the money to support herself, but Kyrah evaded his questions, deciding that he could think what he liked. Although he said very little about it, Kyrah sensed that he was dismayed that she was managing fine without his help, and she'd had no problems as a result of being alone and inexperienced, as he'd put it. Much to her relief, he made no further reference to his proposal of marriage. And she didn't contemplate too deeply the reasons for his attention. She simply enjoyed his company for what it was worth, certain that Ritcherd would come for her any day.

It didn't take long for Peter to guess why Kyrah spent so much time at the pier. More than once he repeated his speech about what a wretch Captain Buchanan was, telling her she was a fool to get her hopes up that he would actually go to the trouble to find her. His motives seemed kind enough; he seemed genuinely concerned for her welfare. Still, Kyrah fought to hold on to the feeling in her heart that Ritcherd *did* love her and he *would* come for her. But weeks continued to pass, and still Captain Buchanan did not come to Hedgeton. The illness Kyrah felt from her pregnancy began to subside, but each week she was more aware of the life growing inside of her by the way her figure swelled. Her clothing hid the evidence fairly well, but she was grateful for the cooler weather that made it possible to wear her cloak whenever she was with Peter.

With time she came to be on friendly terms with the market vendor, and discovered his name to be Mr. Birch. She was grateful for his kindness and the distraction he offered, and she was pleased to discover that he shared her interest in the birds along the shoreline. He knew them well, and they had many conversations about their habits and displays. It was the avocets that fascinated Kyrah the most. They had a unique way of eating, and their extravagant courtship rituals were enchanting. Somehow the avocets gave her hope that Ritcherd, who symbolized to her the greatest bird of all, would find her. He just had to!

"Still waiting for the elusive captain?" Peter said lightly as he approached Kyrah on the pier.

Kyrah made no response as she quickly stuffed her sewing into the satchel so Peter wouldn't see that she was making baby clothes. She was relieved that he didn't seem to notice. But then, many times she'd worked on them almost right under his nose, and he'd paid little attention to what she was doing.

"You know," he said softly, sitting close to her, "there is an inn not far from here called the Harbor. The crowd isn't too pleasant, but the food is great. Would you care to dine with me?" Kyrah glanced at him, saying nothing. But he seemed to have grown accustomed to her silence. "Come along," he said, taking her hand. "I'm certain you could use a change of pace from eating at the boardinghouse day after day."

"Actually the food there is very good," she said.

"Nevertheless," he said and continued walking, "a change of pace would do you good."

Kyrah couldn't deny that he was right—on all counts. The crowd at the Harbor was typical of the brash sailors and merchants that dominated the town. But the food was delicious, and the change of pace did feel good. After they'd eaten, Peter took her arm and led her from the inn, aimlessly walking through the dark town of Hedgeton until they came again to the pier.

"You know, Kyrah," he said, standing close to her, "you're very beautiful." Kyrah turned away from him, not wanting him to say such things to her. "I mean it," he went on and his voice softened. "I think you're beautiful. I know you probably find it difficult to believe, but I do love you, Kyrah."

She turned to look into his eyes, wishing she could read his mind. He seemed sincere enough, but she found it difficult to completely trust him.

"Kyrah," he whispered when she made no response, and she felt his arms go around her. She didn't find his embrace distasteful enough to recoil, but she was more concerned that he might detect that she wasn't nearly as slender as she used to be. Preoccupied with her lack of waistline, she was surprised to find his lips against her face. At one time she would have been revolted, but now she felt entirely indifferent. Of course, Peter had changed. She knew that. He was not the same man she had worked for in Cornwall. Nevertheless, that didn't change the fact that she felt absolutely nothing for him. She told herself she should make her feelings known, and not lead him on this way. But she felt somehow hesitant to speak up. She wondered if old habits made it difficult for her to oppose him, or if she was simply stunned by his apparent affection. She watched him closely as he kissed her face, still searching for evidence of his sincerity. Trying to discern her own emotions, she had to admit that his presence was somehow comforting. He was the only tangible connection she had to the life she had known before. And when he behaved this way, she couldn't deny his charm. He was so different from the man she had come to know in England, and she wondered if he had simply found it difficult to know how to express his feelings appropriately. Could it be possible that he really loved her?

His lips touched hers, startling her to the realization that she was allowing him to tread into territory that belonged to someone else. She quickly turned her face, feeling as if she had just betrayed Ritcherd. She suddenly missed him so deeply that she felt a tangible pain in her chest. She pressed a hand there as Peter touched her chin and looked into her eyes. Not wanting him to see the emotion rising there, she turned her back to him, murmuring, "Please . . . don't."

He said nothing more as he escorted her back to her room. But the loneliness seemed to close in around her after he left. Preparing for bed, Kyrah glanced in the mirror and ran her hand over where Ritcherd Buchanan's child was gradually becoming more evident. This manifestation of time's passing struck her in a way that she had not allowed herself to feel. She crawled into bed and tried to sleep, but her mind roiled in growing turmoil and confusion. She began to wonder if Peter might have been right. Perhaps Ritcherd would have realized by now that they were not well suited to each other. She knew Ritcherd loved her. But how much? And perhaps love was irrelevant. Facts be faced, she was alone in this hole of a town, unwed and pregnant. Her fears began to take hold, squelching the ebbing belief that Ritcherd would find her and make the circumstances right between them. She forced herself to take a long, hard look at where she might end up if Ritcherd didn't find her and she was unable to find passage back to England—or even if she did. Wherever she might end up, she would be the mother of an illegitimate child. She had the diamond necklace, but no matter how much income she got from selling it, the money would run out eventually. She had no means to support herself beyond the menial labor that she had once done. And people who valued their reputations would not be hiring an unwed mother; it was a taint that would never leave her. Only Ritcherd could erase such a blemish, but he was not here. And time's passing increased the probability that he wasn't coming.

Consumed with the stark reality of her position and its accompanying fears, Kyrah cried herself into a numb exhaustion. She finally drifted to sleep, only to wake up again soon after dawn with her fears catapulting through her mind all over again. Spurred by a helpless desperation, she sank to her knees by the bed and poured her heart out in prayer, certain that nothing short of a miracle could save her from an impending doom. She didn't find any immediate answers, but she left for the pier right after breakfast, determined not to let go of the hope that Ritcherd would come. When it became evident that no ships had come in since the previous evening, she walked the pier, asking all the usual places about getting passage to England. She wasn't surprised to hear the same old answers, but at least she felt like she was trying; she was doing everything she could. She could only pray that God would somehow make up the difference.

Kyrah left the pier early when it started to rain, and she managed to avoid Peter. That night she prayed herself to sleep rather than succumbing to her fears. But she woke up to find the sky drizzling and gray. And Mrs. Dodd informed her at breakfast that her rent would be all used up in two more days. Kyrah paid for another week, but the time passed quickly, so she paid for another. Her pregnancy became increasingly difficult to hide, and Peter appeared each day, seeming more determined than ever that she should marry him. She felt somehow detached from herself as she listened to him tell her over and over how much he cared for her, how he would see that her needs were met, and he would do his best to make her happy. He reminded her once again that they were two of a kind, and that he understood her because of the social status they shared.

Kyrah tried to remain hopeful, tried to find something logical to hold on to that might give her strength to resist the means Peter was offering to solve her problems. But each day the confusion and discouragement became stronger, gradually stifling her hopes and beliefs. One day she stayed at the pier later than usual, knowing she was out of time. The rent would be used up tomorrow, and she was almost out of money. She would either have to sell the necklace and begin to face life as an unwed mother, or . . . Could she even entertain the thought? Had she become so desperate that she would actually consider it? Yes, she decided firmly, she had. She could marry Peter. Once she allowed the thought into her mind, it took hold and began to seem so easy. She could stop waiting and wondering. She could stop fearing the future for herself and her child. She could have security and return to England without the scandal and shame of her circumstances. There was something cold and horrible at the core of her that was repulsed and disgusted by the idea. It would solve her problems now, but what would it do to the rest of her life? Could she live with such a decision? On the other hand, could she live with the scandal and shame and probable poverty of her circumstances if she didn't accept his offer?

Trying to look at the positive, Kyrah had come to believe that Peter Westman really did love her. He'd been so kind, so sincere. But sincere or not, she knew she could never love him. It was Ritcherd Buchanan who held her heart captive, and he always would. But too much time had passed. The few ships that had come from England during her stay here had not yet brought him, and Kyrah had to admit that he probably was not coming.

As afternoon faded into evening, Kyrah was grateful that Peter had only shown himself for a few minutes that morning. It was easier to feel hopeful when she looked out over the sea. But when it began to get dark, she forced herself to head home. She was deep in thought over her dilemma when a hand reached out of an alleyway, pulling her into the shadows. For a moment she recalled the time Ritcherd had abducted her. For a moment she wished with everything she had that it was him now. But it quickly became evident that it wasn't, and suddenly her fears for the future were put into heart-stopping perspective.

She was overcome with the stench of body odor and liquor as she was dragged by two men deeper into the alley. One of them kept a hand clamped firmly over her mouth while they discussed what a beauty she was and how much fun they could have with her. She fought and squirmed with all the energy she could muster, while a part of her hoped she would not survive this—then her problems would be solved. They nearly threw her to the ground and held her there, while she prayed that she *would* survive, if only for the sake of her child.

"Hold it right there!" Kyrah heard a familiar voice call out, followed by the cocking of a pistol. The men released their grip and put their hands up. She scrambled to her feet and could barely make out Peter standing at the entrance to the alley, a pistol in each hand. She couldn't help recalling a similar situation on board the *Libertatia*. But she was too filled with gratitude to question the coincidence.

"Peter!" she cried, and ran to put him between herself and her abductors. He kept the pistols pointed at them as he backed out of the alley, keeping her securely behind him.

"Think twice," he said, "before you lay your hands on this lady again. You might find yourselves dead."

The men ran the other way, and Kyrah nearly collapsed with relief. "Are you all right?" Peter asked, putting the pistols into his belt. Kyrah nodded and attempted to get control of her breathing, fearing she might pass out if she didn't. "Are you sure?" he added, touching her chin.

"Yes, thank you," she said, and he guided her silently back to her room at the boardinghouse. Kyrah hardly noticed that he came into the room with her. He guided her to a chair, and she realized she was shaking. She held her cloak tightly around her and couldn't find the will to protest when Peter slid the other chair close beside her and put his arms around her. He whispered soothing words that encouraged the tears she was fighting to hold back. Sobbing against his shoulder, the full reality of her circumstances came crashing down upon her. She cried for the fear of what she'd just been saved from, and she cried for the loss of every hope she had been clinging to. When she finally managed to stop crying, a numb dread settled into her like a cold wind that chilled her to the very core.

"Will you be all right, my dear?" Peter asked tenderly.

"Yes, of course," she said, while her words felt distant and obscure. "Thank you . . . for being there."

"I'm glad that I was," he said, kissing her cheek. He cleared his throat slightly. "You know, Kyrah, it terrifies me more than ever to think of you alone in this dreadful place. Let's get married . . . soon, and I'll take you away from here."

Kyrah looked into his eyes as if she might find the answers there. Not certain whether she'd found them or not, she stood quickly and began pacing.

"What is it that keeps you from saying yes?" he asked in dismay.

"My heart belongs to another man," she stated.

"Ritcherd Buchanan," Peter stated with obvious disgust.

"Yes," she said sadly and continued pacing. In her mind she tallied every aspect of the situation with frantic urgency. The facts stood out sharply, just as they had for days now. But it was the child's welfare that concerned her most. It deserved better than to be born illegitimate, with no security, shamed for life. She deserved better than to do hard labor all her life to support a child—or worse, she could end up in prostitution. But would Peter accept Ritcherd's child? If he loved her, he would have no choice. It was a part of her. Peter was offering what she needed: a husband, security, protection. Forcing herself to think reasonably, she decided to find out exactly where he stood.

"Peter." She stopped pacing and stood to face him. "You know that I'm not in love with you. I've not led you on."

"I know that," he said.

"And you know that I love another man. I believe I always will."

"I feel confident that time could change such feelings," Peter said.

"But now. We have to talk about now."

A light of hope came into Peter's eyes that urged her to go on.

"You're right when you say that I should get married. I should not be alone. But there are more reasons than the ones you have spoken of. You must understand that there is a part of Ritcherd Buchanan that will always be with me. You have to accept that."

"Kyrah," he said, taking her hands, "are you saying what I think you're saying?"

"I suppose I am." She glanced away, then met his eyes directly. "Will you accept me for what I am now—and for the way I feel?"

"Oh, yes," he said with obvious pleasure.

"Even knowing that . . . well, Ritcherd and I were very close. And he has left a very real part of him with me . . . that I will never be free of. That's the real reason I need to get married, Peter. You must accept that, if you accept me."

"Of course," he smiled, but she wondered if he'd even been listening. "I love you, Kyrah," he added gently. "Nothing else matters. I will take you just as you are, and perhaps one day . . ."

"Don't speak of that for now," she said, turning away. "We'll take it one day at a time."

"Whatever you say, my dear," he said with a smile and kissed her. And with his kiss, her little remaining hope disappeared.

When Kyrah was left alone, she realized that her decision had been the result of fear and desperation. She sat numbly on the edge of the bed, searching for any degree of strength inside of her that might ward off the fear and help her to know if she was doing the right thing. But she could see no other way. She didn't *want* to marry Peter. But she simply could see no other way.

Before crawling into bed, she prayed for strength and guidance, feeling at the same time that she didn't have enough faith left to propel her prayers past the ceiling. She lay awake far into the night, while an inner voice seemed to whisper that she shouldn't do it, that she should just hold on, have faith, and believe in her own strength. But the fear overruled and she finally slept, resigning herself to her fate. The following morning, Kyrah went to the pier as usual and stood numbly in the same spot for hours, gazing out to sea, knowing this would be the last time. She couldn't wait another day. At first she felt too numb to cry, but eventually the tears trickled down her face, quickly drying as they met with the salt-tinged breeze.

"Are ye all right, Miss?" Mr. Birch's voice startled her.

"No," she said, turning back to look at the sea, as if a ship might appear on the horizon—a ship that might rescue her from her plight. The old man took her hand and urged her to sit beside him. She hadn't intended to tell him her story, but as the words poured out, along with the tears, she felt somehow better—even if it didn't change what she had to do.

When there was no more to say, Mr. Birch asked, "Why are ye goin' t' marry someone who's not th' cap'n?"

Kyrah swallowed hard and simply repeated what she'd already told him. "I'm in trouble. I can't wait another day."

The old man's brow furrowed with concern, but he didn't ask what kind of trouble she was in. His compassion and listening ear were appreciated, but he couldn't help her. No one could help her but Ritcherd. And she couldn't wait another day.

"I want to thank you for your kindness all these weeks," she said, taking his hand. "I probably won't be seeing you again. We'll be leaving here as soon as we're married. He says that we'll move south, and eventually return to England." Kyrah sighed. Repeating it to him made it all sound so horrible. But she felt helpless to do anything about it.

Kyrah didn't leave the pier until the sun had gone down, and long past midnight, sleep still eluded her. As the hours slipped by, she felt herself losing something that she would never find again. There was a dream in Kyrah's heart of a life she should have shared with Ritcherd. Despite how hard she'd tried to keep that dream, fate had seemed to work against it in the years since Ritcherd had gone to war. And it now appeared inevitable. She had to stop waiting.

As the new day dawned over a sleepless night, she felt those dreams drifting away forever, and resigned herself to live without Captain Ritcherd Buchanan. The times they'd shared together were far in the past. It was too long ago. They'd been too long apart.

Watching sunlight filter through the window, Kyrah thought of the stories she'd heard of men going to the gallows at dawn. At this moment she was certain she knew how they felt. Again, a voice seemed to whisper inside of her that it wasn't too late. She didn't have to go through with it. And once again she tallied the facts and her fear overruled. She could see no other way.

Feeling like a puppet, moving by the will of some power beyond her own, Kyrah packed her things and returned the key to Mrs. Dodd. Peter came for her right on time with a hired carriage. As they rode together toward the little church on the outskirts of town, he proudly told her how he had everything arranged.

While they held hands to be married, Kyrah watched Peter through a fog of confusion. It wasn't until she had spoken her vows that a thought occurred to her. Until that moment, she had believed that her despair was in admitting defeat. She was removing herself from Ritcherd's life forever. But now she realized it was more. The reality was that she would be Peter's wife, and there were aspects of being married to him that she knew would be unbearable. As he slid a gold band onto her finger and kissed her to seal their marriage, Kyrah's thoughts went to her fear of ending up in prostitution. Then she looked into his eyes and realized that there was little difference between that fate and what she had just done. She had sold herself for the sake of being saved from shame and poverty. But the shame would always be with her. She felt certain that by tomorrow morning she would feel so completely defiled that Ritcherd Buchanan would not want her, even if she was free. But there was little point in speculating over such things now. As she left the church wearing Peter Westman's ring, she had to face reality. Captain Ritcherd Buchanan was lost to her.

Kyrah's thoughts wandered as they rode in the carriage, and she was startled to the moment when it drew to a halt much sooner than she'd expected. "Where is this?" she asked. A quick glance out the window told her they were still in Hedgeton.

"This is where I've been living," he said as the carriage door opened. She was thinking that he would be stopping to get his things, but he stepped down and held up a hand to help her. "And now this is where you'll be living."

Kyrah stood beside him and said, "But you told me we would be leaving here . . . that we would—"

"Well, I changed my mind," he said in a tone of voice that chilled her. It reminded her all too keenly of the man she had worked for in Cornwall. He took her bags into one hand and her arm in the other, leading her toward the door of the little house as the carriage rolled away. Everything inside of Kyrah was telling her to scream and run. Something was wrong—horribly wrong. She felt as frightened and helpless as she had when she'd been dragged down the alley by a couple of drunk sailors.

Once they were inside, Peter let go of her arm, but she could feel where he'd held her by the pain that lingered. He tossed her bags onto the floor of the front hallway and leaned against the door. Kyrah watched him closely, trying to convince herself that his concern and affection for her all this time hadn't simply been some overblown charade. She tried not to show her fear, but knew she had failed when he shook his head and laughed. And she could almost hear the devil laughing right along with him.

"Oh, Kyrah, Kyrah. You sweet, gullible fool. Your innocence warms me, I must say. But now that I've got what I want, there's no point in pretending any longer, is there."

"And what is that?" she asked, her voice barely steady.

He laughed again—a triumphant, wicked laugh. "I've got *you*. Who'd have dreamed when I won that card game that I would be getting such an opportunity in the bargain? You see, Kyrah, you're as big a fool as your father. He was gullible too, you know. But I wonder if you *do* know that he left a great deal of money behind. And you and I are going to find it, my dear. With you as my wife, it's *my* money now, wherever it may be."

"It doesn't exist," she insisted, as if she could talk him out of the vows they had just exchanged. "I searched everywhere."

"Well, obviously I knew you hadn't found it, or you wouldn't have been working for me—and what a pity that would have been. But I'm certain it exists. You just don't know how to hunt for money the way I do, my dear. However, that was only part of my motive for marrying you." He laughed again as he folded his arms and moved to lean against a little table. "You can't imagine how thrilled I was to realize that Ritcherd Buchanan, beloved war hero, had a soft spot for you—which was quite contrary to his mother's sentiments."

"What are you saying?" she asked when he made no further explanation.

"I'm saying, my dear, that we are here compliments of Jeanette Buchanan—which probably doesn't surprise you. But I think the price she was willing to pay me for this marriage certificate would probably make your head swim. Between your father's hidden treasure and the bounty on our marriage, I'll be set for life. And you, my dear, will have the benefit of sharing that life with me—once we get other matters out of the way."

Kyrah discreetly eyed her bags at his feet, knowing that she could never survive without the necklace hidden in the lining of one of them. He was no longer blocking the door. She just had to grab them and run. But she barely took a step toward them before he was in front of her like a flash of lightning, as if he had predicted her next move precisely.

"There's no point in running, Kyrah," he said, so close to her face that she could feel his hot breath. "You wouldn't want to go into public anyway, with that nasty bruise on your face."

Kyrah's puzzlement over his statement ended when he backhanded her across the face with such force that she found herself on the floor. She tasted blood and saw stars while Peter spoke to her in a harsh whisper. "You probably think you're so clever, tricking me into marrying you with another man's baby growing inside you. Did you think I hadn't noticed? Did you think I was really so stupid?"

Kyrah bit back the protests that came to mind, knowing that anything she said would only make him more angry. He hit her again. "You won't make a fool out of me, Kyrah," he screamed and any trace of his calm demeanor dissipated as he struck her over and over, cursing and raging.

He told her she was nothing more than a worthless serving wench, and the pompous Ritcherd Buchanan had made a whore out of her. He said that she should have listened when he'd told her that the captain would only use her and toss her aside. And Jeanette Buchanan had been right in trying to keep her son away from a deceptive little tramp. Gradually Kyrah ceased her screaming and protests, numbly letting him hit her while she cried inside, wondering what kind of madness she had subjected herself to.

She felt a blessed relief when he finally stopped and left her lying curled up on the floor. Through swollen, throbbing eyes she looked up at him, silently questioning the way he was glaring at her. She instinctively clutched the buttons of her bodice with clenched fists and slid away. As if he'd read her mind, he laughed again and said, "Oh, don't worry about that, Kyrah—at least not yet." His voice was calm again, malevolent and cold. "I have no desire to share a bed with you when Captain Buchanan's brat will be there, too. No, there will be plenty of time for such niceties. Considering he was home from war about a week before you left him, it shouldn't be too difficult to figure when the brat will no longer be a problem. And that's when I'll be back, Kyrah. The rent is paid on the house for another six months, and there's plenty here for you to eat. I assume you can manage. But you certainly don't have the means to run—as if you could go anywhere looking like that. And even if you did run, I would find you. You're mine now, and I've got the document to prove it."

Kyrah barely clung to consciousness, vaguely aware of noises that indicated he was packing. She heard the door slam and succumbed to the lure of oblivion, wishing that she would never wake up again.

Kyrah drifted in and out of coherency through an eternal night. More than once she dreamt of Ritcherd, lying in some makeshift military hospital, writhing in pain after being shot in the arm. Then her dreams merged into reality as she awoke to find herself in more pain than she'd ever comprehended. And if the physical pain weren't horrible enough, the scope of what she had done made her curl around the pillow and groan. How could she have been so stupid—so thoroughly and utterly stupid? Was she so naive? So gullible? Obviously she was. She had made choices that had thrown her into this mess—choices that could never be undone.

In the deepest part of the night, Kyrah felt as if the darkness would swallow her whole. She felt tempted to curse God for allowing such horrors to happen to her. Then she recalled the repeated whisperings from within that had seemed to warn her. She had ignored those whisperings and given in to her fear instead. And now it seemed her life was over.

As daylight finally filtered into the bedroom where she lay, Kyrah barely managed to open one of her eyes and survey her surroundings. The room felt cold and barren, void of any color or warmth. When her brief perusal intensified the pain in her head, she closed her eyes against the light and attempted to relax. Unable to bear the helplessness and despair surrounding her, she cried into her pillow, heedless of the resulting pain. And while she cried, she prayed. She prayed for forgiveness, and she prayed for strength. At the moment, she just needed the strength to make it through the day, to find something to eat. And she prayed that her baby would survive what her body had been subjected to. She told herself she should be grateful that Peter hadn't forced himself upon her. And while there was no question concerning her relief, there was a degree of humiliation in being rejected by someone so low. What kind of woman was she, that a man like Peter Westman could disparage and degrade her so thoroughly?

Kyrah was barely aware of the room's brightening with the light of morning, while nightmarish images of the previous day flashed repeatedly through her mind. Her relief in knowing that Peter had left was overshadowed by the fear of what her fate might be when he returned. What kind of life would she face? What would he do to her child?

Kyrah's growling stomach finally forced her to get out of bed. She fought the pounding in her head and managed to open both her eyes enough to focus. As she rose unsteadily to her feet, every muscle in her body protested. She took a few steps toward the bureau mirror and cried out at the sight of her own reflection. Her face was so swollen and discolored that she hardly recognized herself. And with the way it hurt to move, she suspected the rest of her body was equally battered. She knew she couldn't go back to the pier and hope for Ritcherd to miraculously disembark from one of the few ships that came here. It would be a very long time before she could even leave the house. And even longer before she could face the reality of what her life would be like, married to a madman.

Ritcherd's relief was indescribable when the goods were finally delivered and the transaction went smoothly and without incident. By sunlight the following morning, the *Phoenix* was sporting the colors of the colonies and sailing toward the only port where Garret was certain they'd meet no trouble. Ritcherd was amused, when he went with George to retrieve the colors, to see that the ship was also carrying British and French flags, as well as the Jolly Roger they'd been flying the majority of the time until now.

The *Phoenix* dropped anchor at the dock of Hedgeton, and Captains Garret and Buckley went ashore to check out the situation. As soon as they started moving through the streets, Ritcherd was immediately grateful for his reformed appearance. This was obviously a place common for pirates and privateers, or one trying to pass themselves off as the other. An aristocrat would have probably been beheaded before he reached the tavern. A woman like Kyrah would have been sorely out of place, but Ritcherd still watched for her continually. He formed an image in his mind of what she might look like walking among people on the street. Picking out every woman he saw, he realized that none of them was even Kyrah's type, let alone coming close to her beauty.

Ritcherd followed Garret to an inn called the Harbor. He didn't feel the least bit conspicuous as they entered and found a table in the corner, but he was keenly aware of all eyes following them. He concluded that Garret had a commanding presence that was difficult to ignore.

They'd only been seated a few minutes when the innkeeper approached them and set two drinks on the table. "Cap'n Garret!" he laughed as they shook hands.

"How are ye, Leon?" Garret said.

"Doin' well. And business is good."

"Glad t' 'ear it," Garret said. "I'd like ye t' meet m' new partner, Cap'n Buckley."

"A pleasure," Leon said, shaking Ritcherd's hand as well.

"Th' pleasure's mine," Ritcherd said, glad they weren't meeting in a dark alley. For all Leon's friendliness, there was a suspicious air about him.

Leon sat down and exchanged small talk with Garret for a few minutes while Ritcherd sipped his drink and discreetly observed his surroundings. He realized that everyone here looked suspicious. It was as if no one was willing to completely trust anyone else. There were practically no women in the place, and most of the ones here were serving drinks and flirting with the sailors. He wouldn't find Kyrah here.

When Ritcherd turned his attention back to Garret, he was whispering something close to Leon's ear. Leon nodded and walked away. Garret followed him. They disappeared into a back room, and Ritcherd realized he didn't like the feeling of being alone. The cutlass and pistol in his belt were suddenly a great comfort—and knowing he had the ability to use them added to his peace of mind. He shuddered to imagine Kyrah alone in a town like this. For the sake of distraction, he pulled Kyrah's brooch out of his pocket. He toyed with it absently as he often did when he felt idle.

Garret returned a few minutes later and leaned across the table. Ritcherd expected the usual answer, but his heart beat quickly as Garret whispered, "The *Libertatia* docked here six weeks after it left England. It couldn't have stopped anywhere else. According to the timing, it's perfect. There was one woman on board."

Ritcherd realized he had lost all sense of time, and it was a good thing Garret hadn't. It seemed like years since he'd seen Kyrah. "So now what?" he asked, hearing a tremor of excitement in his voice.

"We ask around. Find out if anyone's seen her." Garret lifted his brows deviously. "Maybe she's still here." Ritcherd smiled and Garret went on, "Several of the crew have friends or family in this area. In fact, this is where I came across a number of them in the first place. So, unless something comes up to change our plans, I think we'll settle in here for a while. You can take your time and give the place a thorough search. I'll be seeing that we get the supplies we need. And we can all get in some land time." He lifted his brows and added, "It keeps life in balance."

Garret grinned and took a swallow of his drink. Ritcherd resisted the urge to jump out of his chair and begin combing the streets this very instant. While he was formulating some measure of a plan in his mind, he was surprised to feel the brooch open in his hand.

"I did it," he said and Garret looked puzzled.

"Did what?"

"Nothing, really." Ritcherd chuckled, looking at the open clasp. He wondered if he'd worn it out, but examining the clasp closer, he could see that he really had opened it.

"It was kind of a challenge," he told Garret, trying to fasten it again. It took a great deal of effort to maneuver the finger and thumb of his right hand, but he *could* do it.

"So," Garret said, "the right hand's not so useless after all."

"No," Ritcherd chuckled as he undid the brooch again, almost fascinated by his own fingers, "I suppose it's not."

Garret smiled and finished his drink. The captains returned to the ship, where Garret gave detailed orders of what they'd be doing the next several weeks while they remained in port. By alternating shifts, they would take turns at keeping watch on the ship, seeing to the necessary work, and having some recreation. The *Phoenix* would undergo some necessary maintenance and be checked thoroughly for seaworthiness, and supplies would be purchased and brought aboard.

After the men were assigned their tasks, Garret turned to Ritcherd and said, "While I'm overseein' all o' this, I want ye t' stay in port and remain persistent on that little problem we discussed earlier t'day."

Ritcherd smiled and nodded. When the men dispersed, he turned to Garret, who added with a smirk, "Now, while you're searching for your lady, I'm going to find one of my own."

"Anyone in particular?" he asked as they left the ship together.

"Aye. I've been to this port many times. And with any luck she's not forgotten me."

Garret smiled and saluted casually, leaving Ritcherd to begin his search.

Within a couple of days, Kyrah was grateful to be able to get around enough to care for herself, in spite of the intolerable pain that accompanied her every movement. But the bread, cheese, and apples that she'd found in the kitchen were quickly used up. The only other food she found was a generous supply of flour, yeast, and some basic baking supplies. Was that what Peter considered "plenty" for her to eat? The means for her to make bread? If she couldn't go into public until her face healed, she had little choice. The bit of money she had left hidden in her satchel would do her little good if she was confined to the house. And even making bread would be a challenge with the weakness and pain that plagued her.

Through the following days, Kyrah relied on prayer more than she ever had in her life. She found strength she could never explain as she managed to care for herself. And somewhere deep inside she found the hope that she could one day get beyond this and find some measure of happiness. She clung to that hope and encouraged it to grow. Her present circumstances were a blatant reminder of what could happen when hope became replaced by fear.

A week after Peter had left, Kyrah was surprised to hear a knock at the door. She set her sewing aside and peered carefully through a curtain in the parlor to see who it might be. A pleasant-looking blonde woman stood on the little porch with a basket over one arm. Her hair was pulled back tightly and plaited. She wore a starched apron over a skirt and bodice that reminded her of the maids who worked at the inns and taverns.

Kyrah feared that the bruises on her face might frighten the woman away, but she felt compelled to open the door. She hesitated with her hand on the knob and realized that her experience with Peter had made it difficult for her to trust other people. Uttering a quick prayer for discernment and guidance, she opened the door just a bit and tried to ignore the woman's astonishment. Through the brief silence that followed, Kyrah guessed this woman to be near her own age, perhaps a little older.

"May I help you?" Kyrah asked as the woman glanced away, seeming embarrassed.

"My name is Daisy," she said brightly, turning again to look at her as if nothing in the world was out of the ordinary. "I'm your neighbor. I'd heard that the man living here had brought home a bride, but I'd not seen anyone coming or going. With the lights on at night and all . . . well, I wondered if everything was all right." While Kyrah was attempting to come up with a suitable answer, she narrowed her eyes and added, "But it's not, is it."

Kyrah glanced down. "You must forgive my appearance. I was afraid I might frighten you off, but . . ."

"Don't be worrying about that," Daisy said. "Is there something I might do to help you out? I don't want to make you uncomfortable, but . . . well, do you need anything in town I might get for you? It would be no trouble."

Kyrah felt such immense relief from the offer that she was tempted to accuse Daisy of being an angel sent from heaven. She simply said, "That would be wonderful. I have some money, but my supplies are depleted and I don't want to go out looking this way."

"I'd be happy to do it," Daisy said. "What do you need? Fruit, vegetables, meat, milk?"

"A little of everything would be good, I suppose," Kyrah said. "But there's only me, so I don't need much."

"I've got to get along to work now," Daisy said, turning to leave, "but I'll stop back on my way home."

"Wait," Kyrah called, "let me get the money for you."

"Ah, fie," she said, pushing her hand through the air. "You can pay me when I bring it back, then I'll know how much."

"Thank you," Kyrah said and watched through the curtain as Daisy walked away. She sighed and closed her eyes, grateful for this tangible evidence that God was looking out for her.

Daisy returned later as promised, with her basket full of supplies and a lot of friendly chatter. They sat together in the kitchen to visit, and Kyrah realized just how hungry she was for company. Following some friendly small talk, Daisy said, "You'll find I'm not the type to waste time on formalities. If we're going to be neighbors, we need to start acting like it. But first I need to know your name."

"Kyrah," she replied, deciding to forego the rest. She doubted she could even bring herself to say her new legal name aloud.

"Are you alone here?" she asked.

"My . . . husband is gone for now."

"Was he the one who gave you those souvenirs on your face?"

Kyrah looked away quickly and Daisy went on, "I'm sorry if I said something out of line. That's none of my business. I've been accused of intruding where I'm not invited, but you look like you could use a friend, and maybe it would do you good to talk about it."

"But I don't even know you," Kyrah said.

"Sure you do," Daisy said with a gentle smirk. "We're neighbors. You know my name. Let me tell you about myself. I came from England, where I was raised by my snippet of an aunt. I left as soon as I had a chance. It was miserable! I live in the cottage down the lane—all by myself. I work in town serving meals and drinks. I was married for nearly two years, but he was killed in the war. I've been on my own for going on three years now. So you see, you know all about me. Now it's your turn."

For a long moment Kyrah searched her feelings. Instinctively she trusted Daisy, and she ached to have someone share her grief. Perhaps it was Daisy's genuine candor that made it easy to say what she'd wanted to be able to tell someone for months now. "I too came from England," she began, and the story unfolded with more detail than Kyrah had intended to give. Daisy's amazement and compassion felt somehow healing to Kyrah. She shed a few stray tears, and she was astounded to see Daisy's eyes fill with mist more than once. Was her story so tragic? Yes, she had to admit, it was.

"Oh, you poor dear," Daisy said when Kyrah finally finished. She took Kyrah's hand across the table and added firmly, "Well, you're not alone anymore. If you need anything at all, I'm only a few steps away. I get lonely for female companionship myself."

Daisy ended up staying to chat while Kyrah prepared some of the food she'd purchased. Together they washed and cut vegetables to add to a simmering broth. It was well past dark when they sat to share their meal of soup, along with some bread that Kyrah had made the day before. The soup tasted so good to Kyrah that she ate three bowls. And Daisy's company was equally satisfying.

Daisy finally went home when they could both hardly stay awake, but she returned the following day on her way to work, just to make certain

Kyrah was all right. Her visits quickly became a daily habit that Kyrah greatly looked forward to. Daisy's friendship lent some diversion to her long days and helped her deal with some of the horrors she had been through.

Through their long conversations, Daisy made Kyrah realize that she had to keep trying to get passage back to England. "Things like that don't just pop out of the blue," she said. "You've got to keep trying."

Despite her admission that she'd be lonely without her, Daisy insisted that Kyrah belonged with her mother at home, and she offered to do all she could to help find an England-bound ship that would take a lady passenger. "I know those kind of people," Daisy said. "I see them every day. I'll start working on it."

While Kyrah often wondered what she would do without Daisy and her continual optimism and listening ear, Daisy often expressed appreciation for Kyrah's friendship in turn. It was apparent that her husband's death had been difficult, and even though she didn't have much spare time on her hands, her loneliness was evident, although she admitted to having more than one "friend," as she called them. And she was occasionally off to spend time with one male suitor or another—although she didn't seem to take any of them too seriously. They were sailors who came and went from port with long intervals in between. After the love she'd shared with her husband, she wasn't certain if she could ever find happiness again. Kyrah often wondered the same about Ritcherd. Could there possibly be a way to undo what stood between them? Could there be another chance? If not, she felt certain that true fulfillment would evade her forever. No matter what her future might bring, without Ritcherd there would always be a hole in her heart.

For days that seemed endless, Ritcherd diligently questioned every person who didn't look like they'd rather shoot him than talk. The majority of the people were close-lipped and unwilling to help. But Ritcherd was careful to watch people's eyes when he described Kyrah, and he felt confident that no one had lied to him when they said they'd not seen her.

Each day at the same time, Ritcherd met Garret at a certain table in a tavern called the Captain's Wheel. Garret often made humorous references to the name, and said if they were to meet anywhere for a drink, it would have to be there. Ritcherd was endlessly grateful for Garret's daily encouragement and lighthearted attitude concerning his search for Kyrah. And he came to depend on their daily meeting to keep him going.

Ritcherd had lost track of the days they'd been in port when he came across a man sitting casually in front of a cobbler's shop. From his rough appearance and crafty eyes, Ritcherd doubted that his main occupation was really making shoes. He almost didn't ask him, but he couldn't pass anyone by, or he'd always wonder if they might have been the one who knew something. He asked the usual questions, and his heart quickened when he saw recognition in the man's eyes. He seemed hesitant to talk, but when Ritcherd handed him some money, he stuffed it up his sleeve and said, "Yeah, I seen 'er."

Ritcherd's heart raced as he sat down. "When?" he asked, trying to stay calm.

"Been a long time."

"Did ye speak with 'er?" Ritcherd asked.

"Yeah. She wanted me t' buy somethin' from 'er."

"What?" Ritcherd pursued.

"It were some diamond earrings. Pretty things. I made a healthy profit from 'em, too."

Ritcherd's stomach churned with mixed emotions. He didn't know whether to jump up and down or cry. She'd been here. He knew that. He had a lead. But what kind of desperate situation was she in now, if she'd had to sell her earrings a long time ago? He knew her, and he knew she wouldn't have sold them if she hadn't needed the money very badly. He told himself he should be grateful to know that she'd brought them with her and they had given her the means to meet her needs. There was a degree of peace in knowing that she hadn't been left here penniless.

"'Ave ye seen 'er since?" Ritcherd asked. If she'd had to resort to selling the necklace, she'd have come to the same place.

"No," he said flatly, "I ain't."

"If ye see 'er again," Ritcherd said, "could ye tell 'er that Cap'n Buckley is aboard the *Phoenix* and needs t' see 'er?" He hoped she would realize it was him.

"If I see 'er," the man replied, "I can tell 'er."

"Thank ye," Ritcherd said and gave him more money. "Thank ye very much."

The man looked into his hand and smiled. "My pleasure."

It was several days later before Ritcherd found the boardinghouse where Kyrah Payne had stayed. His heart jumped freshly when he saw her signature on the registry. He knew it well. Although the woman he spoke with was hesitant and ornery, she told him everything she knew when he offered her money in return. Kyrah's stay there had begun the day the *Libertatia* had arrived in port. She had paid for most of her stay in advance, and had eaten the two daily meals that were included with the fee. She'd left each day after breakfast and come in each evening before supper. She had been extremely quiet and kept to herself, and no one there had learned anything about who she was or where she was from. No one had cared to.

"And that's it," Ritcherd stated.

"As far as I can remember," the old lady said. "Oh, wait. There was a man come in with 'er a time or two."

"What did 'e look like?" Ritcherd asked, feeling more than a little unsettled.

"Seems like 'e was dark, about yer age. Didn't look like 'er type. But then," she added, "ye don't either."

When the woman had told all she knew, Ritcherd walked back onto the street, feeling no closer to finding Kyrah than he had before. When she'd left the boardinghouse, she had done so without any comment as to where she was going, and she'd not been seen since. He walked slowly to the pier and gazed out to sea, wondering where to go from here. It was almost more frustrating to know that she'd been here and left than not to know anything. He kept thinking: if only they'd gotten here sooner. He glanced toward the *Phoenix*, resting peacefully at the dock. The painting of the vibrant bird with the sun behind its wings somehow gave him the motivation he needed to keep searching.

The following day began a stretch of more than a month that Ritcherd tore the town apart searching for Kyrah Payne. He knew where she had purchased almost everything she must have bought since she'd arrived. But no one had any idea where she was now. He went again to the pier as he did each evening, and gazed longingly at the painting of the phoenix, as if it might give him an answer. He could hear the seagulls crying above him and gazed upward at them flying easily in circles above the sea. If only he could fly, he thought. He could find her if he could fly.

Chapter Fourteen

Liasons

"You know," Daisy said one afternoon while they shared tea on the little back porch of Kyrah's house, "you should be thinking about what to do if you don't get passage before that baby comes. I don't think you should take any chances on being here when that husband of yours returns."

"I've been thinking about that," Kyrah admitted. "I suppose I just don't want to face the possibility."

"Well, not facing it isn't going to solve the problem, honey. If you ask me, and you probably wouldn't, but I have to say that you'd have done well to be facing up to what life's given you a long time ago."

"What do you mean?" Kyrah asked, feeling defensive without fully understanding why.

"I mean that a person might not have any control over what life dishes out, but they can certainly decide what to do with it. You can't change the past, but you can figure out what got you here and make certain you don't ever end up in such a mess again. Sitting here not thinking about what to do to get out of this mess isn't going to fix it. Your time's running out, honey. If there's any hope for you and that baby to have any freedom and peace, you're going to have to make some decisions—and soon."

Kyrah sighed and looked away. She broke the silence with the words that had tumbled around in her mind for months. "If only Ritcherd had come. If he—"

"Now, wait a minute," Daisy interrupted, leaning over the table toward Kyrah, "there's something I have to say about that. I've been biting my tongue since the first time we talked about your dear Captain Buchanan. But I would hope you can see by now that I am your friend, and I would never say anything to you if I didn't have your best interests at heart. Is that true?"

"Of course," Kyrah said, even though she suspected that Daisy's advice would not be pleasant.

"Well, as I see it, you've spent so many years depending on Ritcherd Buchanan to make things right for you that you don't know how to make things right for yourself—or at least you think you don't. You managed to take care of yourself and your mother all that time on your own. You managed well enough after you arrived here. And I think you could have kept managing just fine. You're smart. You're capable. And you're brave. You've faced things that would have made a lot of women crumble. But you've survived. And you're stronger for it. You don't need Ritcherd Buchanan."

Kyrah was so stunned that it took her a moment to gather her words. "But I love him," she protested.

"Love and need are two different things. It's good to have someone to love, to have companionship, to share your life. But any human being is capable of surviving on their own. What would I have done if I'd believed that I couldn't make it without my husband? Where would I be?" Daisy's eyes penetrated Kyrah as she added with careful enunciation, "When a woman relies too heavily on a man to solve all of her problems, eventually she will lose herself completely. A woman needs to stand strong as an individual before she is capable of giving a man the kind of love that keeps a relationship alive and strong. Otherwise, he will lose his intrigue with her. What kind of interest does a man find in a woman when she is little more than an extension of himself? A man wants a woman who has backbone, who keeps him guessing, keeps him challenged."

Daisy leaned back and sighed. "Now, it might take a while for you to digest all that. So, I'm just going to say one more thing and give you some time to think about it. Ritcherd Buchanan is not here. And if there's any hope of the two of you finding *real* happiness together, you're going to have to figure out what *you* have to do to be happy first. Whatever decisions you make from this day forward, make them from the heart, make them according to what you know is right, so that you can become the best person you can become. You got yourself into this mess. You've got to decide what you're going to do about it—with or without Ritcherd Buchanan. And then . . . if the two of you ever do cross paths again, you can determine if you still have what it takes to make it together."

Kyrah inhaled deeply, as if she could more fully absorb everything Daisy had said. "Do you think such a thing is possible?" she asked.

"You tell me," Daisy said. "In my view, anything is possible, but not if somebody else has to figure it out for you." She stood up to leave and added, "Think about it. We'll talk tomorrow."

Daisy's words stayed with Kyrah through the remainder of the day and a restless night. She prayed to be able to sufficiently comprehend what Daisy was trying to teach her, and to be able to apply it to her life in a way that would make a difference. Watching the sun come up through her bedroom window, it all began to make sense. She could look back over the difficulties of her past and see that she had no control over certain things that had happened. She could also see that she had made choices that had affected where she was now. And now she was at a crossroad. She had decisions to make—not only about what to do with her life, but perhaps more important, the attitude with which she did it. As it became clear what those decisions needed to be, she marveled at Daisy's wisdom and insight, and she thanked God for sending her such a friend.

Kyrah knocked at Daisy's front door, knowing it would be a long while before she'd have to leave for work. She answered the door with her hair hanging free, wearing a cotton robe over her nightgown.

"Hello," Kyrah said. "Do you think we could talk a few minutes?"

Daisy smiled and motioned her inside. "I'm just glad you still want to talk to me. It's like I told you from the start, I tend to intrude where I'm not wanted, but—"

"I'm grateful for your intrusion, Daisy. That's one thing I came to tell you. In many ways you have been the answer to my prayers. But I didn't realize until now how much I needed your wisdom."

Daisy hugged Kyrah tightly before they sat together in the kitchen. "Where did you gain such wisdom, anyway?" Kyrah asked.

"I never considered myself wise," she said with a shrug of her shoulders. "I just watch people and the way they behave. My aunt was one of those women who couldn't say boo without her husband to hold her up. I saw the problems and unhappiness firsthand. But we don't need to talk about them. Tell me what's on your mind."

"I've been thinking a great deal about what you said, Daisy, and . . . you're absolutely right. I got myself into this mess. I didn't want to marry Peter. I knew it wasn't right. I was afraid—plain and simple. And I let the fear overrule what I knew in my heart. Looking back, I believe that many of the poor choices I've made in my life have come from fear. And I don't want to be that way anymore."

"That's the spirit," Daisy said exuberantly.

Kyrah smiled and went on. "I have to decide what I want and do my best to make it happen. I've been blessed with the means to have my needs met, and I need to make the most of what I've got to work with."

"So, tell me what you want."

"Well . . . I want to be with Ritcherd. I love him, and I know he loves me. But he's not here, and I can't concern myself with that until I have the chance to see him again. And who knows when that will be? In the meantime, I have to find a way to get back to England. It's my home. It's where I belong. And you were right, I should be with my mother. One of my biggest fears has been what other people might think, the scandal I might cause—for myself as well as for Ritcherd. I know now that it doesn't matter what anyone thinks. I have to do what's right for me. And no one else knows my heart, or the struggles I've been through. So, let people think what they will. I'm going back to England to raise this child where I can be with my mother. And if God is willing, Ritcherd and I will be able to get back together. But I'm not going to count on that. I can hope for it, but I will do what I have to do to make a good life for me and my baby—with or without him."

Daisy smiled and squeezed Kyrah's hand across the table. "You're a fast learner, honey."

Kyrah sighed. "Well, it might be easier said than done. But it's a start, I suppose."

"We'll keep doing what we can to find you passage to England," Daisy said. "But what will you do if that doesn't happen soon?"

"Well, first of all, I'm going to put a lot more effort into trusting God and asking for His help. I'm learning more and more that we just can't make it in this world without Him. I think I've known that for a long time, but perhaps a part of me believed I wasn't worthy of His help because of the mistakes I'd made. But I believe that His love for me is unconditional, and He will help me in spite of my weaknesses, as long as I put my trust and faith in Him."

Tears burned into Kyrah's eyes, as if to verify the truth of what she'd just said. "Anyway," she continued, dabbing at her cheeks with a handkerchief, "I'm going to pray that the opportunity to return comes along soon. And in the meantime, I'll be preparing to leave regardless. If I'm not on my way to England by the end of the month, I will sell the necklace, set aside sufficient for my passage, and find a place to live. Which brings me to another important point. I will not stay married to that animal. No matter how difficult, or how long it takes, I will divorce him, because I deserve better than that. I will not be used and manipulated for his purposes. And I certainly will not tolerate his abuse."

"Good girl!" Daisy cheered. Then she came off her seat and hugged Kyrah tightly. "You're going to be just fine, Kyrah. And I'll do whatever I can to help you. You can even move in with me for a while if you need to. It might be cozy, but we'd manage. And I'm not so bad at protecting myself from obnoxious men. A woman has to be to work in a town like this. I can give you some pointers."

Kyrah let out a long, slow breath. Having repeated her thoughts to Daisy made them seem more real, more plausible. She felt stronger and more determined already. She would get beyond this and find happiness— and God willing, she would find it with Ritcherd Buchanan.

Through the following days, Kyrah began to notice the changes within herself taking hold. As the final traces of Peter's abuse healed and disappeared from her face, a new light seemed to shine through her eyes. She felt as if a new and better woman had emerged from the depths of hell she'd been subjected to, and she would continue to rise and to grow. And she would be a good mother to this child, whatever the cost.

Once again, Ritcherd found himself at the pier, gazing out to sea as if it might give him the answers. He closed his eyes and lifted his face toward the sun high above him, finding a degree of comfort in thinking that Kyrah could feel the warmth of the same sun. He pondered the endless hours he'd spent combing this hole of a town for a clue—any clue—as to where he might find the woman he loved. He'd prayed more than he ever had in his life, and something inside of him refused to give up the hope that she was here somewhere, just beyond his reach. The gulls and other sea birds sang and performed their usual rituals, as if they somehow shared his grief. He became lost in their song, wishing for the thousandth time that he could fly.

"Might ye be a cap'n?" A gruff voice startled Ritcherd from his thoughts, and he turned to see a scruffy-looking old man with gray whiskers that far outnumbered the hair on his head.

"Aye," he replied, "I'm a cap'n."

"I thought so," the man said simply, then turned and walked away.

Ritcherd followed, having to take big steps in order to keep up. "Why did ye want t' know that?" Ritcherd asked.

"It's a long story."

"I've got lots o' time," Ritcherd said with a sad note in his voice.

"I suspected ye might," the old man said as he came to a wheeled cart where fruits, breads, and cheeses were displayed. Sitting down near his wares, he put his legs far apart and eyed Ritcherd curiously.

"Tell me yer story," Ritcherd urged as he sat down close by.

"Well, I thought ye might be a cap'n by th' way ye been comin' t' the pier every day and gazin' out t' sea that way."

"Do all cap'ns do that?" he asked, amused by the theory.

"Certainly not," the man said with a bit of a smile, and Ritcherd liked him. "But I recall a woman who did."

Ritcherd's heart raced. "Tell me!" he insisted, and the old man looked as though he'd expected such a reaction.

"She were a pretty 'un. Dark, curly hair; tall and kind o' sweet lookin'. Mighty out o' place in a town like this. She came every day t' th' pier and looked out t' sea. When a ship 'd come in she'd stand way back 'n watch everyone get off, kind o' bitin' 'er lip like she was full o' nerves or somethin'. She'd always get somethin' t' eat. Little bits o' things 'ere an' there, an' she liked to talk about th' birds."

Ritcherd discreetly wiped a hand over his face in an effort to keep from showing how this affected him. He had no doubt this man was talking about Kyrah. He watched the old man closely, trying to comprehend her being here as he described her so well.

"One day I asked 'er who it was she was waitin' for. She was kind o' quiet, but she looked out to th' sea and said: 'the cap'n o' my 'eart.'"

The old man was silent for a moment and he scrutinized Ritcherd carefully. He seemed certain he'd found the right captain by the emotion Ritcherd couldn't possibly conceal. "She told me 'er name was Kyrah."

Ritcherd looked into the old man's eyes, then he turned away when he felt his emotion beginning to overcome him. There was a long moment of silence before the man went on.

"There was a day she come to th' pier and looked extra sad. She always looked sad, but this day it was worse. I asked 'er what was up, and she said she couldn't wait another day. She told me she was in trouble and she was gonna . . ." The man paused, seeming hesitant to go on.

"What?" Ritcherd insisted.

"She was gonna be gettin' married."

Ritcherd's heart leapt into his throat. It was the last thing in the world he had expected to hear. His chest became constricted and he found it difficult to take a breath. He wanted to yell at the old man and tell him he was crazy. But even if he could have found his voice, he had no reason to believe this man would lie to him. His eyes were too genuine, too filled with concern.

When the old man went on, Ritcherd did his best to force the pain away in order to focus on what was being said. "I asked 'er why she was gonna marry someone who wasn't the cap'n, and she just repeated what she said afore. She said 'I can't wait another day. I'm in trouble.' She said they would be leavin' 'ere, but she didn't tell me where she was goin'. I ain't seen 'er since."

Ritcherd pressed a trembling hand over his mouth to keep from crying out. *Kyrah was married.* She was gone. She should have been his. They should have been together. What had gone wrong? It took everything inside of him to keep his composure as he numbly stood up and offered the old man a handshake. "Thank you, sir," he managed to say as he swallowed his grief. He could fall apart later.

"I wish I could o' done more."

"Thank you for being here for her when she needed someone to talk to," he said, then quickly bit his lip.

"Twas my pleasure, Cap'n. Ye don't see ladies like 'er much in a place like this."

Ritcherd offered him some money but the man held up his hands. "I don't want no money, Cap'n."

"I don't want it either," Ritcherd said, throwing it down on the bench where he'd been sitting as he walked away.

"Kyrah," Daisy shouted, coming through the door and running into the kitchen. "Kyrah! Where are you?"

"I'm here," she replied, coming in from the back porch. "What is it?"

"I've got it," she grinned, taking Kyrah's hands as she tried to catch her breath.

"You've got what?" Kyrah laughed, bewildered.

"I've found passage for you . . . back to England."

"Oh, Daisy." Kyrah sat down quickly and put her hand to her heart. "Are you certain? Is it really true?"

"Of course it's true. I'd not steer you false. I've talked to the captain of the ship himself. And it took a little talking, mind you. But I told him that you had the diamond necklace you were willing to pay with, and he said he'd talk to you."

"He wants to talk to *me?*" Kyrah asked, more excited than afraid.

"There's nothing to be worrying about. He's a nice man . . . once you get to know him."

"But Daisy, I'm . . . I'm not certain I should go out like this. I . . ." She pressed a hand over her well-rounded belly that felt as if it would burst at any moment.

"Just wear your cloak. You'll be fine. It's practically high noon out there. I've got to get back to work. I'll walk with you part way if you'll hurry."

Daisy left Kyrah at a corner only a few steps away from the tavern where she'd told Kyrah the captain could be found. She unconsciously put a hand where her baby grew, knowing it would only be a few weeks before it arrived. She hoped the baby would not deter this man's willingness to take her on board.

Kyrah hesitated at the door of the tavern, wondering what kind of low-life existed inside. Entering stoically, she ignored the skeptical glances of the crowd and approached the table in the corner where Daisy had told her the captain would be. She paused when she saw the man sitting there, and scrutinized him carefully before he saw her. From his appearance, it was tempting to turn around and leave. But if Daisy had recommended him, he couldn't be too bad.

"Captain Garret?" she asked, stepping to the table's edge as she pushed back the hood of her long cloak.

"Yes," he said and stood. As their eyes met, time seemed to briefly stop. He had the most penetrating eyes she had ever seen—yet they were kind, somehow, which lessened her apprehension.

Garret told himself to stop staring and motioned for the woman to sit down. The very fact that she looked so completely out of place in this town made him wonder if she might be the woman Ritch was looking for. She certainly fit the description he'd given—except for being quite pregnant. But then, those things happened. As their eyes met again across the table, he found it difficult to look away. He felt instinctively drawn to her for reasons he couldn't explain.

Kyrah met the captain's bold gaze, considering this an opportunity to exercise her newfound courage. She refused to let this man intimidate her—even though she suspected that was not his intention. While his aura itself was intimidating, there was something about him that Kyrah found intriguing.

"So," he finally broke the silence, "what is it that I can do for you?" She was surprised by his mellow voice and eloquent speech, but she couldn't deny feeling a bit unnerved as he continued to stare at her with deep-set, intense eyes.

"I'm looking for passage back to England," she said quietly. "I hear you have a ship that will be going there soon."

Garret had been apprehensive when Daisy asked if this friend of hers could go back to England with him. But she had pleaded and begged and convinced him that she'd been good to him and he owed her many favors. Now as he watched this woman, he was glad he'd consented to see her. He sensed something fine about her. Her determined air was inspiring some-how, while a barely concealed trepidation showed in her eyes. Instinctively he wanted to do everything he could to help her—whether this was Kyrah Payne or not.

"Might I ask your name?" he said and held his breath.

Kyrah was caught off guard. She recalled Daisy once mentioning that it might be wise to use an assumed name in order to avoid her husband. She quickly came up with her mother's maiden name. "Mrs. Griffin," she said.

"Mrs. Griffin," Garret repeated, and knew she was lying. But he stuck to the business at hand. "Well, it's not my ship," he said, "but I'm sailing it. I don't suppose the owner would mind if we took a woman on board."

"I have this," she said, pulling the velvet box from beneath her cloak. She opened it discreetly, just enough for him to see the brilliant diamond necklace.

It looked much more expensive than Daisy had made him think. He closed the box quickly and pushed it toward her. "Don't let anybody else see that," he cautioned with a smile.

"Will you take me to England," she all but pleaded, "in exchange for the necklace?"

"I will," he said coolly, "but that necklace is worth a great deal more than passage to England."

"Would it be better if I sold it and—"

"You could probably get more for it in England," he said. "You can pay me when we get there."

Kyrah sighed and briefly closed her eyes. The relief was indescribable. At last, she would be going home. Home to the Cornish wind, the church ruins, her mother. *Ritcherd.* The thought made her heart quicken. Oh, to see him again!

Kyrah reminded herself she was not alone and focused on the captain. She resisted the urge to tell him he was an answer to her prayers, not certain how he'd take such a comment from a stranger. "When are you leaving?" she asked.

"A week, maybe two at the most. We've been in port nearly three months. It's about time we got moving."

"That should be fine," she said, biting her lip slightly.

Garret wanted to ask if she'd be bringing the baby or having it on the ship, but he figured they had the means to handle it either way. Not wanting to offend her, he opted to say nothing about it.

"Where can I contact you when we're ready to sail?" he asked.

Kyrah explained where she lived, and told him she'd be ready to leave and waiting for his word.

"I'll send someone to get you," he said.

"Thank you so much, Captain. You are my deliverer." She stood and was surprised when he took her hand and gave it a lingering kiss.

Their eyes met again while Garret held her hand longer than he knew was appropriate. He wanted to blurt out the words on the tip of his tongue: *Does the name Ritcherd Buchanan mean anything to you?* But since she would be sailing with them, he figured it was only a matter of time before he would know if she was the one.

"Thank you again," she said, graciously retracting her hand.

"By the way," he added, "the ship is called the *Phoenix*. That's where you can find me if you need anything."

She smiled again, and he couldn't help thinking how pretty she was—in a sweet and simple way. Women like her just didn't exist in places like this. If she wasn't Kyrah Payne, he wondered where she might have come from. For that matter, if she wasn't Ritcherd Buchanan's woman, he might consider pursuing her himself.

"Perhaps I'll have a look at the ship," she said.

"Feel free," he said proudly. "I'll even give you a tour if you like."

"I'm certain I'll see it well once we set sail."

"Indeed," he smirked, and Kyrah thought that Daisy had been right. Captain Garret was a very nice man.

"Thank you again," she said, and he nodded slightly.

Kyrah wrapped the cloak tightly around her and pulled the hood down around her head as much as possible in order to avoid the odd glances she had gotten on her way in. The tavern was more crowded than when she'd arrived, and she had to push her way past several people to get to the door. But her mind was caught up in the arrangements she had just made. *She was going home.*

Once Ritcherd was beyond sight of the old man, he slipped into an alley and leaned against the wall. "You can fall apart later," he mumbled against the cold bricks where he pressed his face. He was vaguely aware of a few passersby giving him an odd glance and hurrying on. But in a town like this, they would just assume he was drunk. He slid to his knees and wrapped his arms over his head as the reality kept pounding through his mind. *In trouble . . . Married . . .* He couldn't believe it. How could it be possible?

Ritcherd was shocked to the moment as a couple of seedy-looking sailors eyed him like two tomcats spying a mouse. This was no place to fall apart. He had to get back to the ship. But . . . Garret would be waiting for him. *All right,* he told himself, *just get to the tavern. You can fall apart later.* He consciously forced his emotions to a place where they wouldn't be felt, and walked toward the Captain's Wheel, as numb as if he'd been frozen from the inside out.

To the rhythm of his boots on the boardwalk, questions without answers drummed through his mind. Married? Why? And who? What kind of trouble? He'd bet it had something to do with Peter Westman. But married? He thought of Kyrah in another man's arms and his heart caught in his throat, making his insides churn. How could he bear it? He couldn't. He just couldn't! The emotion threatened again, and he forced it back as he approached the tavern and pushed his way through the door. It was more crowded than usual, and several people pushed past him on their way out. He noticed a woman in a burgundy cloak and tried to see her face, but it was covered. He'd become accustomed to looking at every woman lately, always wondering if it might be her. But as he brushed past her, he knew it wasn't. This woman was too big around to be Kyrah.

He found Garret in the usual spot and sat across from him, noting that the seat was warm. He'd been talking to someone. Arrangements for supplies, no doubt.

Garret was still lost in thought over the woman he'd just met when Ritcherd sat down across from him. He was ready to tell him about her, but the look in Ritcherd's eyes let him know something was horribly wrong.

"What's happened?" he asked.

It took Ritcherd a minute to focus on Garret and form the words in his mind. "She's not here anymore," he said. "She's married. She left here a long time ago . . .with her . . . husband."

"Are you sure?" Garret asked in a raspy whisper.

Ritcherd nodded. His entire countenance was so filled with despair that Garret almost felt his own heart breaking.

"How do you know?" Garret asked, not willing to believe it. "Who did you talk to?"

"An old man at the pier," Ritcherd said. "He described her perfectly. He knew her name. She told him she was in some kind of trouble and she was getting married. He hasn't seen her since."

"It's unbelievable," Garret said.

Ritcherd gave a grunt of agreement and resisted the urge to press his face to the table and cry like a baby.

"I'm sorry," Garret whispered, and Ritcherd knew he meant it. "So, what now?"

"I don't know. I suppose this is where it ends."

"Don't you think it's worth at least finding out why?"

Ritcherd shook his head, unable to even think straight. "Time's running out. We've got to leave soon."

"I said we'd not leave for England without Kyrah," Garret said.

"But if she's married . . . well . . . maybe she doesn't want me to find her."

"And maybe she does." Ritcherd looked at Garret and wondered how this man kept giving him hope when it seemed there was none left. "If you stop looking, you'll never find her."

"I don't think I could ever stop looking," Ritcherd admitted. "I'll probably die of old age, still looking for her. It's become a habit to look at every woman I see. And I'm always disappointed when it's not her."

Garret couldn't resist asking, "Did you see that woman who just left here, wearing the burgundy cloak?"

Ritcherd nodded. "I didn't get a good look at her face, but it wasn't her."

Garret blew out a long breath. He couldn't help being disappointed—at least for Ritcherd's sake. On the other hand, their lady passenger could prove to hold his interest. He wondered if such a woman would ever give someone like him a second glance. On a more positive note, he told Ritcherd, "That woman will be sailing with us."

Ritcherd was roused from his own thoughts. "What?"

"You heard me, Captain Buckley." Despite his adamance he spoke softly, as they always did when they weren't speaking like sailors.

"Why? Isn't it a bit odd to take a woman on board a privateer?"

"Would you say that if you'd found Kyrah?"

"You always get me." Ritcherd sighed humbly.

"She needs passage back to England. That's a difficult thing to come by these days. I did it as a favor to an old friend. She seemed desperate and I like her. Maybe she'll like me too," he grinned.

Ritcherd felt the emotion threatening to bubble to the surface. The only coherent thought he could put together was a mumbled, "I've got to get to the ship."

Garret let him go, figuring he could use some time alone.

Once Ritcherd got into the cabin and closed the door, he sank to his knees and curled around his arms. He couldn't believe that emotional pain could be so real, so intense. He cried so hard that every muscle in his body became rigid and tense. When he had finally exhausted every bit of strength, he curled up on his bed and stared at the wall.

Ritcherd knew he hadn't slept, but when Garret spoke to him, he couldn't recall hearing him come in. The cabin was dark except for the dim glow of a lamp.

"How you doing?" Garret asked quietly.

"Not good," Ritcherd said. "I can't decide if I would rather kill myself or kill my mother. Maybe both."

Garret gave a disgusted sigh. "Well, forgive my lack of sensitivity," he said with a trace of sarcasm, "but that is the most pathetic thing I have ever heard. I would have expected better than that from you, no matter how you might feel."

Ritcherd turned and glared at him. "Well, you have no idea how I feel, now do you?"

"Maybe not, Captain Buckley," he snapped. "But you're never going to find peace with this when you've got an attitude like that. You have a right to your feelings. You've had a deep loss and you're entitled to grieve. And you have a right to be angry with your mother, and obviously you're going to have to come to terms with that eventually. But harboring self-pity and hostility will bring you to no good."

Ritcherd sighed and resisted the urge to argue. He didn't have the strength.

"Forgive my asking," Garret said, "but have you prayed for help in this?"

Ritcherd suddenly found the strength to stand up as he growled, "I have prayed more than you could possibly imagine. A lot of good it's done me."

"Well, don't be blaming God for the way it's ended up. Sometimes things just happen. But I wonder how far your prayers are going to get while you're wanting to kill your mother—and yourself." Garret lifted a finger to stop Ritcherd's attempt to retort. "Now before you get that nasty temper of yours all worked up, let me finish. You're going to have to do what you feel is best. But there's something I have to say. If it were me, I would need to at least know what had happened. And I would keep searching and praying until I did. Maybe she's home by now. Maybe your information is wrong. Maybe it's not as bad as it seems. But sooner or later, you will come face-to-face with her. And then you'll know. So stop thinking about how much you hate your mother, and think about how much you deserve to be happy—in spite of your mother. You're obviously going to have to make a life for yourself—with or without Kyrah. So you can get drunk and stay that way until you die in the gutter, or you can look around and see how much worse it could be. You can act like a man and find a way to be happy in spite of what's happened. And then when you find her, the two of you can determine what to do with what you have left."

Ritcherd took two steps backward and sat weakly on the edge of his bunk. He thought of the crew of the *Phoenix* and the tragic stories he'd heard them tell of their lives. He thought of all he'd been blessed with, in spite of the difficulties. And he knew Garret was right. He had to come to terms with this. He couldn't give up until he found her—one way or another. And then he had to find a way to get on with his life. With or without her. The very idea threatened to rip his heart out. But he had to find a way to be happy. He just *had* to.

Ritcherd prayed himself to sleep, hoping God would help him beyond his anger to a place where he could find hope again. And perhaps eventually he would be able to find peace. The following day he didn't bother continuing his search. Instead, he wandered around with Garret while he went about his business. He still felt in a state of shock. And just as Garret had suggested, he felt that he had to grieve. It was as if Kyrah had died—or perhaps worse. Not knowing was perhaps the most difficult thing of all.

So he followed Garret around, feeling like some kind of ghost without the will to do anything for the time being except go on existing. But he found some comfort in staying close to Garret. He knew his partner would keep him from doing anything stupid until he came to his senses.

They spent many hours at the Captain's Wheel, where Garret laughed and talked with many different men—some he obviously knew well. Ritcherd just listened with half an ear, staring at his drinks more than consuming them. He had no desire to end up drunk in a place like this. Odds had it that Garret's profound words were very appropriate in this situation: drunk men become dead men.

Two days after his discovery of Kyrah's marriage, Ritcherd followed Garret to the usual table and listened while he reported their current status of supplies. They were distracted when a crowd started to gather around someone telling a boisterous story about sighting whales somewhere that Ritcherd had never heard of. When the story ended, Ritcherd was the only one in the tavern who wasn't rolling with laughter. Keeping his back to the action, it was easier to remain in his own thoughts.

Garret leaned back to listen as another story began. He seemed to be enjoying himself, but Ritcherd felt bored and disinterested. When that story ended with gales of laughter, the crowd dissipated a bit and the man who had been the center of attention sauntered casually to their table, holding out his hand to Garret.

"Ah, Captain Garret," he said smoothly from behind a neatly trimmed mustache that matched his mane of curly black hair. The length of his hair wasn't unusual; the fact that he didn't wear it tied back was. Ritcherd had to take a second glance, almost to convince himself the guy was real. His appearance had a flawless, almost mythical dimension. "I was hoping to see you here. How have you been doing?" He was obviously American.

"Not so bad." Garret grinned and returned the handshake. "And you?" he added, motioning for him to sit down.

"Never better," he replied but remained standing.

"What can I do for you?" Garret asked, and Ritcherd was surprised not to hear the sailor's drawl. Obviously this was someone Garret knew and trusted.

"It's what I can do for you." He grinned. "You asked me to check up on what John Sloane told you about." He glanced warily toward Ritcherd. Garret nodded to indicate Ritcherd could be trusted. "Well, I'm certain it's the same man who swindled one of my men in a game just last week when we docked in Southport." Garret lifted his brows, obviously pleased by the news, but he made no comment. "Just thought you'd like to know." The mustached man grinned, gave a casual salute, and walked away.

"Thanks," Garret called and was answered by a casual gesture to indicate it was no problem as this man seated himself at a nearby table with some of his shipmates.

"Who was that?" Ritcherd asked quietly.

"That," Garret whispered, "is *the* Captain Cross."

"Never heard of him," Ritcherd said dully.

"You just did," Garret grinned, "and if you ever get in a bad situation, just mention his name. You'll either get treated like royalty or thrown to the sharks."

"That's quite a choice."

"Well," Garret laughed, "it all depends on whose side you're on. Captain Cross is on ours."

Ritcherd was surprised to have their conversation interrupted by a burly man who approached their table, looking almost as bad as he smelled.

"Cap'n?" he asked. They both turned so he added, "I'm lookin' for Cap'n Buckley."

"Here," Ritcherd said blandly, wondering what on earth this lowlife would want with him.

"I understand ye're lookin' for a certain lady," the man said, and Ritcherd's interest perked considerably.

"I am," he stated, trying to remain cool. Garret's expression became intent.

"I think I seen 'er," the man stated smugly.

Garret and Ritcherd exchanged a cautious glance.

"When?" Ritcherd asked. "Tell me what ye know."

"What's it worth t' ye?" the man asked. Ritcherd saw Garret smile, knowing that nothing in this town came free.

Ritcherd pulled a significant amount of money from his pocket and laid it on the table, but he left his hand pressed firmly over it. He wondered if this man actually knew something that might help him. Garret stood up, motioning for the man to sit down, then opted for the same side of the table as Ritcherd when he sat back down. They both faced him, but did their best to keep a distance.

"So talk," Ritcherd demanded, meeting the man's eyes pointedly.

"I was paid t' kidnap 'er," he stated, and Ritcherd went immediately tense.

"What?" he said too loudly. "By who?"

Garret interjected coolly, "'Ow do we know ye're talkin' about th' same lady?"

The man gave a detailed physical description that made Ritcherd's heart beat faster.

Garret still had trouble believing the woman he'd talked to wasn't Kyrah. She certainly fit the description. But if Ritcherd said it wasn't her, he wasn't about to argue.

"Is it th' same lady?" the man asked, and Ritcherd nodded to indicate it was. "All I know for sure is that I was paid a good price t' pull th' lady off th' street an' make it look like I was gonna have m' way with 'er . . . if ye know what I mean."

"Look like!?" Ritcherd said, forgetting his accent. His insides roiled to think of Kyrah subjected to this despicable-looking creature. "What do you mean look—"

Garret put his hand down firmly on Ritcherd's arm to quiet him, and Ritcherd had to admit that he was grateful for Garret's calm presence.

"Go on," Garret said to the man.

"I didn't hurt th' lady," he said adamantly. "All I did was pull 'er down th' alley a bit, then th' one who paid us . . . 'e showed up with a gun t' make himself look like a 'ero. She left with 'im."

"Who was it?" Ritcherd asked, now more calm.

"I don't know 'is name," the man replied. "'Twas m' buddy took th' money from 'im, but 'e left town, so ye can't talk to 'im."

"What did 'e look like?" Garret asked. "The one who showed up with th' gun?"

"He was a big man, with dark slick hair, an' kind o' snaky lookin'. That's all I can tell ye. It was dark, and it's been a long time."

Ritcherd fought to stay calm. He knew this man was talking about Peter Westman, and he was more certain than ever that Kyrah's trouble had something to do with him.

"Then ye don't know where th' lady is?" Garret asked. "Or th' man who paid ye?"

"No, I don't, sir," he said with a nod to indicate he'd finished. Again Ritcherd was grateful for Garret's being able to think clearly and stay calm. He wondered how he could possibly remain reasonable on his own when his despair just seemed to settle deeper every day.

"Thank ye," Garret said, and Ritcherd sighed as he slid the money across the table. The man took it and left.

"Do you know who it was?" Garret asked, moving back to the other side of the table to face him.

"Yes," Ritcherd replied, "but it doesn't make any difference now."

Garret assumed by Buckley's expression that the subject was to be dropped. He just bought a drink and listened to another of Captain Cross's stories before they returned together to the *Phoenix*.

Garret found it difficult to sleep that night. His thoughts were consumed with the mysterious Mrs. Griffin. He couldn't discern if he simply felt an instinctive desire to protect her, or if he was attracted to her. He'd been acquainted with many women in his life—some better than others. But he wasn't one to take advantage of women or indulge in a way of life that many men in this business did. And he'd never gotten too serious with any woman; he'd never found one that made him want to. Daisy was one of those women. He truly cared for her; they were friends, and he liked it that way. Knowing she felt the same way made it easier to spend time with her and not feel like he had any obligation after he left port.

Garret had put a great deal of effort into analyzing the women he knew with respect to his analogy of the sea. He knew that when he found a woman who made him feel the way the sea did, he needed to stop and take notice. Was that the way he felt about Mrs. Griffin—or whatever her name was? Could she be provocative? Breathtaking? Challenging? Perhaps. But only time would let him know for certain. He didn't know her well enough to be able to tell.

Somewhere in the middle of the night, Garret came to the conclusion that he had to see her again—before they set sail. And for whatever reason he felt compelled to pay her a visit, he hoped the outcome would be favorable.

The morning dragged as he took care of some necessary business aboard the *Phoenix*. Following lunch, he told Ritcherd, "I need to take care of something in town—alone."

Ritcherd just scowled at him and walked away. It wasn't the first time he'd gone to visit a woman, and Ritcherd would know he'd have been welcome to come along for any other matter of business. For a moment Garret considered taking Ritcherd with him, but he decided against it. He rationalized that he didn't want to overwhelm the poor woman. But he had to wonder deep inside if he feared that Ritcherd Buchanan's broken heart might prove to be competition for attention from the grieving Mrs. Griffin. He couldn't recall now what Daisy had said about *Mr.* Griffin—or whatever his name was. But he knew the husband was out of the way.

Garret knew it was Daisy's day off, and he knew from the way she'd talked that there was an excellent chance she'd be visiting Mrs. Griffin, who had become a very close friend. He wasn't opposed to calling on Mrs. Griffin when she might be alone, but he hoped that Daisy might make her feel less uncomfortable. And perhaps she might consider a visit from him inappropriate. For whatever reason, he hoped Daisy would be there.

Kyrah heard a knock at the door and exchanged a glance with Daisy. No one had ever come to the house *except* Daisy in all the time she'd been here. Since Daisy had her hands busy stirring the soup they'd been preparing, Kyrah peeked carefully between the curtains to see who it might be. Her heart quickened to see Captain Garret. Had he come to tell her they would be sailing soon? She couldn't help hoping. Eagerly she opened the door, but it took her a moment to gather her senses. She'd forgotten how penetrating his eyes could be.

"Mrs. Griffin," he said. "Forgive me for intruding, but I—"

"Come in," she said, opening the door wider. "Daisy is here and—"

"Yes, I know. I must confess that my visit has two purposes. I did wish to have a word with Daisy, but I also wanted to see that you're well."

"I'm fine, of course," she said, feeling touched by his concern. "But thank you." She tried to cover her disappointment when it became evident that they weren't yet ready to sail. "Daisy's a bit busy in the kitchen. Would you like to—"

"Who's there?" Daisy called.

"It's Captain Garret," Kyrah called back.

"Well, bring him in here where I can give him a good talking-to."

Kyrah led Garret into the kitchen. He laughed when he saw her, and she watched a different side of him emerge. "And what did you wish to talk to me about?" he asked, setting his gloved hands on his hips.

"You've been mighty neglectful of me," Daisy said with a wink while she wiped her hands on her apron.

"I'm a busy man, Daisy."

"What kind of busy?" she asked over her shoulder as she covered the pot on the stove.

"Business busy," he said.

Kyrah sat by the table and motioned for him to join her. "Thank you," he said, sitting down and crossing a booted ankle over his knee. She listened to the two of them banter for several minutes while she discreetly observed this man, wondering why he made her think of Ritcherd. Perhaps it was simply the presence of a man who obviously had character and integrity. The leather of his boots creaked when he moved. The muscles in his arms stood out as he rubbed the back of his neck. She suddenly missed Ritcherd so immensely that she absently put a hand over her heart and sighed.

"Are you all right?" Garret asked, startling her.

"Of course," Kyrah said. "Why do you ask?"

"You look so . . . sad."

"Just . . . missing someone," she said, and Garret couldn't help wondering if her broken heart could possibly help mend Ritcherd's—and vice versa. But only if he could fathom being selfless enough not to woo her himself.

"Ah, well," Daisy said, "women in port towns get to be pretty good at that."

Garret smirked toward her and Kyrah felt inclined to say, "Forgive me if I'm being too presumptuous, or . . . well, perhaps I should ask Daisy such questions privately."

"Go ahead and ask it, honey. I've got no secrets from the brute."

Garret laughed, as if he thoroughly enjoyed being called a brute. Then he motioned toward Kyrah.

"Well," she went on, "I was just wondering if the two of you are . . . you know . . . romantically involved."

Daisy tossed Garret a saucy little smile before she said, "Nah, we're just friends."

"Friends?" he echoed, pretending to be insulted. His eyes made it evident he was teasing. "After all those kisses you've given me, you tell me we're *friends?* Where does that leave all my hopes and dreams?"

"At sea, Captain," Daisy said a little too seriously. "So, we're kissing friends. What's wrong with that?" She spoke more to Kyrah. "Although he'll get nothing more than a kiss from me. A woman can't afford to give more when a man's coming and going all the time."

"Some of them do," Garret said.

"None that you've been visiting, I should hope."

"Of course not, my love . . . Oh, forgive me. My *friend.* You should know me better than that."

Daisy smiled at him. "I do, yes." Then she said more to Kyrah, "That's what makes Garret stand out in the crowd, you know. He's keen on avoiding the diseases that many sailors are prone to catch while they're in port."

It took Kyrah a moment to perceive what she meant, then she felt herself turn warm. And to make it worse, Garret obviously noticed. He smirked again and said, "Now, Daisy. You're making me blush. Mrs. Griffin here might be able to handle that kind of talk, but you'd do well to mind your mouth when I'm around."

"You're a scoundrel," Daisy said.

"Perhaps," he replied. "But just how many kissing friends do *you* have?" he asked, humor teasing the corners of his mouth.

Daisy shrugged her shoulders as she sat down and took his hand across the table. "Just two or three. And you?"

"Only you, Daisy. Only you—at least in this town. And maybe, just maybe, when this war is over . . ." He left the sentence unfinished.

"Don't be talking that way to me, Captain. You're just like the rest of them; the sea's in your blood. And I'm not marrying again until I find a man who will stay in port for more than a month at a time."

"Very wise," Garret said. "And in the meantime . . . we'll just be friends." He kissed her hand, and Kyrah's thoughts of Ritcherd drew her away once more.

Garret discreetly watched Mrs. Griffin's eyes turn distant again. He felt his curiosity growing over her, and had to ask, "So, Mrs. Griffin, what brings an English lady such as yourself to this part of the world during a war?"

Her eyes became so hard so fast that Garret was actually startled. She stood up and turned away, saying curtly, "It wasn't by my choice; that's for certain." She glanced over her shoulder and added, "Forgive me, Captain. I think I should lie down. I'll leave the two of you to visit."

When he was alone with Daisy, she said, "You must understand that she's been through a great deal."

"Yes, that's evident," he said. "But . . . what?"

Daisy narrowed her eyes on him. "It's not like you to be so curious. What's on your mind?"

Garret shook his head. "Nothing. I'm just concerned."

"Well, she's going to be just fine. You get her back to England, and she'll be fine."

"I intend to," he said.

Daisy invited him to stay and eat, but he declined in spite of how good it smelled. He returned to the ship to find Ritcherd fencing with Patrick, and working up a healthy sweat. At least he'd quit sulking. Better that he fight all that emotion into the open, rather than letting it simmer and stew.

That evening Ritcherd was writing furiously in his journal, and Garret figured that was good as well. He decided to do the same, hoping it would clear his head. But he fell asleep again with thoughts of Mrs. Griffin in his mind. He couldn't help feeling that there was something significant about her. If only he knew what.

Chapter Fifteen

Heart to Heart

The day following Captain Garret's visit, Kyrah decided a walk to the pier would do her good. The walk seemed long, but the fresh air felt good. As soon as she arrived at the pier, she realized that she'd chosen a bad day. It was apparent that a vessel had just arrived and there was a great deal of commotion, with people everywhere and cargo being unloaded. But she'd made up her mind to see the *Phoenix*, needing to give some reality to her prospect of returning home. Carefully she pushed her way through the crowd of sailors and merchants until she could see the docked ships clearly. The *Phoenix* was easy to pick out. She caught her breath at the sight of the great bird painted on the hull with the sun at its back. For some reason, it made her think of Ritcherd. She had never been able to determine exactly what type of bird Ritcherd might be, but scrutinizing the *Phoenix*, she understood why. It was no real bird that Ritcherd resembled. It was the mythological phoenix. In truth, if not for his baby growing inside her, she might believe at times that he was little more than a myth. The time they had spent together following his years at war seemed so dreamlike and elusive.

Kyrah pushed back the hood of her cloak and shaded her eyes from the sun in order to take in the whole of the ship. Her heart leapt to think that it would carry her home. She wondered what might be waiting there. What kind of struggles had her mother gone through since she'd left? She wondered if Ritcherd was still there. Had he tried to find her, or had he remained at Buckley Manor and found a life without her?

She was distracted from her thoughts when one of the sailors stacking crates near the *Phoenix*, shouted up toward the deck, "Cap'n, Cap'n!"

Kyrah moved her eyes to the deck and was not surprised to see Captain Garret appear at the rail.

"What do ye want?" Garret shouted with a grin, and Kyrah noticed he spoke with a sailor's drawl, very unlike the mellow voice she'd heard him use previously. She wondered if he was somehow traveling incognito.

"Look yonder," the sailor pointed skyward. "It's th' albatross. It must o' followed th' Lady into port."

Kyrah looked up to see the albatross with its huge wings, soaring and dipping. The sight took her breath away. She'd read about the albatross, but had never seen one. And she wouldn't have expected to find such a bird here.

"It really must be lost," Garret shouted, his eyes focused on the bird. He couldn't deny his fascination When they had arrived more than three months ago, the albatross had followed them right into Hedgeton, and disappeared soon after they'd docked. It had apparently found another ship to follow for its sustenance, and it too had brought the albatross to Hedgeton.

"Aye, Cap'n," Charlie called back. "Is Cap'n Buckley around? I thought 'e'd like t' see it—'im 'avin' such a fancy for th' bird."

Kyrah's heart leapt at the name *Buckley* connected with the title *Captain*. But surely it was coincidental. She couldn't help wondering why there would be two captains on board the same vessel, and she turned her attention to Captain Garret. He fascinated her for reasons she couldn't quite grasp, and she had to admit to being intrigued with the thought of sailing with him. Her feelings certainly weren't romantic by any means; nevertheless, she hoped to get to know him better.

"Eh, Buckley!" Garret called over his shoulder. "There's good fortune for ye now! Your friend 'as found us again."

"Really?" Kyrah heard a voice call back and her heart quickened. Could it be possible that even from a distance, that one word had struck such a strong chord of familiarity?

Ritcherd's eyes went to the albatross and he felt, as always, a surge of awe in beholding it. But at the moment he didn't know whether it was giving him hope with its presence or just some kind of abstract compassion for his grief. Where it had once given him the courage to believe he would find Kyrah, now he had begun to believe that even if he did find her, it was too late. He had searched and speculated to his limits. There was nothing left inside of him.

Clasping his hands behind his back, he ambled toward the rail and leaned against it next to Garret, while they watched the bird's display.

Kyrah's legs almost wilted beneath her when this Captain Buckley stood next to Garret. Everything inside of her melted into a sensation that made her feel hot and cold all at once. She didn't understand the connection, but she had no doubt it was Ritcherd. His hair was changed, his clothes were different. But it was him! She would know that face anywhere. In the moment it took for the reality to settle in, her heart began to pound. Oh, how she loved him! And he'd come for her! He *had!* Was it he who owned the *Phoenix*? It suited him well. As she took in his presence, the sailor shouted again, "Cap'n Buckley! Our luck's bound t' get even better now, eh?"

"Aye," the captain replied, his eyes remaining on the albatross. "At least that's what all o' ye superstitious sailors are bound t' think."

Kyrah's heart leapt freshly as he spoke, and the baby inside of her moved as if to respond to her emotion. She thought of the two voices she'd heard Captain Garret use, and wondered over the reasons as she scrutinized Ritcherd Buchanan, alias Captain Buckley. When the reality of his presence struck her, Kyrah forced herself back to the present. He had come for her! And what had she done? She'd gone and married another man. She'd given up on him. She'd betrayed him. She recalled Captain Garret telling her they'd been in port more than three months. Oh, if only she'd held out just a little longer! How could she ever justify what she'd done? She needed time to come to terms with her feelings, to know how to handle this, what to say. She knew she had to leave before he saw her. If he was to be aboard the ship she was sailing home on, then it was only a matter of days before they would be together. While a part of her ached to just run into his arms, she couldn't face him so unexpectedly.

As soon as Ritcherd spoke, she turned quickly away and pulled the hood of her cloak over her head. But she felt his eyes moving toward her just before she was able to move into the crowd.

Ritcherd sucked in his breath and tried to convince himself he wasn't going crazy. It was bewitching how he'd moved his gaze from the great bird soaring overhead, only to see Kyrah's face among the crowd of people on the pier. Through his months of searching, he'd begun to wonder if he would know her when he saw her. But it only took a second to be certain it was her.

"Kyrah," he whispered, and Garret turned abruptly toward him. But before he had a chance to ask, Ritcherd was running onto the pier, calling out her name.

"Kyrah!" She heard him shout, his deep voice ringing strong above the bustling on the pier. "Kyrah!" he repeated, his desperation evident. She wondered what he had gone through to get here. But she couldn't face him now—not yet. She hurried as quickly as she could manage in her condition. She heard him call her name again. He was getting closer. Her heart raced faster. The child turned inside of her. She pushed her way through the crowd and moved quickly to a side street, hiding herself in a doorway.

Ritcherd became frantic. He felt as if he'd lost his mind. It seemed as though he'd been searching forever, and with one glimpse she was gone again. He pushed his way almost brutally through the crowd, looking desperately for her. But it was as if she'd disappeared into nothing. She was gone.

He wandered the area for more than an hour before he finally returned to the ship, realizing his efforts were futile. He paused on the pier where he had seen her standing. The crowds were gone now, and he tried to imagine her here. But how could she have been here and not seen him? How could she not have heard him calling her? What had gone wrong?

His gaze moved to the albatross that was still flying nearby, and he wondered if the bird really did have the power to bring luck. Had it shown him that Kyrah was here and given him a grain of hope?

He was startled to hear Garret's voice behind him. "What happened?" he asked.

Ritcherd turned to face him. "She's here. I saw her."

"Are you sure?" Garret asked.

"Absolutely." They walked onto the *Phoenix* together and sat down in the cabin while Ritcherd told him exactly what had happened. Garret listened patiently while he speculated over why she might have fled. And he rehearsed his determination to find her.

"You're awfully quiet," Ritcherd said when he realized how long he'd been talking while Garret had just listened with an occasional indication that he understood.

"What can I say? I agree with you. You need to find her, but if she doesn't want to be found, it could be difficult."

"But *why?*" Ritcherd asked and began pacing.

"I don't know," Garret said. He watched Ritcherd pace back and forth for several minutes while his mind worked over a number of elements in this situation. Something didn't add up—or perhaps it added up a little too well. Wanting a little more evidence before he started poking around, he said, "May I ask you a stupid question?"

"That's all I've been doing: asking stupid questions; questions with no answers. Go ahead."

"I was just wondering . . . did you ever give Kyrah any really nice gifts? You weren't together very long, but . . ."

Ritcherd couldn't see the point, but he simply said, "Yes."

"May I ask what?" Ritcherd looked suspicious and he added, "Just curious."

"I gave her a diamond necklace and earrings. I told you a long time ago that I spoke to a man who had bought the earrings from her."

"I guess I'd forgotten," Garret said, resisting the urge to take Ritcherd to meet Mrs. Griffin. He figured it would be better if he had a little talk with her first. And he was going to do it right now.

"Where you going?" Ritcherd asked as Garret headed for the door.

"To see a woman," Garret said and left, but Ritcherd wondered why he seemed angry.

Ritcherd stood to follow him out.

"Where are *you* going?" Garret asked.

"I'm going to look for Kyrah," he said, and disappeared into the dark streets before Garret even got past the pier.

Once Kyrah was certain that she had evaded Ritcherd, she walked slowly home. Knowing he had come for her filled her with unspeakable joy. But at the same time, it made what she had done seem all the more deplorable. She intended to divorce herself from Peter Westman, and her deepest hope was that she could still have a future with Ritcherd. But that would take time—and a great deal of understanding and forgiveness from both of them.

While Kyrah had been hoping the baby would wait to come until she was aboard the ship, now she wished that it might come before they sailed. She felt so unattractive in this condition, and would far prefer to see him again when she was back to normal. She had often fantasized about showing the baby to Ritcherd, and she speculated over what his reaction might be to realize he was a father. She imagined him taking her in his arms and pledging his love and commitment to her forever. But then the reality of her marriage would come crashing into her fantasies, reminding her that the facts had to be faced. She was married to another man, and she could only hope and pray that Ritcherd's love for her was strong enough to carry them beyond whatever might lie ahead.

Kyrah was grateful to know that Daisy was working a double shift to fill in for a woman who was ill. She had no desire to repeat what had happened and have Daisy scold her for running. Perhaps it had been cowardly. She knew it wasn't fair to Ritcherd. But the situation was just too complicated to face at a moment's notice. On that count, too, she hoped that Ritcherd would forgive her.

Kyrah had barely managed to eat an adequate supper when a loud knock came at the door. She peered through the curtain then opened the door.

"I'm sorry," she said to Captain Garret, "Daisy's not here."

"I know," he replied with an intensity in his eyes that unnerved her. She wasn't by any means afraid of Captain Garret, but the timing of his visit made her wonder if he knew more about her than she wanted him to. "I wanted to talk to you."

"Very well," she said, motioning him inside. "Would you like something to drink, or—"

"No, thank you," he said. "I'll get right to the point. It's something I've wondered since the moment I laid eyes on you. I think my instincts told me it was true right from the start, but there was evidence otherwise, however illogical. But now . . ."

"Now?" she repeated when he hesitated.

"There are too many things adding up here. So, I'm just going to come right out and ask."

Kyrah steeled herself, determined not to lie—but equally determined not to allow herself to go against what she felt she had to do.

"Does the name Ritcherd Buchanan mean anything to you?"

Kyrah glanced away quickly, unprepared for the way just hearing his name made her feel.

"I thought so," he said. When she didn't respond, he moved toward the door, adding tersely, "Thank you. That's all I wanted to know."

"Wait!" she insisted and he turned toward her, his hand on the door-knob. "Whatever it is you're assuming, Captain Garret, it is merely assumption. Don't go throwing your assumptions around if you don't know what you're talking about."

"Forgive me, Mrs. Griffin, if that's really your name. But I never go throwing *anything* around. And I have a whole lot more than assumption. I have intuition. I have a number of facts. And I have something right here," he pressed a fist below his heart, "telling me all I need to know."

"And what exactly do you think you know?" she countered.

Garret stepped toward her, and Kyrah resisted the urge to back away. She refused to be intimidated by any man, ever again. "I know your name is really Kyrah Payne, and I know that one Captain Ritcherd Buchanan is at this very moment tearing this town apart searching for you. I know that *you* are well aware that he is here, and you know where to find him. But you're not doing it. Now, I don't care what's happened between the two of you, or how much has changed, he deserves to be told to his face where he stands. He deserves to hear from you that you're done with him, and to at least know what's happened."

Kyrah forced back her rising emotion and lifted her chin. "You're absolutely right, Captain—for the most part. I used to be Kyrah Payne. But I'm married now, under circumstances that are too horrible to even speak of. Yes, I know Ritcherd is here and I know where to find him, but I've only known for a matter of hours. And yes, he deserves to be told where he stands, and to know what's happened. But there is one point where you are wrong." Her voice broke as she held up a clenched fist. "I am not done with him." She squeezed her eyes shut briefly and swallowed her emotion. Forcing a steady voice, she went on. "My deepest hope, Captain, is that this will somehow be a beginning for me and Ritcherd. But I am currently in more of a mess than I ever dreamed possible when I was deported. And I have no idea how, or even if, it can be undone. I need time to think this through before I face him. I know this is difficult for him, but I just need a little time. Please, don't tell him . . . not yet. I'm begging you."

Garret took another step toward her. She looked up into his eyes and marveled to see them more piercing than ever. In spite of their brief acquaintance, he was the most intense person she had ever known. His sincerity was evident when he said, "I have known many men in my life. I've killed a number of them in the name of freedom. I have trusted even fewer. But I have never known a man like Ritcherd Buchanan. I have seen him sweat blood over you. I have seen his heart bleed all over the floor—and this from a man who does not wear his heart on his sleeve. He has been crazy with grief and fear on your behalf. And you're asking me not to tell him that I know where you are?" He shook his head while his eyes penetrated her more deeply. "You're asking more than I can give."

He turned to leave, and Kyrah grabbed his arm. "Please, listen to me." He glanced down at her hand where it held him tightly, but she didn't let go. "You must understand that I had given up hope of ever seeing Ritcherd before I got back to England. I didn't think I would have to confront this so soon."

Kyrah didn't realize she was crying until the tears spilled down her face. "I am married, Captain. I was manipulated and deceived into this marriage, the same way I was manipulated and coerced onto the ship that brought me here against my will. Except that this time I *agreed* to it. I said *I do* to a man I loathe, knowing in my heart that Ritcherd was the only man I could ever love. Now, how do I explain to him—the man I pledged my life, heart, and soul to from my childhood; how do I tell him how I have willfully shattered everything we ever dreamed of sharing?" She tightened her grip on his arm and pressed the other hand over her belly. "And how do I tell him with *this* between us? I need time, Captain Garret." Her voice lowered to an imperative whisper. "Please, just give me a few days. And then . . . if I don't tell him, *you* can. Promise me."

Garret sighed. He squeezed his eyes shut then opened them again. "Very well," he said. "Three days."

Kyrah grabbed hold of his other arm as well. "Promise me," she repeated.

"I promise you, Kyrah."

Kyrah nearly collapsed from relief. She hung her head as a sob erupted from her throat. She was surprised to feel his arms come around her, but she could hardly resist the comfort he offered as he urged her head to his shoulder.

Overcome with his own emotion, Garret couldn't resist the urge to just hold her and allow her to cry. He understood now why he'd been drawn to this woman. He also had to admit that he felt more than a little disappointment. Kyrah Payne was incredible! And in some small way, he'd fallen for her. He recalled now the way Ritcherd had described the sea, and how perfectly it had matched his own description. Could his grandfather's little analogy have such verity? Seeing that he had fallen for the woman Ritcherd loved, he had to believe that it did. He could only hope there was at least one more woman out there who could inspire him the way she did.

Kyrah held tightly to Captain Garret and cried without restraint, unwilling to admit how comforting and strong his embrace really was. She finally got hold of her senses enough to step back, wiping at her face with an embarrassed chuckle. "Forgive me," she said. "It's just that . . . I can't tell you how much it means to me . . . to know . . ." Her voice cracked again. "To *know* that he came for me, that he didn't give up. All that you said about . . . his heart bleeding and . . ." She chuckled again to avoid sobbing. "It stirs me so deeply, but at the same time . . . it makes it all the more difficult to face what's come between us. If he'd given up on me, it would have been easier to tell him that . . . I'd given up on him."

"Listen to me, Kyrah," he said, touching her chin with his finger, "the kind of love that you and Ritcherd share is capable of overcoming anything.

The very fact that your paths have crossed this way is—in my humble opinion—bold evidence that you have what it takes to make it past this."

Kyrah furrowed her brow. "What do you mean?"

He laughed softly. "In matters of love and war, and everything in between, there are two great opposing forces in this world. The one will fight to keep anything good from coming to pass. It delights in misery and evil and oppression. But the other will always triumph when something good is at work; when good people reach out and ask diligently for His help, He will always reach out to give it." Kyrah felt the implication sinking in, but it didn't fully make sense until he added, "Just sit down and think about it, and you won't be able to deny that the hand of Providence is evident in bringing the two of you back together this way." He touched her face and kissed her brow. "Everything will be all right. No matter what it will take to put your lives back together, the love you share will carry you through."

Garret saw fresh tears brim in her eyes, and he resisted the urge to be with her just a little longer. He moved toward the door and added, "Is there anything you need?"

"No," she said in little more than a whisper, "thank you."

"I'll send someone for you when we're preparing to sail. It won't be long now. Don't let them alarm you. My men look a lot scarier than they really are."

"I'll be ready," she said. "And . . . perhaps I'll see you before then."

Garret nodded and reached for the knob. "Is he well?" she asked, making him turn back again. "Beyond the . . . heart bleeding and all of that . . . is he well?"

Garret nodded again. Then he smiled. "Not as well as he'll be in three days."

Ritcherd rose early for the first time in several days to begin searching again for Kyrah. He felt hope as he scanned the faces of people on the streets. This was not such a big place, and if he had seen her once, he would see her again. That evening he returned to the ship and poured his heart out to Garret, who listened but said little. Still, his encouragement meant more to Ritcherd than he could ever say. He rose early again the next day and continued his search. By the third morning he felt doubts beginning to settle in again, but Garret slapped him on the shoulder and smiled, saying, "I have a feeling you're close, my friend. I'll say it again: we will not set sail for England without Kyrah."

Ritcherd appreciated Garret's determination as he walked the same streets again and again. But he couldn't see how such a promise was feasible under the circumstances. They were planning to sail by the end of the week.

That afternoon he returned to the pier, where he saw a woman looking out to sea, wearing a long cloak. Her dark, curly hair was blowing in the wind. His heart went mad as he ran toward her and took hold of her arm. "Kyrah," he murmured.

The woman turned, startled. "Excuse me?"

"I'm sorry," he said, feeling sick as he let go of her arm. "I'm truly sorry. I thought you were someone else."

"Really now." The woman lifted her brows mischievously, and Ritcherd had no trouble guessing her profession. Her heavily rouged cheeks and the cut of her dress made it evident. "Well, if ye can't find 'er," she said coyly, "I might could keep ye company."

"No thanks," Ritcherd said bitterly and moved away.

He hurried back to the *Phoenix* and stood at the stern, gazing out to sea. It took some time and effort, but he finally convinced himself that he hadn't really seen Kyrah. He'd just wanted to for so long that he believed he had seen her. Kyrah Payne was married to another man. She had left this port a long time ago. And not even the best of luck could bring her back now.

He was oblivious to the dark clouds rolling in until Garret said close beside him, "Looks like we're in for a storm."

Ritcherd just grunted to indicate he'd heard.

"What's on your mind?" Garret asked.

"I can't do it anymore," he said. "I think I'm losing my mind."

Garret said nothing. He just listened.

"I want you to know," Ritcherd said, "how much I appreciate every-thing you've done for me. Your encouragement means more than I could ever tell you. But I'm not going to hold up the ship for this any longer. You told me once that the number one law on this ship was that nothing was worth any of these men's lives—not even a woman."

"That's true," Garret said, wondering if Ritcherd would be so appre-ciative if he knew the information that he was purposely withholding. "However, I made you a promise, and I always keep my promises. If we actually end up sailing without her, we'll come back. And we'll find her."

Ritcherd sighed and resisted the urge to break down and cry. "Perhaps she's already returned to England. Eventually she'll go back to her mother, or at least send for her. If I can't find her that way, well . . . I can start advertising in newspapers, and . . . like you said, I just have to know what happened. But I can't go on like this. I can't."

"You don't have to," Garret said, putting a hand on Ritcherd's shoulder. Then he walked away. Ritcherd continued staring at the sea. He felt sick inside. Sick and angry and scared. Staring into the water, he recalled hearing once that drowning could be quite painless once you stopped struggling. Was that the answer? To stop fighting? Could he just accept that she was gone and forget about her? Could he find any measure of happiness without her?

For two days Kyrah stewed over how to tell Ritcherd what she'd done, and the horrible situation she'd gotten herself into. Daisy continued to work long hours, and Kyrah didn't have any opportunity to discuss her dilemma and get some advice. But in her heart she didn't need advice. She knew what she needed to do. She just had to look him in the eye and tell him. It was as simple as that.

She went to bed with her mind made up that first thing in the morning she would just walk down to the pier, walk aboard the *Phoenix* and talk to him. But she woke up not feeling well and stayed in bed, hoping more rest would help. By late morning she realized that her labor had started, and her concerns shifted with the reality of the pain. She was grateful to know that Daisy would stop in for a few minutes between shifts, and she had promised that no matter what kind of trouble she got into at work she would be with Kyrah if the baby came before she left port. While she was waiting for Daisy to come, she pondered having her take a message to Ritcherd. Suddenly the idea of bringing his baby into the world without him seemed terrifying. But she was hurting too badly to move very far, and no message ever got written.

When Daisy arrived, she flew into a calm frenzy, making certain that everything was prepared. Faced with the reality of giving birth, Kyrah counted her blessings once again in having Daisy's friendship. She'd helped deliver a number of babies in her day, and Kyrah felt a lot better about having Daisy's help rather than soliciting the only doctor available—a man reputedly careless and insensitive.

Outside it began to pour, and Kyrah decided it was best not to send Daisy walking to the pier in the rain, especially when she was afraid to be alone. She found some comfort in knowing that Captain Garret would tell Ritcherd where she was, and with any luck, he would tell him soon. While she had made up her mind to tell him herself, she wondered if it might be better this way. As the pain intensified, she put all her effort into praying that Ritcherd might come to help her through this. Of course she knew she could do it without him. She could do whatever she had to. But she wanted him beside her. She wanted to feel her hand in his and know that he still loved her. If Ritcherd Buchanan loved her, nothing else mattered.

Ritcherd lost track of the time as clouds continued to gather overhead. He was startled when Mort hollered at him, "Hey, Buckley! Cap'n Garret needs t' see ye in th' cabin—right now, 'e said."

Ritcherd went quickly below deck. "Is there a problem?" he asked, entering the cabin.

"Yeah. I'd say there's a problem!" Garret said, standing abruptly from behind the desk. "Fortunately for us, we've got ears in the right places."

"What? Tell me!"

"The redcoats will be in this port before morning."

Ritcherd didn't need anything more explained.

"We're a suspicious-looking bunch, and I'm not taking any chances. We're sailing with the tide."

"Are we ready?"

"We will be."

"What about the storm?"

"I think the worst of it will be over before high tide. I'm not concerned."

"Well then, there's no problem."

"But there is. You've got to go and get that woman who'll be sailing with us."

"Why me?" Ritcherd asked, and Garret couldn't suppress a smile. For whatever reason Kyrah had not shown herself by now, her time was nearly up. He figured it would be three days in a couple of hours—and he'd bitten his tongue long enough. But rather than telling Ritcherd something that would be difficult to explain, he simply had to send him on a needed errand with a perfectly logical explanation.

"Because the men are preparing the ship," Garret said. "I need them. Face it, Buckley, as a sailor you're useless. And you need to hurry. Curly went to get a horse from that livery on the corner. He'll be back in a few minutes. So get on it and go tell her we're sailing, and we'll send someone with a carriage to get her in two hours."

"Yes sir," he saluted elaborately, grateful for a distraction. "How do I find her?"

Garret told him where she lived, and Ritcherd left to carry out his orders. Curly had a horse waiting for him on the pier, and he rode quickly through the rain. He had no trouble finding the modest house on the outskirts of town. He knocked loudly at the door, waited a minute, then knocked again.

"What?" a woman growled as the door flew open. She appeared to be about his own age, and was dressed like a tavern maid. Her blonde hair looked like it had seen a long day, and her expression was bordering on frantic.

"Forgive me," he said. "My name is Captain Buckley. I was told to let you know that the *Phoenix* will be sailing with the tide. We'll send a carriage for you in a couple of hours."

"I'm not sailing anywhere," she retorted, seeming distracted by subtle noises coming from somewhere in the house.

"But . . . I was told that—"

"Oh, I know. Garret sent you. But . . ." A sharp cry came from the other room and the woman hurried away, calling over her shoulder. "Come in and close the door. It's freezing out there."

"Who's there, Daisy?" Kyrah demanded once the pain had subsided. "What's going on?"

"Captain Garret sent someone to get you. They're sailing with the tide."

"No," Kyrah groaned. "Oh please, God, no! Not now!"

"Hush, girl," Daisy insisted. "You need to be thinking about getting this baby here. Something else will turn up. Now calm down or you're just going to be hurting all the more."

Kyrah nodded, knowing Daisy was right. But her mind was in a panic. She *had* to sail with them. But she just *couldn't!* Oh, why didn't anything in her life work out the way she planned? Another pain came on and Daisy stayed by her side until it subsided, then she pressed a gentle hand to Kyrah's face, saying firmly, "You stay calm. I'll get rid of the bloke and be right back."

As soon as Daisy left the room, Kyrah knew she had to at least send a message for Ritcherd. She had to let him know what had happened. He'd come so far to find her. She couldn't expect Garret to have to tell him everything. She only prayed that he would at least tell Ritcherd before they sailed. Still, she couldn't count on that. And she couldn't leave him to wonder, or there might never be a chance for them again. After enduring another pain, she managed to sit up, wishing she could have been on board the ship before her labor had begun. She set her eye on some paper on the bureau while she could hear Daisy arguing with the man at the door, even if she couldn't make out what was being said.

"But Garret told me she needed passage urgently," Ritcherd insisted, his frustration mounting. "And we can't wait."

"I know that," Daisy said with increasing impatience. "But she can't go right now."

"Why not?" Ritcherd demanded. He couldn't believe this. "Is she ill? Is she—"

"She's having a baby, if you must know."

Ritcherd was so stunned he didn't know what to say. But he *did* know that Garret would not be pleased with the news Ritcherd had to give him.

"Can't she have it on the ship?" Ritcherd finally managed to say.

"And who's going to deliver it? You?" Daisy snapped. "She needs *me* to get that baby here, and I'm not going anywhere. Besides, she can't be moved until that baby gets here."

"Well, how long is it going to take?" Ritcherd asked.

"How should I know?" Daisy was beyond control now. "Just tell Garret we'll find another way. Thank you and good evening."

"But . . ." Ritcherd stammered. "Garret will . . ."

"Get over it," she shouted, opening the door. "Good night, Captain Buckley."

While Kyrah was enduring another pain, she heard Daisy shouting. Her urgent desire to send a message to the ship became meaningless. "Ritcherd, wait!" she called just as the door slammed, and she doubted that he had heard her. Mustering all the strength she had, she came to her feet and moved into the hallway, knowing she had to get to the door before another contraction came.

"What on earth are you doing?" Daisy insisted. Kyrah tried to push past her but ended up going to her knees, holding tightly to Daisy's arm as the pain hit.

Ritcherd hesitated on the porch, wondering if he was going mad. Had he heard what he thought he just heard? His name? Kyrah's voice? *A baby?* In a matter of seconds he recalled everything he knew about the woman who had arranged passage with Garret—which was practically nothing. He had brushed past her in the tavern, concluding that she couldn't be Kyrah because of her size. But she was . . . *pregnant!* "Could it be?" he murmured into the night air. Had they been gone so long? Or maybe he was mistaken. But he would never know if he didn't turn around and go back into that house. His hand was trembling as he reached for the knob, and it didn't even occur to him to knock. Once inside, he held his breath as he absorbed the scene before him. She was kneeling in the hall, curled over so far that he couldn't even see her face. Still, there was no mistaking that it was her. The hair, the shoulders, the voice.

"Don't let him go, Daisy," she cried, the pain intensifying her words. "You have to go after him. Don't let him go."

"I'm not leaving you alone," Daisy retorted. "Now just—"

"No!" Kyrah screamed. "You have to get him! You . . ." Another pain overtook her, making it impossible to speak.

Ritcherd suddenly froze as he recalled his mistaken encounter with a woman on the pier that afternoon. Was he hearing things? Seeing things? He wouldn't believe it, *couldn't* believe it, until he saw her face.

Kyrah and Daisy both felt the cool air at the same time and realized the door was open. Daisy straightened up but remained on her knees. The door closed just as Kyrah felt the pain recede, and she lifted her eyes enough to see the pair of boots planted directly in front of her.

"Ritcherd," she murmured, lifting her gaze upward.

Ritcherd could hardly breathe when her features came into view. He reached out to take her face into his trembling hands. When the feel of her skin verified that he hadn't lost his mind, something between a sob and laughter erupted from his throat.

"Oh, Ritcherd," Kyrah cried, pressing her hands over his. He sank to his knees as much from weakness as his need to be close to her.

Kyrah felt the world freeze around her; even the pain seemed to relent, or perhaps time just stood still long enough for her to absorb his presence. She couldn't believe it! But it was *him!* He was *real!* As their eyes met, she could almost literally feel his love. He'd come for her! Just knowing that one fact made every question that had haunted her fall into perspective. There was no room or reason to doubt his sincerity or his commitment. He had crossed an ocean and searched for months in order to end up here, now. That was all she needed to know.

She found her voice enough to say, "You came for me. You did."

"I did," he laughed, and she laughed with him.

"How . . . did you find me?"

His eyes burned through her as he said, "I walked through hell in bare feet. And I'd do it again."

Ritcherd pressed a kiss to her brow, wondering where to begin to tell her all he was feeling. He'd barely looked into her eyes again when she doubled over and groaned with such anguish that it scared him.

"What is it?" he demanded, holding her against him. "What's wrong?"

"Any fool can see she's having a baby," Daisy snapped as she came to her feet.

Ritcherd looked up at the blonde woman who had answered the door. Mimicking her tone of voice, he asked, "And who might you be?"

"I'm the one who's going to deliver this baby. And I know who you are. It's about time you showed up. Now help me get her back to bed before she hurts herself."

As the pain receded once again, Kyrah clutched tightly onto Ritcherd's arms, almost fearing he might disappear. She closed her eyes briefly, thanking God for sending him to her now. Her prayers had truly been heard and answered.

Ritcherd carefully scooped Kyrah into his arms and followed Daisy to the bed, where he laid her down. Their eyes met, and his heart threatened to beat right out of his chest. *He couldn't believe it!* He could hardly accept the reality that they were actually together. How could he possibly digest the fact that she was having a baby? He sat on the edge of the bed to face her, well aware of her fingers digging into his arms as the pain came and went once more. In the brief absence of pain, their eyes met. He saw moisture appear in hers only a moment before his own vision blurred with mist. But he took hold of her face and had no trouble finding her lips with his. He didn't care if she was married. He didn't care if she was in labor. He could only feel the evidence that she was here, and she was real. And the response he felt in her kiss gave him the hope that there might still be a life for them—together.

"Kyrah," he murmured against her lips and kissed her again. There was so much he wanted to say, so much he wanted to ask her, but only one thing mattered for now, and he said it with all of the desperation and conviction that he had felt through his eternity of searching for her. "I love you," he said and kissed her again. "I love you."

She laughed with indescribable relief before she was overtaken by the pain again and he held her until it relented. She touched his face and started to cry so hard that she could hardly speak. "Oh, Ritcherd," she managed, "I'm so sorry . . . I . . . was so . . ."

"Shhh," he whispered and pressed his fingers over her lips. "We'll have plenty of time to talk later. Let's just get you through this, all right?"

Kyrah nodded, then groaned as she endured another contraction. Ritcherd held her close, wishing he could somehow take the pain from her.

When she relaxed again, he felt her hand in his hair and heard her words near his ear. "I love you, Ritcherd. I love you."

Ritcherd buried his face into her hair and wept. That was all he needed to know. The relief and hope he felt was comparable to the anguish and despair they had replaced. He cried without restraint while she held to him, withstanding one pain after another.

Ritcherd became so distraught with watching her suffer that he couldn't help the sharp tone when he said to Daisy, "Where's the doctor? Is he—"

"I told you," she said firmly, "I'm going to deliver this baby."

"But she needs a doctor," Ritcherd protested.

"I won't have that doctor anywhere near me," Kyrah growled between pains.

"He's a crook," Daisy said. "And a perverted one, at that."

Ritcherd attempted to swallow his frustration. He felt somewhat better when Daisy explained, "You mustn't worry, Captain. I've done this before. And the pain is all quite normal. I'll do everything I can to see that she gets through this all right."

"Thank you," Ritcherd said, "for everything. For . . . being here for her."

"It's been my pleasure, actually."

As the pain continued to get worse, Ritcherd asked Daisy, "How much longer?"

"It's going to be a while, if you must know. First babies generally take their time. But I'm not in any hurry, so—"

"Good heavens," Ritcherd murmured, realizing he'd lost track of the time. "I've got to go back and—"

"Don't leave me," Kyrah cried, holding to him tightly.

"I won't be long," he said, touching her face gently. "I just have to get a few of my things, and tell them I'm staying."

Kyrah looked as if she wanted to protest, but she couldn't speak. Daisy wiped a damp cloth over Kyrah's face and said gently, "He'll be back before the baby comes. I promise." She added to Ritcherd, "You hurry, now. Don't make a liar out of me."

"I'll hurry," he said.

"And tell Garret to . . . well, to be careful," Daisy added.

"I will," Ritcherd said, just now making the connection in his mind. Daisy had to be Garret's *friend,* who had made arrangements for Kyrah to sail with them. If he weren't so distracted, he would have hugged her.

Attempting to soothe Kyrah, he pressed a kiss to her brow, lingering there as if he could absorb her presence to get him through the minutes until he returned. As he eased away, she grabbed his arm, saying with a strained voice, "Tell Garret . . . thank you . . . for me. He . . . he didn't tell you . . . it was me . . . because he . . ." She groaned and clenched her teeth while Ritcherd tried to take in what he'd just learned. Garret *knew?*

"Get out of here," Daisy said, nudging him, "or you might not make it back in time. There's no way of knowing how fast it will go."

Ritcherd galloped through the rain toward the *Phoenix* while his anger took hold. All of the desperation and frenzy he'd been feeling rushed to a point right between his eyes, pounding there with a fury that made him wonder how this man, who had become his most trusted friend, could have purposely withheld something like this from him. He shook off the rain as he went below deck and entered the cabin to find Garret seated at the desk.

"It's about time you got back," he said as Ritcherd slammed the door. Coming to his feet, he added, "I was about to send somebody to—"

Ritcherd drew back his left hand and hit Garret square in the jaw. Before he recovered, Ritcherd took him by the shirt and slammed him against the door. "Why didn't you tell me it was her? How could you stand back and watch me tear myself to pieces when you *knew* it was her!"

Garret touched his lip and calmly looked at the blood on his fingers. In a gravelly voice he said, "You have a nasty temper, Captain Buchanan."

Ritcherd dropped his hands and took a step back, but his eyes made it clear he wanted an answer. With no warning, Garret threw an equivalent blow to Ritcherd's face, then grabbed him by the shirt, turned and slammed him against the door. "Because she made me promise not to tell you—and I gave my promise reluctantly. *She* was tearing herself to pieces, wondering how to tell you she was married to another man and about to have a baby. And I do *not* break a promise to a lady, no matter how much it was tearing *me* to pieces to watch you suffer."

Garret stepped back and tugged at his waistcoat to straighten it, as if the issue was closed.

"I'm sorry," Ritcherd said.

"As you should be," Garret retorted. Then his voice softened. "And I'm sorry, too—sorry that I couldn't keep my promise to her and keep you from suffering at the same time. I told her I would give her three days, and that's when I sent you to get her."

Ritcherd took a minute to digest what Garret was saying. The events of the past two hours flooded through him. "I need to sit down," he said and moved unsteadily to a chair. "Forgive me, Garret. I just . . . I don't know what to think." He looked up to meet Garret's compassionate gaze. "After all this time . . . I've found her. But . . . she's *married.* How am I supposed to deal with that?"

Garret sat down. "I've gotten every impression that, for whatever reason she got into this marriage, she's eager to put it behind her. I believe she loves you and she's hoping to start over."

Ritcherd took a deep breath, attempting to inhale Garret's calm perspective. "Yes," he admitted, "I believe that, too."

"Then the two of you will find a way—together."

Ritcherd nodded, then became distant again as his thoughts wandered.

"So, what else is wrong?" Garret asked.

Ritcherd chuckled without humor and shook his head. "She's about to have a baby—any time now." Again he met Garret's gaze. While he was aware that he needed to return quickly to Kyrah, he felt the need to take a few minutes and gather his wits, or he'd never be able to help her through what lay ahead. And he had no idea how long it would be before he could talk with Garret again. He'd gained a deep respect for Garret's insight and wisdom. And if he'd ever needed insight and wisdom, he needed it now. But he felt so thoroughly overwhelmed that he couldn't even put his thoughts together enough to know what else to say.

When Ritcherd remained silent, Garret drawled, "So . . . she's going to have a baby, and that would mean . . ." He motioned for Ritcherd to finish the statement.

"It would mean that . . . that . . ." Ritcherd stammered his thoughts into the open. "I don't know what. She couldn't have been married *that* long. Was she raped? Did she find somebody else and—"

"Now, wait a minute," Garret said, holding up his hands. "The only way you're going to find the answers to those questions is to ask her. But in my humble opinion, the answer is obvious."

Ritcherd thought for a minute, but he had to admit, "If it was obvious, I wouldn't have to ask."

"How long have we been gone, Ritcherd?"

"I don't know. It seems like forever."

Garret stood and picked up the large leather-bound book that always lay open on his desk. He set the book on the table in front of Ritcherd.

"What's this?" he asked.

"You're the owner of the *Phoenix.* Perhaps you should be more familiar with the ship's log. Take note of the dates."

Garret turned back several pages and pointed to a date at the top of the page. Ritcherd read aloud, "14 September 1779." Garret's finger moved down the page and Ritcherd followed with his eyes, reading silently: *Ship purchased by Ritcherd Buchanan, now officially christened the* Phoenix; *set sail at morning tide.*

Ritcherd looked up at Garret in question. He just turned back to the page where it had been open and pointed at today's date at the top. *28 May 1780.* Ritcherd's heart beat faster. He was certain they'd been gone longer than that. As if Garret had read his mind, he said, "Count the months, Ritcherd. Use your fingers if you have to." Garret chuckled. "It would seem your indiscretions have been manifested . . . you scoundrel, you."

"Merciful heaven," Ritcherd breathed. Had he lost track of time so completely? *Yes,* he had! And he'd been so ashamed and distraught over what had happened between him and Kyrah that he'd completely forced it out of his mind. But Garret was right—again. He *had* been a scoundrel. And his indiscretions *had* been manifested. He tried to comprehend what Kyrah had been through as a result, and a tangible pain developed in his chest. He pressed a hand there and groaned, but it only worsened.

"Yes," Garret said in a gentle voice, "heaven is merciful, Ritcherd. You've found her, and we all have much to be grateful for."

"Yes, we do," Ritcherd agreed distantly while he tried to absorb the reality that he was about to become a father.

Garret startled him when he said, "Now that we have that cleared up, we'll have to chat later. We've got to sail. Where is she?"

"Good heavens!" Ritcherd muttered under his breath. "I've got to go back."

"You didn't *bring* her?" Garret shouted.

"She's in labor," Ritcherd muttered, throwing a few of his things into a bag. "She can't be moved right now."

"You left her *alone?*" he snapped in a voice that was unusually agitated.

"No! Of course not! Daisy's with her. But I have to get back. That's what I came to tell you. I'm staying with her. Come back for us as soon as you can get safely into port."

"I will," Garret said. Ritcherd figured he had what he needed and turned to face Garret. "I promise," Garret added.

Ritcherd quickly embraced him. "Thank you," he said. Their eyes met briefly, then Ritcherd opened the door. "I have to go."

"Take Patrick with you," Garret called.

Ritcherd stopped and turned. "Why?"

"He's delivered more than a few babies in his day," Garret said, as if Ritcherd should have already known.

"Patrick?" Ritcherd laughed. "A doctor?"

"Aye, Cap'n Buckley," Garret said with a sarcastic chuckle. More seriously, he went on, "He's the ship's surgeon and must be with us when we sail in case he's needed. We never know what we'll come up against. But he has time to check her and make certain everything's all right."

"Thank you," he said again and turned to leave.

"Ritcherd," Garret said and stopped him. "I'll be praying for you—both of you."

Ritcherd smiled. "And I'll be doing the same for you. We'll see you soon."

Patrick was ready to go in less than a minute. He mounted the horse behind Ritcherd and they reached their destination quickly. Ritcherd entered the house without knocking and dropped his things in the hall while he and Patrick shook off the rain and removed their wet coats and hats.

"Kyrah," Ritcherd said softly as he returned to her side. He sighed just to see her, to touch her, and to feel the evidence once again of being with her. With his new discovery, there was so much he wanted to say. But this wasn't the time.

She opened her eyes, and the exhaustion was evident in her expression. "Ritcherd," she murmured and took his hand. "You came back."

Through his brief absence and the ensuing pain, Kyrah had almost begun to wonder if Ritcherd's appearance had been a hallucination.

"Of course I came back," Ritcherd said. While Daisy was skeptically appraising the man in the doorway to the bedroom, he explained more to Kyrah. "The doctor from the *Phoenix* is here. He can't stay, but he'll make certain everything's all right." Kyrah nodded and looked past Ritcherd's shoulder as Patrick came closer.

Kyrah might have felt apprehensive if she hadn't realized by now that Captain Garret and his men tended to look much worse than they were.

"How are you feeling?" Patrick asked tenderly, taking Kyrah's hand into his. Ritcherd was amazed—though he shouldn't have been—to hear a complete absence of Patrick's accent. It was immediately evident that Patrick was a well-educated man.

"Awful."

"It will probably get worse," he said with a compassionate chuckle. "But I want you to remember that it's all very natural. The pain doesn't mean something's wrong. That's just the way it works. Can you remember that?"

Kyrah nodded, then groaned as another pain struck her and Patrick waited patiently for it to subside. "I want you to roll onto your side," he said gently. "Until you get nearer to having the baby, this position might ease the pain a bit. Captain Buckley," he added, turning to him, "if you press firmly here," he pushed Ritcherd's hand against the lower part of Kyrah's back, "during the pains, it might ease the pressure for her a bit."

Another pain hit and Patrick pressed as he'd shown Ritcherd to. When it was over, Kyrah turned to the doctor and smiled feebly. "That feels a little better. Thank you."

Patrick checked Kyrah and reported that everything seemed normal, with no apparent problems. He told them she could start pushing soon, then he talked quietly with Daisy while Ritcherd stayed close to Kyrah.

"Any more questions?" he asked, glancing at all three of them. When no one said anything, he said, "Well, I must be off then, or they'll sail without me."

"Thank you, Patrick," Ritcherd said.

"Wish I could stay," he replied. "Babies are the best part of being a physician—but you don't get much opportunity for that on board a privateer." He chuckled. "I've got all the children between the ages of two and eight in a little village in Yorkshire to my credit. Someday I'm going back to see how they're doing."

Patrick wished them luck and left quickly. Ritcherd had to admit he felt a little better about the situation. But he still had trouble comprehending that Patrick—the great fencer—was really a doctor.

"Has he gone?" Kyrah asked when the pain briefly relented.

"Yes. The *Phoenix* will be sailing soon. He has to be on board."

"They're leaving without you?" she asked with concern.

"They'll come back for us. It's my ship," he smirked. "They have to."

In the midst of Kyrah's weak smile, her head lolled to the side and she moaned, but she didn't seem as uncomfortable as she had before they'd taken Patrick's suggestions. Daisy motioned toward the kitchen, letting Ritcherd know she would be close by if he needed her. He nodded and watched her leave the room.

Kyrah sighed deeply, feeling a slight reprieve from the intensity of the contractions. She took hold of Ritcherd's hand, marveling at the reality that they were together. She touched his face and watched him turn and press a kiss to her palm. She fingered the gold ring in his ear, and they exchanged a smile.

"You had to become a pirate to find me?" she asked.

"Something like that," he said, then she squeezed her eyes shut and groaned, tightening her hand in his.

"Is it gone now?" Ritcherd asked when she relaxed. She nodded, and their eyes met as if they could somehow bridge the time they'd been apart.

"Ritcherd," she said, "there's something I have to tell you."

She endured another pain before he said, "It can wait, Kyrah. Whatever it is, it doesn't matter."

"But it does," she said, determined to have the worst out in the open and have it over with. She knew she would never be able to get through this while she was dreading having to tell him what she'd done.

The pain came and went before she continued. "There's no way . . . to tell you except . . . to just tell you." She took a deep breath and closed her eyes, unable to look at him. "I'm married, Ritcherd."

She waited to hear his shock and disgust, his demand for an explanation. But she only heard him sigh and whisper, "I know."

Kyrah opened her eyes. "You know? Garret told you?"

Ritcherd waited for the pain to subside again. "An old man at the pier told me," he said.

Kyrah wanted to ask exactly how that had come about, but this wasn't the time for getting into a detailed conversation. Knowing her time between pains was brief, she got to the point. "I'm so sorry, Ritcherd." She couldn't hold back the emotion. Seeing the question in his eyes, she attempted to explain through her tears, "I was all alone . . . and so afraid. I didn't know if . . ." She squeezed his hand tightly and waited for the pain to subside. "I didn't know if . . ." she continued, "if you would come . . . or if you could find me . . . even if you did. But I was wrong, Ritcherd. I made a mistake. I don't know if you'll even want me now that—"

"I love you, Kyrah." He took hold of her shoulders and his voice became fierce, however quiet. "I want to share my life with you more than anything else in this world. But more than anything, I want you to be happy." She saw his chin quiver and he bit his lip for a moment. While she endured another pain, he gained control of his emotion. "Tell me to go away and leave you in peace, Kyrah, and I will. I don't want to . . . but . . . if that's what you want . . . I will."

Ritcherd heard the words come back to him and wondered where he'd found the strength to say them without falling apart. Perhaps the strength had come from the evidence that she still loved him. But he wondered if that would make any difference. The knowledge that this was *his* baby only deepened his fears. He swallowed the lump in his throat and added carefully, "Just tell me what you want me to do, Kyrah—anything, and I'll do it." He waited patiently for her to be able to speak again. But when the pain subsided, she said nothing.

Ritcherd took hold of her chin and forced her to look at him. Drawing what little inner strength he had left, he asked, "Do you love him, Kyrah?"

Kyrah shook her head frantically. Fresh emotion choked her voice and she barely managed to say, "You . . . misunderstand me."

"There is no room for misunderstanding here, Kyrah. We've been through too much, we've come too far." She groaned with pain, and he could tell it was getting worse again. Recalling how they had come across a difficult bridge in the past, he took both her hands into his, kneeling on the floor beside her. He looked into her eyes and said firmly, "We can talk when you get this baby here, Kyrah. Right now, there are only three things I need to know. Tell me what you want. Tell me what you need. And tell me how you feel."

Kyrah laughed through her tears as the memory of his saying that very thing somehow gave her the hope and strength she needed. It was easy to say, "I need your help, Ritcherd. I need to get away from here . . . as quickly as possible. When the *Phoenix* comes back, we're coming with you."

"We?" he asked.

"Me and . . . the baby," she said, and he smiled. At least she wasn't talking about her husband.

He waited for her to continue. "And when we get to England," she said, "I need you to get some legal help for me."

Ritcherd felt confused. Did she mean straightening out the reasons for the deportation? Was there some aspect of the trouble she'd been in that he didn't know about? "Of course," he said. "But . . . why?"

"I need to get a divorce, Ritcherd . . . as quickly as possible."

It took a minute for him to grasp what she meant. While she withstood another pain, he laughed to avoid sobbing. When she focused on him again, he said, "Are you trying to tell me that . . . you want . . ."

"I was getting to that," she said. "I want to marry you, Ritcherd . . . if you can live with a *divorced* gambler's daughter."

A sob broke through his laughter. He pulled her close and buried his face into her hair. "Oh, Kyrah," he murmured, "I love you. I love you." He drew back to look into her eyes. "Nothing else matters as long as we're together. Do you hear me?" She nodded, and he held her through another pain. "I know we have some difficulties ahead of us, but we will see them through together. Do you understand?"

She nodded again and touched his face. "I'm so sorry, Ritcherd. I was such a fool. I never should have—"

"Shhh," he whispered, pressing his fingers over her lips. "It is I who am sorry; sorry that I got you into this mess. I have so many regrets that I don't know where to begin. But . . . we'll have all those weeks at sea together, and we can talk to our heart's content."

She laughed softly until it became a groan. "I love you, Ritcherd," she finally said. "That's how I feel. I love you more than life. And I will never—never—allow anything or anyone to ever come between us again. *Never!*"

Ritcherd inhaled deeply, as if he could drink in her determination. Something in her had changed. He could never put it to words, but she was stronger, finer, more beautiful than ever. In a word, she was breathtaking.

"We must be together, Ritcherd," she added with a finality that seemed to end the need for any further discussion.

"We will be," he said. "As God is my witness, Kyrah, we will be together."

Ritcherd remained on his knees with her hand in his, praying as much as doing his best to ease her discomfort. The storm faded and night settled in as deeply as her ongoing pain. Ritcherd stayed next to her every minute. He whispered words of reassurance and encouragement, doing everything he could to make her comfortable, wishing there was something he could do to really make a difference. He felt so thoroughly helpless, which made him increasingly grateful for Daisy's calm presence as she moved in and out of the room, staying closer as Kyrah's labor worsened. As the hours passed, he wondered what exactly Patrick had meant when he'd said she could start pushing soon. He wanted to know his definition of *soon*.

"Ritcherd," Kyrah said feebly and surprised him. She'd hardly said anything at all for more than an hour. She reached out and touched his face as he bent close to her. "Are you really here, or am I just hallucinating?"

"I'm really here." He smiled and pressed a kiss to her brow, but he didn't have time to say any more. While he'd believed that this couldn't possibly get any worse, suddenly it was. Rather than coming and going, the pain became constant. Ritcherd kept his focus on Kyrah, while Daisy instructed Kyrah on what she needed to do now that the baby was ready to come. Kyrah groaned and pushed, digging her fingers into Ritcherd's arms while she nearly went mad from the pain. She raged and protested, swearing that she couldn't possibly do this, and she cursed Ritcherd for causing her so much trouble and grief.

She went through the ordeal of pushing more times than he could count before Daisy finally said, "It's almost here, honey. You can do it!"

Ritcherd's heart beat madly with fear and anticipation. She pushed again, and he heard Daisy gasp. Following a tense minute while Kyrah attempted to catch her breath and Ritcherd didn't dare turn around, a loud wail filled the air.

"It's a girl, Kyrah," Daisy reported, and he felt a lump of emotion catch in his throat.

Kyrah gasped with a laugh of relief as Daisy set the wiggling infant into her arms. Then she cried. Ritcherd blinked the mist out of his own eyes and had to say, "She's beautiful, Kyrah." He marveled at the baby's perfection while it wailed and waved its tiny arms about. She was alive. And real. It was a miracle!

After scrutinizing the baby, Kyrah looked up at Ritcherd and smiled affectionately. "I love you," she whispered. "Thank you."

Ritcherd felt the lump in his throat intensify. All he could do was nod and press a kiss to her brow.

"I'm so cold," she said and shivered visibly.

Daisy handed Ritcherd a blanket and he tucked it carefully around her. Kyrah smiled weakly at him as he pressed a kiss to her cheek. She glanced again at the baby and fell almost immediately to sleep.

Daisy took the baby into the kitchen to clean her up. Ritcherd sat in a chair near the bed and leaned back with a sigh. Watching Kyrah sleeping peacefully at last, he silently thanked God for finding her when he did. Despite the ordeal she had just suffered, he felt almost weak from her beauty. Leaning forward in the chair, he brushed the back of his fingers over her face that still held traces of sweat, then he moved his hand meekly through her tangled hair sprawled over the pillows.

"I love you, Kyrah," he whispered, "and I will never let you go again. *Never!*"

About the Author

*E*lizabeth D. Michaels began writing at the age of sixteen and has since immersed herself in the lives created by her vivid imagination. Beyond her devotion to family and friends, writing has been her passion for the majority of her adult life. While she has more than seventy published novels under the name Anita Stansfield and is the recipient of many awards—including two Lifetime Achievement Awards—she boldly declares the historical novels published under the Michaels name to be dearly close to her heart. She is best known for her keen ability to explore the psychological depths of human nature, bringing her characters to life through the timeless struggles they face in the midst of exquisite dramas.

For more information on the author and her books, follow her on Instagram or go to anitastansfield.com.

Scan to visit

www.anitastansfield.com

You've dreamed of accomplishing your publishing goal for ages—holding *that* book in your hands. We want to partner with you in bringing this dream to light.

Whether you're an aspiring author looking to publish your first book or a seasoned author who's been published before, we want to hear from you. Please submit your manuscript to

CEDARFORT.SUBMITTABLE.COM/SUBMIT

CEDAR FORT HAS PUBLISHED BOOKS IN THE FOLLOWING GENRES

- LDS Nonfiction
- Fiction
- Juvenile & YA
- Biographies
- Regency Romances
- Cozy Mysteries
- General Nonfiction
- Cookbooks
- Children's Books
- Self-Help
- Comic & Activity books
- Children's books with customizable character illustrations

BRING LIGHT
INTO YOUR LIFE

Books, Products & Courses at
www.cedarfort.com

CEDAR FORT
Publishing & Media

SAVE ON 15%OFF
YOUR NEXT ORDER
WHEN YOU USE
DISCOUNT CODE:

SAVE15